The Adoption

David Schein

Fomite
Burlington, VT

Fomite
58 Peru Street
Burlington, VT 05401
www.fomitepress.com

8/13/2021

*This book is dedicated to
Hermann Hunzinger who brought me to Ethiopia
and showed me the world of Wax and Gold.*

Tony

Thank for your
+ support
friendship
of my work.

+ pass it on

Enjoy.
David

2022

Thanks to F, M, N, S and T for life stories, Amharic advice and fact-checking that contributed to *The Adoption* as well as many other Ethiopian, German and American friends whose lives are extrapolated and fictionalized in this book. Thanks to Hermann Hunzinger who first brought me to Ethiopia and who many years later bought me a plane ticket to France and provided a haven in the Ardeche for me to work on this book. Thanks to Ethan Viets Van Lear for the lowdown on East Rogers Park, and to Cynthia Gallaher, Amanda Lichtenstein, Cynthia Moore, and my daughter Aurora Schein who read early drafts and provided feedback. Thanks also to Aurora for helping me fine-tune the book cover. Special thanks to my sister Susan Schein who cast an eagle eye on the manuscript and to Marc and Donna of Fomite Press for believing in this story and encouraging my writing.

Kalkidane's Family

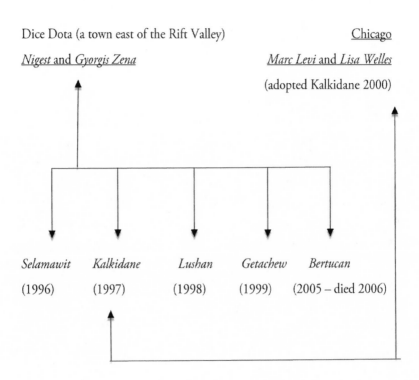

Dice Dota (a town east of the Rift Valley)   Chicago

Nigest and *Gyorgis Zena*   *Marc Levi* and *Lisa Welles*

(adopted Kalkidane 2000)

Selamawit	Kalkidane	Lushan	Getachew	Bertucan
(1996)	(1997)	(1998)	(1999)	(2005 – died 2006)

Glossary of Ethiopian words and terms – Pg. 427

Other Characters
(PRINCIPALS IN CAPITALS)

Mother Tenege – Midwife, and practitioner of female circumcision

The Aunties – Nigest's sisters– *Malekeda, Feriwot* and *Almanesh*

TSEHAY and *RODEAT* – the Tekle sisters. They run the Andamu Children's Center

Dawit – Rodeat's son

Zalman – Driver for the Tekles

Emma Welles– Lisa's mother

Lieutenant Giron– Ethiopia Immigration Officer at Bole Airport

Seleshe – Ethiopian friend of Marc and Lisa in Chicago

FIKIR – The boy who found Kalkidane's family. Nephew of Adane Ermes, son of Eden Kalmata. He becomes the protector of Nigest's family

Adane Ermes – Executive Director, Illinois Ethiopian Association

Kiflu, Zena, Mektid and *Antoneh* – Fikir's friends in Dice Dota

Girma –Rich mafioso type in Dice Dota from whom Gyorgis borrows money

Miranda – Kalkidane's school-friend in Chicago

(Fat) Tadesse – A cohort of Gyorgis

Yewok and Zeff – The sons of Tadesse

Izzak – Khat-chewing friend of Gyorgis

Kidist – Nigest's neighbor

Yemisrach – Nurse at the Norwegian Hospital

The Derg – Meaning "committee;" the Coordinating Committee of the Armed Forces, Police and Territorial Army that ruled Ethiopia from 1974-1987

HELEN aka Heaven – Friend of Selam; she has gone to Adis and works as a "bar girl" in the nightclub, Seven Nights

HELMUT – German boyfriend of Helen. He builds roads for the UN

Crystal – Helmut's wife in Hamm, Germany

Marlene – Daughter of Helmut and Crystal

Betlihem and Seble (Sebbie) – Friends of Selamawit and Helen

Mullanae – A friend of Fikir's

Hanna and Mukbar – Friends of Fikir

Tati – Proprietor (Madame) of Seven Nights

Henok and *Ernst* – Bartender and pimp respectively at Seven Nights

Ayana – Friend of Lushan's

Abraham – Cab driver in Chicago

Dejen – Fikir's uncle– owns his own van, drives for the Americans

Demissie – Boy cousin who lives next door to Selamawit, Lushan and Geta

Golya – Acquaintance of Gyorgis

EDEN KALMATA – Fikir's mother

Dawit Kalmata – Fikir's father who was imprisoned by the Derg and who died in jail

Issac Silverstone – Head Rastafarian at the Rastah Museum in Shashamene– originally from Bed Stuy, Brooklyn

Megdes – Street girl, friend of Genet

Maritu – High School girlfriend of Helen and Selam who went to Chinese Acrobat School and who now lives in San Diego

Eskadar – Friend of Lushan's in Dice Dota

Ato Mikal – Proprietor of Southern Sun Employment Agency in Dice Dota

Amudah – Employer of Lushan in the Arab Emirates

Sharnah – Wife of Amudah

Mahmud – Son of Amudah and Sharnah

Wolf – Friend of Helmut

Elijah (Eli) Johnson – Kalkidane's American boyfriend

ABEYNESH – Ethiopian Airlines employee in Dubai who helps indentured runaway Ethiopian maids; she is the lover of Hedyat Pakir

HEDEYAT PAKIR – Gujerati captain of the dhow, Sea Tiger, which transports freight from Gujerat to Dubai to Somalia

SAGAR – Son of Hedeyat Pakir

Ying Wjen – Social Director for African students at the Wyqiao Acrobatic Art School

Makeda, Kifle, Ferawayne and Sintayehu – Fikir's Ethiopian classmates at the Wyqiao Acrobatic Art School

Mr. Otto – Employee of the German Embassy in Beijing who helps Fikir and his friends get visas for Germany

Captain Abinet – Soldier who claims to have fired in the air at the Dice Dota student massacre

Ali Dulani – Wealthy Ethiopian-Yemeni industrialist; the largest land-owner in Southern Ethiopia

IMAN MUHAMMUD – Builder and guardian of the Cave of All Religions, a combination mosque-church and shrine to religious tolerance on the outskirts of Shashamene

Mola Abera – Ethiopian Musician who founded an environmental movement with street children in Adis Ababa

Ato Abdellah – Ethiopian farmer, living on the outskirts of Shashamene

Officer Abselo – Immigration Official, Bole Airport

Ahmed – colleague of Officer Abselo

Captain Melech – Ethiopian army officer who operates drone surveillance on the demonstrators in Shashamene

Captain Netaye Worede – Ethiopian army officer who secretly conspires with Unity March organizers to prevent non-violence and who later becomes prime minister of Ethiopia

Jolenee – Eden Kalmata's cousin's wife – a sergeant in the Ethiopian army

Captain Jemberee Tessoma – Jolenee's lover

Isaias Afewerki – Leader of Eritrea, formerly head of Eritrean Liberation Front

1997

Come On Baby
Lisa: **Chicago**

"…active labour may take about eight hours. This is average though, and it could be much shorter or longer than that" – www.babycentre.co.uk
"…a first labor lasts 16 hours on average, however, this can vary tremendously." – www.pregnancyandbaby.com
"For first time moms, the average length of early labor is six to 12 hours." – www. mayoclinic.org

Break water, gush, wet flood down my leg. Marc, forget about the movies. Marc, I'm in the bathroom.

Five minutes

five minutes

five minutes between contractions.

This is it, get the bag, we're going. Call Dr. Sharon.

You called her? You *beeped* her. Did she call back?

Oh that's great, we don't know where she is, that's fucking great.

Give me the bag. I've got to check something before you put it in the car.

None of your business. Oh fuck…

JESUS, JESUS, COME ON LITTLE BAYYYYYYBEEEEEEEEEE, BAAAASTARD, SONOFABITCH, MOTHER FUCKERRRRRRRR, FUCK THAT HURTS.

OK, OK, You check the bag. *Underwear,* I'll need seven pairs, cotton, nothing fancy.

OK. Skip it. Zip it up, put it in the car. Come *on*, baby, let's go. Wait, there's the phone. Is it Dr. Sharon?

She's at her kid's friend's birthday party? She'll meet us there? OK, let's go.

Wait. You're forgetting the bag, you're forgetting the motherfucking bag. Good one. Put it in the car, and then come back and help me. Go. GO. You're sure you can drive?

What? Are you crazy? No, I can't drive. Look, this is no time to be a wiseass.

Did you lock the door? OK, here let me get in the car before the next one hits. All right. Let's go. Go. Go. Go. Go. Go. Daddy.

Don't speed, that's all we need. Woah, here they come again, that's four minutes.

BAAAASTARD, SONOFABITCH, MOTHER FUCKERRRRRRR, BAST-ARD, MOTHERFUCKER BASTARDCUNTFACESONOFAMOTHER-FUCKINGBITCH. Fuck, that fucking hurts.

Marc, look, the guys are there with the wheelchair. Give me the bag and go park.

OK fellas go wheel me in and let's get the show on the road. Marc, give me the bag, now go park.

Doctor Sharon glad to see you, are you going to try to turn it? One more time? No?

MOTHERFUCKERRRRRBASTARDSONOFABITCHMOTHER-FUCKER HOLYSHITWOOOOOHHHCOME ON BABY, COME ON BABY, COME ON BABY, COME ON BABY.

SHIT. SHIT. SHIT. SHIT. SHIT.

OK, give me the epidural.

Owwww, that pinches.

OK, OK, that's better, I feel that, I feel that, I don't feel that, I don't feel that. No, I don't feel that.

When Kalkidane Was Born
Selamawit: Dice Dota, Ethiopia

According to a 2011 study published in the Ethiopian Journal of Health, many Ethiopian women prefer delivering at home in the company of known and trusted relatives and friends, where customs and traditions can be observed.

The night my Aunties pushed the men and boys out of the tukol and sang high to Mother Maryam, "Bless this child, bring him from heaven, make him strong, Maryam protect him," was the night my sister Kalkidane was born.

When the big ropes squeezed Nigest's tummy she groaned and yelled and we all cried so loud so that her sound would not be alone. Even though I was the littlest I screeched the highest. When the Aunties went out of the tukol, I went too. The men waited outside with their torches, drinking tej by the fire-pit. The Aunties put the birthstones on each other's shoulders and stagger danced in the compound, crying, "Mother Maryam give us the burden, take the pain from Nigest, put it on our shoulders." Then we went back in the tukol.

The ropes squeezed her tummy more and more. I could see them, like snakes under the skin. Mother Tenegne took us aside and said the baby was going to come out now. Momma pushed and yelled and we screamed with her, the Aunties and me and Lushan, so loud that the neighbors knew it was Nigest's time. I got at the end of the bed and saw everything; the brown head coming out and Mother Tenegne putting her hands inside Momma, pulling her out, and the tube that looked like what came out of the ox when Father killed it, all blood and yellow fat. She held the baby by the feet and showed us the girl part. The Aunties gave the cry so the men would know it was a girl, "Ulelelelelelelelel". Mother Tenegne tied the tube tight in two places close together with string and cut the tube between the knots with her razor. Then she tied the end that came out of Momma to Momma's leg and slapped the baby's bottom. It gulped in air and made a sound like a kid goat, "Maaaaaaaah." All the Aunties clapped and laughed when she changed color and her skin began to glow bright.

Then Momma sighed, "Ooooh, Ooooh give me the baby," and Mother Tenegne said, "Not yet, wait until the rest is out." Auntie Malkeda brought butter and rubbed Momma's belly while Mother Tenegne pressed a big bottle on her tummy and Auntie rubbed more butter on Momma's tummy and pressed some more until there was a wet sound and a piece of meat came out of Momma, all green and yellow and bloody and Mother Tenegne held it up for all the women to see. Mother Tenegne put the meat in a dish and the women prayed seven times to Maryam, "Oh Mother Maryam, thank you for giving Nigest this child, Oh Mother Maryam, give this baby health and make her strong, Oh Mother Maryam, she will be your daughter, Oh Mother Maryam, her sons will honor you." Auntie Malkeda told me that seven times was for a girl. I asked her if the same stuff that came out of Momma was in me. "No, not yet", she said, but it would be, when I was a woman. I asked her, "Will I have to be a woman?" and she said, "Yes."

She poured water on the baby, while Auntie Feriwot held her and the baby's goat cry got louder, "Maaaaah, Maaaaah." They held her up for Momma to see. Momma put the bracelet on her ankle, the same bracelet that Lushan and I have, and then they gave her the baby and Momma held her and put her to her tee-tee. I wanted to hold her too and they told me, "No," but they let me pet her head while she drank from Momma.

What Happened In The Hospital
Marc: **Chicago**

She was conscious from the ribs up but, cut off by a screen she couldn't see what I could, the scalpel cutting red through brown skin, her stomach muscles pulled back, then the womb so red and glistening, incised, and the baby pulled out dark and still, legs tucked up to show the lips. Our daughter not to be. My first thought, this will heal, my second, this will hurt forever.

They'd tried to turn her, three times pushed the bulge far to the side but always the head swung back across the belly like a tide-bound buoy, feet-hooked to pelvis and looking up. The mystery solved when they'd cut in to get her, seized her, found her, lifeless, dead, her idea lost, her hope a fiction, an ephemera.

Her mother just eyes above the oxygen mask, still half there, stunned, died to hold her. "Can I hold her?" Our cold dark nameless dream thing. She held her for a minute and gave her back to the wind. The dark spongy pouch they placed on her ribs that for one wild moment I thought was Lisa's heart was the after-birth, big as a bowl.

2001

First Day In Ethiopia
Lisa: Dice Dota

Adopt An Ethiopian Orphan • Your New Child Is Waiting For You • Bring Him/ Her Home With Our Help!

Momma:

I'm drinking my second cup of Ethiopian coffee black and thick with sugar on the patio of the Hotel Taytu in Dice Dota. It's 11 in the morning and Bad, I know, but Yum, you bet. That's how they drink it here and when you want a waiter, you clap your hands and they come running, really, clap, clap and they jog up to your table. Old slave culture, Black on Black. And I am the Black Queen Bwana Lisa.

We got here yesterday but Ethiopia started the day before in Frankfurt when we changed planes for the flight to Adis. All these elegant Ethiopians dressed to the tits, heading home with baggage carts full of VCRs, Computers, Blenders, Speakers, TVs. Fruits of the West that they can't get there. And then there were couples, like us, adopters, all White except me. What's with that? When Black adopt White we'll all skate across hell.

One gal in line. Mrs. Born Again from Texas, said that she and Mr. Born Again were adopting their third Ethiopian kid, that they had Bosnian and Cambodian too but Ethiopia had so many orphans it was *all she could do not to take them all.* I had to bite my tongue when she told me how easy it was for her to adopt through her church. All I could think about was all the bullshit Marc and I went through with the adoption agency. Was that because we're mixed? No doubt.

This afternoon we pick the baby. I am so scared. What if we pick the wrong one?

11

Mama, it's late morning, I'm sitting on the hotel patio looking down at maybe two hundred people on the main boulevard, and I can't see one White face, not one. And that's a new old feeling. Ever since you got us out of Robert Taylor Homes I've been the fly in the milk and now I'm Brown on Brown.

Which don't mean shit here cuz everybody is. So there's none of that brothah sistah thing we have back home. Long before I open my mouth I'm pegged as a rich American, even when I'm not with Marc, could be by my shoes, my clothes, my walk, I don't know how. When the woman in uniform at the Customs and Immigration desk asked us the purpose of our visit and we said we were adopting, she gave us a look that almost spit, same look I used to see Sandy Lewis give the DFC lady when she came around the building to check up on her kids. She issued us a business visa, not a tourist visa, which was twice as expensive. Same freeze from the Customs official when we showed him the toys we were bringing for the baby. Smile stuck, eyes hard, the tone behind his "Welcome to Ethiopia," saying "Rich motherfuckers, leave us our kids."

So now the scholarship girl from the Projects is the Rich American Bitch just landed in Pisspooropia to snap up a Bargain Baby, their largest export. Once we got out of customs, there was a huge crowd with signs from all these agencies saying "Children's Hope," "Mercy of Hope," "All God's Children," and there was our name on a sign, "Marc and Lisa," held up by Tsehay Tekle, the adoption lady from Andamu Children's Center. She was butter brown, had a big head of dreads, and a smile as wide as a plate. She spoke English like a German, because, she told us, she'd married a German and lived there for fifteen years. I was so glad to see her. She ran interference as we cut through a swarm of porters and rolled our luggage cart down to the parking lot where our driver, Zalman was waiting with his mini-van. Big blue-black guy. Good English. He'd driven for the UN he told us. He loaded up the van with his stuff and then we drove to a motel close to the airport so we could catch some sleep before we drove to Dice Dota.

Marc crashed hard but I was too excited to sleep. I went out to the motel patio. No sigh of Tsehay and Zalman so I walked past the guard who was dozing in his booth at the hotel gate with his machine gun, down the hotel driveway about half a block down the main drag to the airport, Bole Road, six lanes of total chaos; taxis, vans and trucks honking and changing lanes, hordes of people walking at the side of the road, kids herding cattle, goats, and donkeys carrying plastic barrels and boxes, stopping traffic. And beggars, guys with no legs living on the street, and unbelievably sad women with malnourished babies with flies in their eyes, holding out their hands. I gave one of them a quarter because I didn't have any Ethiopian money and the next thing I knew all these little kids were swarming around me, screaming, "You, You, You, Money, Money, Money," and the beggar women pushing their babies at me as the kids jostled me. I held my purse tight and got my elbows down. I wondered if I'd have to start swinging. Thank God for this skinny old man in a suit who rescued me. He yelled at the beggars and swung this little stick that I've noticed lots of Ethiopian men carry, smacking the women and kids right off me, and then he bowed and said, in English: "I apologize." I thanked him. Bowed back. He bowed again. And then he walked me back to the hotel, slapping his stick in his hand.

Marc, Tsehay and Zalmon were all waiting for me. Zalman read me out, told me that if I went out on my own I would be eaten. I asked him how they could tell I was not Ethiopian? He laughed and said that Ethiopians can smell gold from five meters.

We packed our stuff in the van and headed for Dice Dota. It took an hour just to get out of the city, the road was so clogged with trucks, buses and vans, but then we crossed an eroded canyon and a river and the traffic thinned out. Momma, you have to see this countryside, it is so different, no big fields of corn and beans like you see in the midwest, just little tiny plowed plots set out in a dry land, few trees, and dry mountains in the distance, like Nevada. On the side of the road; thatched huts and heaps of grain piled right by the house, cactus, hedgerows, men plowing with oxen, naked children playing outside; no one is fat. The road is alive with horse-drawn carts packed with people, kids herding goats, camels, donkeys, cattle, sometimes you have to wait 10 minutes for a big herd to cross the highway. Folks sit under umbrellas by the side of the road and jump up when you whiz by, trying to flag you down to buy from their little piles of tomatoes, bananas, melons or charcoal. There are people everywhere, you see them way off in the fields sitting under shade trees, or walking behind their goats or digging in the dry dirt with hoes and shovels. I get the feeling that people have been here forever and that nothing has ever changed.

Proof being: all the systems are from ancient days. Get this – it's an hour before noon but it isn't 11 AM. It's 5 in the Day. The day starts at 0 in the Day, which is 6 AM. 7PM is 1 in the Night. It isn't 2002 – it's 1995. The year has 13 months, not 12. Ethiopia was never colonized so they never adopted the Gregorian calendar, they have an ancient Coptic one and it does just fine. Yesterday we took a "cultural taxi", *a horse and buggy*. Really there are hardly any cars in this town. The poor horse was covered with scabs. Momma, Marc's come downstairs and Tsehay from the Children's Center just arrived. We're going to see our baby. Right now. My God, I can't help but think that the spirit we lost is coming back to us, and that this time, she's going to stay. Love, Lisa.

Marc and Lisa Visit The Children's House
Rodeat: Dice Dota

The cozy and surprisingly fast developing city of Dice Dota lies 325 km South East of Adis Ababa, the capital of Ethiopia. At an altitude of 1,800 m. above sea level it has a pleasant climate and also is in a beautiful location on Lake Gumare. Previously, it was the capital of the Andamu Province and now it is the capital city of the Southeast Peoples Region (SEPR).

Greetings Miss Lisa and Mr. Marc, I am Rodeat, the sister to Tsehay. I welcome you to Ethiopia and to Dice Dota. We are thankful that you have come this great distance from America to help our children.

Come now to the children's house so that you can see the boys and girls in our care. You said you wanted a girl. That is good because all parents in Ethiopia pray for boys because girls are a burden, and so there are many more girls abandoned here than boys. For this girl the life you will take her from is one of the most severe poverty. Jesus will bless you for making this child your own and giving her the chance to grow up healthy and find the love of a mother and father in America.

Come on now, we must go into the minibus. I apologize if these beggars are a bother. We are a poor country and many foreigners are not used to this. Please – do not give coins to children – because that gives them the reason to think that this will be a good profession. If you want to give to them I suggest you buy pens and give them away. They need those for school.

Yes, here you see St. Abraham. It is known throughout Ethiopia. On Holy days there are thousands here worshiping outside the church. I will take you if you want, if you are here next Sunday.

Yes, we take Muslim children as well as Christian. We are easy with this.

We are not like the Arab people. A child is the same under Allah or Jesus. No, we do not have any Muslim children presently.

Did you bring gifts? For all the children? Good. Often foreigners bring gifts for only one child and that makes the other children very sad. Please do not show the children gifts until we have all met and discussed which child is the one you want.

Here we are, this is our compound. The children are waiting to meet you.

Got Baby
Lisa: **Adis Adaba**

Andamu Children's Center • Building a future for the Children of Ethiopia • Because our Children are our Wealth

Hello Momma.

MOMMA, I'm so glad you are there, I can't talk long, it's like $10 a minute. Unbelievable.

In Adis. In the hotel. We're back from Dice Dota. No, there's no Internet here, Momma, You don't get it, there's no infrastructure here, it's just coming in.

Forget that, *Grandma Emma.* YES, We got the baby. This morning. She's so beautiful, I can't tell you, she's three, out of diapers mostly they say, almost your color, not quite as red. She has the most beautiful eyes and face, she's fat and healthy, she loves to laugh and eat. They say she doesn't talk. Her name is Kalkidane, but we are going to call her Kay Lee. Not *Kali,* Mom, that would be like a curse, we're not crazy. *Kay Lee.* Rhymes with Bailey. Kay Lee Emmeline Levi, Emmaline for you, her Grandma. Yeah!

Momma, hush your mouth, Kay Lee does not sound like a porn star! It sounds happy.

Her parents died of AIDS. No, she didn't cry at all.

No, the paperwork was easy. Not like in Chicago. Look, Momma, this call costs a fortune. I'll give you all the details when I see you. We're flying in a couple of hours.

You'll be at the airport? Oh Momma, I can't wait to introduce you. We'll call you from Frankfurt if we are late.

Look, I gotta go. We're going to the market. It's the biggest in Africa.

Yeah, and there are thieves in Chicago too. Don't worry. Marc has a money belt. Love you, love you, love you. See you tomorrow or whatever day it will be when we get home. Bye, *Grandma*.

My Blessing To The Child The Americans Bought
Lieutenant Giron: **Bole Airport**

They were different from most of those people who take children – a Black woman and a White man, Americans. The girl looked exactly like my second daughter, Kassa. Exactly. It broke my heart that they had bought her. I looked the girl in the eye and told her, "Never forget, you are Abesha." I swear, she nodded that she understood. The people asked me what I had said to her. I told them, "I wished her a good life." The girl had gold around her ankle that set off the machine. I asked them, "Are you taking gold from Ethiopia?" Then I let them through.

Kalkidane Is Gone
Nigest: **Dice Dota**

The number of Ethiopian children adopted into foreign families in the U.S., Canada, and Europe has risen from just a few hundred several years ago to several thousand last year. The increase has been so rapid — and, for some, so lucrative — that some locals have said adoption was becoming the new export industry for our country." Kathryn Joyce – The Atlantic Monthly, Dec. 21, 2011

We walked to the Center to meet the Americans, Selam, Lushi, Geta and me. I had to stop many times, because I was so heavy then, and I had Geta, who was just then walking, in my arms. Selam helped me. She is a good girl. When we got there Weyzero Rodeat and Tsehay said that the Americans had been confused about the plane and had had to leave suddenly that morning with Kalkidane. When I asked Rodeat for the rest of the money she said they had left without paying her but she would be contacting them in America and when the money came she would let me know. Oh my God I thought now I am in trouble. Gyorgis bought a television from fat Tadesse and is expecting this money to pay off what he owes him. And we were going to use the rest of the 100,000 birr for school uniforms and medicine for the other children. "When will the money come?" I asked Rodeat.

She told me she would let me know. She swore it to God.

I could not believe this. "Oh my God," I cried: "Kalkidane, my daughter, are you gone so far away without my chance to say goodbye? Who has taken you? Will I ever see you again? Will you ever know your mother?"

2002

Kay Lee Goes Pottie And Says "Helicopter"
Lisa and her Mother: **Chicago**

Hi Momma, what's up?

The Princess? As good as she can be.

Nope, we're all done with that. She's figured it out. Were you worried?

Well, yes, 5 is late, but you know regression is common with adoptees. You gotta remember, the kid went through some big changes.

Yes it is a milestone. They should issue certificates: So and so, age 5 has mastered the art of the potty and is fully licensed to use sanitarily inspected commodes unaccompanied by an adult. Signed, Y. P. Butts III, Pee and Poop hD.

Oh God, yes, it's a flood, it's a torrent, it's a miracle. This is the age of genius. Yesterday we were in the back yard. A helicopter was over the lake and she looked up and pointed and said, very seriously, he-lo-cop-ter. She pronounced each syllable like the lady in language lab. And then in the evening she looked up and saw the moon and said, "Mun."

I don't know. We had Seleshe and Eva over and Seleshe was speaking to her in Amharic and she got a very serious look on her face. I don't know how much she remembers.

Yeah, I know. We're going to take her to the Community Center and get her started. They have Amharic, folk-dancing for all the kids, stuff to keep them in touch with their culture.

Look, Momma, it's nice out and I want to take her to the park. Are you good for Thursday babysitting?

Great, Marc and I are going out.

I don't know, a meal, maybe some dancing. We haven't done that in ages.

You are a dirty old lady. That's why I love you. We'll bring her by at five.

Thanks Momma. And bye.

The Story of You (Kay Lee)
Marc: **Chicago**

Dad, tell me the story of me.

Kay Lee, I've told you the story every night this week.

Tell it again. Tell it to me again.

Did you brush your teeth?

I brushed my teeths and I brushed my hair.

Did you kiss Momma goodnight?

I kissed her.

Did you really?

I forgot.

OK, move over. Once upon a time there was a little brown girl named Kalkidane who lived in a country called what?

Dice Dota

Right. No. Ethiopia. The town is Dice Dota. The *country* is Ethiopia. She lived in a little blue house behind a tin gate and a cactus fence on a dirt road where children played and goats ate everything. She lived with many other brown children and two ladies called Mamita One and Mamita Two. You see, Kalkidane and all the other children had no mother and father, so the Mamitas and the other children were their family and the blue house was their home.

Did her mother and father die?

Yes they died from a bad disease called AIDS.

Did they…

Let me go on. Kalkidane loved her Mamitas and she loved to play in the road with her brothers and sisters, but still she missed having a real family. One day your Momma and Daddy came to visit the blue house. They came from far away across the sea from…where?

Meerka.

Right.

Chicago.

They were looking for a little girl to be their daughter because they had had a little girl who died and they missed her. They met all the children in the blue house and gave them all presents, rubber balls and dolls and little animals. Your Mommy and Daddy spoke what?

English.

Right. And people in Ethiopia spoke another language. What?

Maric.

Almost. *Amharic*. Say it. Am-har-ic.

Am-har-ic.

Good. So, they spoke different languages so it was hard for them to understand one another. The Mamitas told the children that your Mommy and Daddy's names were Lisa and Marc. Lisa and Marc loved all the children but they loved a girl named Kalkidane the most. Who is Kalkidane?

Kay Lee.

Right, so they asked Mamita One and Mamita Two if they could be her mother and father and take her to live with them in America. The Mamitas said, do you promise to always love Kalkidane and take care of her forever and ever? Lisa and Marc said yes, so the Mamitas said, "OK." Kalkidane was sad to leave the Mamitas and her brothers and sisters and the goats, but she was also excited to have her own mother and father and to go to America.

Can we get a goat?

No.

I want a goat.

They don't let you have one in the city.

I want one.

Too bad, you can't, now don't interrupt, sorry, *please* don't interrupt. Kalkidane said goodbye to the Mamitas and to the other children and got in a van with Lisa and Marc and the driver. They drove to the big city, Adis Ababa, and they got in a little room in a tall building. When they pressed a button the door in the little room closed and the room rose way up to the

7th floor. Kalkidane was scared and she cried. Do you remember that? Are you sleepy?

Story.

Then the door opened and they got out and went into another room where there was a man and a woman who signed many papers and put a big stamp on them. Then they went to the airport and stood in line for a long time and Kalkidane got very tired and wished she was back in the blue house with the Mamitas and she missed her brothers and sisters and the goats. She was hungry and tired and she cried some more. Your Momma picked you up and took you to the bathroom and gave you a cookie and a drink of water. Finally we got into the plane and after a while the plane started to go so fast that you were scared, but then you looked out the window and saw the city and land getting smaller below you and you laughed because you knew you were not just a girl anymore, you were a bird. Do you remember that? Are you asleep?

Who's Your Momma?
Marc and Lisa: **Chicago**

Seleshe says she has a mother. He says she told him. He says she knows Amharic and she wonders where her mother is. Seleshe says she says she didn't die. And that she wants to see *her* and these other names – who he thinks are her brothers and sisters.

But Tsehay and Rodeat said her parents died of AIDS and she was given to the orphanage. That she had no one. That she'd been abandoned.

Seleshe says that's probably bullshit. It happens all the time in Ethiopia. A family gives a kid up for adoption so the kid will have a better life, the orphanage promises the family money, tells them that they will have a new American family, and that's the last the family hears of the kid. And people who arrange the adoption pay off the government and take most of the money.

No, no, no, that can't be. They said she was an orphan.

Did we see any papers? Death certificates? Proof?

We signed papers.

Yes, but that was to get permission to take her out of the country and bring her into the US. But we didn't see any proof.

But we assumed.

Right we *assumed*. I showed Seleshe the paperwork we got from the Center. It gave us custody yes, but there was nothing that said they had the custody to give.

Oh Jesus, you mean…her family…if she has a family…could ask to get her back?

I don't know about that. But if she does have another family she has to know them. We can't take that away from her. Or them.

This could be really complicated. What if we just didn't go down this road?

Maybe she'd forget them? It would all sort of recede into a murky past and come back when she goes through therapy after she's killed us for not telling her.

LISA!

I know. I'm a bad selfish girl. I don't want to share my doll. I want to be her one and only mother like I am now.

Maybe you could think of it as a gift, giving her back her birth family, the same way they gave her to us.

Fuck, Marc, you sound like those bible thumpers on the plane. Shit! Bastard! I hate this. What should we do?

Lisa, here comes the waitress, get it together. What do you want?

A shot of Dewars. A double. No, a triple. Just to start with.

Lisa…

And a beer back.

Lisa, let's go slowly with this. We can ask Seleshe to come back over. And then we can all play a game, you know, like house, and we could…have crayons and we could draw…a family…and…

Ato Adane Puts His Detectives To Work
Adane Ermes: Ethiopian Community Center: **Chicago**

More and more we see these people. They adopt a child who they are told is an "orphan," and bring it to America. The orphan cries and cries and they wonder what is wrong with the child? They hold it, they feed it, they kiss it, but still it cries. Then, once the child learns some English, they learn that all along the baby has been crying for the mother who sold it, and wondering, my God, where are my brothers and sisters? So it becomes obvious to the adopters that their "orphan" is not an orphan and they come to the Ethiopian Association crying for help to find the birth family. We have had five cases this year.

We try to track down the Ethiopian agency that played this trick, and we help find the birth family, and when we finally do, there is so much love, the American family cries and cries and says we are so sorry, we didn't know, now you are our Ethiopian family, and the Ethiopian family cries and cries and says thank you thank you, we thought we had lost our child. Then they immediately ask for the money that the criminals who arranged the adoption had promised would be sent to them. And usually the Americans are glad to send it; they are guilty that have taken a child away from its family, they feel good to help the other brothers and sisters, and they are scared that the family will want them to return the child. Until, the next year, when the Ethiopian family asks again, for school tuition for the other children, for medical bills, and please send shoes. And then in the next year – for their cousin to start a business and their big daughter to go to Business College, and their father to have an operation. The requests get bigger and the American family begins to get angry; they only contracted to adopt a child, not to support a whole clan. They stop communicating, they cease answering the requests and finally they cut off all contact. And the Ethiopian family gets angry because they have tied their dreams for the future to the American money and now there is no answer to their asking. So both families are angry and speak badly of each other and the child who was adopted becomes confused and torn. Why will her American family not help her brothers and sisters? And is her Ethiopian family a bunch of thieves? I have seen it happen many times.

They gave me the details, the name of the child and the names of the criminals who sold her. My sister is in Dice Dota and knows everybody there. I will offer her son Fikir fifty dollars to find the girl's parents. He will find them, no problem.

Fikir Gets An Assignment From Uncle Adane:
Fikir: Dice Dota

What, Mamoo?

Uncle Adane? For *me?*

Give it to me.

Hello. Uncle? Uncle Adane? Are you back for a visit?

In Chicago? You are calling from Chicago?

Are you in health? And my aunt and my cousins?

We are all well. Yes, I graduated in sociology from Gonder last year. But no job. I play the immigration lottery and pray to God.

Oh yes, what you will, I will do it.

850 birr? To find a family? This is too generous. This will really help me. Wait, let me write.

Andamu Children's Center? Rodeat? Tsehay? I know them. Those are the Tekles. They have their own private children's house. Kalkidane? That is the girl?

I will find them. How will I let you know?

No, there is not email yet. Only in the Irish Library. But it is coming. My friend will start a café like they have in Adis.

Three days? That is more than enough time. I will have this information for you when you call.

Thank you Uncle, Please visit. If I win the DV I will see you in Chicago. And my cousins. OK, three days.

Goodbye Uncle Adane. And, thank you. Mamoo!

Mamoo! Come here. Uncle Adane has a job for me.

It was nothing to find Nigest. In Dice Dota the street is our television and everyone has a big mouth so you can find out everything about every family.

First thing in the morning I put out the word to Kiflu and Zela through Mektid at Coffee Metra that I had some work for them and that they should find me there at Seven in the Day. They are my brothers and best friends and are always there for a job. We met and had coffee. I gave them the information from Ato Adane; the girl is Kalkidane, she knows some Amhara words, she was taken by the Tekles; there is a mother, two sisters and a baby brother; the father had one leg; the Americans who took her are a Black woman and a White man. My boys put out the call to all their connections. By the time we met on the next day it was a sure thing. Zela's cousin Antoneh had told him about Gyorgis, an Amhara married to Nigest an Oromo from his mother's clan. He lives in Atoneh's kabele, had lost his leg in the Ogaden and had sold his daughter to the Tekles. The family name is Zena. I knew Antoneh from school. He brought me to Gyorgis family in the evening. The father was not there so I spoke with the mother Nigest. She cried and hugged me and wouldn't let me go. "God sent you," she said. For three years I am fighting with these Tekle witches to find my daughter."

Nigest was with me when Adane called. We arranged that the Americans who had taken Kalkidane would telephone our house in the next days and I would translate for Nigest.

The next week Adane sent the money to Western Union. I gave thirty birr each to Kiflu, Zela and Antoneh and with the rest I bought some cool shoes.

2003

In Defense Of Kalkidane's Orphan Status
Tsehay: **Dice Dota**

(Hold up five fingers.)
Five little monkeys sitting on the bed
(Hold up one finger and roll your hand down towards the floor.)
One fell down and bumped his head
(Tap your head with your fist.)
Mama called the Doctor and the Doctor said
(Put your pinky in your mouth and thumb to your ear like a telephone.)
No more little monkeys jumping on the bed
(Put one hand on your hip and wag your index finger.)

I don't know why there is all this trouble. We were only trying to find a good home for the girl, like we do for all the children. I knew her family; they were hungry hyenas and they would have bitten Weyzero Lisa and Ato Marc and kept biting if they had known who was taking her. They would have drunk their blood until they had nothing left.

Come on, we took them to the Center. The childrens were waiting for their presents and sang their monkey song like they always do when farange come, and then played with their presents until dinner. They were happy because they knew that the Mamitas would serve them meat. Ato Marc and Weyzero Lisa watched them play and picked Kalkidane, just as Rodeat and I knew they would. They always choose the fat and pretty ones and she was a well-fed child. And we had dressed her especially.

The childrens are so smart. When farange come, I can always tell, they are wondering who will be chosen, they are always giving looks at them at dinner and trying to be the one who has a smile. We never tell them who is leaving until the next day when we say goodbye.

Yes, she *was* an orphan. She *was.* You do not understand! In this country you do not have to have your parents dead; if you are abandoned you are an orphan. When someone brings us their child that means they are giving them up. Everyone here knows this, it is only the farange who make this confusion and, my God, this causes such problems.

Yes we give them a little money. That is so that they can feed their other childrens. They would not give up a child unless it was for that. What, do you think, that our people do not love their childrens?

No little monkeys jumping on the bed
(*Children put their toys in toy boxes.*)
None fell off and broke their head
(*Children line up in front of boys' sink and girls' sink.*)
Momma called the doctor and the doctor said
(*Children pray and arrange their mosquito nets.*)
Put those little monkeys back in bed.
(*Children get into bed.*)

How We Drank Milk and Peed In A Toilet
Selamawit: Dice Dota

After the boy said that they had found my sister Kalkidane in the USA my Father made Momma take us back to Weyzero Rodeat's house to try to get our money. I had to carry Geta because Momma is so big now it is hard for her to walk. It was too hot and it was too far. Lushan walked by herself and didn't cry. When we got to the gate, Momma knocked and knocked. The man, Ato Zalman, called from behind the gate, "What do you want?"

Momma said, "To speak with Weyzero Rodeat.

"She's not here now."

Momma gave me the sign that she was going to tell a lie by pretending to cut her tongue with her fingers and called over the wall. "Please Ato Zalman, it is Nigest. Tell her I must talk to her about taking my son Geta."

There was whispering from behind the gate. Then Weyzero Rodeat's voice said, "Zalman, I am back from the market. Is that Nigest? Nigest, my sister, please come in and visit."

Ato Zalman opened the gate and there was Weyzero Rodeat with a big smile and very nice, with her round face and shiny skin, gold in her mouth and a good smell of soap. She took Momma by the hand and put her arm out to carry Geta, smiling and pinching his fat cheek and saying, "You are a beautiful boy." I was glad she took him; he was so heavy he was killing me. As she led us to her house at the end of the compound the children watched us through the windows of their house. Did they think that we were orphans like them? How could they? We were with our own mother.

Her house was too big and beautiful, with four rooms and every room with a window and a roof and electric lights. Her son, Dawit, was there in the room with big furniture, sitting in a chair *watching a television*. I knew him from school. Everyone knew he was an only son and that he was rich and had a television. She clapped for the girl to make coffee and bring milk. *Milk?* Did Dawit have milk every day, I wondered? Did he have Fanta? The girl brought two glasses for Lushan and me and we both looked at Momma to be sure we could drink. She nodded and Weyzero Rodeat laughed and said, "Drink, drink children, the Germans sent a cow like a big black and white factory. We have too much milk."

Then she took Momma and Geta into the kitchen and Lushan and I sat in the room with Dawit and drank our milk. I drank mine very slowly to make it last. I had never had a glass so big of my own before. Lushan watched me and only drank when I drank. It was too good, cold and with all the cream that stayed on your tongue after you swallowed. On the television was a big green man with a body like a triangle, and many muscles. He had guns for hands. He was speaking in a voice like a hyena; English, I knew it from school. He fired his gun-hands at thousands of yellow spiders that came out of a car that flew in a red sky and when the spiders fell and died blue blood splashed out of them and Dawit made gun sounds, duh, duh. But he would not talk to us or look at us. He showed an angry face, I thought, because his mother had let us into her house and given us his milk. He was wearing sports shoes and his clothes were very new. He wore a jacket that was shiny like metal with a big red English letter on it, the "C", from "CAT" that I knew from school. He was a very rich boy. Everyone knew this.

We waited and waited and drank our milk. I had to pee-pee. I asked Dawit where? He pointed to a door inside the house. I got up and opened the door. There was a toilet. I was so happy. I had pee-peed and pooped in one at the hotel when Uncle Afaz got married, my auntie had showed me how and I loved them. This one was white and clean and water was inside it and there was no stink. I came back to show Lushan. I wanted to teach her. She was watching the television where now a man and a woman were giving cookies to some children. The children were laughing and biting the cookies and then the cookies danced and sang a funny song about how they were the best cookies and that all children would like them very much. Lushan would not come, she wanted to watch the cookies, so I pulled her off the chair and dragged her into the room. She cried and tried to bite and Dawit said "Shut up," so I closed the door. "Look," I said and pulled the handle and we watched the water go around and around. I put the seat down and sat and made a pee-pee and wiped with the paper that was there on the toilet. Then I let Lushan pull the handle again and we watched the pee-pee and the paper go away. Then it was Lushan's turn. I held her so she would not fall in and pulled her panties down and she pee-peed and she wiped and pulled the handle and again we watched. It was so white and clean that toilet room, I wanted to stay in there forever.

I Tricked Rodeat
Nigest: **Dice Dota**

I said to Rodeat, "Look, I was thinking, those Americans who took Kalki, the boy Fikir said that God will not let them have any more children. Won't that be so lonely for her, to have no brothers and sisters, to be alone, how could this be for a child and for a father and mother to only have one little one at the table? What if they took Geta too? Then they would be Abesha together, both of the same seed. And, if Geta goes to America, there will be more for Selam and Lushan and the new baby." She fell for my story and made tears come to her eyes, but I knew when she said, "Oh yes, the girl will be so lonely," she was thinking: *more money.*

Weyzero Rodeat had always looked at me as a slave, someone she might pay to clean her kitchen and sleep under the table, but when she thought for one minute that there was money to come from selling Geta she became my closest sister. These landowner families still think it is the Haile Selassie time and that everything is theirs. And those Tekle women go blind when they smell gold; they are famous for this.

She told her servant to give the children milk and while Geta drank on my lap she telephoned her sister and told her the idea of the Americans taking Geta too.

"Tsehay says she will speak with the Americans about this."

I asked if I could speak with Tsehay.

On the phone I said, "Wezyero Tsehay, I am blessed for you speaking to Ato Marc and Weyzero Lisa about taking Geta. But I would like to speak to these Americans to see what would be the agreement about Geta."

"I will call them and ask them," replied Tsehay.

"Thank you," I said, "but I must hear their voices. It is from their voice that I can tell who is a good person." Oh that caught them. When Rodeat heard what I said to Tsehay, the thought flickered behind her eyes: *if Nigest talks to the Americans then they will know everything about the money. And then Nigest will want us to pay her what we stole from her.*

I knew Tsehay thought the same as her sister. Blood can know without words. Her lie was no surprise. She said: "These calls are very expensive Nigest and when it is day in America it is night here. I will make the call from Adis in the middle of the night when the cost is low."

How she twisted and turned! But I would not let her keep her teeth in me. I danced around her words and said, "Thank you Tsehay but I do not want you to have so much trouble and such a cost! I will come back to Rodeat's early in the next days and then we can make the phone call. Rodeat will translate. And I will bring money for the call, so do not worry. You have already spent so much. You are a good friend and I know you will help Geta join his sister in America. In the name of Saint Gabriel, I thank you."

I gave the telephone back to Rodeat, took Geta from her and left the room with her on the telephone with Tsehay. Oh yes, I knew they would plan a trick, but I had a trick of my own to put against theirs, and we would see who the winner would be. In the other room Dawit was watching the television. The girls were not there. I could see they had drunk their milk because their glasses were on the table.

I said, "May you have health, Dawit, where are the girls?"

My God, what a spoiled boy. He did not greet me, he did not rise for his elder, and he behaved like a little dictator. These landowner families, they pass on the ruling mentality and you cannot kill it. Mengistu tried but no matter how much of their blood he drank, he could not change their ways. One thing I can say about those communists, under them, the poor man had a better chance to become big than when the Haile Selassie people sat in their palaces and squeezed everyone.

I heard the girls and called to them. They came out happy from behind the white door. Lushi said, "Momma I went pee-pee in the toilet. And there is no stink." Oh how I pray that they will get education, those girls so that they will live in a good house.

I brought them back into the kitchen to say thank you to Weyzero Rodeat. She was still talking on the telephone to her sister, but she stopped when she saw us. Her trick was not finished. The girls bowed and thanked her for the milk.

"Not to trouble you my sister, but when should I come for the phone call?" I said. "We should do this soon or who knows what can happen? The small rains will bring malaria and Geta is so young. And I love him too much and do not want to change my mind."

You see how I was making my trap? She did not want to lose any money so she had to put her foot into the net.

"May we come the day after tomorrow?"

She fell like a rabbit. "Yes, at Three in the Day. That will be the morning in America." Then, as if she remembered that the coffee needed more sugar, she made it too sweet, taking my hand, kissing Geta and looking into my eyes to read my heart.

"Oh sister, you give up too much for these children. Mother Maryam gives you her blessing."

"What can we do? Our children are our life," I said, avoiding her look, by pressing her close so I could look beyond her through the kitchen window. In the yard the children were playing and the Mamitas were cooking injera. How much money does she get for each child, I wondered. She had given me only 10,000 birr for Kalki.

As we walked home all Lushi and Selam would talk about was the toilet. "Where did the water go?" they asked. I did not know. I had to find that boy Fikir.

Connection!
Marc and Lisa: **Chicago**

Marc: It was almost too fast. I was half hoping it would take a while and Lisa was hoping that we'd never find them, but no, the African telegraph turned on full amp; drum signal went out on Tuesday and on Thursday we are talking on the phone to Nigest Zena and Adane's nephew, Fikir, who is translating. It seems we have a whole new family. That's a whole lot more love than I was counting on. And what about the money?

"Hello, hello. I am Lisa calling from America."

"Hello, hello, is this Mrs. Lisa?"

"Who is this?"

"This is the nephew of Ato Adane. I am Fikir, who found the family. I speak English."

"Oh Hello Fikir. Of course. I am Lisa. My husband is here, too, Marc."

"Hello Fikir."

"Hello Mr. Marc."

"We are the people who adopted Kay Lee."

"I'm sorry Mr. Marc. We do not understand. Who is Kay Lee?"

"The girl, Kalkidane, we call her Kay Lee. Fikir, is her mother there? Can we say hello? Does she speak English?"

"No."

"Hello Nigest? Nigest?"

"She says hello, Mr. Lisa and Mr. Marc."

"Hello Nigest."

"Excuse me Mrs. Lisa and Mr. Marc. Nigest asks – can she hear Kalkidane?"

"Fikir, what are they saying?"

"She calls her a little monkey. And she asks if she remembers Amharic and if she remembers her mother and father. Now the girl answers her and asks where is her father's leg? Now Nigest answers and says it was stolen by the Somalis in the War of the Ogaden. And now Nigest talks to you and wants me to translate. She would like to thank you so very much. She apologizes for not meeting you in Dice Dota. She came to see you at the house of Rodeat but Rodeat said you had left. That was her trick."

"Fikir, tell Nigest that Rodeat and Tsehay told us that Kay Lee was an orphan. That her mother and father had died of AIDS."

"Mr. Marc and Mrs. Lisa. Nigest says that they gave you a lie. They did it for the present. She says they stole the present that you gave to her."

"Fikir, we gave presents to all the children at Rodeat's house."

"Mr. Marc and Mrs. Lisa, she is not talking about the presents for the children. These are small things. She is speaking of the money for Kalkidane, the 100,000 birr that Tekles promised. When she did not get it her husband beat her. He had bought many things and had no money to pay the ones he owed. He had to give them back. Nigest needs to know if you will send her that money. And the 20,000 that you will send every year for the other children. Was that also a lie from Rodeat?"

"But I only adopted one child, not a whole family."

"Madame, I do not think you understand the culture of our country. The family would never have given Kalkidane to Rodeat unless she would get money to help the other children. Do you think that we don't love our children?"

Oh Jesus.

"Look, Fikir, tell Nigest, that we will do the best we can."

"Mrs. Lisa, Nigest says thank you. And if her new baby is male she will name her new baby after Mr. Marc."

"Her new baby? "

"Oh yes, Nigest is pregnant. She is due any day."

44

Lisa: My stomach was flipping through the whole conversation. This kid Fikir was a little operator; he worked the conversation like a pro. First he breaks it to us that we've been tricked, that Kay Lee is no orphan, rather she's got a huge family who expect us to support them. *I don't ask for how long? Does that mean the grand-children too?* I don't scream when he says that, all I do is look at Marc and make the crazy sign with my hand in circles by my head. Then he tells us that they have to get the money we gave to Rodeat and Tsehay and if we'd call to Rodeat's house in two days, Nigest will also be there and we can make Rodeat confess.

Marc is listening. He nods, so I say OK. The plan is to call them on Thursday at "Nine in the Day" ostensibly about adopting Kay Lee's brother, but really to bust their chops for the lies they told and the money they stole. Hey, I'm ready to take them on, but while I'm trying to figure out what time is "Nine in the Day" the line goes dead.

Gyorgis Has To Give Back A TV
Gyorgis: Dice Dota

Izzak, my brother, here is the khat. Chew it, it is just fresh of the truck.

Now I want to say this about that fat bastard Girma. Don't let anyone tell you that I am scared of him. If I had my fucking leg I could beat him. I have known him since I was a boy, I went to school with him and he cried a hundred times when I knocked him down and rubbed his face in the dust. He is like a woman, weak and smart, and will only fight you when your back is turned. If I had my fucking leg I could beat him, but now, what can I do? He has his sons and brothers. What chance would I have against them unless I shot them and if I did that a war would start; they would kill me and then my family would roam the streets like dogs.

Here, give me the leaf. Thank you. It is strong, no? Those people in Yir Gallum, they grow the good stuff.

So when Rodeat stole the money the Americans paid for Kalkidane there was no choice. I had to give Girma back the television and the generator. If I had my fucking leg I might have had a chance to scare him off, but not now. I was beaten. But I also know that we will beat Rodeat and get our money, and then, in the long war, I will be the winner over Girma and his brothers. I will get that television back and the generator and I will buy a bajaj.

It was a good trick that Nigest pulled on Rodeat — to call the Americans when she brought Geta. And God was behind the plan because they got the call through, which only happens these days with a miracle. Even better that Rodeat didn't realize that we would bring Fikir to translate and that I would be there too to add to the tension. Those Tekles do not want to fight me, because I know exactly how much money they have given Ato Sema in the

Children's Office to keep his eyes away from their Center. I know this because Ato Sema's sister was my girlfriend before the accident.

Did you know that? Oh we had a very good time, but then she was married and we had to stop the fun. I kept this secret from everyone but now I tell you because you are my friend. But you must never tell this. Sema's sister's husband would beat me, and If Nigest finds this out she will put a spell on me and I will get sick.

Izzak would you like a St. George?

Selam, bring beer for me and Izzak. Come on! Why are you so slow?

Marc And Lisa Get Cut Off
Marc: Chicago

So they call us and a woman says, "Hallo, Mr. Marc?,"and then the carnival begins; before I can say anything there's shouting in the background and then, *thunk,* someone drops a phone 9,000 miles away, then static, then more *thunks,* then shouting; sounds like people are fighting over the phone. On our end it's not much better; Lisa is trying to grab the phone from me, and I'm slapping her away and giving her the finger-over-the-lips sign, don't make a fucking sound, shut up and back off, let me handle this, for *Chrissakes,* just *listen.*

A woman screams and this kid Fikir gets on the phone. He's very nice.

"Excuse us Mr. Marc, we are having a little argument. Are you fine?"

I tell him I'm fine and I ask him if he's fine and he says he's fine. I say, "What's the matter?"

"We are quarreling with Rodeat, but don't worry, we are all friends. We want to know how much money did Rodeat take from you?"

"$5,000 dollars."

"And did she tell you that Kalkidane was orphan?"

"Yes, of course."

"Here is the mother of Kalkidane, Nigest."

He puts Nigest on the phone now; she's talking, no rather screaming Amharic in that high pitch that the women there have and I don't understand a thing, then, Fikir gets back on the line and says:

"Listen to Rodeat, *the thief…*"

At which point Lisa loses it and makes a dive for the phone and I dodge her but then we drop the phone. We are both scrabbling under the table to get it, but I grab it first, wave my fist at her like I'm gonna paste her in the mouth, and say, "Sorry."

"Now you will hear the thief confess herself."

And then there is a woman crying and a man's voice yelling until everything quiets down and there is the voice, I think, of Rodeat, who says, "Hello Mr. Marc, I hope you are fine."

I tell her I am fine.

Fikir says, "Tell them."

Rodeat says, "I am sorry for the misunderstanding, yes, there is the family of Kalkidane that we have just discovered…"

Obviously that is too much for the rest of the Kalkidane family, because then there is more yelling. I think it is Fikir who says: "Mr. Marc, she is lying…"

And we get cut off and Lisa freaks the fuck out.

2006

Lushan Prays To Mother Maryam
Lushan: **Dice Dota**

Mother Maryam I am praying to you, so please listen. First, I thank you for keeping my mother safe and giving us our sister Bertukan. She is a beautiful baby though my father and mother are not happy that she is another girl. The other baby before was a boy but he did not live and this made everyone sad. It was God's will and I accept that. Now we have Selam, Me, Geta and Bertu, and, then there is Kalkidane in America. That is a good family and that is enough.

Mother Maryam, you know that I am very grateful for my family but please, be aware, if you send any more babies there will be some problems. Even if we sell the new baby to the Americans it will not be a good idea. Nigest gets more and more tired each time she has a baby and I do not want her to get sick and die because then who would be my mother in this world? Already there are so many of us and there is the problem that Geta gets every-thing first because he is a boy, so there is less to eat for all of us, especially me and Selam. You know I would like milk, but who can buy milk? Since my father spent the American money they only give milk to the baby. Then finally the biggest problem is I want to keep going to school but they say that they will buy Geta's uniform first because if a boy goes to school he will find money for the family. My mother says that the Americans will pay for my school but I do not believe her. And even if they send money I know my father will take that money and spend it on khat and a bajaj.

Mother Maryam, I know what you can do when you come to the kabele. Skip our tukol and visit the next compound where Kidist and her husband live. They only have one baby. And then go to my Auntie Feriwot. She only has two babies and her husband works for the Chinas and has a motorcycle. They have a television. Give them a girl for me to play with.

Goodnight Mother Maryam, I want to sleep before the baby starts to cry and my father's curses wake me. Please keep me safe and tell the Americans to send money for my school uniform before the new grade starts, and, if they do, don't let my father chew it up with his friends. If you can manage that I will be a very good and helpful girl.

Your daughter, Lushan.

A Skype To Fikir In Dice Dota
Marc: **Chicago**

Voices, timbre and words, oxymoronic *live image*, disintegrated into dots, transmitted by waves, snagged in space by satellites, bent, beamed and reassembled dot by dit across a screen 9000 miles away. For all this disembodiment and reassemblage, we appear to each other in "real" time, no delay, they call it "live," and me thinking with all the *re-formation*, is there any shred of meaning left or has the code become the message and the meaning just the conduit for the code?

This is everybody's first Skype. We'd arranged it with Fikir, Adane's nephew, the one who found Kay Lee's family and who we'd talked to at Rodeat's before we got cut off, Fikir, the cool kid with the English, he's the one who picks up the Skype. Lisa is videoing my laptop screen. We'll show the video to Adane to confirm that this is indeed the right guy. After getting played for fools by Kidist and Tsehay we figure that the Ethiopian truth is somewhat mutable; we better keep records. Kay Lee, Lisa and I crowd around the MacBook.

Switch to record.

Fikir says: "Hello, hello, Mr. Marc, Mrs. Lisa. We are here in the Tesfay Phillipos Computer Shop."

I say: "Hello, hello Fikir can you see us, we can't see you, can you turn on the video camera for Skype, we think it is in the box on the upper right side." A forehead appears, light skinned, hair in dreads. Then a face, too close and blurry, a young man. This must be Fikir. His face moves in and out of focus.

He says: "I can see you."

I say: "Fikir, can you put her brothers and sisters in front of the camera so she can meet them? Kay Lee, get in front of the computer."

A girl appears on the screen. Six ? Seven? Same perfect mouth and almond eyes as Kay Lee, longer nose, and rounder face. In English: "Hello sister, I am Lushan. Are you fine?"

Kay Lee gives me a look. I nod, yes, you are fine. "Yes, sister, I am fine? Are you fine?"

"Yes, thank you."

She suddenly vanishes from the camera. Loud talking in Amharic, a man's voice, a woman's and the girl's. Then Fikir's face in the camera, smiling: "My dear Miss Kalkidane, here is your other sister."

Half the face of an older girl appears close up in the camera. She's darker than Lushan. "Hello Sister, I am Selamawit."

"Selamawit please back up so we can see your whole face."

She doesn't get it. Her half face continues. "I have 9 years. I am in the Grade 4 and I am first in my room. I must have a uniform to continue or they put me out. So must my sister and brother."

I look at Lisa. Obviously she's been coached.

"I miss you so much."

"Fikir, please ask Selamawit to move backwards." Now Fikir's voice, harsh and high in Amharic, and then a woman's, scolding. Selamawit pulls back and we can see her whole face now. She has Kay Lee's longer face, but is darker, her lips are more full and her nose is longer. But for her skin tone, she's the spitting image of a Jewish girl from Queens. Sheba.

"Kay Lee, say something." She gives me a look. I mouth the word "pretty," and whisper, "tell her she is pretty."

"You are very pretty."

"Thank you. You are so pretty. When do you come?"

Kay Lee gives me another look. I shake my head.

"I don't know."

"You must come. I will show you all things in Dice Dota, the Church of Abraham and Gumare Lake. And then I will come to Chicago."

Suddenly she's gone, obviously yanked away from the camera. Here's Fikir again, his mug filling the screen.

"Kalkidane, now here is Nigest the mother. She is speaking only Amharic. Are you remembering your cultural language?"

Now Nigest appears. This is the first time we can attach a face to the voice we'd heard on the phone. She is lighter than Kay Lee, round-faced like Lushan. Kay Lee lives in her nose and mouth. Hard to tell her age; her face is unwrinkled but there are dark bags under her eyes. She speaks Amharic really fast. Kay Lee listens. Can she understand? Nigest stops abruptly and looks to the side. We're seeing Nigest but hearing Fikir's voice off camera. "She tells, Kay Lee, I miss her so much. Please send pictures of the life in America. Please visit Dice Dota with Mr. Marc and Lisa in this year and to bring presents for your brother and sisters."

Kay Lee is still in front of the computer. Lisa is mouthing something to me. *Isn't there a brother?* I signal Kay Lee to move away, put my face in the camera and interrupt Fikir.

"Hello Nigest. I am Marc." I point to myself and repeat, "Marc." She nods, she understands. I continue. "Nigest, I have a question. Where is the baby? And where is Kay Lee's brother? Fikir, please translate."

Fikir speaks in Amharic. Nigest holds up a caramel baby to the camera, maybe 3 months old, shock of black hair, eyes sealed in sleep, and speaks slowly its name.

"Ber-tu-kan."

Fikir: "The new Queen. Bertukan. Her name means 'orange.'"

Kay Lee starts to crack up. I put my finger to my lips. *Chill.* She mouths: *Cute.*

Fikir: "The brother is playing. He is Getachew. He has six years."

Now Nigest hands off the baby. She puts her face in her hands. When she removes them her eyes are wet. Her hands come together as if in prayer and she looks directly into the camera, nodding her head. She is asking for something. Fikir translates.

"Mr. Marc I apologize but she is asking Mrs. Lisa when she will send the money of Rodeat's promise?" He stops talking and says something in Amharic. Nigest tosses her head, obviously flipping him off.

"Mr. Lisa, Nigest says that Selam and Lushan need school uniforms and shoes. They cannot go to school without them."

Lisa can't take this. She sticks her mug in front of the computer and speaks slowly, as if that will make it easier for Nigest to understand her, even though Nigest doesn't speak a word of English:

"Hello...Nigest...I...am...Lisa. I...want...you...to...know...that... we...are...not...rich...Americans...we...are...artists. We...will...help... your... family...as...much...as...possible. But...we...are...not...rich."

I'm thinking that will make as much sense to the Ethiopians as a Captain Kangaroo rerun. How could they think we were anything but rich? We paid $5,000 for one kid, we pay 60 bucks for shoes. Fikir now speaks Amharic. I assume he is translating for Nigest. I'm worried about Kay Lee hearing all this. Here, the reunion with her Ethiopian family and her real mother has deteriorated into a *hit*. I remember the chant of the Ethiopian street kids: You, You, You. Money, Money, Money. Same deal.

Then Nigest speaks again. She is wiping her eyes. Fikir translates: "Nigest thanks you very much Mr. Marc and Mrs. Lisa. She knows you must keep your promise." I can tell Lisa is about to go off on the word "promise" and I signal her to suck it up, which thankfully she does. They need help and we'll do what we can. Fikir tells us that he will send us the bank information by e-mail so that we can wire money for the uniforms. And then: "Now will Kalkidane say goodbye to her mother and sisters?"

The two girls crowd into their mother so we can only see part of their faces. They push their prettiness into the camera blocking Nigest. "Thank you, sister," they say. Then Nigest gets her mug in front, speaking more in Amharic. I hear the word "Abesha," which I know means "Ethiopia." Fikir doesn't translate. Kay Lee nods as if she understands, then says "Dehna Hugni." Where did that come from? Fikir comes on the screen and says "Thank you," and "Goodbye." The screen goes blank.

Later when Kay Lee is playing with her friend, Lisa and I have a big argument about money. How much should we send? She's in grad school and my job is ending in a month. We decide on $100. *That's all?* That's all.

2007

Selamawit Fights With Her Dad And Channels Beyoncé
Selamawit: Dice Dota

So my father becomes a bigger bastard every day. This day is the feast of
St. Michael. We have been to church in the morning and there is no school.
Nigest is working, cooking a feast for the German farange at the GDZ Center.
I am mad because I can't work with her; I have to stay with Lushan and watch
Bertukan, so for me there will be none of the Orange Fanta they give you at
the GDZ. This whole afternoon would be so *boring* except for a very good
thing; I have a funny English book from Mr. Lisa and Marc in America,
which I am reading with Lushi. It is the funniest book and we laugh and
laugh. There are pictures and pictures of very stupid monsters and a very bad
boy and his boat. The monsters think the boy is a God and so they dance. It
is so funny. I understand most of the words except for rumpus: r-u-m-p-u-s.
Is it the name of the dance?

My father's leg is getting worse; he has some sort of infection where it was
cut off. It hurts him badly. I can tell – the pain squeezes his face. He orders
Nigest or me to change the bandage on it for him when he gets it dirty, which
is too often. I hate to do it. All he does now in the morning is go to the corner
with his crutches and wait for the khat truck. When he has bought it he then
comes back to his chair, where the new goat is waiting. When he has chewed
his khat and spit it out for the goat to eat, then he must have his injera and his
coffee and when the khat is all chewed and it is Eight in the Day, his friends
come with their tej. They sit with their dominoes and drink and talk about
the people who kept them down in their life, blaming everyone but themselves. They are old disappointed men, and the more they drink the more they
try to order any woman or child around, "get me this, get me that." Unless it
is my father, I nod my head and don't get them anything. I stay in the tukol,

where they do not come in. If it is my father I have to do what he asks but then I go out to get away from him and stay away until it is dark. I never want to see men like this in my life.

After we finish the book Bertukan wakes up in her basket and cries for Nigest's tee-tee so we give her sugar water on our finger and injera. Then we show the book to her and we read it again, taking her finger to touch the pictures. We play the book; there is the brown doll that they have sent that we call the *Mister Barbare*. She has beautiful clothes and we pretend she is the boy Max and we put him in Bertukan's basket. We dance like the monsters and play that we have feet with teeth, and grab Bertu like we will eat her. She laughs and laughs; we dance with her like we are wild, round and round the compound, dancing and screaming so loudly that Gyorgis starts yelling at us to shut up. Then, to show off for his friends, he grabs the Mister Barbare from the basket and throws her over the fence. Now Bertu is crying and my heart is cold, I would kill my father I am so angry with him but I will not show this to the world. I know he will destroy anything that I like, just to keep me down, so when he goes for the book I am ready; I snatch it to my breast and run with it through the gate before he has a chance to tear it. Ha! There is my mother coming back from work with food from the GDZ and at her feet lies the Mister Barbare, so nothing is lost. She asks me to help her prepare the dinner. I know she will protect me, so back I go into the tukol. The first thing I do is to hide the book in the place I keep my underpants, where my father is forbidden to look. Then I come back out into the compound, hiding Mr. Barbare behind my back. Nigest is giving tee-tee to Bertukan and the men are picking up their dominoes and getting up to go back to their houses. I do not make eye contact with any of them but I quickly give Mister Barbare to Lushi. Oh she is happy to see that Mister Barbare is not lost. I take her to the kitchen house and while Lushi grinds the misir and cuts the potatoes I cut the onions and make strips from the ox Nigest has brought. It is beautiful meat and red. I can hear Nigest and Gyorgis arguing as they do every night about the money he spends on khat and beer, but I don't care about them at all, I am too happy with this beautiful meat and I have the song from Beyoncé to sing while I chop the onions. Lushan sings it with me. We know all the words; we have learned them from the tape of the Denmark woman that we play over and over at the children's center. I love Beyoncé. How can she be so beautiful?

> *If I were a boy even just for a day*
> *I'd roll out of bed in the morning*
> *And throw on what I wanted…*

Kay Lee Channels The Same Song As Her Sister
Kay Lee: **Chicago**

...And go drink beer with the guys
And chase after girls
And I'd never get confronted for it
Cause they'd stick up for me

I was listening to the radio with Momma and we were dancing. She loves this song.

"Why does Beyoncé want to be a boy? I don't want to be a boy."

"Beyoncé doesn't want to be a boy but in the old days in America and in lots of places in the world right now, boys can do things that women can't and it isn't fair. So Beyoncé is imagining that if she was a boy things would be more fair for her."

"What things?"

"Well for one thing in a lot of places it's OK for men to have more than one girlfriend or boyfriend or even wives, but if women have more than one boyfriend or girlfriend or husbands, they call her a name, *whore*, and in some countries the men beat her and even kill her. You are lucky to live in America where that is against the law and the law says that boys and girls are equal, even if sometimes the law doesn't work. "

"Why did they kill her and not the boy if he has more than one girlfriend? "

"Honey it's all about power. Once you kiss someone or, even if you don't and they are just attracted to you and they never told you, then they often get really mad if you hug and kiss someone else. They want to stop you from doing that with anyone but them. They want to own all your hugs and kisses and pettings. It's like when you get mad with Sasha when she plays with Linda and not with you, or when you get mad at me when I don't want to play with you but want to talk to Marc. But lover jealousy is a thousand times worse than friend jealousy or mother jealousy. Don't get me wrong, making love feels really good, is a great thing to do when you are a grown up and people will be happier and kinder if they find the time to do it a whole lot more, but most people don't want their lover making love with anyone else, they only want them to make love to them."

"Do you get jealousy when I kiss and hug Sasha?"

"Honey, I don't have sexual love for you, I have mother love. That is not jealous. But if Marc was hugging and kissing another woman, you bet I would, if it was a sex attraction, and not just a friend or family, I would ask him to stop that right now. And if I did that with another man or woman, he would get really angry and maybe he would find another wife. Look, Kay Lee, people are attracted to many people especially when they are beautiful and they want to pet them and hug and kiss them, but they have to control themselves because people can get jealous, they can lose friends and husbands and wives and children. In some countries women and girls are killed or beaten if their husband or even a man in their family finds out that they are attracted to someone."

"But how, if you love someone, can you beat and kill them?"

"Honey, this is what I think: in the skeleton of every human being, is a Jealousy Bone that makes them love with a selfish love and not a kind love. I have it me and I gotta use the Bone of Grace to take over the Jealousy Bone whenever it starts hurting. If I could teach people to love people without wanting anything back, I would be like Buddha or Jesus and there'd be no more wars or hurting each other. But we're lucky because here, in America and in some of the European countries it is against the law for men and boys to hurt girls or women if they want to love someone else. Don't you ever let anybody tell you how to love."

"Even you and Marc?"

"Yes, even us. You are our daughter and if we think you are in love with a bad person we will tell you what we think. But we will not, we cannot stop you."

"Why wasn't my mother Nigest jealous?"

"What do you mean?"

"Why wasn't Nigest jealous when you took me away? I was her daughter and she loved me but then you got me and you love me now. Is Nigest mad at you?"

Then Lisa looked sad, and she hugged me.

"Why do you ask? You look sad."

"I always think she loves my brothers and sisters and not me."

"But she does love you."

"Then why did she give me away?"

"She gave you away because she loved you. She's so poor she was afraid that you wouldn't have enough to eat so she gave you to us so we could be your other mother and father. She cried and cried when she gave you away. But her love wasn't selfish. She did that so you would have a good life."

I said, "I know" and I hugged her. Then I went to my room and looked at the pictures of my brothers and sisters. I miss them so much.

Nigest Speaks Telepathically To Lisa And Marc; Bertukan Is Sick
Nigest: Dice Dota

Dear Sister and Brother: Everyday we think of you and thank you for being the mother and father to Kalkidane and for the help that you send for our family. We have a big problem here now because our newest daughter Bertukan is sick from malaria and there is a need for medicine. She has fever for three days, she will not eat or drink, she is too weak, and so I take her to the Norwegian hospital. We walk and walk it is so far, I am carrying her and her sleeping is so heavy that I hope she will not die. I do not take the other children to help. There is so much infection at the hospital I do not want to expose them.

Before the gate to the hospital the people with their tents and their fire circles are camping by the wall. They are the ones whose family members are in the hospital; they cook them food and wait to take them home. They are from all tribes; Amhara, Afar, Sidama, Andamu, Konso, Somali. We show Bertu's red eyes to the guard; he opens the gate and so we take our place in the line to the front door where the woman at the table decides. Finally, it is our turn. The woman feels Bertu's fever, looks at her eyes, feels for her heartbeat and tells us to go in. In the hospital every bed is taken, many people sleep on the hallway's floor. We find the Doctor room and wait there until the Doctor enters. She is a European female who cannot speak Amharic. The nurse is the Ethiopian woman, Yemisrach, I know her. They put Bertu on a table that has wheels next to a big tree of plastic bags that hold the medicine. She cries and cries when the Doctor puts the needle in her arm and connects a tube from the end of the needle to one of the bags on the tree. That is how they give her food and medicine. After the crying she falls asleep. Yemisrach then helps me push the table and the tree into the hall. We have to be very careful because if we do not keep them together the needle will rip out of Bertu's arm.

After two hours Yemisrach calls me back into the room. We push Bertu and the medicine tree back in. She tells me that there is no room in the hospital, and at the end of the day we must go home, and that we must make her eat and should give her the special medicine, sulfadoxine. She asks me if I can pay for the medicine and I say to her, yes, even though I do not know the price and I am afraid if I say cannot pay she will not write me the paper. She gives me nets to put over the beds to keep out the waba and she tells me that I must use these in the night and that also I must cover the water, because there is the waba's breeding home. Are there tires, she asks, where water stands inside? I tell her we have no tires. She gives me the paper. Then she wakes Bertu up and calls for the Doctor who comes into the room, takes the needle out of her arm and then leaves the room. Yemisrach puts cotton on the arm in the place where the needle was and asks me to hold it in place. I do this while Bertu cries and cries. Then Yemisrach says, when there is no blood we must go, and she goes out. After some minutes there is no more blood on the cotton and I take Bertu out by carrying.

On the way out of the room, when carrying Bertu, I hear children crying and I look inside another doctor room where the sound comes from; oh my God, there is Tsehay Tekle with four little children in there, very little, three girls and one boy, with the Doctor and Yemisrach and, ah-ha, I see now, the Doctor gives them vaccinations so the Tekles can sell them. I listen by the door. Tsehay is complaining to Yemisrach about the parents of the children; they don't care for their children, they only want money, and the farange are very stingy, they do not understand how hard she works to find the best future for the children. If she did not love them she would not do this work, it is not for the money.

When I hear these lies I want to scream, but no, I am afraid if I say anything Yemisrach will take back the paper for the medicine, so I just spit and walk on, carrying Bertu who is now awake. It is getting dark and the people are making fires to cook food for their families and making their beds on the hospital fields. I cannot carry Bertu all the way back so I find a ghari to take us to the medicine store. I give the Medicine Lady the paper. Oh my God.

She asks for so much money. I tell her that I cannot pay. She tells me that she is sorry but I should come back when I have the money.

Marc And Lisa Make Fiscal Sense
Marc and Lisa: **Balsam River, Wisconsin**

Peepers, peepers. Wisconsin pines at my parents camp on the Balsam River, Lisa dressing, curve of spine as she steps into her panties, hip swell, rouge on soft bronze, nape of the neck and pale of palm, beautiful gal, she gets me going. No privacy here though, sleeping with the Kay Lee in the same room, so…down pecker, down, I guess I'll check the mail.

In the woods of wild flowers they got cell phone towers.

Where's Kay Lee?

She's down by the river. Don't worry, she knows not to go in the river alone. Look, here's an email from Ethiopia, news from Fikir, they've got another problem and only need 1,000 birr for medicine because the baby has malaria and 2,500 birr for school tuition, school tuition, which if Nigest doesn't pay, the school will invite the children to leave, so they want to know if we can send…that's…$300. He also says that Selamawit is first in her class, they miss us terribly, when are we coming, and may we have too many blessings for our Easter.

But we can't afford three hundred. We just sent five last Christmas when Gyorgis got that thing in his stump. That was four months ago. And now we owe Kay Lee's preschool three grand for last spring. By the end of the year that will be six. Do you have any idea how we're going to pay for it? I'm adjunct faculty, they could cut my courses in a minute, and you're going to school.

So let's tell them that we're broke, and we just can't right now.

But what about the baby?

What about *our* baby?

Will you write Fikir back? I'll go look for Kay Lee.

Thanks a lot.

She's typing and sighing. I take the steps from the deck to the path that winds through the pines down the wooded bank to the water. A sunbeam shoots through a hole in the clouds, comes through the pines and shimmers on the river, which is lower than I've ever seen it, because of the fucking drought. I'm hoping it snows like hell this winter and thinking of the time I packed in, stayed at the cabin and skied on a three foot snow pack on the river and the banks and forest all around.

Kay Lee's out of sight but I can hear her singing down river in *Kayleelee,* her made-up language. You know when you hear her that she's channeling something Ethiopian; the hissing and rolls, and she does that multi ah-ah-ah-ah-ah minor trill they do in their music. I give her the family whistle and she yodels back, "coming." I watch her round the river bend, picking her way through the rotted beaver dam to the sand bank, hopping and leaping from log to rock to log and then down to the sand, jumping brown gazelle girl, my daughter. I take her hand and together we walk up to the camp. It's clouding up now fast. When we come inside Lisa's done typing.

Hey, I say, if it's nice out tomorrow, let's take Kay Lee to the Water Park in Menominee. She really wants to go. It's not that much, $40 adults, $20 kids.

This makes Kay Lee very happy. Please Mommy. Lisa says, great, she'll pack lunch to save money. BOOM! Now there's lighting and thunder over the river. I wonder if the rains have come to Ethiopia. And about the girls: do they *need* to go to that private school? They've got public schools, don't they?

A Storm Takes Bertu
Selamawit: **Dice Dota**

This is a bad place in the summer; it rains every afternoon and everything turns to mud and then the malaria comes, and if it doesn't rain there is food insecurity and drought, the animals starve, the price of all food goes up and all the tribal people come to the city to get the UN wheat. Now it rains and rains and even with the cloths over the bed there are still mosquitoes and the baby is dying. She is so hot and does not eat or drink or cry or move. She will leave us. Now my mother, Lushan and my aunts are in the tukol praying around her. The Americans say they can send no money for medicine and Ato Girma will not loan us any more because of what happened with the bajaj. I know my father thinks about selling Lushan and me, but the chance is not good, we are too old for adoption and too young to work in Dubai. And, I will run away before I let him give me to any man or sell me as a servant. He can beat me and beat me. I will not go.

Oh! This lightning is very close and the noise so loud. The air is electric and crackling. Oh no, now they are going ""Wayne wayne wayne wayne lijaaan." Did the lighting take the soul from Bertu? It is over. I should go in and cry with them and hold my mother to keep her from self-hurt. Oh Maryam, be a good mother to Bertu in heaven. And will you stop this rain?

Feeling ~~Guilty~~ Responsible
Lisa: Chicago

So Marc said don't send the money for the medicine, we need it for our kid's $6,000 a year preschool. And then the baby died.

FUCK!!!

ME, cuz what am I doing blaming Marc? Jesus, Lisa, why do you immediately go for blood when things go bad? You agreed with him, you thought he was making *fiscal sense*, didn't you? *And he was.*

He was, she was, a little baby girl, she...*was.*

Kay Lee, come here. I've got something sad to tell you. Come sit on my lap.

You know that your Ethiopian mother had a little baby last year, a little girl sister, named after an orange, Bertukan, they called her Bertu? Well she had a bad disease they call malaria and we just heard that she died.

Yes she got a shot but it didn't work. And we were...trying to get some money to send them to buy some medicine but she died before we could do it.

No, it's too late, I'm sorry honey, I know, I know, you'll never get to see your little sister. That's sad. But you have your sisters, Selam and Lushan and your brother, Geta.

No, we don't have to send them medicine, they're not sick.

Yes we'll try to call them this week. We'll find out, OK? Now, go play.

MOTHERFUCKER! SHIT! FUCK POVERTY!

Dear Fikir, please tell Nigest, Gyorgis, Selam, Lushan and Geta how sad we are to hear about ~~the death of~~ Bertu. ~~I feel~~ We are so sorry that we couldn't help the family more, but we are in a bad situation here with money.

73

Kay Lee what are you doing? OH SHIT. Don't touch those. Did you put any of them in your mouth?

I'm sorry I yelled at you honey but these can be poison if you take too many of them.

I know it was an accident. Here I'll help you pick them up. Why were you playing with them?

Oh, honey, you dear heart, we can't send them all these pills. These are all our medicines.

No I know you want to share. But you can't share pills. These pills are for our American germs not for Ethiopian germs. If they took them they could make them sicker, they could even make them dead. And their pills could make us dead, if we took them.

No, I know they don't have any pills. We *are* trying to send them money so they can buy their own pills but we don't have enough money now to do that, that's the problem.

No, Grandma doesn't have enough money, either. She has to pay her rent.

No, no, we can't sell your toys, they won't bring in enough money. Honey, they are very religious, if they get sick, they pray for God to keep them safe.

He tried everything, but Bertu was just too sick.

No, honey, God isn't always a man. You can say, "She tried everything." God can be either a boy or girl.

What? Kay Lee, how do you know about Maryam?

Oh, who else do they talk about there?

Christos, that's Jesus. I thought you were just learning the language at the Association. And dancing.

OK we've got them all picked up. Kay Lee, please, you can't play with these pills or try to send them to anyone. They are like poison. You have to be very careful. OK, go play.

Yes, God can be a cat. God can be what you want.

Dear Fikir, please tell Nigest, Gyorgis, Selam, Lushan and Geta everyone how sad we are to hear about the death of Bertu. I feel We are so sorry that we can't help

74

the family more, but we are in a bad situation here with money. ~~I am a student and Marc's job is not secure.~~ If things get better for us we will try to ~~send money~~ do something, but we ~~don't know when~~ cannot promise. All of our love to Nigest and the kids. Lisa, Marc and Kay Lee.

2008

Kay Lee Shows Her Friend Miranda Pictures
And Reads Her A Letter
Kay Lee: Chicago

Miranda, look, this is my real mother. Her name is Nigest.

No, I don't know how old she is.

And these are my sisters. The older one is Selam and the younger girl is Lushan. They are so beautiful. They are, like, learning English. They wrote me. Oh my God, I want to see them. They are so sweet. Listen, their English is perfectly freaky.

My beautiful sister Kalkidane: This letter I am writing you with our sister Lushan who learns also English in our school. Are you fine?

I have twelve years. I am in the Grade 8 and will have my examinations in one month. Lushan has ten years. She is in the Grade 5. And our brother Geta is in Grade 4. If I make success in my examinations I will be accepted in the high school. Before I find the fees for the high school and the uniform I pray to God that I will win first place and go to University and I will be a nurse and have my own living.

We are very sad when our sister Bertu died. We miss her so much.

When will you come to Ethiopia? We miss you and love you so much and pray to see you and Lisa and Marc the beautiful.

We think you forget us. Here is the photo of us and your mother, Nigest, and of Bertu before she is dead. Please send us your photo.

Your sisters, Selamawit and Lushan.

Oh my God, Miranda, look, they put black around the baby picture. That's my little sister. That *was* my little sister. Her name was Orange. She got sick and they couldn't pay for the medicine, so she died. They are like, so poor.

Miranda, I have to see my sisters. I have to go there.

It's really expensive. Lisa says it's over two thousand dollars. We can't afford it. But I have to see my sisters and my mother. I have to. I'm going to. I'm going to do a project. At school. Like they did for the food bank.

Miranda, will you help me? Will you be my sister?

Geta Runs Away And Goes To Live On The Street
Geta: **Dice Dota**

I was nine the night I ran away. It wasn't that I wanted to live as a street boy, I hated to leave my mother and sisters, but I'd had it with my father beating me up. This time he was so slow and drunk with his one leg that I got him down. You can't go home after you have beaten your father.

What should I have done? Let him hurt me? It was after-school in the winter. My work was to watch the goats while they grazed in the road near our compound. As usual when I was doing this job I played with my friends who were also watching their family's animals. We had a football made from string and paper. It was getting dark and I was making a good try for the goal when the soldier's truck came fast around the corner and the billy goat, Bruk, he was so stupid, he thought the truck wanted to fuck his wife, Labella, the mother goat, so he tried to fight the truck, he ran at it with his head down and the truck went over right him and almost took his head off. Now Bruk was down in the road; his legs were shaking and blood was pouring from his throat. The truck stopped.

We all watched him die, shaking and bubbling blood from what was left of his neck, my friends and I, and the Captain who had come out of the truck. When he was dead the Captain ordered us to put the goat into the truck, but before anyone could obey, I ran and picked up Bruk, held him close to me and faced the Captain. I knew he wouldn't grab me because he didn't want to get blood on his uniform. I said to him, "No, this is my family goat, you cannot eat him, and you must pay us 100 birr because you have killed our goat and we must get a new one." The Captain made to hit me, but I ducked and backed towards the wall holding the goat. He put his hand to his pistol. I held the goat tighter and looked at him with fighting eyes, and said, "You cannot have my goat." Believe me, he could have killed me but I was not going to give him Bruk. The Captain looked at my eyes and he knew this; then he looked at the other man in the truck who shrugged at him. The Captain laughed and said, "OK you tough little bastard, go feed your family." He turned to go back to the truck but I called out to him, "Where is my 100 birr?" Slowly he turned back to me. He took his pistol from the holster on his belt and pointed it at me. I didn't move. Then there was a big shot. It was so loud. All the kids and goats ran, but not me. I couldn't move. Was I dead? The Captain was laughing. He had fired into the air. He got back in his truck and with much dust the truck jumped ahead and down the road.

I just stood there holding Bruk. The smell of him was strong and sour and my heart was drumming so hard against my ribs that I could hear the beat. I had won the war with the Captain. I had faced his pistol and been brave, so when I heard my father yelling I was not afraid.

You see, some little bastard neighbor kid had run to our compound and told him that a truck had hit Bruk, and so now here he was, crutching towards me, with his beating stick, twitching with withdrawal from his morning khat and drunk on tej, ready to bite me for his useless life. My mother, Selam and Lushan, followed him, pulling at his clothes, trying to calm him down; he swung at them with his crutch, yelling and cursing, "I will beat him like a slave, I will teach him to pay attention."

It was the same old noise, him with his red eyes, cursing and roaring in his throat, Momma screeching, my sisters crying, and the neighbors cracking their gates open to watch the show, but this time I did not add my curses to the bad music. I just let the sound go through me like the empty air it was.

My father had me against the wall of the compound. I did not run or cry when he cursed me and raised his stick. "You will obey me," he brayed, and brought the stick down, but I had seen it coming and thrust the dead goat forward so the stick hit the goat instead of me. Then I kicked his crutch out from under him and pushed the goat into him to knock him down. Now he was on the ground under the goat and I was on top, pressing dead Bruk's face into his face. "Ahhh, Ahhh," he cried, and I said "Fuck You" in my father's ear and pushed the goat's mouth hard into his, to make him kiss it and block his cry. Momma and my sisters pulled on my clothes and cried, "Stop, stop." and his hands came around to grab me, but again I was too fast and jumped up and away from him, for his fingers were like hyena teeth; once he'd grabbed me he would never let me go until he had killed me. I picked up his beating stick and broke it on my knee, threw the pieces over the wall, and then with one look to my mother I was gone, running fast, turning corners right and left through the dusty roads of the kabele, until I came out into the Town Center.

Now it was almost dark. I sat on the steps outside the Telephone Building, watching the lights come on in the hotels and the crowds of people going home. It was so different from the calm and quiet of my compound at night. The people called out to the gharis for their neighborhoods and the drivers lined up with their horses to pick up their fares, while others who could not pay walked together into the side streets. As the lights came on, the prostitutes came out to the street in their short dresses and high shoes, waiting for the businessmen and farange to pick them and buy them supper. People came into the Telephone Building and went up the stairs to the restaurant on the top floor. I could hear music from the restaurant. The smell of cooking wat made my stomach hurt; tonight there would be no supper in the compound from my mother; no washing up from the basin before bed, no prayers on our knees before the picture of Christos in the house; no whispering with my sisters in the bed after we got under the blanket together and listened to the sounds of the grown-ups talking, laughing and sometimes making fucking sounds.

Where would I sleep? Suddenly there was a hand on my shoulder. "Why are you on our stairs, Mr. Boy?" I looked up; there were the shoeshine boys who worked all day on the Piazza, with their wooden boxes, cloths and polishes. I told them that I had fought my father and could not go home. They told me to get off the stairs, the stairs were theirs at night, the little kids slept by the Meskarum Hotel across from the Kodak store and I should go there. I told them I would stay with them and help them in their shoe business, but they just laughed and pushed me out. I went to the corner of the Meskarum and there on the side of the hotel in the palm trees were boys and girls lying on the ground around a charcoal pan, some sleeping, and some talking. One of them, a big boy, sat looking out to the hotel. He was the watchdog, I could tell, and he might stop me if I came into them fast, so I sat on the hotel stairs so he could see me while I studied the soldiers and the prostitutes coming in and out of the hotel. The soldiers were two kinds, airforce and army. I knew this because my father was in the army before he lost his leg and he had taught me everything about the military. The Meskarum was where they went for their women. The prostitutes were young and beautiful. You could smell them 20 feet away, they used so much perfume. Their short skirts showed most of their legs and ass. This was all part of their spider web; first the soldiers smelled them and then they saw them and then they were caught. The whores took them by the hand and led them in. I thought I recognized one of the women, Aster, the older sister of my friend Girum. She had just graduated 10th grade the year before.

Meanwhile I was giving strong asking looks to the guard boy. He looked back at me, so finally I got up and went to him. Before I even asked he nodded yes, so I laid down next to some of the others. I had no mattress or blanket or anything for a cover, so I pulled my t-shirt down over my shorts and put my head inside like a caterpillar all curled up into myself. So tired from all the emotionality and fighting of the day, I fell asleep immediately.

I dreamt of hyenas. The guard boy has fallen asleep when out of the side street trots the mother hyena and her children. She stands while her children pull at her teats. I jump up and stare at the hyena, asking with my eyes: "What do you want?"

"My children are hungry," says the hyena, "give me that little girl." The hyena points her snout to the smallest girl in the pile of children.

"Me too," I tell the hyena, "I am hungry. You give me your little ones and you can have the girl."

The hyena laughs and laughs, "Never, never, a good mother will never give up her children."

"Go away," I tell Mrs. Hyena, "or I will get a gun and kill you and your children."

"Then who will eat your dead?" laughs Mrs. Hyena, "do you want them rotting here on the streets?"

The streets are suddenly full of dead horses surrounded by buzzing flies. The smell is awful. Mrs. Hyena laughs. I throw stones at her, but she doesn't move. Laughing, she and her children feed on the horses.

When I woke up, it was raining. The kids were moving all around me getting under the trees out of the rain and I followed them and remembered everything. I realized that now there would be no one who would try to control me. I was totally free. But, how was I going to survive? Who was going to feed me?

Gyorgis Offers Selam To Big Fat Tadesse
Gyorgis: Dice Dota

Tadesse, here, have a chew. It's the best from Yir Gallum and is just off the truck, fresh. I got it an hour ago.

Ha – I see you are looking at Selam. Do you see how she is filling out? Beautiful. Listen, I know what you are thinking, and don't worry, it's OK. Look, you are a man, how can you not think about having her, her face is like a movie star and she will have tits and hips like her mother. They're coming, you can see. Remember Nigest when she was young? She is the same, but with even better nutrition, she will be stronger.

Look at her, pounding the tef, look at her arms, look at her back. Listen my brother, I want to tell you: this beautiful girl, my Selam, she could be yours. Now that your wife is dead, she can take care of your little ones, she can have more children for you. She is strong, she can work like a donkey. Her mother has trained her; she cooks, she takes care of babies, she knows it all and she is smart; she is first in her school, no one in the Market can fool her, she can write better than you, she can help you in your business.

Tadesse, think about it. Who will take care of your children now that your wife is dead and your mother is so old? Your sisters cannot continue, they have their own children. And here is Selam. She is thirteen now, the boys are after her already, and soon I will find her a husband. If you wait you will lose your chance. And, if you agree, I will take her from school and she can begin to help you before the marriage.

Tadesse, my brother, I understand your situation, it is your second time around, you have to think of your children, you have to continue your business. I will not make this hard for you. I only want enough to buy a bajaj, so I can have hope for my family. Look, we are not in the days of Haile Selassie, we are modern men, we don't have to go through a circus like stupid Ashenafi. You do not know his story? I thought you were at the wedding. Oh man, someone should bring him more brains. He spent 100,000 birr on his daughter's wedding for a dowry of only 50,000. And then he lost his job and he was ruined, so had to move his whole family in with his daughter. Her husband's family now treats them like slaves.

Here's more khat. Chew it.

SELAM, COFFEE FOR ME AND TADESSE! QUICK!

Look at her; she knows you are looking and so she looks away. She is a modest girl.

After coffee I have tej. Listen, I know that this might hurt her chances, but I don't care, I'm telling you because you are my friend; she is not cut. No, her mother refused and I thought, why not, we are a modern family, if she is not cut, she will be more passionate for her husband, and in these times, a husband may want this and it would also give her a chance to marry a farange. They hate that. If this a problem for you, if you want her to be cut, we will go to the practitioner, but I know you Tadesse, I remember in the brothel, you are so strong you would keep three wives satisfied and she is a good girl, she will not go with younger men for pleasure if you do good work at night, ha, ha. But this is your choice.

If you don't want her, then another man will snap her up. Tadesse, I tell you, Selam is your best choice. And because you are my friend, if you agree, then I will turn away all the others. I promise.

Here she comes with the coffee. We'll talk more about this. Come on, chew.

Selam, here is our friend Tadesse, you know him, you have seen his copy shop in the Piazza? He tells me he is looking for smart girls to work. Maybe you will have a chance.

Selam, where are your manners. Say thank you to Tadesse for this.

That's a good girl. Now, bring us tej.

This girl is not respecting me. She is making plans with her mother and she does not ask permission. Her surprise is coming. She thinks she will go to school but how can she do that if the Americans send no money? Where will she get the money? She wants to learn? Tadesse will teach her some things…ha ha…oh yes… he is a big guy; she will not walk for a week after her wedding night. She will have to take a ride in my bajaj.

Selam Tells Sebbie About Her Big Problem
Selamawit: Dice Dota

Solomon, I would like to hear about your football game, but I have to talk to Sebbie now, it is very important. So please. Go. Away. Thank you.

Sebbie, I am crazy today, I have to talk to you, Come here. NOW, I HAVE TO TALK TO YOU NOW!

It's about my stupid father. I hate him. God forgive me, I want him to die. He says he will kill Geta and now he wants me to marry Ato Tadesse, you know, Tadesse of the copy shop, he's as old as my Dad, his daughter is in Lushi's class, I would be her mother, and he's huge, he's a big fat crocodile, I will kill myself before I will let me touch me. It's all about the bajaj, Gyorgis wants to buy one, he can't work because of his leg so he thinks he can get a dowry and buy a bajaj. I can't believe it. My own Father is selling me to a fat old crocodile for the price of a bajaj. And what if he wants me to get cut? I don't care if he beats me, I don't care if he kills me, I will kill myself before they cut me and make me marry that fat old man. I will kill him. I will email my American family and they will take me, I will run away to Adis like Helen did. I will go to school up there. I heard that she was working there and that she was going to school.

Maybe I should call her. Hey Sebbie, you know how to get in touch with Helen? Your cousin Betlihem was her best friend. Where is Betlihem? My father is selling my life for a bajaj. Sebbie, we have to find Betlihem.

Betlihem And Selam Contact Helen At The Internet Café
Betlihem and Selam: **Dice Dota,** *Helen:* **Adis Ababa**

Helen. Andamu Girl.

Betlihem.

Can you chat?

Yes. I am at the Internet café in Kasanchis with my boyfriend.

And I am at Metro. Are you well?

Fine. You? Your mother? Your sisters?

Helen, they are all fine, thank God. Selam is here with me. Do you remember her? She has this problem, the same you had; her father arranges her marriage to an old man. She refuses. She plans to run to Adis to find work and go to school. She wants to know, how is your life?

I am working in a restaurant called Seven Nights. My boyfriend, Helmut, is German. We will go to Germany in the spring and get married and I will learn German and become a nurse. I am waiting for a visa.

Helen, this so lucky.

Is Selam the beautiful girl who lives in the street near Sebbie? She will have no problem finding a job here.

Do you have a phone?

Not now, but Helmut will buy me a phone soon. Selam can find me at the restaurant Seven Nights in Kasanchis. Tell her to ask for "Heaven." That is my waitress name. I will help her.

Selam says God bless you. You are her savior.

Maybe. Look Betlihem, Adis is rough. Tell her be careful and to bring some money. She will need some. I am out of time. Ciao.

Meanwhile, Helmut Emails His Wife
Helmut: **Adis Ababa**

Crystal, I am just taking a moment at the Internet Cafe before I start my appointments. Everything is OK here, the work is successful. I will be traveling to Desse to make the contract for the asphalt tomorrow.

It's the same old thing here, dirt, beggars, injera, everyone trying to cheat you, everyone is beautiful, everyone is dull, endless suppers with Ethiopian colleagues in their houses with their families and old mothers. They all fish for a way to get out, to come to Germany or the States.

I fly back to Dusseldorf next Friday and will be home in the evening. Be sure that you call the electrician to come to put the new fixture in the bathroom. And tell Marlene to be a good girl and to help her mother.

I miss you terribly my little turnip, but you don't like the beggars and the food and I am working all the time, you would be so bored. I miss you in bed and look forward to some fun. It is lonely here.

Darling, I have to go now, my appointment has come. I will see you Friday. Tschüss.

And Plans The Future With Helen/Heaven
Helmut and Helen: **Adis Ababa**

My God, look at her typing away in that crazy language. She looks so good in that dress I bought her, those beautiful legs, so fresh, and oh, that skin that belly, that cunt where the dark meets the pink, oh Jesus, if I take my pill we can fuck again this afternoon. Why not? Is there anything better to do in this life and I have no appointments until Thursday.

Heaven, Can you finish?

Helmut, please, I have told you, do not call me Heaven. That is only for Seven Nights. I am Helen.

I am sorry. Helen, Did you see your friends on the Face Book? Let's see, who is that? She's beautiful...but not as beautiful as you. Do you want some more coffee? Let me pay for the Internet.

What is the matter with that boy? Does he give me this look because I am a farange with an Ethiopian girl? Too bad for him, not me. I have the pretty girl, he doesn't.

Please, two Macchiato. You're welcome. Thank you.

You want to see the pictures again? All right, here, look on the camera.

This is the town of Hamm. This is the castle from very old days when my family was the boss of the whole city. These are the houses in the main street. Now, see here, above the shop with the sign that says 'Tabac,'" those windows. That is where we will have our flat. Do you like that, on your leg, my hand?

Kay Lee Gets Money
Kay Lee: Chicago

Can you believe it? Mrs. Romanes, we got $1,075. That's so amazing.

The 5th and 6th grade's door-to-door drive got $350. Awesome Miranda organized them. They went out three evenings to different neighborhoods. Walk for Dice Dota brought in $500, fifty kids walked five miles for ten dollar pledges, and I want to thank you so very much for walking with us, Mrs. Romanes, that was so cool. Sherri Melosky's parents gave $100 and Mama Mekelle Restaurant donated 10% of all dinners for last Saturday night, and that came to $125 so the total was $1,075.

My parents say that I will need $2,000 for the trip, Mrs. Romanes, I can't believe it, we've got half that, I'm halfway to Ethiopia and seeing my brothers and sisters and my real mother. I'm crying already just to think of it. And we have a great plan to get the rest; Ms. Conrad in the Art Room said that she will have all the grades make Valentine Cards for Ethiopia. I have pictures of my sisters which I will copy on the copy machine and paste on the inside of the cards along with stuff that I will write about my family there, and we'll sell them for two dollars. And then at Easter we'll do "Eggs for Ethiopia." And on Mother's Day we'll sell "Chocolates for Ethiopia." And that's how we'll get enough so I can buy a ticket. And then when I get back I can bring all these pictures and maybe, what do you think, our school could adopt my brother's and sister's school? And did you know, since, like, coffee comes from Ethiopia, we could bring back a whole lot of coffee and sell it? Oh, Ms. Romanes, there's the bell. I'll come back after class.

Kay Lee Gives a Speech At Harriett Tubman Magnet School
Kay Lee: **Chicago**

I just want to say thank you to Principal Romanes and to everybody who helped and, of course, a special shout out to Miranda and her family. It was so awesome what you all did, I mean, what *we* did. I didn't know what I was getting into when I started this, I mean I thought it would take like a thousand dollars and when I did the research it was more like six, and I'm thinking, how am I going to do this? But now, with the door-to-door and the walk, the auction and the restaurants, and then Miranda's grandma's donation and all of you, Mom and I are going to go there and bring $3,500 for medicine and for school uniforms, and tuition for my brothers and sister, and help for their school. It's so amazing what you can do when you don't know you can't.

And we did it. But you don't know what "it" is, so, like I want to tell you where the money will go and show you pictures. Can you show the first picture? Oh good. That's my big sister, Selamawit, isn't she pretty? She had really good grades in middle school and passed her examinations, so some of this money will help her go to a private high school so she has a good chance to go to University. Next…that's my second older sister and little brother, Lushan and Getachew. They are going to get new school uniforms so they can keep going to public school because you can't go if you don't have a uniform, it's not like here. OK, next slide. That's my birth Mom, Nigest. We're going to give her money so she can buy mosquito nets and malaria medicine because, well, my family lost our little sister. Slide please. That was Bertu before she died of malaria and they couldn't afford medicine, so we don't want that to ever happen again. And also some of the medicine will go to my birth father Gyorgis. He was a soldier and he had his leg amputated and he needs medicine too. They didn't send his picture.

Oh my God, I'm taking too long. I'm just going to say one more thing, that is, we're gonna post news of the trip on the PTA web blog and next year there will be a hall display of pictures of my family and their animals and their schools and stuff. And maybe someday they can visit here and thank all of you guys in person for making their world so much bigger by making our whole world a little bit smaller. From me, and my American parents, Lisa and Marc and my family there, Nigest and Gyorgis, Selamawit, Lushan, and Getachew, and to all the staff, students and families of Harriet Tubman Middle School, thank you.

Kay Lee And Lisa Have A Fight
Kay Lee and Lisa: **Chicago**

Kay Lee, we've got to do something special to thank Miranda's Grandma. We'll put their donation in the bank with the other money you raised, and when you're old enough to go there you can...

Oh no, Kay Lee you can't just go there alone.

You are going to have to wait until you are older.

I don't know. Sixteen? You are going to have to wait until you are sixteen.

No, you can't fly there all by yourself. You are way too young to do that. I know you fly to Grandma Levi's here. But that's in the USA and it's a whole lot safer. It's different in Ethiopia, really different. And your family there, they don't have a car. Or a phone. They live far from Adis. How would they meet you? And how would you communicate. They don't speak English.

Yes, but that's school English. What if you got sick? What if you wanted to come home? What if you got kidnapped? They have bandits there who kidnap and ransom foreign children.

No, I know you are Ethiopian but that's just how you look, that's not who you are. And they are not really your family. You don't know them.

What? Oh that's absurd. You wouldn't want to stay there. You'd miss your TV and your friends. And what about your dad?

Watch out kid, that's really nasty. Of course I'm your mother. Nigest is your birth mother, but I'm the one who raised you.

Kay Lee, don't you curse me. You know that's against the rules.

Hey Marc! Hey MARC! I need some help here.

KAY LEE, you come back her right now. Marc, MARC, I need you!

WHAT DID YOU CALL ME? Don't you curse at me, you little fucker, I am your motherfucking mother for God's sake, I AM YOUR MOTHER!

Gyorgis Decides That Lushan Must Be Cut
Gyorgis: **Dice Dota**

That little bitch Selam says she will not marry Tadesse and so she tries to wreck all my plans to buy a bajaj, but no, I will show her who is the father. Nigest and Lushan are against me too, they are talking and I can hear their thoughts; *if only he would die.* They think I don't know what they are planning but I will give the first bite of any food they make for me to the dog, just to be sure there is nothing funny going on. I will get the marriage money from Tadesse so she will marry and I will bring the practitioner here to get Lushan cut so she does not become so proud as her sister and can find a good husband. If Nigest opposes she will learn that any beating she got before from me was just training for the main event.

Always these women work against me, and now with my bad leg they think they will win. But they are so stupid and transparent that nothing they plan can escape me. I will stay ahead of all their conspiracies and when I have my bajaj they will see the truth. I will buy them the things they want. I will take them to the doctor when they are sick. Geta will come back and submit to my discipline and he will go to University. The girls will be married and they will give me grandchildren. They will see then that I had to be a hard man so the family could survive. I will make them apologize and they will thank me. And I will beat them.

Kay Lee Calls Miranda
Kay Lee: **Chicago**

Miranda, MIRANDA, can you talk? Fuck Matt. Tell him you'll call him back. This is an EMERGENCY.

I just ran away. I got completely pissed off at my Mom. She won't let me go to Ethiopia.

I know, we raised all that money, your grandmother gave us all that money, and now she says I have to wait until I'm sixteen. That's bullshit. I'm not waiting. I want to see my family. They need me. They need medicine. How many more of them are going to die before we help them? And anyways, Lisa and Marc are not my real family. And she's not my mother and she's jealous of my real mother and doesn't want me to see her. I hate her. I told her to fuck off.

I know that was wrong. But she says fuck all the time, so?

I don't know. I'm at the IHOP now. I'm gonna call Grandma Emma, I'm going to call Seleshe. I'm gonna email Fikir to tell my family that I'm coming, I'm coming. Can you come to the IHOP?

Homework? I've got homework too. But I'm not going to school, I'm sorry. Why should I go to school when my sisters can't go to school because they can't afford the uniforms? I'm not going to go unless they let me go to Ethiopia. And I'm not going home.

OK, I'll come over. DON'T tell your folks that I've run away. They'll just call my parents. Tell them we're doing geography. Bye.

Geta Tells Fikir About Gyorgis' Intention
To Get Lushan Cut
Geta and Fikir: **Dice Dota**

Hey, Geta, GETA, is that you? Hey man, how are you? You still on the street?

I'm good, yes, God be praised, yes, my family is all well, we are blessed. Do you want some breakfast? Coffee?

Come on man. Sit down. No, Come on. Look at those bones you call a body. That street life makes you skinny. Order what you want. I've got a job with One World Circus. I do the gymnastics for the HIV shows. And I am teaching the little kids. Yes, for pay. You should come back and learn. Why did you stop?

Boy! Waiter! Coffee! Eggs! Pineapple! And no injera, bread.

So tell me, what's going on? How do you live? Hey man, you gotta get off the street and back in school. You are too smart for the shifta life. You'll get sick. Look, really, you need to come talk to my Mom, we might have a place for you to stay if you can't get along with your Dad. Really. Will you do that? Konjo, brother, konjo, in ten years, if you aren't playing forward for Manchester United you are going to be Prime Minister, I know it. If you get back in school and work hard you will get to University.

So tell me about your family. Selam? No I know, Selam told me about your dad and Tadesse. She said she would run if they try to force her.

So now what? Lushan? Gyorgis again? Tell me.

That fucker. Who does this any more? It's illegal. You know, Gyorgis and all those old men like him are the biggest problem in this whole country; they grew up under the boot of Haile Selassie and Mengistu so all they know is to dodge the blows of those above them and kick the ass of anyone below them.

They are only into personal advantage and keeping everyone down. When these old guys die, the sooner the better. They said nothing when the dictator imprisoned my father for fighting for the new ways. They got rewarded for going along with his torture and execution, even though they had been brothers in school and sports. And now they do anything to make sure that nothing happens, because something new might threaten their position of patriarch, which is bullshit because people don't respect or listen to them anyways. They chew khat all day then get drunk and beat their wives and children because these are the only ones who they can reach with their stick. God damn them. Geta, we're not going to let your father cut Lushi. We're not. When is the practitioner coming to your compound?

Here's your breakfast. Eat, eat, we've got time. I am calling Kiflu to get in touch with Anteneh, Ebi and Zela. And Mukbar. We will form a little army and go visit the ceremony. There will be no cutting unless it's your father's dick.

Eat, eat. Hello…Kiflu?

Marc To Lisa: "Chill Out"
Marc: **Chicago**

It wasn't the money, it wasn't the timing, it was the flutter of fear for the loss of the child, the memory she still carried of the baby gone and the pull of the tribe on the growing soul she'd borrowed from the nest she'd so carefully feathered. We say that we do it all for the kids but truly we serve ourselves when we raise them, they give us reasons that we need, to reach beyond our bodies, otherwise we would look only to ourselves and at a thin reflection; we are made to increase and keep our people close so we can see ourselves in their eyes.

Lisa, Lisa, give it up, we're going there, we're going with her, and we're bringing her back. You can't deny her brothers and sisters, this is elemental, it transcends humanity, it's beyond being mammal, it's the call of the flock, the herd, the life force of family for which we must give way. She has to know and we need to know too, these people who gave her life.

I'll take time off, we'll borrow, I'll sell books, but she's going. We are going. We have to. We have to let her penetrate the mystery of who she is and why she was chosen, and so does her family there. Or else - we'll all be tripping over this history like a hidden staircase in a dark hallway. We will fall and fall again. We have to turn the light on the sepia, move our constructs of who we think we are, the words and photos we send of how we want to be seen, off the paper, so we can, see, smell, hear, touch, taste the truth of each other.

Lisa Relents
Lisa: **Chicago**

Hi Mom.

I know she called you. She called everybody.

No, she came back. She was at her friends'.

I told her she couldn't go until she was sixteen and she got mad and cursed me out so I got mad and did the same. So she ran away. For a day.

Yeah, I remember, I stayed away three days. It was about Joshua Denham. You said I couldn't go out with him, I got mad and called you the B word, you slapped me and I was out the door. She's just a chip off the old block.

No, I gave in. Marc persuaded me. I'm going with her. I don't want to, but I have to.

For a lot of reasons. I thought I was adopting an orphan girl, not a whole hungry family. If I'd wanted that I would have become a missionary or something. And, Momma, it feels like you have to cross a big couple of universes to communicate with Kay Lee's people. We're talking about bridging chasms of money and privilege and the luck of the draw and goddamit, Mom, I'm used to being the underdog and now I'm the overlord, the owner, the stingy bastard, fat Lady Moneybags in the big house, and I hate the fucking crap out of it, sorry, excuse me, my mouth, I know, Mom. My heart is too small for this and I'm scared of all the work I'll have to do keep it open when I'm over there. That's why I don't want to go. I'm gonna have to be a nice person.

No, I know, it's the same deal here, there's more than enough desperation to go around right next door, Cabrini is five blocks from the Gold Coast and there's a homeless guy dying on the street right outside the Chicken Shack, but here we're all in the same show. You all know your lines, the plot, your character, the other actors, the costumes and the play. But there - you got a part in a show that's written in code. When we were there last time, *nothing* was what it seemed. I couldn't tell if a social call was a shell game until I got asked for a thousand bucks from a person I'd just given a present to. Anyways, we're going. I don't know what we're going to do about money, but we're going.

I was afraid you'd say that. Thank you. It's 2 grand. I didn't want to ask.

No, I get it. Kay Lee has to figure it out. And if she wants to move back there...well OK, I'll get another child, a real orphan, from here. A White one, from Mississippi, just to fuck everybody up.

No, I know, I am scared she'll want to stay, but that's not a rational fear. But I'm worried about us all getting swept up in something as big as Africa. She wants to save her brothers and sisters. My problem is...there are so many, millions. I can't be all their mommas.

We'll fly over winter break. She'll miss a week of school. Yeah, I'll give her your love. And tell her the same thing you told me, back in the day, about cursing the one who feeds you. This whole Ethiopian thing makes me fucking crazy. Oops. Sorry. Bye.

The Farange Are Coming
Kay Lee: **Chicago**

Dear Cousin Fikir:

I have awesome news. Mom and I will be coming to Ethiopia in five weeks, for two weeks. I raised an insane amount of money at my school and now I can come back to my home and meet my real family. Tell them, I want to meet everyone and I want to take Amharic lessons too. Will you teach me?

Mom bought the tickets and today we are going to get our vaccinations. We will be flying through Germany.

I can't wait to meet my mother and sisters and brother, and of course my dad. I have missed them so much.

I have to go to school now. All my love to my fabulous Ethiopian family and everyone in Dice Dota. I can't wait to come home.

Let me know if you get this mail by writing me at Kay Lee Levi, 1234 Farwell, Chicago, IL 60660 USA or emailing me at kaygirllevi@yahoo.com.

Do you have email in Ethiopia?

So much love, Kay Lee.

About The Victory Of The Anti-Cutting Army
Fikir: Dice Dota

Let me tell you, it was a great victory with all the aspects of a military raid: reconnaissance, planning, approach, battle and surrender. We met at the Café Metro, and using the Chinese war book of Sun Tzu that we got from the Irish Library, we planned our campaign. Here's how it went:

For the initial preparation and reconnaissance, on the Thursday before the cutting day, Geta waited for Lushan as she got out of school and gave her the plan for the Saturday rescue; she was to pretend to go along with her father's wishes and was to tell Nigest to also play act as if she was accepting her husband's authority. The important thing for Nigest was, when the practitioner came into the compound, to let her in, but to leave the gate unlocked. Also Hanna would tell Selam to say that she had to study with a friend that day and to leave the house early.

On the day of the battle, Hanna, who lives across the road from the practitioner, Weyzero Tenege, watched from her house all morning and when Tenege left her house, carrying the special wooden box of razors that all practitioners use for cutting, Hanna called me at the Metro from her family phone and then followed Tenege on her bicycle as she went to one house and then another to pick up her assistants. When I got Hanna's call I called Antoneh and Ebe who were waiting at the stadium near Nigest's. They came there by the path by the Pharmacy College and played soccer in the street by Nigest's gate until Weyzero Tenege and her helpers came to the door of the compound. In the meantime Mukbar, Geta and I came from the direction of the Metro and waited around the corner from the gate, peeking around the corner.

Tenege called out at the gate and when Nigest opened it, she and the assistants went in and then, right behind them, all at once, we followed; Ebe, Antoneh, Mukbar, Geta, Hanna and me.

Gyorgis was standing with his crutch by the outside stove and was about to greet Tenege. He stopped when he saw us come in behind her and as he began to speak Antoneh and Ebe came quickly behind Tenege at either side and Mukbar grabbed the box from her arms and dumped the two razors into the dust. Tenege screamed and Gyorgis roared and started towards us swinging his crutch but we had anticipated this. I came from behind and tripped him up so he was on the ground, then grabbed his crutch, pinning him with its point, like you keep a dog at bay. Then, while I held Gyorgis down, as we had planned, the rest of us broke the razors with our shoes until they were just bent metal and wooden handles separated from the thin bands of iron. We sang out the motto that we had composed at Metro

End cutting and abduction
Ethiopians stand against it
Girls and Women, Men and Boys
All together make the choice
Equal chances in our lives
No forced marriage, No more knives.

While we sang and broke their knives Weyzero Tenege and her two old ladies darted in for us like old pecking chickens, but Hanna and Mukbar came forward and slapped them back. They scratched themselves and cried as if when we'd stepped on the razors we'd broken their fingers, "Oh no, don't, Ayeeeeeeeee, you are from the devil, God strike you, Help!" It was almost comical because this had nothing to do with God, this had to do with how they made their living. More and more they could see their cutting business gone and their livelihood in pieces in the dust. Lushan ran from the tukol where she had hidden and came to stand behind us. Nigest stood in the middle of us all and said nothing, she could not show support for Lushi but it was clear from the look in her eyes; this was a victory.

After breaking the razors we stood in a line against the old women. I took the crutch off Gyorgis who sat in the dust, cursing and threatening. Then I had fun with him. The only kind of talk the old ones understand is semi-legal bullshit, so I played dictator, pretending that we were representing the kabele, saying: "Ato Gyorgis, shut up, stop your cursing immediately. I am sorry to come in without an invitation, but we are the Anti Genital Mutilation Army and we represent the law of Ethiopia as ordered by Prime Minister Meles. This cutting is illegal. You must not do this or you will be taken to prison. You must tell all your friends about the law and the danger if they break it. Come on, get up and brush yourself off."

I gave him his crutch back and helped him to his feet. He crutched away to the door of the tukol and stood there, glaring. The ladies were still crying so I said to them, "Tenege and you ladies, now listen, Betlihem can take you to the Woman's Center so you can get the midwife training. It is a UN program: they will train you if you promise to give up the cutting. Come on now, stop crying and start thinking. Pick up your box."

Ha ha, they obeyed like dogs. Ebe gave Tenege's box back to her. Betlihem motioned to the old hags and they followed her out of the compound door, Tenege cradling the box as if it was an injured child. Before we left we stood before Gyorgis and I told him, "OK, you just remember if we hear anything about Lushan getting beaten you will see what happens. We will complain to the kabele and you will be arrested. And we will tell the Americans."

Geta stood before his father and said, "And you don't beat our mother either or we will come back and you will be sorry." Gyorgis shook his head at Geta as if he was flicking off a fly, but he said nothing. I picked up the broken razor parts and holding them carefully in my hand I led my army out of the compound. Laughing, we marched back to Café Metro and celebrated our victory for the future with cappuccinos for all that I could not afford.

The Lack Of Respect For Tradition In Dice Dota
Wazero Tenege: Dice Dota

These kids are forked-tongued devils; they should be whipped in public and sent to prison for taking away my living and dishonoring the reputation of these young girls. They do not accept the authority of God, they reject Jesus and all the old ways, they want all women to be prostitutes and leave the home. They think I like hurting the girls but that is not the case. The problem is that no respectable man will marry them unless they are excised and closed up and I am the wisest woman to do this. I was trained by my mother to make a clean cut just as her mother trained her. I keep my razors sharp and purify them with fire. Not to do this is to go against the will of the Lord and all our tradition. When all women are uncut our culture will vanish, Ethiopian women will be as farange, showing their thighs and stinking between their legs, fornicating like donkeys. With sex organs like a man's and that entire stink, there will be no way for a baby to come into the world and who would ever want them?

2009

Concerning Traveling To Ethiopia
Center For Disease Control: **Chicago**

Routine: Recommended if you are not up-to-date with routine shots – measles/ mumps/rubella (MMR) vaccine, diphtheria/pertussis/tetanus (DPT) vaccine, poliovirus vaccine, etc.

Yellow Fever: Required for all travelers entering Ethiopia.

Hepatitis A or immune globulin (IG): Recommended for all unvaccinated people. Transmitted through food or water.

Hepatitis B: Recommended for all unvaccinated persons especially those who might be exposed to blood or body fluids, have sexual contact with the local population, or be exposed through medical treatment (e.g., for an accident).

Typhoid: Recommended for all unvaccinated people traveling to or working in East Africa, especially if staying with friends or relatives or visiting smaller cities, villages, or rural areas where exposure might occur through food or water.

Polio: Recommended for adult travelers who have received a primary series with either inactivated poliovirus vaccine (IPV) or oral polio vaccine. (OPV). They should receive another dose of IPV before departure. For adults, available data do not indicate the need for more than a single lifetime booster dose with IPV.

Meningococcal (meningitis): Recommended if you plan to visit countries that experience epidemics of meningococcal disease during December – June:

Rabies: Recommended for travelers spending a lot of time outdoors, especially in rural areas, involved in activities such as bicycling, camping, or hiking. Also recommended for travelers with significant occupational risks (such as veterinarians), for long-term travelers and expatriates living in areas with a significant risk of exposure, and for travelers involved in any activities that might bring them into direct contact with bats, carni-vores, and other mammals.

Malaria: Areas of Ethiopia with Malaria: All areas less than 8,200 ft (2500 m) and none in central Adis Ababa. If you will be visiting an area of Ethiopia with malaria, you will need to discuss with your doctor the best ways for you to avoid malaria, including: taking a prescription antimalarial drug, using insect repellent and wearing long pants and sleeves to prevent mosquito bites; sleeping in air-conditioned or well-screened rooms or using bed nets

All of the following drugs are equal options for preventing malaria in Ethiopia:
• Atovaquone-proguanil
• Doxycycline
• Mefloquine
Note: Chloroquine is NOT an effective antimalarial drug in Ethiopia and should not be taken to prevent malaria in this region.

Fikir Asks Not To Ask for Too Much
Nigest: Dice Dota

What is a Diaspora Account? It is a deposit account targeted for Ethiopians in Diaspora to open and use foreign currency in Ethiopia. Individuals and companies can open this account. This account can serve as collateral to get loans in local currency from domestic banks in line with the opening bank's credit policy. Deposit is made in one or more of the following currencies: US Dollar, Pound Sterling or Euro – Basic Information for Ethiopians in the Diaspora – Ministry of Foreign Affairs: Diaspora Engagement Affairs General Directorate, September, 2011:

Since Fikir and his friends stopped Lushi's cutting, Gyorgis did not raise his hand to me. Still, he kept chewing and drinking with his friends all day and though he said nothing I could hear the devil's voice screaming inside him; he would never be satisfied until he got his bajaj and there was no good way for him to do this. He would not work and his infection was getting worse and worse. At night sometimes he would try to make sex with me, but he refused to use a condom and he was so weak now I could keep him away from me. He did not fight. It was all for show. If he had turned to smoke in the middle of any night and drifted away forever I wouldn't have missed him for one minute. In the dark part of my heart I hoped that he would die soon.

Fikir and I kept the details about Kalkidane's and Mrs. Lisa's visit away from Gyorgis so he could not plan a bad surprise; that man was always plotting. On the morning before they were to fly in, Fikir came by with Antoneh and Kiflu and told us that the Americans were coming. He told us to listen while he gave us a lesson in managing farange. He was very strong in what he said; he had learned from his Uncle Adane who also lived in Chicago and who knew Kalkidane and Mrs. Lisa. He said that we should be very careful not to ask the farange for too much. They are not all rich like in the movies, the same way that Ethiopians are not all starving, which is how they see us on their television. They will have presents; they will want to give, in the same way that we will, but they will get nervous if the asking never stops. When he said this he looked hard at Gyorgis. For once, Gyorgis said nothing, he just spat out the khat he was chewing, but his look said bajaj, bajaj, bajaj. I knew that I would have to watch him carefully during this visit. This feeling got even stronger after Fikir left when Gyorgis, with a big smile, told me that when the Americans came he would give me 100 birr to go buy grass for the floor and food for a feast. Where did he think he would get this money? Was he selling something in advance to get his bajaj? On the way to the market I thought about Geta. I missed him and wanted him back home, but if he were with his father they would kill each other. He was lucky that Fikir and his mother were watching out for him. Street life teaches children to be shiftas but now he was off the street, sleeping in the grain shed in Fikir's compound, eating with his family and going to school. This reminded me to make injera and take it to Weyzero Eden, to thank her for feeding my son.

Lushan & Ayana Anticipate The Visit Of The American Sister
Lushan and Ayana: **Dice Dota**

So, Lushi, when she comes, what do you think, will she bring lots of presents?

Of course she will, they always do these farange. How could she not? She is so rich.

But she is Abesha.

Yes, but when they come back they always bring presents.

What do you think she will bring?

I hope she brings a television.

Yes but that needs electric and your father will never even turn the light on. Everyone knows he owes Fat Tadesse money. He would sell it.

No, I will tell him that he can show football games and his friends will pay.

Maybe they will bring money.

I hope she brings those good shoes for sports and walking.

I hope she brings more books about Max and his boat and the let the wild rumpus begin.

I am going to ask her to take me back there.

Where?

To Chicago in America.

What, how can you ask her that?

I can just ask her: Can you take me? She is alone. She needs a sister.

Does she speak Amharic?

She is Abesha. All Abesha speak Amharic.

No, the Oromo, the Mursi, the Afar, the Hamar, they speak their own language.

Well she is not a pagan, she is just like us, part Amhara from our mother and Oromo from our father. And if she has forgotten Amharic I will speak to her in English and teach her Amharic. I am number one in my class.

Can I go?

Ayana, how could you go? You are not of our family.

Yes, but I am your friend, and if you go, you will need a friend.

But I will have my sister. And won't you miss your mother and your family?

Yes, but then I can send them money from America and I will bring presents. They would be happy.

And where will you find money in America?

They have so much money there. I will be a doctor like Dr. Jane at the Family Health and get a lot of money and bring it here.

My father says he hates America.

How can he say that? Everyone loves America.

He says that all the farange are there and they have no respect for Abesha. All they have is money. They think we are their slaves and they treat us like dogs. He says he will never go there.

What's wrong with him?

You know. He is drunk and crazy and all he talks is shit. He hates any people that have one more birr than him.

What would you do if they took you to America?

The first thing I would do would be to sit on the toilet, they all have toilets there, and make a big pee and then sit there for a really long time and make the water run. When it went out I would make it come back in. And then I would pee again. I used to do this with Selam at the Tekle house and I always loved how clean and white the toilet was. And I would learn.

What would you learn?

Nursing. Or Violin. Or Driving. Or Lawyer. Or swimming with the big fish like the woman in the movie. Or Fashion.

Or Pharmacy.

Or Medicine.

Or Teacher.

Or Basketball.

Basketball?

For women? They have it.

They do?

Yes. And they have women who fly airplanes. They have too much. Look Ayana I must study. I will go and hide now with my homework. So I will see you tomorrow.

I am so excited. I will visit you in America, OK?

OK. In Hollywood.

Is that near Chicago?

It is part of Chicago. Near California.

My Uncle is in California.

Abesha is everywhere. OK, go now. Here comes my father.

Selam Prays To Mother Maryam
Selam: **Dice Dota**

Oh Mother Maryam I am so sorry, I pray for you to help my mother, please help her, I have caused her such trouble. I refused to obey my father and she tried to protect me so he beat her.

And I cannot help her, Mother Maryam I cannot go home. My father wants me to marry old Tadesse and I have refused him. I refused him in front of my brothers and sisters and my mother, I refused him in front of all the neighbors and this shames him and now he is a mad dog. I told him right there on the street in front of the compound, I screamed to him I will not be cut and I will not be married to Tadesse or to anyone, and I will not. So he chased me and I ran and my mother got in his way so he beat her with his crutch and she fell down. I could not stay to help her.

Mother Maryam, I'm scared, I have to go away now, to Adis. When I ran from my father I went to find my brother and he told me: Tadesse's sons are organizing to take me. And they will, Maryam, my father will be sure that they abduct me, so Tadesse will rape me and I will be married, my father will get money and I will be their slave. This is how my father got my mother when our grandfather sold her, and he will be sure that the same thing will happen to me.

Mother Maryam I pray that you will protect me tonight. I am here now by the lake with Geta's friends, the street kids, the yegodana lejoch, in the trees across from the old army base. This is where they sleep at night, all together in a child mountain so the hyenas do not sneak up on them. That is my worse fear, that a hyena will bite me and pull me away.

Before the sun rises I will go to the bus station. Geta's friends gave me 30 birr for the bus, 30 birr that they got begging. Oh, please help these kids

Mother Maryam. They have left their families and they need their mothers. They were so good to me, and they have nothing.

Oh, I am so sad, if I could only go to school this morning, if only I could go home to my mother and to Lushan, if only I could stay with what I know. I am not ready to make my own way in this world. Now I hear the storks moving in their nests, and the monkeys are waking up. It's time to go to the bus station. Today I will go to Adis. My God, who can tell what will happen? Only God knows.

Abraham Drives Lisa And Kay Lee To The Airport
In His Yellow Cab
Abraham: Chicago

I picked them up on the North Side near Foster and Ashland with all their bags. The man kissed the woman and the girl goodbye. The woman was quite attractive. Her accent was American, but the girl, she looked Abesha. Adopted, I thought. I have seen so many, but never have I seen a Black American take an Ethiopian child.

"Where do you go?"

O'Hare was happy for me because with traffic and a dollar for each of the four big bags, the fare might run up to $35. Once I crossed Western on Foster, the woman asked me where I was from.

"I am from Africa, Ethiopia. You know it?

Ah, so you have been there. And are going back today? But you are not Ethiopian, I can tell.

Because American ladies are different from African. My expert opinion is – you are more on your guard."

The girl interrupted and said she was Ethiopian. Excited, she poured out a big story about going back to help her family in Dice Dota with money she had found with the help of her school. She said she would bring them medicine and money for her brother and sister's school fees and for their school uniforms. She sounded just like the Swaggart people. I wondered what kind of family she came from. Looking at her I guessed they were Amhara. I am Oromo. I wondered if they would come back with their hearts so big. And with any of their shoes.

"You are lucky to go there. Your family will be very happy."

I can bring no presents. I cannot see my mother. They will not let me back. But next year, when I become US citizen, then…

"Dice Dota is beautiful. I was there once. It is so green. I am from Desse, in Wollo, in the north. It is more dry than Dice Dota. It is famous as the capital of famine photography."

The woman caught her laugh. I was surprised she got my joke.

"No, no, I would not live there even I could. It's better here for my kids. Ethiopia is poor and the Tigray tribe runs the government and the army, and sits on all your chances. I drive cab here but I make more money than an engineer there. And here, I can get a lawyer if there is trouble. There, ha, the government does anything it wants."

The smell of the charcoal, coffee, eucalyptus, injera cooking in the big pan, the sharp light on the dry hills, the cries of us boys taking out the cows eeeeyah, eeeeyah, the oil rag smell of grandfather's rifle, never forget, never.

"Kalkidane. That is a good name. Do you know what it means?"

She knew it: Promise.

"I know your family misses you very much. And you are learning Amharic? From Seleshe at Community Center? My children do the same. Do you know my son Johannes? And my daughter Deem, they call her Aahyito. It means Little Rat. She is five years.

Abeshanetshin atrishie." Never forget you are Abesha.

"Alesam Abate." Yes, Father.

The beautiful mother asked me what we are saying. I did not want to trouble her.

"I said 'May St. George keeps you safe on your journey.' And your daughter said, 'Thank you father, may you be in health.' She is very smart.

Look, we are here already. It was fast, right? I told you I am an expert driver. Terminal Five. Turkish Airlines. I will get the bags. That will be $35 with luggage fee. Safe journey to you Miss Kalkidane Keep Your Promise.

Oh, you are too generous.

Kiss the ground for me."

The tip was twenty-five dollars. They could not afford that.

Selam Sleeps In A Kid Mountain
And Barely Escapes Tadesse's Sons
Selamawit: **Dice Dota**

Oh my God that night was too long, I couldn't sleep a minute, I just lay in the child mountain, listening to their breaths and murmurs, and then when the boy next to me, this little boy with the voice of a girl, put his hand on my breast and whispered he will fuck me, I scratched him and pulled his ear so hard that he cried and I hissed back to him to show respect or I would kick his ass and throw him out for the hyenas. Anyway, I said, you are too little and I am virgin and just forget it, so he went back to sleep with his head on my shoulder, stupid boy. When the first sun glow came up over Mt Hermon, I rose and whispered goodbye to my brother, then I left them all sleeping and with my money folded in my shoe I walked in the dark along the path by the lake where the hippos come in to feed and people bring old horses to die. There, in the marsh by the army base, standing in the mud, was one of them, its ribs just a cage of bones, sinking slowly, too weak to pull its legs out, with its eyes rolled back to the whites and screaming in a terrible wheeze, kccchaaaaa, kccchaaaaa. The sound made my stomach turn. I had to look away. I prayed that God would send a soldier to shoot him; otherwise, he would have to wait all day for the hyenas to take him down. At the gate by the Bale Hotel when I turned to take the path to the road I said goodbye to my Gumare Lake, thinking will I ever see you again, will I ever walk with my friends on the levee and eat kola and talk about how life goes, will I ever be a girl in this world again?

I walked through the hotel garden where the colobus live in the big trees. The hotel people feed them to keep them there for the tourists, and now that the light was coming they were waking up and chattering at me: "Girl in the garden go away, go away, we want all the food, nothing for you, nothing for you." These zinjero shit everywhere, they steal everything and are bandits, and yet the farange love them, they come all the way from Germany to take their pictures because there are no monkeys where they live.

I took the path that bypasses the hotel guard's little house at the end of the driveway and comes out through the trees to the main road. Already just before sunrise it was a wonder to see who was on the road going to Piazza. I had lived in this town all my life but never was out so early in the day in the Center; there were the firewood men, bringing their donkey wagons through the town to pick up their loads on the outskirts, the women coming in from the country to cook breakfast and clean the houses of the rich, and the goat and cattle boys with their sticks, calling out to their animals as they drove their family herds to water at the lake. The town was waking and moving like a person and I made a picture of her in my mind to take with me to Adis. My Dice Dota, my mother town. At the Abraham Cathedral I made the cross and prayed for safety. Then I came up the street to the gate of the Depot. Many people were walking with me; everyone knew to be early so to get their place in the minibus. It was a good thing that I stopped to take my money from my shoe before I passed through the gate. There, talking to the guard, I saw the sons of Tadesse, Yewok and Zeff. Watching for me. Watching to take me in a car to a house where they would lock me in a bedroom until their father came, where I would fight him and he would beat me and lie on me and take my virginity. There would be a cheap wedding, my father would get money and buy a bajaj and I would be in Tadesse's house, a slave to him and his mother and his sons. Soon I would be pregnant and how then could I leave my babies? That would be my life.

It was lucky for me that they were laughing with the guard when I approached; they did not see me. But how was I to pass close by them to get to the minibus inside the Depot? Oh, this passage made my stomach flutter. I turned my back away from the Tadesses, and tied my gabi to cover my hair and wrapped it over my mouth and nose, leaving only my eyes above it like an Islam girl and curving my back and bringing my shoulders together to hide my breasts and make myself smaller. Here was a donkey wagon coming into

123

the Depot, full of red bananas tied in leaves to sell to the travelers, driven by a man standing on the wagon. On it sat a woman with a baby tied in her gabi, dangling her legs and holding the hand of her small boy who sat next to her. As the wagon passed I ducked and ran beside it, calling to the woman, "Please mother, give me a ride into the Depot, I have walked so far and I am so tired." When she nodded, I thanked God and jumped on the wagon, sitting with my back to the Tadesses and taking the little boy's hand as if I were his sister. I kept my eyes down as we came into the Depot, waiting for the bad thing to happen, for Yewok and Zeff to see me, call out and pull me off the wagon and beat me. But no, they did not see me. Once through the gate, I thanked the mother, jumped off the wagon and ran to where minibuses to Adis were waiting.

A boy stood by the door of the first minibus I came to. How much to Adis? 40 birr. I nodded, even though I only had 30 birr and went in and sat where I could not be seen through the front window, in the very back seat next to an old Islam man. The mini was filling up with all sorts of people heading to Shashamene, Ziway, Debre Zeit and Adis; young men and women, families with children, elders, a beggar nun who the boys yelled at for holding her hand out to the other passengers, a farange with enough bags for three people; every new person who came into the mini brought it closer to leaving, and for me, to escaping from the nightmare of Fat Tadesse. Finally after what seemed to take forever, when the mini boy could not squeeze in another body, the driver took his seat, turned on the motor and his music, and drove slowly out of the Depot. I kept my head down and prayed. Thank you, Maryam, you have protected me. Now please make the heart of the mini boy kind. When he finds out I do not have the whole 40 birr, do not let him throw me off the mini.

Judy Jones Tells Kay Lee She's Going To Adopt Ethiopian Orphan # 3
Judy Jones: Flight 204, Istanbul – Adis Ababa

Excuse me dear. Do you speak English?

Oh yes you do, it sounds like you do it very well.

Umm. I was trying not to wake you, but I have to use the rest room. I'll just be a jiffy.

Here I am again. I'm sorry to bother you.

Oh my stars, it's such a long flight, isn't it. We started from Abilene to Dallas where we had to wait two hours for an eight hour flight to London, then a four hour layover and a four hour flight to Istanbul, and now four more to Adis, goodness it's a long haul. And you are from...?

Now that's a big city, Chicago, I mean there are so many different kinds of people there, not like Abilene, I mean there are some African Americans and of course it's Texas so there are Mexicans, but mostly, Abilene is White. But we're doing our best to change that. And you were born in...

Oh, I knew it minute I sat next to you. I have two Ethiopian children, Alan and Betty, and you could be their sister. I just love your people. You have such a special look. I'm going back now to adopt my third baby. The government is making it so hard now, with these new laws. This is my second trip for this baby.

No, she's an orphan.

Oh, no, she really is.

Oh, that's terrible, you mean they lied?

Oh my stars, that must have been so hard.

No, I'm sure, we work with our mission there and they have all the documentation. These kids have lost their families because of AIDS.

Oh, you do? You are going back to see them? How wonderful to have two families. Sometimes I wish Alan and Betty had some sort of connection to their heritage. But then that might be confusing.

Well you know, I mean, they might wonder who their real family is. Oh no, I'm sorry, I'm not suggesting that you have an identity crisis dear, I mean, how could I say that? I don't even know you. Look here, our new baby is named Fasika, this is her, we found her last year, isn't she beautiful?

Well yes of course, you have to get back to your... Oh, *that's* your mother? Is she American?

Oh well, yes, why shouldn't she be? Well, dear it was wonderful talking to you. I'm Judy Jones and I didn't... I didn't get your name.

Selam Gets Through The Border
But How Will She Pay For Her Ticket?
Selam: **Dimaa Kaloo (Red Pasture)**

For two days all I'd thought about was Fat Tadesse lying on top of me and pushing his thing into my body and that had made all my muscles so tight I could hardly pee or squeeze out a tear, but once we left the Depot I cried and cried and couldn't stop. How embarrassing. I pulled the gabi over my face and pretended I was sleeping but the sobs made me shake and the old man in the Islam hat sitting beside me asked me, "What is the matter, my daughter?" When I told him my mother had died he made a prayer to Allah to keep her spirit safe in heaven. I am Christian but still, his prayer was a blessing; it stopped me crying. I lowered my gabi and watched through the window as the mini passed out of town, up the Lake road and by the place they call Red Pasture, where the border is with Oromia, the place where the Arsi bring their donkeys down to the lake from the dry lands. There were always fights there among the different tribes about water. My father said he had fought them there when he was with the Derg, but I don't know, who could believe such a liar?

I had forgotten that there was a checkpoint at Red Pasture. The driver showed his papers to one soldier and the boy opened the door so that another soldier, a female, could take a look at all the passengers. Who were they looking for I wondered? There had been no problems since after the election. But, oh my God, I realized when I saw the soldier, I knew her. She was the sister of Mukbar from my school who I had played with when I was a little kid. And she knew me, and my family. Her family had been proud when she had gone into the army. Now as she inspected all the passengers her eyes caught mine and even though most of my face was covered, I knew she recognized me because she nodded and was about to speak, but before she could greet me I shook my head and made the *don't talk* sign, *please don't*. What if someone on the mini knew Tadesse? Or my father. She nodded again and left the bus. I thanked God for a good sister, but oh Jesus I thought, will I ever be anywhere where no one knows me?

Once we passed into Oromia the boy began to collect the money. How would I tell him I only had 30 birr? I was in the back of the mini so he came to me last. When he came to me, I took out the birr that the yegodanna lejoch had given me and showed him, saying, "Please my brother, this is all I have and I have to get to Adis, please accept this."

"What?" he says back to me, "so I must pay the difference? My boss will want his money."

"But brother, he won't know…"

Then the old Islam man next to me asked the boy, "Can you not show mercy? Her mother has died and she is an orphan."

"Yes," I lied, "I am going to Adis to look for my aunt. There is no one else in my family."

"Ahah," he says, "this is an old story, father, all these girls run away from their families to become bar girls. They are tired of living in a tukol with their families and the goat. They want clothes. They want money."

This brought the tears back, so I could lie with more power. "How can you insult me?" I said to the boy in a crying voice, so loud that the rest of the passengers turned to look. "My mother is dead and you call me a prostitute?" Now I cried louder.

The woman in front of me now joined in. She was my mother's age, dressed up to travel and with a tattooed face so you knew she was Amhara. A little girl sat next to her. "Yes, you should be ashamed," she told the boy, "look how young she is."

"That's all very well," said the boy, "but this mini doesn't run on tears. Who will give me the ten birr she needs to go to Adis? Otherwise she will have to get off at Ziway."

The woman looked away. The Islam man did too.

"You get off at Ziway," the boy said to me.

"Please brother." I looked at him direct in his eyes. He wasn't so much older than me.

"You get off at Ziway," he repeated and went back to his sitting place above the wheel.

Lisa and Kay Lee Land At Bole
Lisa: Dice Dota

Marc, I can't sleep so I gotta write.

Bole was like fucking old home, as was Istanbul, same long halls and glass walls, filtering you down from the plane portal to the big chamber where you step up to the line and then to the official in the booth who looks at your papers. Always the panty wetting at the luggage belt: are my bags all here or is one on its way to New Delhi? Funny how I dreaded leaving the airport because then I'd have to be "Mrs. Lisa," accountable to a context, a place. I felt fine being irradiated by fluorescence in a plastic chair watching dressed up people on a screen talking in a language that I didn't understand, better than I did when the pin ball stopped bumping me from airport to airport, and I rolled into the uncontrolled climate at the exit door, beyond customs into *customs*. No more safe limbo, I am *here*, and there *they* are, the people with whom we made an intangible deal with no details. Our "promise." Did you write anything down? I didn't.

We got through immigration, bought our visas, found our bags and rolled through customs without a hassle. They didn't question that we were bringing 40 pair of shoes. Another orphan project, yes, OK. Then out to the patio outside the main Bole building. First trip to Adis was hot sun, blue-brown, dry, dusty and bright, but this time rain at 8,500 feet made for a cold and soggy morning, like Chicago April, not my idea of Africa at all, but then again, ask anyone and you'll hear, "Ethiopia is not Africa." Still, the same smell of car exhaust, coffee, garbage and eucalyptus, the view of the hills of the city, green now, sprawling beyond the airport parking lot, the same wiry old porters grabbing for your luggage cart.

Kay Lee was beside herself, she held my hand tight, poking me to look at the people waiting outside on the patio; an old guy in a shawl with a long staff; two women in modern dresses, ornate braids and blue tattoos on their cheeks and jaws; a Somali queen with intricately braided dreads, a brilliantly colored embroidered dress and cool sun glasses. In the gaggle of porters and drivers on the landing Kay Lee saw my name on a sign, "Mrs. Lisa Levi" held up by a thin young man. She grabbed his arm and pulled him to me. "Mrs. Lisa, Miss Kay Lee. I am Fikir." Yes, it was Fikir the guy on the phone and the Skype. He batted away the other porters and took our cart. "Come on, we have Ato Dejen's mini to take you to Dice Dota." We followed him through the lot to a battered blue van. Fikir slid the side door open, and put our bags in the back. "Come on, the family is waiting." We got in the back, Fikir in the front, next to a wide saddle-colored man with a face like a big leather bowl who turned from the driver's seat and gave us a grin full of brown teeth. Ato Dejen greeted us, "Welcome to Ethiopia." Kay Lee, showing off her Amharic, shot back at him "Amar say ko nal lo" and then whispered to me, "What happened to his teeth?"

Selam Tricks The Nice Farange
Selam: **Between Shashamene and Adis**

In Shashamene the Islam Man got out with some other passengers but before he did he wished me the protection of Allah and I said, "Thank you father," sad that he would not stay sitting next to me and be my guardian all the way to Adis. When new passengers got on the mini I hid my face in my gabi in case any of them were from Tadesse or my father, but no, thank God, I did not recognize any of them. Many were Woleyta and speaking that language; they had transferred from the bus from Soto and with them were two young farange, a man and a woman, with big carrying bags, which the mini boy tied on the roof. The mini boy squeezed the girl into the seat next to me where the Islam man had sat. As she sat, she smiled at me, a tall girl with orange hair and orange splotches on her face that were part of her skin. I wanted to touch her hair because Ethiopians never have this color hair unless they put in red mineral like the people from the Omo. I had known a German girl who worked for the German NGO in Dice Dota; once she let me braid her hair. It was the color of new brick, so soft and beautiful like a model you see on television.

We passed the famous Black Lion painted on the wall of the Bob Marley Church on the way to Shashamene. I had passed it before on the way to Lake Langano and I had seen Rastah priests in Dice Dota with their braided hair and tape recorders always playing reggae; they would sell their hats and Bob Marley shirts, and all the farange would buy ganja from them. Our teachers told us to stay away from them or else we would become addicted. On the front of their house was the lion and a big picture of Haile Selassie. As the mini passed it the farange girl became very excited and called out in English to the farange man in the front, "Look, Dave."

I am not shy with farange. More and more are coming to Dice Dota to work in the NGOs and whenever I meet one, I try my English with them and, if they are American, I always ask for my sister. So I asked the girl, "You know One Love, Bob Marley?"

She smiled and nodded yes, and asked me "Do you speak English?"

"Yes, a little," I said, "I am Selam. What is your name?"

Her name was Jen.

"Are you fine, Jen? Where are you from?"

She was fine. And she was from USA.

"Do you know my sister in Chicago? She is Kalkidane. She lives with Marc and Lisa."

She did not know Chicago or Marc or Lisa. She was from Vermont, a place I had never heard of. She had been in Jinka to see the Omo people. Now she was going to Lalibela.

"I have never gone," I said.

We were coming close to Langano where all the farange go to swim because the water is red and has no bilharzia. I pointed to the road to the lake when we passed it. "You know Langano?"

Yes, she said, she had been swimming there with her friend, Dave. She pointed to the farange man. I understood her meaning; he was not her husband.

Then she asked me where I was going. I told her my lie, that my mother died and that I was going to look for my aunt in Adis. She asked for my father. I said he is dead too, from HIV. The mini boy was watching me as I talked to the farange woman. I watched him back and cast my eyes to her and back to him. Did he understand?

Soon we were passing the big flower houses south of the town of Ziway. I had heard so much about them, but I had never been north of Langano in my life and it was such a surprise to see them, these houses one after another, each the size of three farms under a plastic roof. So many have been built that people now are coming to Ziway from Dice Dota and other towns in Ethiopia to find work. The flowers are picked and then are taken to the airport in Bole and flown to Europe, all in the same day. It is a miracle. My first thought was if I was a flower instead of a person then I would not need a visa,

I could fly to Europe in one day and marry a farange like Helen will do. But my second thought was, yes, but if I was a flower, then I would be dead in a week. As we came into the town the minibus boy rose to collect his money. Before he could ask the man Dave for the fare I snapped my fingers so he came to the back of the mini. Again I cast my eyes to the farange woman so he could read my game.

"He wants you to pay for you and your friend."
"How much?"
I asked the boy, in Amharic how much for the two farange? He smiled and said 50 birr each. I told this to Jen and she went into her pocket and gave 100 birr to the boy. He had just made a good profit and my fare to Adis was covered. The woman in front of me turned to look at me and smiled. Everyone loves to fool the farange; they have so much money. The woman, Jen, thanked me for helping her and I told her, "No problem."

Kay Lee Writes Miranda From An Internet Café
Kay Lee: **Dice Dota**

Miranda, I'm at an Internet café in Hometown Dee Say Do Tah in Homeland E–Thee-o-Pee-Yah in the continent of Ah Freak Ah and it's Amar-Fuck-ing-Dazing.

The plane ride was like 190 hours from Chicago to Istanbul and packed so full you couldn't stretch or lie down. Then we had a layover in Istanbul, from 12 to 4 AM; this because Turkish Airlines was the cheapest flight my Mom could find from O'Hare to Adis Ababa. Problem was the fuckhead Nazis who designed the Istanbul airport built the chairs so you could not lie down anywhere, like at midnight there were 1,000 empty single fixed seats with trays but you could not find a bench to save your butt, they did not want you to lie down, so my Mom took a pill and we found a luggage cart with an empty wagon and curled up in the back of one of those carts. Nobody said shit. I almost had to carry Mom to the plane for Adis at 5 AM she was so knocked out. The plane wasn't crowded so I moved seats to let her stretch out, went forward and sat next to a creepy blue haired White racist Christian bitch from Texas who was coming to kidnap her third Ethiopian baby and who couldn't believe that I wasn't an orphan and that Lisa actually was my adoptive Mom.

Anyways, this is a day later and so much has happened and I still don't know what time it is. I think its 11 in the Day which is late afternoon here. First, the boys here are really cute, nobody's fat, they are buffed, they have beautiful faces but sometimes brown teeth because there's something in the water here. They all play soccer and do gymnastics and they are really polite; they call me Ms. Kay Lee, they won't let me carry anything, they love to flirt, and being guys, they try not to look at your boobs, or your ass, but they do. Their English is amazing, I mean really amazing, they will not swear, but they know all the words from Hip Hop. Ho, MuhFuh, Bling, and they know Reggae, One Love, Bob Marley, Jammin, they have it down. They like to rap in Amharic and in other Ethiopian languages and it cracks everybody up when they rap one language, then another, with the different tribal dances, they just laugh and laugh. They are all Christian and so religious that they cannot handle me telling them that I am an atheist, they just say, "How can that be?" They all have five brothers and sisters, they all pay a lot of attention to their clothes and how they look. The boys all want to come to the United States and study engineering and the girls all want to study nursing, though if you ask them more, the boys all want to be professional soccer players like David Beckham and girls all want to be Beyoncé. Sound familiar?

We drove from the airport straight to Dice Dota to see my family. Five hours, wow, maybe people are all the same underneath but the road is so different; folks on the side of the highway under umbrellas on a dusty plain in the middle of nowhere, waving at you madly as you whiz by, selling tomatoes, bananas, cabbages, melons, charcoal and you think: is that their job? Do they stand by the road like this every day waving potatoes?

Lots of animals everywhere, donkeys, horses, cows, camels, sheep and goats, in the country, in the towns and in the city too, crossing the highways, main roads, side streets, herded by little boys and girls with sticks. It's very cool. I wish it were like that in Chicago. Can you imagine the traffic jam while you waited for a herd of donkeys to cross Lakeshore Drive? It's like: you keep your meat and milk close, you protect your bank account as it crosses the road.

Seeing my real mother…wow, was so unreal, Nigest, everyone says she looks like me. She's Lisa's age and she's already had five kids!!! She looks so tired. My father Gyorgis, oh, is he a trip, he looks almost ancient, more like my Grandpa Mike, he's got one leg and gets around on a crutch, is missing teeth and laughs all the time. Him and Nigest don't speak English so who knows what they're really saying? Fikir translates but I get the feeling he's changing some and leaving out more. So we're having this big meal with them, they've obviously been cooking all day, and they are serving us meat, which my Mom tells me is special, like they killed one of their goats for us, and I'm watching them, thinking; these are my blood, they are in me, and how much of me, my reactions, what I like, and don't like, how I get mad, my gestures, my laugh, even my BO, how much comes from them?

And then where is my brother and my sister? Somehow, my older sister Selamawit isn't around, they say she's working in Adis. So my Mom says, "but we brought her school tuition," and she gives Nigest and Gyorgis a look that I call "the corncob" which means *What's Up Your Butt?* and they start arguing and Fikir doesn't translate until we ask him to, and then he says it's unimportant, and then my Mom asks where's little brother Geta, we want to pay his tuition too, and we find out he isn't there either, he's living at Fikir's, but he'll be around the next day, and then they start arguing about that, and Fikir doesn't translate. However my sister Lushan and my cousin Demissie are there, and they are adorable, she's almost eleven and he's five, and a whole lot of other people are there who have come to meet me. I can't tell who is a neighbor and who is my aunt. I have three aunties, Alemenesh, Malekeda and Feriwot, (I wrote it down), but where were the older guys, my uncles? And who is my cousin and who is Lushan's friend? Meanwhile my Mom is giving me her funny eyebrow signals that mean "Chill, we will talk about this later," and my little cousin Demissie sees this and he starts imitating Lisa and makes his own funny eyebrow signals and everybody laughs.

The food was great, just like they serve at Gondar Restaurant, injera that Fikir said Nigest made herself, doro wat with an egg, fried fish, gomen, goat tibs, and beer for the grown-ups and Orange Fanta for us kids. They must have spent a lot on us, which is crazy because the houses are so small, hardly any furniture and no plumbing, you should smell the outhouse, P. U.

What's the big surprise? My family is poor, duh, they gave me up for adoption for a reason, right? This meal must have set them back. We all eat in the yard under a fixed tarp. It's not exactly warm either, they're all wearing jackets and they offer to get us some blankets but my Mom shakes her head, gives me the eye, and whispers "scabies."

137

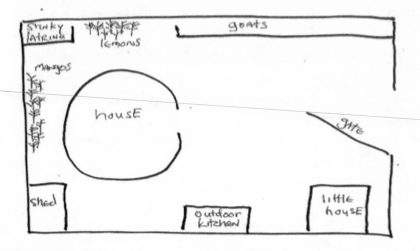

The whole compound is a rectangle, enclosed in a long block about four streets away from the big downtown boulevard that leads from the lake to the Cathedral. The front end faces a dirt road that makes a right angle turn just before the compound's gate. One long side is walled off by thick frondy palms and a concrete block wall. That's where the goat corral is. They are so cute. They stay in there eating grass, and bleating until they get out which seems to happen a lot, and then everyone stops what they are doing and chases them back in and ties the corral gate shut, and then they get out again. In the yard, are lemon, mango, banana palms and pepper trees. The bananas are fruiting, and they are small, red, sour and delicious. On the entrance side is a big concrete wall with jagged glass splinters set into the top, just like you see in the South Side, and a big gate made out of an aluminum sheet with a door cut in it, that opens up to the dirt road. The whole thing opens wide enough for a small truck to get in, but usually they just use the door. When the gate is shut you can't see in. In the back corner of the compound is the stinky two-hole shed where you poop. I have no idea where the poop goes and I don't want to know. I breathe through my mouth and get out of there as fast as I can. Then there's the house which they call the "tukol," a one-story mud hut with two rooms, and next to it is the open kitchen shed. Along the back and sides of the compound are palm frond fences woven with brambles in front of cinder block walls. When the gate is closed the compound is its own world, its own fortress.

So after we eat, they spread the grass, burn incense and do the coffee ceremony, just like they taught us at the Community Center, and we all drink this amazingly strong coffee, the kind that immediately sends me to the bathroom, and that's an experience I won't describe here. Then we take out all the presents, books and pens and colored markers for Lushan and Geta, but since Geta is not there we give the markers to Demissie. More presents: two frisbees, a suitcase of shoes that people have given us, a Swiss Army Knife for Gyorgis, and headlamp for Nigest. The shoes are fun; when they find a pair that fits they vogue around while everybody laughs. Then Gyorgis tries on a pair and it gets a little weird because he only has a right foot so he puts the other shoe on his hand. But he loves his knife and Nigest, her light; Fikir says that she says the headlight is perfect for when she has to walk or cook in the night. Little cousin Demissie was wild about the frisbees. He grabbed them and danced around me and Mom, talking a stream of Amharic, posing while everybody laughed, and when I asked Fikir what he was saying, Fikir said that he was saying that he was "the absolutely top standard football player" and now he would become a frisbee expert too. I showed him and Fikir how to throw it and they caught on fast. When they finally got it together to shoot me one that I could catch, I caught it between my legs. Now I am Demissie's Goddess.

But it's my sister Lushi who really got to me. Oh my God, I just love her and I want her to have everything she needs. Right when we got there she had *Where The Wild Things Are* in her hand, with what I wrote when I'd sent it last year, "To my Sister Selamawit: This is the best book, read it to our little brothers and sisters." While we ate and gave presents she was really quiet but her eyes were on me and my Mom's, and mine were on her because WTF? she looks just like me when I was 10, when my Mom got me extensions and it cost $55 and Marc had a shit-fit. This may sound like a stuck-up douche, but with her dreads all pulled back tight on her head and then falling out of the tie with a million beads and her color the same as me, and her beautiful mouth and eyes, oh God, such sad eyes – she was so beautiful. She was really happy about the books, "Outside Over There" and "In the Night Kitchen" and she wanted me to stay and read them with her, but then my Mom called out, TIME TO GO. She'd been talking with my Mother and Father with Fikir translating, and, like we'd flown all night and she was really wasted, and she gave me her look, *Get Me Out Of Here. This Is Too Much*, and I had to get her back, I owed her for coming with me, she didn't even want to.

Lushan got really internally fucked up that we were leaving. She smiled and everything but she gave me a look from the bottom of her eyes that said: *stay here with me, sister, please stay*, and oh, I felt bad, I mean, I wanted to stay, but I didn't know if she was going to ask me for something that I couldn't give, and that toilet was challenging. Problem solved when Fikir said we should go to the hotel before it was too late and he called Dejen on his cell. We waited around the van arrived and we made a date with the family for the next day after school, and then we went to the hotel. Dejen had already got all our bags up in the room and me and Mom didn't even brush our teeth, we fell asleep in our clothes.

Selam Gets Lost In Adis And Makes A New Friend
Selam: **Adis Ababa**

Coming into Adis, my God, from the checkpoint at Debre Zeit all the way into the Center it was so slow, lines of cars and trucks going both ways and around each other, the mini stopping and starting all the time while people got on and off. By the side of the road were many people walking, just like the busiest time on the Piazza in Dice Dota, but going on and on, crowds and cars and people herding animals for so many kilometers all the way into the Center; past factories, stores, restaurants, hotels and shops. What would I do when I got to the Depot? Where would I go? I watched the farange girl sleeping and thought about her life. Where did she live? With her parents? With her boyfriend? Did she sleep naked in a bed with him like the Sally girl in the Harry movie in a house with a bedroom for every person, like the one in Home Alone? Or in a flat like in Ghosts, in a tall building with an elevator? Did she have brothers and sisters with orange hair? Did her father beat her? Did she have an auto? Did her mother have a kitchen with white stoves and coolers and a machine for washing clothes? Did she work? Was she rich? How could she have so much? Would I ever have such a chance? My mind was running with a river of dreams and questions, jumping to heaven with hopes that I would have everything, and falling to hell with sadness that I had nothing and would so always.

Now we were coming into the Central Depot of Adis. My plan was to ask for directions to the neighborhood Kasanchis and find the restaurant, Seven Nights, where Helen worked. I hoped that they could give me a job there right away. I had not eaten since I left my house the day before. The woman Jen woke up. I smiled at her and she said, "Good luck," and took my hand. The boy opened the door and I went out into Adis.

All the taxi men and mini boys were there, calling to the people for their rides to different neighborhoods. The city was all around me, the sidewalks full and vans and cars going in all directions and I felt so small, like just a dot. Where was I? Where was Kasanchis? I asked a boy by his mini, did he know Seven Nights in Kasanchis? Yes he did. Could he show me the way?

"Oh," he said, "sister, you shouldn't go there, it is no place for a young girl." "Why?" I said, "my sister is there. I am going to find her."

"OK," he said, "and then may God help you find her. Take that mini by the City Coffee shop."

I told him I was traveling on foot. "OK," he said, "it is not too far, take Ras Mekonnen Street," and he pointed towards a road. I thanked him and started walking. The smell from the coffee shops and restaurants made juice in my stomach. As I left the Depot I saw Jen and David loading their big bags on to a mini-van. They were laughing. Jen saw me and waved.

I walked to the big road, Ras Mekonnen Street, and then by the big stadium I had seen so many times on the television at the Swaggart Center, where we all went to watch the Africa Cup. And there in the park above the road was the famous Ghion Hotel where Meles, Khadafi, and Mandela met together and made friendship agreements with their armies. Here in this sector there were too many buses and cars on these streets, and no shops, just big buildings everywhere, with uniformed guards under their umbrellas at the gates to the parking lots, and many men and women in their suits, Ethiopians and farange coming in and out of the buildings with badges on their jackets. The sun was high now, it was around Nine in the Day, and so hot, I had to sit. Where could I find food and water? How would I live?

Outside the guard posts where the farange went in and out were the beggars under the shade trees. This was their office and I wondered if they fought in the morning like they did in Dice Dota over the best position. I had seen this and laughed with my friends on the way to school when the crippled women with their babies punched each other. I went over to their tree and sat down on the ground on the edge of the shade. A dirty barefoot girl beggar with a ragged dress and hair like a savage looked me over in the way that these wild kids do, with old eyes like a woman in the market reading a customer. She didn't even put out her hand; she knew I was as poor as her. At her feet was a tray of chewing gum.

"Little sister," I said, "I am traveling from Dice Dota and looking for the Seven Nights restaurant in Kasanchis. I have no money and I need water. Will you help me?"

"What happened to your money? Where is your family?"

"My mother and father have died from HIV." This lie was becoming so fixed I was starting to believe it, which was not hard because it was not about me or my family. It was a story from a film.

The girl looked at me as if she had heard that lie so many times and couldn't I do better? "And why do you look for Kasanchis? So you can become a little whore and die of AIDS like your mother?"

She backed away from me like a dog dodging a blow from a stick and showing her teeth. It was not a smile. "Kasanchis is where all the girls go to make money from the farange. I am too little to work there but you have titties, you could get rich. Are you virgin?"

I could not believe this girl would speak to me this way. I did not know her. I had never hurt her. What was she saying? I turned from her. The spit in my mouth was like a thick paste. I put my gabi over my head and put my head between my knees. I was too tired to cry.

Who was tapping me on my back? It was her, I knew it.

"Girl you go to hell."

Now she pulled my gabi from my face. She held out a plastic bottle with water.

"I am Genet. Come on. Drink, it's clean. I got it this morning from the church." I took the bottle and wiped it with my gabi, then put it to my lips, holding the water in my mouth, before I swallowed.

"Go on, take more. You don't want to pass out or get the shakes." I did as she commanded and then gave her back the bottle.

"Thank you. I am Selamawit." She took some gum from her tray and held out a stick. "Here, chew this, it will take away the hunger for a while.

Not as good as the sniff, but then gum don't make you sick and crazy. Never do that no matter how hungry you get, OK, promise?"

"The what?"

"Sniff. Don't do it." She brought the water bottle up to her nose and sniffed, rolling her eyes. "Once you start you cannot stop. It makes you too stupid to live." Now she was pulling my hand, "Come on. I will take you to Seven Nights."

She took her tray and we walked down the sidewalk past the big buildings calling out, "Chicle, one birr" to everyone we passed, and whenever she saw a farange she ran behind them, calling in English, "Mister, hungry, hungry, one birr, one birr." She would not stop, she followed close behind them calling and touching their arm until they bought a gum or turned to brush her off. She would always jump back, she could not be hit, she was a mosquito they could not swat. We went by the biggest buildings, UNICEF, GDZ, and National Hotel. By the time we came to the Airport Road she had ten birr.

"Now we must get food," she said. "Do you know how to steal?"

"Why do you steal? You have this money?"

"What, are you stupid? Do you think I don't have a family? I give some money to my mother and then with the rest I go to Merkato every morning and buy this gum. I buy it for 25 cents and sell it for one birr."

"If I get money, can I go with you and buy gum too? I do not know how I will live here."

"You can do what you want, but listen, Miss Selamawit, you are too old for the gum business. Miruts, the gum man, if you have titties, he won't sell to you unless you fuck him. If you are going to be a whore, you might as well make a lot more money in Kasanchis and if you are virgin, oh my God, you can win many birr from the Arabs if your pimp doesn't get it all. And, if you are young and beautiful, you can be a virgin many times. You will learn this in Kasanchis."

Oh my God, I thought. How can this little girl speak like this? Was this what the minibus boy was trying to tell me at the Depot? And what about the waitress job that Helen said I could get at Seven Nights – what will I be serving?

Genet Teaches Selam How To Steal
Genet: **Adis Ababa**

So this Southern girl Selam, she knew nothing and she was too pretty for street life, it was a good thing she met me before somebody's pimp boy caught her and raped her just to break her in and put her to work until she got HIV or pregnant or both. I've seen girls like her plenty of times stumbling around, hungry and crying until someone swallows them whole. The smart ones, they kick out the pimps and the Mammas and get into business for themselves; they find a farange to marry and go to Europe or America. The ugly girls who don't get raped, if they are strong and don't sniff or chew or get sick, they find their way; there are schools and shelters for these girls. Me, when my titties grow and I have an ass, I'm getting off the street that's for sure, because I'm really pretty already. I'll sell myself to some Swedish people for adoption and then I'll learn Swedish, go to a university there and be a model like Iman.

I could see how hungry she was so I took her to the stalls on the way to Kasanchis where they sell fruit and kola. I told her we have to make a trick so we can get some food but first we had to look carefully at the scene before we make our strike.

"But what if we get caught?"

"Run like hell, because if they catch you, your ass will know their sticks. And if a beating is all that happens you are lucky, because if you have no parents to pay a penalty, they put you in the Woman's Prison forever and that is worse than horrible; the food is bad, just injera, shirro and tea if you are lucky and never near enough. You sleep on the floor crowded like sticks in a bundle, there is no soap, you shit in a bucket and there are women with sick babies. I was there once and before I got out a baby died and the mother cried for three

145

nights. No one can sleep there and if you stay for too long you will get an infection and die."

That's what I told her. We walked down the market street and there, at the far end among the ladies sitting behind their tables of fruit and vegetables, sat an old mamma, alone. I didn't see any men or children around her. The location was good; you could run right out of the end of the market and around a corner in case she started to yell.

"OK, Selam, here's the game. You are so hungry and thirsty that you fall on the table so hard that it collapses. She goes crazy, cries and screams, and you cry and apologize, say you are so weak and sick, and then you crawl around and help her pick up her stuff and put back her table. Meanwhile I am pretending to help too, I pick up oranges and bananas and put some in my scarf, then I disappear and meet you over there on the big road on the steps to Dashen Bank. Do you see the sign? OK, are you ready to pass out?"

That girl was scared, I knew it, her eyes were big, but OK, the girl had to do some work or else she would starve, and I had to teach her.

"Come on, look she's almost sleeping. Go." I push her from the back.

She's good though, I can see she has a talent for these street games. She starts walking all stagger stagger like a drunk sniffer up on her toes, then she stops in front of the table, puts her hands up to her face like her head is killing her, sighs, "Ohhhhh, Ohhhhh," rises up and crashes right on the table fluttering her eyes back in her head. A great performance. Now, the table goes down and the fruit and vegetables are rolling everywhere. The old mother yells, "Oh my God, what are you doing, girl?" Selam is on the ground with the tomatoes and bananas, moaning, "ahhh, ahhh." Old Mother is trying to beat her with one hand and pick up the vegetables with the other, so the beating is nothing and I am down on the stones acting like I'm helping but stuffing oranges and bananas into my scarf. Now other people are trying to help, or steal, you don't know, people from the market and shoppers and other kids too, it is a perfectly crazy crowd. I get out of there and around the corner with four oranges, two tomatoes and some bananas and go to the steps of Dashen Bank where I wait for Selam.

Selam Studies The Big Toe
Of The Old Mother And Blocks Her Curse
Selam: **Adis Ababa**

Saint George, this life is too hard. After I fell down I opened my eyes and there was the big bare toe of the Old Mother right in front of my face, the nail like a purple horn and the knuckle all bumps and covered with tough yellow skin, more like the knob at the end of a stick than part of an old woman's foot. She pulled it back but I turned my face away in time, so she only just got the back of my head and she was such an old woman it was the kick of a little kid. Then she started beating me, screaming, "What have you done, girl, what have you done?" I didn't want to get up, no, just to stay on the ground and shut my eyes and get kicked and beaten until the blows stopped and then just lay there until everyone went away and it was night, but no, of course that could not be, so I got my knee up while gathering up the oranges and tomatoes and blocking the old witch's slaps I cried, "Oh Mother, I am so sorry, let me help you, please forgive me, please." Other people from the market were gathering round and putting the table back. I caught sight of Genet scampering away between people's legs. She had gotten some fruit. Now how would I get away?

I dumped the food on the table and went down to pick more up, still warding off the blows. She stopped swinging, and began to gather the food on the table back into her baskets and boxes. She was crying. I felt bad for her, this was her living and I had taken part of it. "Oh Mother," I lied, "I am so sick and weak that I cannot stand, please forgive me. Let me help you."

She shook her head and pushed me away. "Go away, I know your game. You and the other girl, I saw her. I curse you girl, you uncircumcised devil, may you be gang-raped by bandits, may the police lock you up and beat you until you die, may your children fall sick and your mother get HIV and give it to your father, may you..."

I made the sign to send her curse away. The people around us were laughing as I walked out of the market and around the corner to the street. There I could see Genet waving from the steps of the Dashen Bank.

Lisa, Nigest, Fikir And The Kids Go To The Market And Then Have Coffee
Nigest: **Dice Dota**

On the second day of the visit in the afternoon Mrs. Lisa came with Kalki and Fikir and offered to take me to the market. This solved a big problem; we had already borrowed money for the greeting feast, so how could we continue to show hospitality with no food and nothing to sell? My husband was angry when he saw Fikir. He knew what Fikir would tell Mrs. Lisa; that he had tried to sell Selam and cut Lushi and had beaten me and Geta, so he would never get any of Mrs. Lisa's money. To put on a good face he made a stupid joke as we were leaving, calling out, "Please, while you are at the market see if you can find me another leg?" When Fikir translated this, Mrs. Lisa brought her eyebrows together and cast a dark look back at Gyorgis, but he had been chewing and would hardly have noticed if she had shot him in the head, he was so intoxicated. He's lucky I am Christian, I thought, otherwise I would follow my worst thoughts and no one would know; they would think he died from alcohol.

On our way to the market Kalkidane walked ahead with Lushan and the sight of the two sisters made me remember how, when I was a girl, walking with my sisters, it felt as if our blood flowed through our fingers to each other. Oh, I thought, if only I could walk with all my children for all my life. Is this what all mothers feel, that our children are always part of our body; and so the pain comes when we push them, or when they tear themselves, away?

At the market, Fikir spoke with Mrs. Lisa. She tried to put money in my hand but I closed my fist saying, "Thank you but no, you are our guest," so she shook her head and gave the money to Fikir who handed it back to me. I bowed and kissed Mrs. Lisa. Fikir and Lushan wanted to take Kalki and Mrs.

Lisa on a tour of the market. I told Fikir that he must bargain for Mrs. Lisa
so that people will not take advantage and she will not win the reputation of
a stupid farange, easy to trick. Then I bought injera, beef, chicken, eggs, kik
alicha, gomen, tef, coffee and fruit. When they came back they had many
presents; table cloths for me and to bring back to America, sports shoes for
the kids, cultural dresses for Kalki and Mrs. Lisa, and ice cream for everyone
from Ato Gabebbe's ice box. Fikir said Mrs. Lisa offered to buy us a taxi to
take everything home but he had refused because that money would just go
for nothing. So we all ate our ice cream and then walked to the Center with
our bags.

It was Fikir's custom to drink coffee with his student friends at the Metro
and on this day Mrs. Lisa could pay for us, so that is where we went first. I
understood that Fikir wanted to show himself with the Americans so his name
would spread as an experienced fixer and guide for farange but this display in
public to his friends and the others on the patio made me nervous because
when thieves see you with Whites or diaspora relatives they notice. They find
out where you live and then after watching, if they decide that you will be
their next job, they offer robbers from other towns a share of the profit if they
will attack you. I know this because once, after my sister's friend's brother had
visited with presents and returned to Germany, strange men came in a van to
my sister's friend's house with Kalashnikovs. No one knew them. They took
the computer and the television he had given them. Everyone knew she had no
husband there. She said that they would have hurt her if she had fought them.

But even though he was sometimes foolish Fikir was my savior and protector and his English was the cord to Kalkidane. As we sat at Metro I watched
her throw the flying toy in the courtyard with Lushan and our eyes were
sometimes meeting even though she was laughing and running. She was playing like a sister, and looking at me to know me better. I thanked God for this
sight and then prayed that all my children would be careful and have joy.

Nitty Gritty Table Talk At The Café Metro Between Nigest, Fikir And Mrs. Lisa While The Kids Play
Nigest: Dice Dota

"Nigest, Mrs. Lisa wants to know about Selam. I told her she is working in Adis. My answer did not satisfy her. She wants to know more."

"Fikir, tell her that there was problem at home and that she had to leave Dice Dota."

They speak more English.

"She wants to know what problem? That the money they collected was for her school and since she is not in school, what should she do?"

"OK, so tell her everything."

"She does not want me to speak for you. She wants me to translate true words."

OK. I nodded to Mrs. Lisa. Only a liar would call what I said a lie.

"Mrs. Lisa, Gyorgis' friend Tadesse's wife died, and he needed a young wife to be in his bed and take care of his children and give him more babies. Gyorgis knew this, and since he wanted a bajaj, he offered Selam to Tadesse so he could buy the bajaj and a taxi license with the bride price. Gyorgis beat me when I told him that Selam had to stay in school. When Selam refused her father in public, she had to run away because Gyorgis had already accepted the dowry money, so Tadesse's sons were going to abduct her for their father. And now Gyorgis is scared because Tadesse wants his money back and Gyorgis has spent most of it."

What I did not say was what all girls do when they run away.

More English. Now she is talking loudly and with her hands. "Selam, Adis, Dice Dota, Tadesse, Gyorgis, Geta," then more English and frowning. Really she is strong like a Tekle. Fikir shakes his head. He tries to speak, but she keeps breaking in. He nods and laughs and tries to speak again and she breaks in again and he laughs again and tries to speak again, but again she breaks in. Fikir is defeated.

"She says that we must rescue Selam and get her back to school. I tried to tell her that this is not our custom and that God will protect her and that she must find her own way."

"Yes," I nodded to Mrs. Lisa and spoke softly, "We must rescue her."

More English. "And she wants to know about Geta."

"Tell her that as long as Gyorgis is at home Geta cannot live there. They will kill each other. And that if your Mother will continue to let Geta live at your house, we will use some of the America money for his food and school."

More English. Then Fikir says, "She asks you where will the money come from after we have spent what she has brought?"

What could I answer? God will provide.

Kay Lee Emails Miranda About The Ethiopian Way To Pee
Kay Lee/Miranda: **Dice Dota/Chicago**

Miranda, this from the Internet Expert Café in Dice Dota. They keep serving me coffee and I am so buzzed.

Last night was amazing. I slept over. In their house. We ate there, and then when it was time to go back to the hotel they wanted me to stay. But Lisa said no. Then Nigest, and my sister Lushan said please. So she let me.

The whole family lives in two rooms. Combined they are the size of your kitchen. Outside are the goats and chickens. If Lushan came to visit us, I'll bet she'd say: "Where are the animals? Why do you live in so many rooms?" The living room has a couch and cupboards, a table and a shrine to Ethiopian Jesus, Cristos, who looks like Bob Marley. The other room is for sleeping; Lushi and Demissie (I think he is their cousin) in one big bed, and Nigest and my father in the other. All the beds have mosquito nets. My sister Bertukan, which means orange – like the fruit, not the color – died of malaria when she was one and a half. They got the nets after she died.

I can't imagine sleeping in the same room with my whole family. Everybody turns away when you get dressed but I don't know what they do for privacy. It's bad enough hearing Lisa and Marc in their own room and there was that time when I slept over and we heard your parents, but I can't imagine sleeping in the same room with Nigest and Gyorgis, like he's got one leg, not to discriminate against the disabled but, no, no way, I mean, I can't imagine what it would be like. I would definitely have my eyes put out and wear earplugs and burn incense and cry at the top of my lungs and beg them to stop.

Lisa really didn't want to me stay over, she's so paranoid, like she will never get over growing up in the Projects; she's scared that my real Mom will try to get me back because my adoption was illegal. I had to beg her and this guy, he's like my cousin, Fikir, he helps my Ethiopian mother, he said I would be safe, he would sleep there too and be a guard for me.

And she shouldn't worry, I love my family here but no way I could handle their bathroom. You wash outside in a big sink with a little bar of soap that everyone uses. And where you pee and poop is an amazingly stinky cement platform with a hole in the ground. They call it the "shintabet." Like the shit tablet. There's a straw fence around it, you squat and you don't use paper to pee. Lushan showed me how she shakes her butt after she pees. I peed and shook my butt and we held our noses and laughed. Then we went to bed and tickled her cousin and then I taught her the Pledge of Allegiance.

Wouldn't it be great if we named our kids after fruits and vegetables like they do here. It'd be like, Hello Tomato McKenzie, my name is Broccoli Goldberg and this is my friend Coconut Jones?

Now Fikir says its time to go meet my Mom back at Nigest's house. Or maybe I should say, go meet Lisa at my Mom's house.

I'm as confused as ever, XOX K

Fikir, Lisa And Kay Lee See Rodeat With The Mormons And Lisa Gets Mad
Fikir: Dice Dota

You know, most farange, unless they live here for some years, don't know what is going on at all. They don't understand the culture, they are too direct, they say things that seem very rude, they often don't understand the meanings behind words that seem obvious, they pay too much for everything but then they get aggressive when they have to bargain, they are always scared of stealers and yet they invite them by being so careless and showing off all their rich stuff. I can never understand them and they will never understand Ethiopians. It was a good learning for me to be the guide for Mrs. Lisa and Kalkidane so that I remembered how different they are. If I ever go to the West I will be ready to know nothing.

The first meeting was good. Everyone loved to see Kalkidane, and how she looked like them. Nigest cooked well, and there was cold beer and Orange Fanta. The presents were extraordinary and one of the pairs of shoes fit me so now I can keep them very clean for business. The ferrrisbee was the best. I will learn this sport and play that with my friends. There was some tension when Mrs. Lisa wanted to know about Selam and Geta. Nigest and Gyorgis started to argue but I told them right away with a smile to shut up and Nigest's sister Almenesh said they'd better not embarrass themselves before Mrs. Lisa, so they stopped. It is good that Mrs. Lisa and Kalki don't understand Amharic. I can smile and tell Gyorgis to go fuck himself in the ass and he can tell me that he will beat me until I am dead and she may think I am asking him about his health and he is saying that he is well and how is my mother? For me this too funny. Gyorgis understands this joke and it is the only thing on which we come together.

Now on the third day of the visit I went to collect them at the Hotel Taytu. First we had a breakfast and I showed them the mango avocado drink that all the farange love. They had eggs and pastries. I had firfir. Of course, being farange they put milk in their coffee. Talking at the breakfast, Lisa wanted to know about Selam and Geta. I asked her and Kalki to promise not to tell Nigest or anyone what I told them; that Gyorgis was a crazy bad dog who was destroying his family so he could buy a bajaj, trying to force marriage to an old crocodile on Selam, beating Nigest, trying to cut Lushan and fighting Geta so he had to live with my family. I said, watch out for him, I have a posse looking after that family, but he will try to extort you for his bajaj money, he will get any birr you give to Nigest for her or the children and use it to buy khat and beer. Miss Lisa then said that Kalki and her school had found much money and it was for school and medicine for the Nigest family. She asked then how could she help the family if she could not give money to Nigest? I proposed a solution that had been suggested by my mother, perhaps we could set up a bank account for the family and I could act as administrator. She said that after her experience with the Tekles, how could she trust that the money would not get stolen?

Farange get right to the point and I respect that, but this question was so hard and aimed right at me. I had to stop myself from making a protest. But then I understood: how was she to trust any Abesha person? And in truth, as my old Amhara grandfather used to say, money is shit to flies.

Our talking about those Tekles must have drawn them to us. I heard her voice before I saw her, Rodeat, speaking English in the Taytu lobby to a big herd of farange young people that she was obviously leading. This made my stomach turn over. I was hoping that Mrs. Lisa would not see her, but of course, when she heard the loud English, she turned just as Rodeat and the farange came into the restaurant, and before I could say anything Mrs. Lisa got up saying, "Excuse me, Kay Lee, watch my bag please," and went to greet her. I followed her to prevent any aggression.

"Well if it isn't Rodeat," she said.

Those Tekles, you cannot get them off balance. With a smile she greeted Mrs. Lisa, "Oh, Hello Mrs. Lisa, I did not know you were back in Ethiopia, look these are my friends from the Mormon Church of Utah, they are volunteering at our new Children's Village. Friends, this is Mrs. Lisa from Chicago."

Oh but Mrs. Lisa was angry. The color of her face became like dark stone and she backed out of Rodeat's arms, pointing her finger at her, which in our culture is not friendly. I could not believe what she said next, she used the muhfuh word and told the Mormons if they bought an orphan from Rodeat to be sure it didn't have parents. Rodeat laughed as if Mrs. Lisa was mad, and said what a funny person Mrs. Lisa was and began to move the students quickly out of the restaurant and into a van in the parking lot, but Lisa followed her and Kalkidane now, seeing this, took Lisa's bag, and went after them. So did I. We stood on the steps of the Taytu and watched the fight along with everyone else; beggars, guards, waiters, NGO farange and drivers, everyone loved to see this battle, especially between an American Black woman and one of the Tekles. All the people in Dice Dota know their clan is famous for corruption. Lisa called out loudly to Rodeat that she should expect a visit from her and Nigest in the next days and to have some money ready for Nigest. Rodeat did not turn her head to acknowledge this; she waited until all the students were in the van and got in the passenger seat and the driver, Ato Zalman, closed the van and drove it away. I was surprised that the crowd watching did not clap their hands. Everyone hates those Tekles.

"What was that?" asked Kalkidane.

Miss Lisa was so angry that her lips were tight. "That woman was one of the angels that brought you to me. She and her sister arranged your adoption," said Mrs. Lisa. "She is also a lying jive-ass motherfucker and I am going to slap her silly unless she gives back the money she stole."

These were bad words that I knew from Snoop Dog. Mrs. Lisa looked around at the people, put one hand on her hip and with the other made the sign of hitting with her open palm, back and forth, as if the face of Rodeat were in the air. The crowd laughed. They understood.

We returned to our table and the waiter brought more buna. I then told Lisa and Kalki the story of what happened to the Tekles and to the whole baby industry throughout the country. There were too many problems and so many people complaining; the babies were not orphans, the baby's parents were promised money and never got it, the babies had malaria, people were buying one baby and getting a different one, the babies weren't babies – they were six years old, the orphanages were not giving the children enough food, no one was paying taxes on the money they were making from the farange. It was a huge confusion, so the government just stopped all baby-selling and started investigating the people who were doing it. One of the first people they arrested in Dice Dota was Tsehay. She went to the woman's prison for some months and then she and Rodeat had to pay a fine for punishment, but nothing stops those Tekles, they have one hundred lives. Now they have another business: organizing farange volunteers for different orphanages and community centers. It is not as much money as selling babies, but in the long run a much better business. Things are developing so quickly here. There are no more dirt roads in the center, a new hotel goes up every day, the ghari drivers all drive bajajs now. So the Tekles see their chance in all this development. They are investing in hotels where the volunteers stay, restaurants where they can eat, and bajajs to take them around. They have contracts from American universities. They pass the students through every three weeks, and they get a piece of all the food and hotels they book, and from what their bajajs earn.

"Why do all the universities send their students to Africa for three weeks? Who pays for this?" I asked Mrs. Lisa. "Is it the American government?"

"They do this so they can attract more rich students and no, the government does not pay for this. American colleges are really expensive. So the family pays."

My God, I was thinking, is every family in America so rich? And how can these students teach English? They are not matriculated teachers, they do not know Amharic, and even if they had a diploma they could not master any pedagogy because they are only here for three weeks and many of them, even the Christians, smoke ganja with the Rastahs and go to the night clubs where the bar girls and the little college girls fight over who can win an American boyfriend and where the Abesha boys dance like Michael Jackson to try to meet the American girls and have sex. And the "work" these American students do is all a fantasy circus. The orphanage children get so little attention the students could be from the University of Satan; as long as they bring toys and play with them, the children will love them. Any nine-year child can do this kind of babysitting, and what the students pay to travel to Africa and babysit could keep two families alive for one year. They do this so they can say they helped African children but they are really helping the Tekles, the bajaj guys, the van drivers and the hotel and restaurant people.

I should not complain. This game brings money to our city and the Tekles are always smart about the next way to get rich off of the farange. My idea, once Mrs. Lisa and Kalkidane have gone back to the USA, is to ask the Tekles to hire me as a guide, but I cannot ask them while the war is going on between Nigest and the Tekles because I am a fighter for Nigest and I cannot change sides while the battle is on. I am no traitor.

So, there was still the problem of protecting the money for Nigest's children from their father. Back at the table we resumed our discussion.

"OK, Mrs. Lisa, I understand. The Tekles have stolen from you and that is why you are not trusting Ethiopian people. So what is the solution?"

"I don't know, Fikir, but whatever happens we want the money to go to school and medicine. That's what people gave it for. Right, Kay Lee? If it gets stolen what would you say to your school?"

"But Momma, why can't Fikir call the police if Gyorgis tries to get the money?"

When I heard that I tried not to laugh.

I said, "Kalkidane, this is not America. Here, the police will want some money and the person who promises them the most will win what is left. But if we take the money you brought and open an account in the name of Nigest and my mother, one could not take out the money without the other. Mom and I will then will know how much money is in Nigest's hands and we can make sure that she spends the money on your brother's and sister's education and health. We will send you a report when any money is spent. Come on, lets go open the account and then go to Nigest's and take her shopping."

We left the hotel and went to Dashen Bank. On the way Mrs. Lisa said that she and her husband Mr. Marc were artists who had not much money and that she had made no promises. Again I tried not to laugh; all farange I have ever met have told me that they were so poor. This while their cameras are bouncing on their chests and the cost of their footwear could pay for a year of school for me at the Business College.

Genet And Selam Find Heaven At Seven Nights
Genet and Selam: **Adis Ababa**

I thanked God when I saw Genet sitting there on the steps of the Dashen Bank, eating an orange. She did not acknowledge me when I sat next to her. I took a fat fruit from the pile she had next to her, peeled it and chewed it slowly, segment by segment, so that I could feel each separate little sac squirt its sweet sour blood in my mouth. Then there were the bananas she had taken, a nice bunch of small red ones, and after I had sucked the last juice out of the orange, I ate two as slowly as I could. Oh, how sweet and nutty they were.

That Genet would not speak. She just ate and looked out. We chewed together, all the oranges and bananas, every one. From the steps we could see over the southwest part of the city. The sun was moving lower now, and as it dipped closer to the edge of the mountains and buildings, I wondered where I would sleep. I didn't want to sleep with the other street kids. They could beat me. They could take my shoes. It would be cold. I got up. "Genet, thank you for helping me, but now I must go to the Seven Nights Restaurant in Kasanchis. Is it far?"

"No, but everything stands on its head in Kasanchis. You will never find it."

"But I have to. So I will try. Where do you sleep?"

"With my family of course. Do you think I am godana legoch?"

"Sorry."

"And don't you even think about coming home with me. We have seven kids. There is no room in the bed."

"OK, well...goodbye."

"Idiot. Fucker. Come on."

She was little but she was big at cursing. She got up fast and started walking. I followed, I guess, to Kasanchis.

We crossed a big busy street where a policeman controlled when you walked and then for a long time on the other side, by a big church with a long wall. At the back of the church, Genet took a path off the road and there in bush she squatted and so did I with great relief, I was so full of pee and had not known where to go all day. Then we came back to the big road and passed big buildings with the blue UN sign. All the cars and buses and vans were stopping and going, picking up and letting off the people. Walking and walking, all of this time the girl wouldn't speak. The sun went down and the lights from the cars came on and in some of the big buildings. I was so tired. Finally we turned onto a small street walking uphill past shops and restaurants. There were people on the street and taxis letting off many farange, Arab and Chinas, mostly men, but some with Ethiopian women. Just as we passed by a restaurant with guards standing in front of it, two farange got out of a taxi, almost hitting me on the sidewalk with the door as they opened it, one, a big yellow-haired man in short pants and a colorful shirt, the other, also in short pants, smaller with no hair on the head and a grey beard. I jumped to the side. The big buffalo nodded to me as if to apologize, and said in a farange accent, "Ykerta," giving me a look with terrible eyes, blue in the center with red veins around them and showing his yellow teeth in a smile. I cut my eyes away, but from where I stood, pressed against the restaurant window, I watched as he fished in his pocket and took out a money clip of hundred birr notes, a bigger roll than I'd ever seen, then peeling off two of them and giving them to the driver. Wow.

Before the money was back in his pocket Genet had grabbed my hand and pulled me toward him. In a little crying girl voice she said, "Please father...we are hungry, our mother is dead...please father." She held out her hand and her face was suddenly so sad; tears ran down her cheeks if she'd squeezed a rubber ball behind her eyes. The driver, like everyone in Adis, loved to curse us. He called us "little begging bastards," said "fuck off," and began to swing to slap us but Genet danced away and the big farange buffalo called out, "Nein," so the driver would not chase her.

Genet moved back towards the buffalo, pulling me closer, and keeping eye contact, said, "Please, father ten birr, ten birr." The buffalo farange looked at her, threw his head back and made a laugh like a baboon, "Eee-yah-eee-yah-ha-ha-ha," and said something in the German language to his friend who, yes, I couldn't believe it, took a ball of money from the pocket of his short pants, unrolled a blue one and gave it to Genet. 10 birr. Then they went into the restaurant. Genet pulled me by the hand down the street, away from the restaurant, so the driver would not come after us for the money and stopped by a shed store on the street. The money was tight in her fist so you could not see it.

"You see?"

"What?"

"All these men?"

"Yes."

"So, what do you think?"

"They look so rich."

"Yes, and where are the women?" "

I don't know. "

"You will. Come on. Here is Seven Nights. Go see your friend." She pointed to a sign down the hill from us: *Seven Nights, Seven Nights*, on and off it blinked, green, red and yellow.

"And with the men, be sure that they always use a condom, or you should kick their ass."

"What?" She turned her back to me and ran up the street.

"Genet!"

She was gone.

Helen Sends Selam Back To Dice Dota
Helen: Seven Nights/Kasanchis/Adis Ababa

When she came into the club in her dirty dress, with her toothbrush and underwear in a plastic bag, I recognized her immediately, Selam, that Dice Dota girl from my old kabele. I was cleaning the tables and moved close. She asked Henok the barman for "Helen" and he told her there was no Helen there and she began to cry. I hissed to her, "Selam, come over here, it is me," and then to Henok, "This is my sister, she has come all the way from Dice Dota because our mother is sick, please let me talk to her."

I knew the first thing was to keep her away from Tati. She was too young, so beautiful, and very filled out; if Tati got a close look Tati's greedy eyes would stick to her face and body and then she would start counting the money; she would know that she was the kind of girl that farange would buy for several days, and say to Selam like they say to me, "Look at you, Ethiopian women are the most beautiful in the world." Tati would know she had found a gold machine, and she would wave food and money at her to catch her and then give her to that bastard Ernst to break her in. He would keep her in a luscious cage of hotels and fucking and cake and drinks, and always telling her how beautiful she is. How can a starving girl resist that after living in a tukol with her parents, brothers, sisters and the goats, for God's sake? Jesus, the hotel beds are soft and White men feed you well and buy you clothes after you please them. I wasn't about keeping Selam from playing that game if that was her fate, but not yet, no, she was really too young, she should have a look at the life before she jumped to work with fucking and the farange. She should be serious and know how to take care of herself.

"OK, Henok," I said, "I need fifteen minutes." To get her away from there before Tati saw her, I pulled her out the door onto the street and into

Kasanchis Bakery. Her eyes flew like flies to the sweet cakes in the glass case. I could tell it had been too long since she had eaten, so I ordered coffee for both and two cakes for her.

"How are you Selam, and your mother and father and family? Are they fine?"

"My father is drinking and chewing khat so he beats my mother, my brother is on the street for fighting my father because he beats my mother, my father tried to sell me to Fat Tadesse to buy a bajaj, so I have run away, but in health we are fine, except for my father. And you?"

"Fine. I will move to Germany soon. With my boyfriend Helmut. I hope to leave next week. We are working with the embassy now to get my visa."

"Oh that is so lucky for you that he has fallen in love with you."

"Here, look at this picture. This is the town where we will live."

I took the picture from my bag and showed her. It was almost a miracle to think that she would be living in Germany. A crazy thought: *would she have to eat pig?*

"Helen, how can they not know you at Seven Nights? You work there."

"Here my name is Heaven. I changed it so my father will not find me."

"Helen, is there a job you can find me here? I really have nothing. I spent a night in the street in Dice Dota and that was bad, but here I know nobody, and it looks so hard."

"Selam, the work here is not what you think."

"I know, I know, everyone has told me about Kasanchis."

She was polite and didn't say out it loud but the question was shouting.

"Selam, look, eat your cake, and listen. The work here is only one thing. Seven Nights is one of the best places and you can make money here, but you have to be really ready. Once you are in, you have to fight like crazy, every day, all your girl dreams of love and boyfriends and getting married, you have to kill those dreams every day, and then your instinct for the privacy of your body, you have to defeat that over and over, your pussy, your mouth, your ass; they are for others now, and then while you surrender that you must always be fighting for your health, and that is life or death. Think about that. Then there is the owner Tati, she pretends to be your mother, but you have to fight her, always with a smile or she will throw you out, but always you are struggling for your money, and then there are the men, again you fight them with a smile and open your body and pretend happiness while you fight and fight in secret so they don't hurt you and you win their money. They only want to fuck you and some say they love you and sometimes, when they are handsome and nice, you want to love them back, and you have to be so strong with this, you have to keep your heart and mind in one place, your body in another place and your money in another place. Selam, you are not ready for this."

"What about Helmut? Why does he marry you if he can have you anyways? Why does he take you to Germany?"

Oh this girl she goes right to the point.

"Helmut is different. He is my friend. He is a father and a brother and a husband. He loves me. I will have his children. And I will send money from Germany to help my family."

"Maybe I could meet someone like him."

"Selam, maybe you will, but not yet. You are too young."

"I am not too young for Tadesse. He will abduct me and get me pregnant as soon as he can and then I will be trapped with his children for the rest of my life. He will beat me when he wants to and I will be a slave to his mother and his sons and I will have no chance in life. How would that be better? Here I would have a chance. I would have money. Men will always try to get me. Here I will have a selection and a chance to win one. And I will have my own room."

What could I tell her? She was right but life was wrong. I felt for her like my little sister; I could not see her in this hard game. I opened my purse and her eyes jumped when she saw all the green notes.

"Look, Selam, I have to get back to work in a minute in the bar. You can stay in my room tonight. I will be in the hotel with Helmut. Here is 2,000 birr. Two hundred are yours if you do what I say. Tomorrow you will leave early for the Depot and get a ticket for Dice Dota and go to my mother's and give her 1,800. I will tell her you are coming. Stay with her and hide from Tadesse."

"No, I will stay with this boy Fikir and his mother. They are in contact with the Americans who adopted my little sister. They are helping our family now."

"Look, save some of this money so you can return here. I will find you a place and a school in Adis."

"But you are going to Germany."

"Don't worry I will set this up before I go. OK now quick come with me. My room is down the street. Stay there until the morning and do not go out or someone will get your money. Come on quick."

We left the coffee shop and turned off of Zehudie Street to the street of Hotel Bethel where I had my room. I showed Selam my room and bed.

"Selam, I am trusting you. You will give 1,800 birr to my mother. Do not leave the room until you see the sun. Leave the key down with the boy in the lobby. OK, goodbye. Contact me on the internet from the Metro."

I embraced her and left her there before she could say anything, and went back to the street and to Seven Nights. Tati was waiting for me.

"I heard your sister was here. Henok told me."

"Yes Tati, I had to give her a present for my mother who is very sick. She goes back to Dice Dota with my Uncle this evening."

"Oh that is too bad, I would have liked to meet her. Henok said she is very beautiful."

"I'm sorry Tati, my uncle was waiting for her. They will drive in the night with his friend who has a van. She has school tomorrow."

I went back to work, cleaning the tables. Helmut would come in later and he would give Tati some money so he could take me to the hotel. My God, I thought, first it's your father and then it's your boss. Always when you are a girl someone owns you. In a week, when Helmut takes me to Germany, I will finally be free. Please Jesus let seven days go by like one.

Genet Shadows Selam, Knocks On Her Door
And Sleeps in Heaven
Genet: **Adis Ababa/Kasanchis**

That girl, she thought she had me fooled but you can't just shake your tail
and think you're getting rid of a spy like me. I'm a flea. I saw them leave Seven
Nights and go to the coffee shop, and then when they left there I followed her
and her little whore friend to the hotel and watched them both go in and then
in just a minute the little whore came out and went back up the hill to her
nightclub. When she was out of sight I went into the hotel, right to the table
where the boy guard sat dozing, shook his shoulder to wake him up and said,
"Oh please Mr. Hotel Boy, the Seven Nights lady had to get back to work
but she told me to give her friend an important message. What is the correct
room?" He didn't even raise his head from his arms on the desk, he just said
"Number 4," and pointed up the stairs. Really, a robber with half intelligence
could clean out every room in that place and that boy would never wake up. I
knocked on Number 4's door and waited. No answer. Put my ear to the door.
Nothing. I knew she was in there sitting on the bed, with her hands together,
not moving, making her breath invisible, waiting for whoever it was to go
away, scared that a stealer would come in and rape her. These country girls
are so stupid. She would never open the door so I called out, "Hey Selamawit
girl, I am Genet, your friend who showed you Seven Nights and gave you
water, open the door."

"What do you want?" Oh this girl! Here, I save her and show her everything and she still behaves like a donkey.

"I have to talk to you. My mother says you can sleep with us for one
night."

"But Helen told me to stay here and not let anyone in."

"No, you should not stay here. This is a bad place. The men will come in the middle of the night and rape you and beat you. They always do. Open the door and come with me to my mother's."

The key turned and she opened the door. The room was nice. A big bed. Her little whore friend had bought a lamp and put up pictures of Teddy Yo and Christos and the actor Will Smith. I would bet there were pretty clothes in the bureau too.

"Genet, why did you come back? I thought you were going home to give your mother the money."

Oh oh, sticking her nose right into the heart of my lie. My mother, Son of God, did I remember her at all? My aunt putting me on her bed. A sour smell.

"I didn't want to leave you at Seven Nights. Can I come in?"

She moved from the door. I came in and sat on the bed.

"What a great bed. Does your friend stay here?"

"Listen you've got to go. I promised Helen I wouldn't open the door."

"Oh Selamawit. I am so tired from walking you all the way here. And it's so cold and damp to walk home this late. Please just let me lie down here for a second."

She wasn't going to do anything to stop me so I lay on the bed. I was so tired. Before I could fall all the way to sleep she shook me.

"Genet, you can't stay here. I am going back to Dice Dota tomorrow morning. You've got to go to your mother."

This bed was heaven and my sleeping place was really behind the church with all the beggar mothers and their babies, under their plastic sheets. It was cold and wet when it rained and most of the babies were sick and kept you up. She would have had to fight me to get me to leave the bed.

"Selamawit, look, I can't leave you here alone. I must stay and be your guard in case the pimp boys come to rape you. Look I will watch out for you and help you find the Depot in the morning. OK? Look, lock the door quick, do you hear those steps in the hall?"

Ha ha. She heard the steps of no one and locked the door with the key, which she put in her dress pocket. I could see a bulge in that pocket that wasn't there before. She saw me looking and put her hand over the bulge. Her little whore friend had given her money. No worries for her. I am a thief so I am the best thief killer.

"Here you must be tired. We can sleep like sisters, come on lie down. And don't be so nervous. I will not take what is in your pocket."

Of course she wanted a sister, this big girl. She got next to me and I swear she fell asleep with her hand in her pocket before her head hit the pillow. I pulled the blanket over us and joined her in such a warm and dry heaven.

Selam And Genet Ride The Mini With The Chinas To The Depot
Selam: Adis Ababa

Someone was shaking me and I could not move because I was trapped underneath a fat crocodile. How could I push him off? Now he had my wrist in his teeth. I tried to open my eyes but I could not so I cried out. Now, he was pinching my ass. Genet's face was right up in mine and I could smell her warm breath.

"Come on," she said, "Now you have to get up."

She was right. It was past Two in the Day and I had to catch the mini to get to Dice Dota before dark. The bed was like a big soft net and so it was hard to escape. I felt for the money in my pocket.

"It is all there, don't worry, 2,000 birr, I counted it and put it all back. I have never had so much money in my hand. Go count it."

I sat up. It was cold in the room.

"Come on, let's go get a coffee and a cake before we go to the Depot. This time we can take a mini with the money your friend gave you. I will guard you in case any thief tricks you and I will put you in the van for Dice Dota."

And so we went to go to the bathroom in the hotel yard and then to wash. We gave the key to the boy in the front and returned to the same bakery where I had talked to Helen and clapped for coffee and cakes and mango juice with avocado and pina. This breakfast I would have every day in my life if I could. Both of us ate slowly and said nothing. As I let the sugar cake crumbs turn to sweet spit on my tongue I noticed that Genet had good manners with her food, carefully picking it with her fingers and taking small bites. Had she learned this from her mother?

On the corner was the minibus to the Depot. It was so full that the people inside said, "No, no, don't come in, wait for the next one," but Genet being

171

the right height and unafraid of any fight, stuck her head in between the people like a baby goat pushing others aside for the teat. She pulled me in behind her and when the van boy closed the door we all were squeezed together and I was right up against a tall China man who wore a yellow helmet and sunglasses and had pens in his shirt pocket. More and more these Chinas are in Ethiopia. They are different from the White farange; they travel like Ethiopians and do not enjoy luxuries. They work in industry and building roads. My friend's brothers have worked for them and say that they have a high standard for work and will never let you be lazy, and that they always go to prostitutes because Ethiopian women will not have them. I looked up at the China and wondered if he could ever find a China woman to marry and if she would have such a high standard of work; would she open a shop like all the China women do? And, if I married a China man would my family hate me? It was a long ride to the Depot through the morning traffic; the minute the China got off the people next to me had a conversation about how they hated all Chinas. Yes, they thought they were better, they were like Arabs one woman said. Then they started talking about the Arabs and how they were worse than the Chinas, because they took slaves and didn't pay them, while the Chinas paid. Then they started talking about Manchester United. This as the people pushed to come in and out until the boy decided enough people, and jammed the door shut and pressed us all together. At the depot we found the Van Boys calling out for rides south; Shashamene, Dice Dota, and aggressive Genet climbed right in the Dice Dota van and claimed a seat in the third row by the window. I did not want it known that I was going to be in Dice Dota in case some Tadesse friends were on the van, so I put my scarf over my head before I entered and looked at the floor. Genet gave me the seat, got up to leave, but at the door she looked back at me. I heard her mind thinking; we will never see each other again so I carefully peeled 20 birr from the money roll in my pocket, crumpled it in my fist and made the "come here" sign. I reached for her hand, and put my fist in her palm, uncurling my fingers and letting the money pass to her like a secret. She did not look to see how much it was, she just turned to leave.

"Genet, thank you, sister," I called out. "I'll see you back at Seven Nights." She turned back to me and that is when I first saw her smile. Then she was gone.

Fikir Claims Tribal Discrimination
And Asks A Question That Gets No Answer
Fikir and Lisa: Dice Dota

"The Andamu initially welcomed the Italian Occupation of Ethiopia which began in 1936. The Italian colonizers abolished the hated landlord system and thus appeared as liberators from the Amhara oppressors. When the Italians left in 1941 the Andamu tried to organize to prevent the return of the Amhara rulers. This led to retaliation from the Amhara." – Tribal History of Andamu – Dr. Meinhart Eslinger © 2010 Schottespress Bielefeld, ISSN 1201648 -22348-e.

Here is Hotel Taytu.

Fikir, thank you for walking with me. Mrs. Lisa, you cannot walk alone here at night. The shiftas are hunting and they love to catch farange. Last year they beat and robbed a German woman. Even with a bajaj, you must be careful. One shifta with a Kalashnikov can take everything.

How would they know that I am....

...the Black American Woman who took Nigest's Kalkidane and who came back without her husband and had a war with the Tekles in public outside of Hotel Taytu and who is now famous in all Dice Dota? Everyone knows.

And Kay Lee...

Don't worry Mrs. Lisa, I will go back to Nigest's and stand guard all night. She will be safe. And then we will come to you at eight in the morning.

You mean Two in the Day.

Very good Mrs. Lisa.

Denadur.

That is correct. And because you are a woman I say, Denaduree. But Mrs. Lisa, one thing before the good night, I have a question for you. You know that I am university graduate in sociology? I was in University in Gondar for three years. And there is no problem, Mrs. Lisa, if I can help in anyway, I am your son and you see the time I give to look after Nigest and be your guide. Why do you think that is?

Fikir, these children want money.

Bek ah!

Mrs. Lisa, these kids learn to beg, and then they cannot accept any discipline. Tell them that your name is not money, your name is Lisa. You can say Amharic for that: Sieme Birr aydelem. Sieme Lisa naw. Repeat that.

Sieme Birr aydelem. Sieme Lisa naw.

Good Mrs. Lisa, you see, they go away. But you do not answer my question. Mrs. Lisa, are Ethiopian people living in heaven so they do not have to work? No, we are not a lucky people like these Arabs. Muhammad gives them oil. Christos just gives us blood. You do not understand how it is here. I am looking for a job all days for two years but I cannot find one in Ethiopia.

Fikir, I'm sorry. I didn't know. Have you looked in Adis?

Mrs. Lisa, how many times have I gone to Adis? It is not about Adis. It is because I the son of Kalmata, the Amhara. In the Derg time my father became a teacher in the University for people who want to be teachers. He was Amhara. Mengistu was Amhara. When the Derg fell Woyane came to the University and put my father and all the other Derg Amhara in jail. That is where my father died – in the Woyane jail. The Woyane who were Tigre gave all the jobs to the Anduma who had hated the Derg and all Amhara, always, even before the Haile Selassie days, because the Amhara had conquered them. Now the Anduma work all the jobs and there is nothing for Amhara. When I go to look for work I wait in the office of the same men who killed my father. That is why I ask you to sponsor me.

Sponsor you?

Yes, if you say you will be my sponsor, then I will apply at the American Embassy to immigrate to the USA. Then if I am lucky they will let me in.

But what does that mean?

You guarantee me.

Guarantee you?

You make a promise, that I have a job and that you will be responsible for me.

Do you have a job?

No, but I will find one. I am a very hard worker.

But what if you can't find a job?

But I will…

What about your uncle Adane?

He tried but they did not accept.

Fikir, I am very tired. Let me talk about this with you in the morning. Here is some money. Go, take a bajaj back to the compound. And thank you, thank you so much for taking care of us so well…and guarding Kay Lee. You will be rewarded. Thank you. And you will bring Kay Lee in the morning? Goodnight Fikir.

Goodnight Mrs. Lisa.

Lisa Calls Marc From The Hotel (It's Expensive)
Lisa: Dice Dota

Marc? I'm in the hotel.

I know but I had to talk. I'll pay you back.

We're fine. She's happy as a tick on a dog. Having a sleepover with her brothers and sisters in the compound. That kid Fikir is guarding against shiftas. Bandits. They kidnap farange for ransom. It seems to be a tradition. Same old gang-banger shit if you ask me. Small world.

Well, I can tell you what I think is happening but that don't mean squat because it's all poured through linguistic cheesecloth, meaning Fikir translates, and he's only showing the tip of the iceberg, most of the context is underwater and frozen around recent and ancient mambos between families and clans and tribes and who fucked who, who made it big and who didn't, who was related to Haile Selassie, who has a motorcycle, who stole this, who forgave that, who was put in jail by the Derg, who was in the Derg, whose sister married an Italian, whose cousin lives in Las Vegas and all this shit I don't comprehend and never will. There's a lot of eye talk around the table that I don't have a prayer to understand. So everything is loaded and I don't know what the fuck with. Fikir's a good kid who is trying to be some kind of hero to Kay Lee's family, but he's part of that iceberg too, so he's not going to say anything to make himself or the family look bad, even though, one minute, he warns me about how everyone else is only after our money, and the next he puts the bite on me about sponsoring him for immigration.

No surprise, given the cost of my Reeboks could buy two month's family groceries; Kay Lee's relatives hit me from all sides. Same as at home when Cousin Ray is on the phone when her SSI and stamps have run out before the end of the month. And it's no bullshit. She's broke. And so are these folks.

Marc, here's the deal: Kay Lee spends all year raising money for her brother and sisters' school fees and money for medicine and when we get here we find that two of them have run away because their father, Kay Lee's dad Gyorgis, is a stone cold one-legged evil motherfucking freak. He tried to marry off the oldest girl Selam to a friend of his whose wife died, a guy thirty years older than her, so he could get a bride price and buy a taxi, so she said fuck you dad, I'm going to own my own pussy. She split for Adis before we got here. Dad also beat on the younger brother Geta so bad that Geta split too and started living on the street. And he tried to get the younger girl circumcised. He's a classic loco, the guy outside the liquor store who is just too mean to die. He's always crutching around stoned with a weird smile on his face. So much for helping our poor Ethiopian relatives. Ain't no different than Sweet Home Cabrini. I could have gotten just as much ghetto at home and saved the plane fare. What the fuck? I feel like I'm looking at everything through a fun-house mirror.

Like I said, she's happier than a pig in shit. She loves playing with her little sister and cousin and running around with the goats, being the wild African girl that she wants to be, and that makes this fucked up trip, which I did not want to take, and only did because you insisted, worth it. It's great for her to see that folks can have fun and be smart and loving even if they don't live the fat life in la-la-land, and also to realize what she would face if she lived here; one minute Girlfriend's jumping rope dreaming of *Beyoncé*, and the next week she's getting spermacized by some fat old man that her dad married her to because he wants to buy a taxi. Reality is always a good fix. It makes you appreciate the unreal world a whole lot more.

Well, do I have a choice? I'm going to do what we came here for, meaning make sure the money goes for school and medicine for these kids. What's messed up is that I'm going to have to kick everybody's ass to get them to do what they asked us to help them do, and I know that the harder I kick, the deeper I will sink into the African mud from whence I came, and oh Lord will I ever get out of this quicksand?

Look I gotta go. There's a German couple in the lobby showing off a baby they just bought, excuse me, *adopted*, and I must restrain myself when I walk through. I thought the government stopped all that, but this place works in wondrous ways. The truth changes all the time.

Look, my time is running out. I gotta get off the phone.

Look, there are other people waiting in line to use the international phone. I miss you, want you, and we will be home in five days, I gotta get off the phone.

I gotta get off the phone. Five days baby. Goodbye..

Poem For Lisa
Marc: **Chicago**

You're at the well
I'm on the mountain
You haul water
I dream fountain
I pray for rain
You dig the root
I hunt the game
You find the fuel
I make the flame
We get through

Lisa Calls Her Mom To Complain About Ethiopia
Lisa and her Mom: Dice Dota

Mom?

Lisa…where are you?

What, you got Alzheimer's? I'm in Ethiopia.

Lisa, this is not a good time to talk.

Mom, I'm calling from this little booth in the post office where you can make international calls. It's expensive. The Internet and the phones have been down. I thought you might be worried. Did you get my email from two days ago, about how two of the kids that we brought money for have run away? And about Kay Lee's dad? Did you get that?

Lisa, you are going to have to speak up.

Are those sirens?

Yeah. There's some sort of war going on. They were shooting by Homan Avenue ten minutes ago and now there are a lot of squad cars and ambulances down the block. It's the Lovers and the Jokers. Last week they killed two kids on Central. Do you remember that Hudson boy who was in your class? His brother was shot. Oh honey, it's been heavy here. Monica called me. Your cousin Joe's back in jail.

What was it this time?

He was hanging out with Tru and when they went to pick up Angie at day care, Tru made an illegal left turn, got stopped, and of course, never losing an opportunity to mess himself up and everybody around him, he was driving without a license. So of course when he couldn't show ID he and Joe got spread out on the back of the car with guns up their butts, they found a bag of weed in Tru's pocket, so they took them in and once they ran their IDs, they were moved immediately to Cook County for violating parole, possession, driving without a license, etc. etc. No bail for Joe. Monica and Reverend Smythe are taking a collection for a lawyer. I was going to call Marc.

Mom, Marc hardly has a job. We can't help those people.

Those people? Girl, listen to yourself talking 'bout your family.

Mom? Mom? They are just gonna suck you dry. And it ain't no different here. Are you there?

Mom? The electricity just went off. Fuck these phones. Mom? Are you there?

Gyorgis Gives Up On The Bajaj
And Dreams Of The Family Clinic Zena
Gyorgis: Dice Dota

That fucker Fikir has screwed it all up. He spoke badly of me to Mrs. Lisa and now she does not talk to me or acknowledge my presence. Does she think that Kalkidane has no father, that she came out of the air? So, she will give control of the money she has promised to Fikir. I'll bet Nigest and the children will see but little. The rest will stick to his pocket.

Everyone knows the Americans are here and everyone is trying to figure out how to get a bite. Fat Tadesse will smell money and come to get his bride price back, and since I used it to pay back Girma for the TV, everything between Tadesse and me will be complicated. He will stick needles in me over every little thing until he feels he has been paid back. It could go on for years. And even if we find Selam, it is too late for an abduction. With these new laws, Fikir and the students from the Gang of Stop Cutting will fight us and it will be a war that I will lose. Tadesse will not want to fight. He will just want his money back.

Now, the whole idea of the bajaj is dead. And my children are worth nothing.

Getachew, that little bastard, will never obey, and so I can never make him work like my father did me. And Lushan is too young, although they are taking girls as young as 13 to work in Dubai. Golya made a contract for his daughter to work in there for two years, and he got a signing fee. Now she sends money back every month. So maybe this will be the way. If Lushan works in Dubai, I can make monthly payments on the bajaj and when I start making money with one bajaj, I will buy another. Then I will buy back Lushan's contract and then Lushan can come back and go to school and learn to be a nurse. And I will send Geta to the private school so he can go to University and become a doctor. I will rent a house near the Swedish hospital and we will open the Clinic Family Zena; Dr. Getachew and Nurse Lushan and myself as manager. Nigest will clean and cook. Then I will buy a house.

Aww, my leg. Those fucking Somalis.

In the old days, Selam would have had to obey, and I would have beaten Fikir if he interfered. But, with one leg I have no force, I cannot fight, so there is no choice for me now but to be the smartest while I act like the most stupid, and to tell no one what I am thinking. They will think, "Oh there is Gyorgis, he is a drunk, he chews khat, he has no mentality," and they will be entirely surprised when they see my plan has taken shape while they slept. This is a hard plan but I am a warrior, I will never give up. And no one will stop me because they will know of nothing to stop until it has already happened.

Seble Recognizes Selam Who Tells Her
To Keep It On The QT
Selam and Seble: Dice Dota

Selam.

Selam.

SELAM!

Seble, shut up. Come over here.

Selam, why are you dressed like an Islam girl?

Sebbie BE QUIET, don't say my name. Stand in front of me. I don't want anyone to see me.

Selam, what happened to you? One day you were not in school and the next day no one could find you.

I will tell you later.

Did you see Helen?

Please shut up and hold my hand and walk with me now so I am by the wall and you will be on the outside. No one can see my face. And you cannot tell anyone you saw me because if my father hears I am back in town, then it is all over. Tadesse will take me and I will get beaten.

Did you see her?

Yes I saw her. She calls herself Heaven. She is moving to Germany with her boyfriend and they will get married.

What will you do now? Where are you going?

I am going to Fikir's house. Can you walk with me all the way there, and promise if you see anyone you know you will turn away, or act like you are in hurry?

Why did you come back?

It is private.

What?

I am doing a job for Helen.

What?

She wanted me to come here and think.

Why?

Not your business.

Think about what?

I told you, it's private.

Are you going to work where Helen works?

Look, stop, stand in front of my butt while I pretend to tie my sandal. That 's Geta's friend, that street kid. He's one of those who sleep down by the See The Hippo boats. I don't want him to see me.

So what will you do?

I will go back to Adis and go to school. OK, now walk.

How will you live? Maybe you will meet a German.

I don't want to meet anyone. I want to go to school. But anything would be better than Tadesse.

Listen Selam, always use a condom.

Shuttup Sebbie. Don't insult me. I am Mother Maryam's daughter. OK, now there is the door to Fikir's. Stay behind me as we cross the street.

OK, now you knock on the door while I wait behind you. Listen, Sebbie, thank you. Tell no one that I was here. No one. And pray for me and I will pray for you. Someone is coming to the gate. Now go.

Weyzero Eden Lets Selam In And Fikir Shows His Feelings
Weyzero Eden, Selamawit, Fikir and Geta: **Dice Dota**

Who's that?

It's Selam. The friend of Fikir. Selam.

But Fikir said you are in Adis.

How could I be when I am here? Please, Weyzero Eden, open the gate. I do not want any of Tadesse's people to find me. They look to abduct me. My father…

Fikir told me. Come in then and stop making such a racket. Come in. You know the Americans are here.

My God, I didn't know. Did you meet them?

Fikir has been with them. He is their guide. He told me that they brought school tuition for you, Lushan and Geta. But they were upset when they found out that you and Geta were not living at Nigest's or going to school.

I want to meet them. I want them to take me to America with them.

Ha. I think everyone is asking them that. Would you like a coffee?

Can you call Fikir?

No need to. Here he is.

Denah.

Denesh.

Are you fine?

Yes, and you? Why are you here? Did you hear about the Americans?

Yes, I know they were coming but I didn't know so soon.

Why did you come back?

I am doing a job for Helen. She is paying me.

Helen is paying you? She must be rich. Is she working in the bars?

She has a German boyfriend. She will be going there and marrying him. They will live in a big stone house that has a bakery in the front of it. He showed her a picture.

So, Helen caught a big fish. Give her my congratulations.

Where are the Americans?

Does she have a visa?

He is working that out with the German Embassy.

Ha! All faranges sing that song and the young girls fall for it but when it comes time to leave, only the white bird flies from Bole.

Where are the Americans? I want to see them.

Mrs. Lisa is at Hotel Jerusalum and Kalkidane is at your house.

I can't go there. My father and Tadesse...

...And his sons. I know all about it. I will bring the Americans here tomorrow morning.

With Geta?

Geta lives here now. He's off the street. Nigest and I worked it out with my mother.

Listen I must contact Helen's mother. I need to get her a message.

She lives on the road to Nigest and that is where I am going now. Give me the message and I will bring it to her.

No, I have to give it myself. I promised Helen.

Well then I will tell her to come here tomorrow. I must go. Hey look, Geta is coming in the gate. HEY GETA. Here's a surprise.

SELAM! SISTER!

Shhh. Don't call my name. No one should know I am back in town. How are you?

I am fine. Why are you back?

Have you seen the Americans?

No. I don't want to be part of the crowd that is licking their ass.

Geta! Don't you want to meet our American sister?

Every time a farange shows up the line of beggars goes around the block. She can find me if she wants to. Did you find a job?

No. Maybe. I don't know.

You know that Zeff and his brothers are looking for you?

Yes, I know. So you cannot tell anyone I am here.

Do you go back to Adis?

Yes, I hope tomorrow. But first, I must see the Americans. Fikir, will you bring the American and our mother and Kalkidane in the morning? Geta, can you come in the morning?

I have school.

Did you go back?

Yes I went yesterday. And they accepted me if I find a uniform. And I promised strict attendance. So Nigest will get the money for the uniform from the Americans. And Fikir's Mom will let me stay in the grain shed if I promise to excel in school. So I promised.

Can't you skip school to thank the Americans? And to see your sister?

Selam, I don't want to be their monkey. Everyone else is dancing in front of them, holding out their hand. What will you ask them for?

Geta, that is too rude.

True is rude. Look I have to study. Tell the Americans that I thank them for helping with the tuition and the uniform and that I honor them by not skipping school. I am going. Be well sister.

Health to you, brother.

Selam, I'm going with Geta.

Geta, wait outside, I want to talk to Fikir.

Fikir, don't forget, go to Helen's mother and tell her to come in the morning? And thank you. You are like a father.

No, Selam, I cannot accept that, because then I could not be more than that.

Fikir, you make me shy. Go.

Lisa And Kalkidane Meet Selam
At Weyzero Eden's House For Breakfast
Weyzero Eden: **Dice Dota**

The problem with feeding farange is that they do not have the proper bacteria to drink our water, so to feed them you have to spend more on bottled water and beer than on food. On this day when we wake up, we pray and wash. I start the fire, make the coffee and ask Selam to set the table while I go out to buy grass for the coffee ceremony and bread and fruit and Ambo. Geta takes bread, injera and coffee before he leaves for school. He will not change his mind; no matter how much I ask him to meet with Mrs. Lisa and his sister, he will not miss school. I understand, I can hear his feeling; he does not want to wonder why did they choose Kalkidane and not him?

At 3 in the Day they are precisely there; Mrs. Lisa, Kalkidane, Nigest and Fikir, but I had just come back from buying bread and fruit so I am embarrassed not to be ready. This is how Americans and Europeans are: they say a time and then they are there on the minute. They give you no chance to prepare. In Ethiopia, among friends, that is rude. Even in the old days, if slaves were late, it was normal, even the Emperor had to wait for his slaves. And during the Derg, when the town was full of Russians and Czechs and Cubans, to get any thing done took days and days. But now, since we are trying to adapt to capitalism, we are told to be on time at the place where it is agreed to meet and then more business will be done. I think it's a good thing for work but bad for pleasure and relations.

Mrs. Lisa wears shorts and a t-shirt, she is my size, neither tall nor short, slender like me but darker, with round features, her nose and lips more African than Ethiopian. I guess her age at 35 years. Her hair is natural and combed out, she wears big earrings and her fingernails are blue and though she dresses like a teenager, her manner commands respect, much like an official. I have heard the story of her fight with the Tekles and suppose that she is not an easy woman, but one who speaks her feelings and pushes to get what she wants. The girl is certainly from Nigest and Gyorgis, there can be no doubt, the long face and thin bones, small teeth and wide cat mouth, pretty lips just like Nigest's. Her woman's body is starting to come out in her breasts and hips, she looks to be 12 years. She sits between both her mothers, and though she holds Mrs. Lisa's hand her eyes are more often for Nigest. How must it be, I wonder, to have a mother with whom you could not speak? The feeling between them is so strong I can almost see it in the air, a light ray of unnameable wonder and wanting for the other's touch running between them. And Mrs. Lisa's feelings are also visible, a cool blue searchlight, taking in the love of her daughter for her unknown mother, wary of loss, and jealous.

Finally we are ready with the bread and fruit on the table, the bottled water, the charcoal fired for the coffee and the grass spread for the ceremony. Selam stops fanning the charcoal, gets up from the coffee grill and takes a seat. We are all around the table, Mrs. Lisa, Fikir, Kalkidane, Selam, Nigest and myself. Who would begin?

It is Mrs. Lisa, and with no customary greeting as we always do; "We are honored to be here. Are you fine? And your family, yes and yours?" None of that; her first words were, "Is everyone speaking English here except for Nigest?"

We all nod except, of course, Nigest.

"Selam?"

"Yes, Mrs. Lisa, I have English in school since the grade 7."

"And I will translate for Nigest," says Fikir. "To start, I think we must…"

Mrs. Lisa interrupts him without any excuse and gives him a look that says many things, the loudest being: "Shut up, I will lead this."

"So, Selam…we have given money for you to go to school. How are your grades? Were you successful in your examinations?"

Watch out, I think, this woman knows everything already. If Selam lies, she will lose her chance.

"Mrs. Lisa, I…"

Again Mrs. Lisa interrupts.

"Fikir please translate my question for Nigest."

Fikir translates Mrs. Lisa's question into Amharic for Nigest and then, without looking at Selam so Mrs. Lisa will think he is still talking to Nigest, tells Selam that he has already told her about Tadesse and her father and her running to Adis. He tell her if she lies that Mrs. Lisa will find the reason she is looking for to cut us all off.

Me, I have no part in the conversation. My heart is first for Selam, for Mrs. Lisa to help her find her education and then for Nigest and the rest of her family to maintain the connection with their American sister. But my interest is also to advance Fikir's chance to go to America; I will interrupt him by serving the food if he says any foolish thing that would make him lose Mrs. Lisa's trust. For that reason I watch Mrs. Lisa's eyes which are hot, dark and sparking. What does she have to be so angry about? I wonder. I know nothing about her life. And what does she know of ours?

Selam takes a big breath and looks at Nigest who nods yes.

"Mrs. Lisa, you know my father wants buy a bajaj so he accepts marriage for me to an old man, Ato Tadesse. I refused to my father. I ran to Adis to avoid harmful traditional practice, the abduction and rape of me. Mrs. Lisa, school at this time is not possible. I look for a job in Adis for my living, and then I will find a school. I would like to become a doctor."

Mrs. Lisa looks to Fikir. He translates Selam's answer for Nigest. Mrs. Lisa says, "So Nigest, what is your advice for Selam? Fikir, please, ask her."

Is this a trick question? What can Nigest say? Marry the old man? Become a prostitute? Fikir translates Mrs. Lisa's question and Nigest asks him what she should say?

Selam interrupts, "Ask her to take me."

Mrs. Lisa interrupts, "What are you saying?"

Nigest asks, "How should I answer?" And Fikir translates this.

Mrs. Lisa says, "Oh for Christ's sake!" And then she laughs, but the laugh is sad.

"Mom!" Kalkidane is angry with Mrs. Lisa. Then Nigest speaks. She knows the word "Christ," it is the same in all languages and she says that, yes, she has been praying to Christos but she does not have an answer. Fikir translates.

Kalkidane says, "Mom, what about...?" Mrs. Lisa gives her a look that means, don't say this thing, stay out of my way.

Then she asks Selam, "You have no education. What job is there for you in Adis?" She nods to Fikir who translates the question for Nigest.

Aha, she knows everything. How will Selam answer? Selam looks to Nigest.

Nigest speaks and Fikir translates. "In Ethiopia there is only one job for young girls who run away."

"Mom, what does he mean? One job?"

"Kay Lee, he means...being a bar girl, serving drinks to men, wearing short skirts and then..."

"Being a ho?"

The girl's eyes are big. Every girl in the world knows this; once the men start looking at them, there can be money. And more. My cousin Megdes was beautiful. She ran away from a marriage to an old man and it only took her two years of sex work in Adis to find an Italian. Now she lives in Rome with him and their two children and they have a fabric store and an auto. Myself, I was a fool to fall in love with Dagnachew in high school and to believe in the revolution. We would be teachers and end the feudal system. All the farmers would get their own land. Women would be equal. We would talk about Marx. And dance. And then we would kiss. And make love. And build bombs.

Mrs. Lisa looked to Nigest and then to Selam. "Fikir, please translate."

"Mrs. Lisa has told Kalkidane that Selam has gone to Adis to become a prostitute."

"But that is a lie," says Selam.

She is angry now and she stands and stamps, speaking Amharic. "I ran from abduction by Fat Tadesse. I ran so I did not have to kill myself. I do not want to be a bargirl and go with any man. I want to be a doctor. But how will I live?" Now her eyes are full of tears but she does not cry. She sits down, Fikir translates and Nigest takes Selam's hand and kisses it.

Mrs. Lisa's eyes flicker from Selam to Nigest to Fikir to Kay Lee and then to me.

"Excuse me, what is your name?"

She asks me this so abruptly, I almost jump.

"I know you are Fikir's mother, and here I am in your house, and I just realized I don't know your name. I apologize."

"My name is Eden Kalmata."

"Eden, I thank you for inviting us to your house."

"Mrs. Lisa we're honored that you visit us. Please, have breakfast. Will you eat firfir? We also have bread and butter."

It is the right time for an interruption. Selam has told her truth and Mrs. Lisa must let it sit on her heart. I nod to Selam and we rise to bring in the washing bowl, towels, bread, injera, popcorn, pineapple and coffee from the kitchen. Nigest looks to Kalkidane but the girl does not understand and does not rise to help. When I was a girl my mother would have given me a slap if I had not offered to help a guest serve the meal. In America, do parents serve the children?

Selam moves with the washbowl to each of us and then I pass the injera and firfir, serving Mrs. Lisa first, even though I am the oldest. From the side of my eyes I watch her and the girl try to eat the injera. Most farange do not have the practice that we learn as children; to manipulate the injera with their fingers and make a tight bundle. They cannot wrap it with their thumb and two fingers, so the food falls out, and they try again and again until the injera has lost its integrity. I always keep towels and water ready with farange because often when they have failed with injera and the wat is on their fingers, they lick their fingers and then reach for more injera from the common plate. They do not understand sanitation.

We eat. I have faith that the pleasure of the food will calm everyone down and there will be a good outcome from this meeting. Things are not what Mrs. Lisa expected, but how could it be other? They certainly are not what Nigest expected when she gave Kalkidane to the Tekles who had told her she would get money every year so the other children could go to school. The important thing as far as I can tell is that everyone here is a victim of the Tekles, so even though everyone is surprised by everything, and even though the things unsaid are louder than those that are spoken, no one can find a reason to make an accusation. Thank goodness.

I make conversation with the girl. I wonder how much of Ethiopia is still inside her? She was adopted at three years. What does she remember? What is in her blood?

"So, how do you find your country?"

The girl stutters like a bad motor of English.

"Oh God, it is so fantastic. I mean it's so…much the same…but it's so different, we have so much…and…so do you…and…everybody in the world wants the same things, but…I mean in Chicago it's not a big deal to go to the doctor…but here…I feel like I'm coming home to old times…like our street, my mother Nigest…Selam and Lushan…I remember things."

She looks to Mrs. Lisa who is reaching for more firfir. This makes me happy, but then I am worried when I see that the red wat sauce, when she tries to fold the firfir into the injera, drips onto her fingers. She is wearing a white shirt that says "Free Street," and soon it will be red. I signal Selam who rises and takes the water bowl and towel to Mrs. Lisa, serving her.

"And you, Mrs. Lisa, do you feel part of Africa?"

The look with which Mrs. Lisa first answers my question makes me wonder why faranges are so surprised when they find that Africans have any understanding of their psychology. Yet, we are forced to know their history, while they know nothing of ours.

"Mrs. Kalmata…"

"You can say Weyzero. It means Mrs. You should use this when you address a mother."

"Thank you for teaching me this, Mrs. Weyzero."

Mrs. Weyzero? That was funny and made me sputter and when Selam, who had been very quiet up until now, heard Mrs. Lisa say Mrs. Weyzero, which is like saying Mrs. Woman Woman, she choked on her firfir which came flying out of her mouth onto the face of Ms. Kay Lee and then did Fikir give her a strong look until Ms. Kay Lee wiped the firfir off her face and held it up for all to see in her hand and started laughing. The laughter infected Selam and Nigest and then me. It was so comical the way the firfir had jumped across the table. Mrs. Lisa was astonished.

"What's so funny? Did I say something?"

It was hard for me to catch my breath.

"Mrs. Liza, you must say Weyzero Kalmata or Eden, not Mrs. Weyzero. It is very funny to people who speak Amharic. It is like saying Mrs. Woman Woman."

She nodded.

"Wayzero Kalmata, so, let me tell you about myself. I'm a Black American woman from the South Side of Chicago. My people came from West Africa, the British Isles and the Choctaw Nation. The Choctaws originally came over from Asia, so four continents of people gave me my body, my skin and my children's games and songs. I feel part of all of these people as an African-American. And you, Weyzero Kalmata, what do you call yourself? Amhara? Ethiopian?"

Mrs. Lisa understood more about Ethiopia than I thought, that everything is tribe.

"This is a question for my identification paper, Mrs. Lisa. My mother was Gurage and Amhara, my father Tigre and Kambatta, so I too am from four people. I call myself Ethiopian. And, of course, I am African.

African, Mrs. Lisa. I am from a certain generation older than you and younger than your parents. I have studied Marx and Marcus Garvey, Martin Luther King and Nyere, Ghandi, Foucault, Huey Newton and the Black Panthers. I read the book of Haley: Roots. I was part of the EPRP in university. We studied the civil rights. Do you know what the EPRP was?"

I regretted the question the moment I asked it. I did not mean for her ignorance to embarrass her. Who in the rest of the world knows Ethiopia?

"I know Haile Selassie. And then there was a revolution. Oh…. you must have been part of that?"

"Oh yes, Mrs. Lisa, for all Ethiopians one age of the world was done when Haile Selassie fell. I was sixteen in 1965, and Ethiopia was still a feudal society. The Emperor tossed gold coins from his Rolls Royce to people who gave their crops to his landowners for the privilege to farm while their children died of malnutrition. The Emperor and the Church owned everything and the landowners and the priests collected their tribute. This was the post-colonial era. All over Africa countries were becoming independent and everyone knew that there would be a revolution against Ras Tafari. We students were one of the first to make a fight."

"You had guns, Weyzero Kalmata?"

"Yes, Kalkidane, but only a small number of old Enfields that the British gave our fathers and uncles when they defeated Mussolini and put Haile Selassie back on the throne. These were useless. In University I was first place in chemistry and so I was a leader in the EPRP bomb-making club. This was our way. We made many bombs against Haile Selassie."

"And did the bombs…did you…kill people?"

"Kalkidane, I just made them, others planted them, but once, I know, people died from the explosion of a bomb I made. So I must say with regret: Yes."

"Who?"

"Landowners."

"Were there any children?"

"Kay Lee!"

Mrs. Lisa was upset that Kalki would question me. But I thought she was strong to do so, even if she did not understand anything about killing. We Amhara women, we will always argue.

"Ms. Kalkidane, when I was in high school the army would kill you and the landowners would beat you if you challenged the privilege of Haile Selassie. When I went to University there was the Ethiopian Peoples Revolutionary Party, the EPRP, and the Ethiopian Socialist Party, the MEISON. I joined EPRP because my girlfriend's brother Dagnachew was EPRP and he was attractive. We thought we had started the revolution but we were tricked. Two of our leaders were army spies and their assignment was to get students to make trouble so the Army could make a coup. Later, after the revolution, the army became the DERG and they became dictators. They chose MEISON as the true revolutionaries and started to hate all EPRP. They shot us, they put us in prison, and they tortured us. They killed my husband. This was the Red Terror. Then the DERG turned on MEISON and did the same to them. It was a violent time. There was so much Goddamit.

"Weyzero Eden, it's the same in Chicago. My cousins have guns. I hate them."

"Kay Lee, chill."

Mrs. Lisa voice snaps like a rope end. I look at her as if to say: These young people don't understand when violence is necessary. They are lucky.

"Wayzero Eden, I grew up in what people call 'the Projects,' tall buildings away from other parts of the city, built by the government for poor people. They are violent and disorganized, with their own laws and customs, isolated from the rest of the neighborhoods. Many of the boys become criminals and many girls have babies very young. My mother did, but she was also very smart and good in school. She joined the army and left me with my grandmother in the Projects. When she got out of the army they paid for her to go to college to become a teacher. She took me away from there when I was eight years old."

"And your father?"

"He has been in prison since before I was born. I've never seen him. But a lot of my family is still in the Projects so I take Kay Lee to visit her cousins and their children, and we take them out to the zoo or the beach. I know how to love my people there without being sad for them, but Kay Lee doesn't know how to do this. When she was little she would play with her cousins, but now she never wants to visit them. Do you Kay Lee?"

Kalkidane shakes her head.

"Fikir is the same way. I was pregnant when the Derg killed his father. He remembers when I was in prison and he lived with my sister. My stories of the revolution and the Red Terror are old sad songs to him. All he talks about is basketball and going to America."

It is interesting the way the Americans eat everything that is served to them. Here if we do that it means we are hungry. I signal Selam to serve them more wat but they shake their heads. The meal is finished. Nigest and Selam take the plates and the food back to the kitchen. I nod to Kalkidane and she understands and rises to help. I tell Mrs. Lisa: "Let us finish our discussion and then we will have the coffee ceremony." I look to Selam. Now is her time.

Selam Asks Mrs. Lisa To Take Her To America
Fikir: Dice Dota

When Selam begins Mrs. Lisa does not let her get started. She rises from her chair and pulls her off her knees before Selam can kiss her feet.

"Oh no, no, no, Selam, please, don't do that, get up please."

Now she is holding Selam's wrists and looking at her straight on as if she is about to shake a child who had broken something valuable of her mother's. Selam's eyes are wet, she had not even been given a chance to ask, and so she turns away and looks at us, me, my Mom, and Nigest, and shakes her head. What was my mistake? Why did Mrs. Lisa get so angry?

I could have warned her. Faranges hate this custom of asking by holding the foot.

"Mrs. Lisa, do not be angry with Selam. This is our culture, this is what we do to show respect when we go to ask an important favor. It is from the feudal days when you could get in trouble if you did not bow to the landowner. Even if he was kind, if he noticed this omission, he would never give you a present."

"Listen Fikir. Tell them we are all slaves and all masters and I don't want anybody bowing to me and kissing my feet." Now she lets go of Selam's wrists and goes down her knees and Nigest is moving her leg so Mrs. Lisa cannot grab her foot.

"Mom, what are you doing?" Kalkidane speaks in the voice that makes a mother slap a girl but Mrs. Lisa does not notice and she does not stop. Now Kalkidane is looking at Mrs. Lisa, then at us all and then looking to heaven for an angel to fly down and take her mother away.

"Fikir translate." Mrs. Lisa touches her head to the ground. It is almost comical.

I tell them that Mrs. Lisa is like the communists, she does not like the old customs; she believes in the words of Martin Luther King: All people are created equal, for standing together, not for bowing and self-humiliation to the most powerful. We are not dogs for the rich to pet and kick.

Nigest says, "I used to have to beg and beg the communists and still they never had any mercy." My mother makes a little throat sound and the corners of her mouth twitch. Only I know that Nigest has made my mother laugh.

"What does she say, Fikir?" Mrs. Lisa now is standing.

Before I can think up a good lie, Selam is faster. She now takes Mrs. Lisa's wrists and looks up at her, giving her the full power of her eyes.

"She says for you to please not be angry but to listen to Selam."

Mrs. Lisa gives Selam a long look and sits back down at the table. "OK Selam, what is it?"

Selam, standing, speaks in English. "Mrs. Lisa and Kalkidane. I thank you for finding this money for my school. I want more than life to go to school. But I cannot stay in Dice Dota, so this money you have…"

She runs out of her meaning; she cannot find the English to politely ask for what everyone knows she must ask. Maybe there is no polite way to ask for this in any language.

"In Adis I do not know anyone except my friend, Helen. I could get job where she works…but…"

Again the words cannot come and no one speaks until finally Mrs. Lisa: "What, Selam?"

"I could be the real sister to Kalkidane. I would finish high school in America. I would clean and help you and your husband in the house. And I would cook."

As she speaks the invisible line between Mrs. Lisa's eyes and Kalkidane's becomes a flaming rope. The girl's lips part to speak but Mrs. Lisa shakes her head: No, don't say anything. Kalkidane is silent and finally looks away. Selam has not taken her eyes off Mrs. Lisa.

"Fikir, please, for Nigest."

I tell Nigest that Selam has asked to go to America. Nigest looks at me and says, "And will you ask her too?" She didn't know that I had asked already.

"What? What does she say?"

199

"Mrs. Lisa, Nigest says...if it is God's will, she will go."

Mrs. Lisa sighs and makes the same strange motion I saw her do when she fought the Tekles at the Hotel Pina. She shakes her hand as if to make water fly off of them. But there is no water...she is shaking off the answer.

"Sit down Selam." Mrs. Lisa motions Selam to sit. Selam's eyes are full. She has gotten the answer before it is spoken. She will not sit. Mrs. Lisa sees her disobedience and goes on.

"Selam, we cannot take you with us."

There is something so farange in the way she just gives the answer. There is no polite delay. There is no saying that she has to consider any possibility. Not like with me. Her answer to me was that she had to think about it. This gives me hope. Now that she has rejected Selam, there still might be room for me.

"And everybody, you've got to understand. We are poor people in America. We do not have money. We do not have a big house. I am a student and my husband is a writer and artist. The money we bring was collected by school children. We cannot take you with us. We cannot sponsor you."

Mrs. Lisa looks at me when she says this. "Fikir, translate."

I tell Nigest who says, "I could see this. And of course she has no money, she gave all she had to the Tekles."

"Ema!" Selam now makes the same barking at her mother that Kalkidane has made. She knows that Nigest will not slap her in front of the farange.

"Fikir?"

"Nigest says that you have been more than generous. And that she thanks you for what you have done and brought. And that the money you brought will be used for Geta's and Lushan's school – and for medicine, if she can keep it away from Gyorgis, and..."

"How could she say all of that in such a short sentence, Fikir?"

Now she has interrupted me again and the worst thing, she has lost trust in my translation. She looks and listens to everything. It is hard to make a trick with her.

"Mrs. Lisa, yes she did say you have been more than generous, but no, I'm sorry, she did not say the rest, but I know she is too shy to ask for the other children and so I did for her."

"Selam, is this correct?"

"Yes Mrs. Lisa."

Now Mrs. Lisa sits quietly. There is consideration going on. I see it in her eyes and forehead. She is thinking, how much should I give them? What will they ask for next? If I give them money, who can tell where it will go?

Kalkidane will not look up. She has caught the sadness from Selam. She wants a sister. No one speaks.

To break the silence, my mother says it is time for the coffee ceremony and nods to Selam, freeing her to leave the center of attention and serve. When Selam is out of the room my mother stands and starts to bow to Mrs. Lisa but then remembers that she hates this, so she speaks without showing the customary respect.

"Mrs. Lisa, I have a friend from prison days who now works at the NGO in Adis where girls and women go to escape abduction and beating. The House of Adenech. If you made a contribution I am sure they would accept Selam there. The women there make tablecloths and sell them to farange. Selam could live and work there and go to school."

With my mother's words the color of the air in the room changes from smoke to sweet yellow. This is typical. She does not reveal her thinking until there is no competition for argument. She goes along and goes along and then when all the good ideas of others reveal themselves as ridiculous she strikes with a solution. Myself, I don't like this idea of Selam being at Adenech. I know of this place. All the NGOs love it. The girls have to be in at night by 10 PM and they are very strict. How long must I wait for Selam if she goes to this school?

Helmut Tells Helen The Bad News About Her Visa
Helmut and Helen: **Adis Ababa**

So?

Here, sit my dear Helen, would you like a coffee?

What did they say? They said no?

Waiter, please a coffee, no, two coffees, please, and two cakes.

Helen, they don't work that fast, it will take three months. So, I have applied for a visa for you and to be your sponsor. They will examine the application. When I come back in three months we will go together to the embassy and then they will interview us. That is the next step.

So you will leave me here?

Helen, listen to this. I am coming back in three months and in the mean time I will pay for an apartment. Listen, that means no more Seven Nights, do you understand? You will live in the apartment and when I come back to Adis in three months, in February, this is where we will live.

And then I will get a visa and will go back to Germany with you?

God willing.

And be married?

In Germany. If all goes as planned. And the UN will save money if they pay me to keep the apartment and not have to pay hotel.

Oh Helmut, I will work, I will pay my share.

No, no, no, no you must study, not work. And anyway, what work could you do? You must learn a profession. In Germany you can work, not here.

I will work in Germany, Oh my God Helmut, I will learn pharmacy. I will learn beauty hair.

Yes, you will be a very rich woman. You will have more money than me. So, do you accept? Excuse me, I must go to piss.

Lisa Calls Marc And Tells Him About Saying Goodbye To Nigest And What The Deal Might Or Might Not Be
Lisa and Marc: Dice Dota/Chicago

Marc?

Lisa? Where are you?

Sorry to call this early. All the cell phones in the region are down. Fikir says the government cut the switch to punish the South for the last election. I'm using the landline at the post office. It's open for another half an hour. Tomorrow we leave at the crack of dawn for Adis and the airport.

Lisa, hold on I'm half asleep. Hey, stop, stop!!!

Who are you talking to?

Sukie.

Right. Is she giving you head?

Jesus Lisa, what's the matter? She's doing that kneading thing with her paws and purring like a furnace. It's obnoxious.

Sorry, I'm needing too. But I'm not purring. When I get home will you let me just cry?

Oh yeah, you can cry, cry, cry, Baby… and I'll kiss you and hold you and do, you know…everything, and then you can curl up and tell me what's new in the oldest country in the world. God what time is it? I was dreaming. Somehow I had betrayed my sister.

It must be 2:30 AM your time, It's 5:30 here. I mean 11:30 in the Day.

So, what's the matter? Did you give away everything we own? Are we moving there to open an orphanage?

You got it, all of the above, and we've promised to sponsor thirty or forty of Kay Lee's relatives and neighbors for immigration who will live with us in Chicago until they find a place of their own. Baby, I just want a cheeseburger and some Isaac Hayes and to look so poor that even the drunks don't hit on me. It doesn't stop. You know that Selam and Geta ran away so we had this big meeting to figure out Selam and Geta's school thing. First thing, Selam asked if we would adopt her. She says she would be a sister to Kalkidane, oh and by the way, if we took her she'd be a house slave too, she'd cook and clean. Talk about me getting choked up. It was just too much fun telling her thanks but no thanks, maybe later. Wish you could have been there. You would have run out of there screaming. Solution: Fikir's mother, Eden, in whose house we had the meeting because we couldn't let creepy Gyorgis know what was going on, found a safe house in Adis for girls who have run away, so we're using some of the money for that. We're taking Selam there tomorrow on the way to the airport. Geta is living with Fikir and Eden because Evil Muhfuh Hopalong Gyorgis will try to kill him if he comes home, so we're working out giving Eden money for Geta's upkeep. Lushan is home with Nigest and Gyorgis. We bought school uniforms for her and Geta, and left money with Fikir and Eden to use for them in case of medical emergencies, because if we give Nigest money, Evil Muhfah will take it from her.

How much money?

Not near enough. And that's not all. So yesterday Fikir hired his uncle's van and we took Nigest and the kids, but not Geta – who for some reason will have nothing to do with me or Kay Lee – we haven't even seen him once – on an outing to the big attraction in the area, a hot springs by the mountains where Haile Selassie had a palace. We stopped at a place in the Rift Valley where you can see cracks in the ground where East Africa is separating from the rest of Africa and moving towards the Indian Ocean. Fikir says if you wedge a little stake in one of the cracks…in a month it will be twice as wide and the stick will have fallen over. Tha's how fast it's coming apart. We drove by fields where farmers hand-bucked wooden plows behind an ox. Along the road every hundred yards, there were mud huts with thatched roofs, and all around kids herding goats and cattle and women with huge bundles of sticks on their heads. Like Bible days.

So we crossed the Great Rift to the mountains on its eastern side and drove through this one-horse town, Wondo, past the tour bus stop where thirty taxis competed for ten tourists. The khat chewers were lined up on stools by the side of the road, spitting their disgusting green wads into the dirt, and get this, the wads were then slurped up by goats who appeared to be more stoned than the chewers. One Billy with a green mouth stood up on his hind legs like he was going to do a tap-dance or something, and then keeled right over in the road in front of our van and we had to drive around him. The vendors jammed Haile Selassie t-shirts through the van windows until we closed them. We followed the line of taxis up a rutted road to the parking lot of the Hot Spring. The minute we got out of the van we were swarmed by packs of little beggars but our Ethiopian friends took us by the arm and marched us to the gate, Fikir in the lead slashing with a little stick, the rest, kids included, snarling at them, baring their teeth and pushing them away. Once in the gate we bought everyone tickets and changed and the kids all went swimming in this pool heated by the hot spring. Lots of screaming and splashing. Wondo is a big treat, the emperor's pleasure palace, Disney World to them. None of the kids knew how to swim so Kay Lee was teaching them. That's when Nigest gets me aside with Fikir who translates: "Many thanks for your generosity, etc. etc. but what about next year, will there be more money?"

What did you tell them?

Jesus, Marc, I told them we'd do what we could but no promises, tried to explain that we hardly know where our next dime is coming from and when Nigest kept staring at me as if she didn't get it, I actually said, can you believe it: "Don't worry, God will provide." So she finally cut her eyes and I felt like such a slimeball.

Babe, how much is this costing?

About six thousand dollars but most of that was what Kay Lee raised...

I mean this call.

Don't worry, I'll pay you back, wait, there's more, so on the way home I'm sitting next to Kay Lee and her little sister Lushi in the back of the van, and Lushi is whispering something to Kay Lee – she actually speaks English pretty well – and Kay Lee leans over to and she whispers in my ear, "Lushi wants to know if we can take her to live in America with us." I tell her, "No

205

we can't," and she leans over and whispers to Lushi, and we all sit there and we all sit there in silence until we get back to Dice Dota.

Well, maybe we could put a bunk bed in her room.

Marc...what about her little cousin? Should we take him too?

We'd have to get a bigger place.

Marc, I...I love you, but they are closing the PO and I've got to go. Tomorrow we go to Adis. We'll drop Selam off at the woman's shelter and then go to the airport. I'll call you from Dubai.

Lisa, I can't wait to see you. And to hold you.

Yeah, Baby. Marc, they're closing. Bye.

Bye.

Quick Stop At The Rastah Museum
Fikir, Lisa and Kalkidane: **Rastah Museum, Shashamene**

"Ganja is the sacramental right of every man worldwide and any law against it is only the organized conspiracy of the United Nations and the political governments who assist in maintaining this conspiracy." - Walter Wells, Elder Priest of the Ethiopian Zion Coptic Church of Jamaica, West Indies

"Fikir, Look here's the Rastah Museum. See the mural: 'Haile Selassie the Lion of Judah.' Dejen, stop the van. Please. Stop."

"No, Mrs. Lisa, You should not stop here. Not with Ms. Kalkidane here."

"Thank you Dejen. Fikir, I've heard about this place. Can we go in?"

"Mrs. Lisa, the Rastahs, you know, they are all bullshit, their religion is pretend. It is just a show to sell ganja to the tourists."

"Don't worry Fikir. We know all about the Rastahs, Bob Marley, One Love. They are in Chicago. My husband likes their ganja. Kay Lee smokes it with her friends."

"MOM!"

"But I don't like it. It makes me paranoid. So this is where the Jamaicans came? Shashamene?"

"Yes Mrs. Lisa. Haile Selassie invited them before the revolution. A thousand came and he threw hundreds of people off the land to make room for them. All the tourists love them for their ganja. I hate them."

"What about One Love? One Heart?"

"They are parasites and drug addicts. They beat their women and keep them under. They sell drugs to children. They are dirty and they don't bathe. Look, here comes their chief, Silverstone. If you go in you will smell him."

"Hi…you're speakin' English? American? You want to visit our church? Good, come in, we want you to come in. This is my son, Ezekiel and my daughter Ruth. Zekey, prepare the video. Will you be wantin' to partake of the sacrament? There is no obligation."

"Mrs. Lisa, I will wait outside."

"No, please Fikir, come in. I want to understand this better."

"I hate this smoke."

"We won't smoke."

"Yes but he will. I have seen this too many times."

"Come in, come in, we are ready for the presentation.

I apologize, there is a problem with the video but don't worry. Be seated. This is what we will do here. I will make a presentation about the Church of the Rastafari and then if you want you can sample the sacrament and then be makin' a donation. But only if you want to, it is not required.

My name is Isaac Silverstone. I come from Bed Sty in Babylon but I have lived in Zion for 48 years. I came here in 1963 as one of the founders of this colony. I married an Ethiopian woman and have raised my children and grandchildren to worship the true divine Second Coming of Jesus Christ, Haile Selassie Ras Tafarai.

Yeah Mon, of course, Bed Sty is Brooklyn, but we call it Babylon, and any place apart from Zion, where the society of materialism and sensual pleasure is the dominator. Zion is the original birthplace of humankind, the Promised Land that is ruled by Jah.

All right. First, look, look at this book by the author Peter Matthiesson, on page 247 he writes about visiting the Church in 1986 and he mentions my name, see here, Isaac Silverstone. Pass the book, please.

Hello Mister why don't you sit? Oh I know you, you are the Dice Dota guide, the gymnastics boy, you brought the Irish and the Canadians, I remember. You are the no ganja man. Ha ha, that is no matter, we welcome everyone. All right, OK, so now I will tell you about Ras Tafarai, Haile Selassie I, Jah or Jah Rastafari. We be believin' that Jah Rastah is the Second Coming of Jesus

Christ the King to Earth. He proclaimed Ethiopia as Zion and offered us the right of repatriation to the Promised Land. And he gave us Ganja to awaken our spirit.

So now it is time for the sacrament. We grow it here. Can you smell its holy ishence? It opens the door to reason."

"Mrs. Lisa, I will meet you at the van. Come Selam. Kalkidane."

"Oh, you, don't leave. No need to be afraid of the sacrament. It is for every age. Does it not say in Psalms 104:14, 'He causeth the grass to grow for the cattle, and herb for the service of man?' "

"Selam, come."

"Kay Lee, go with Fikir."

"Mom, that smells like really good dope. Are you going to…"

"No, I told you. It makes me paranoid. Now, go! Brother Issac, we have a plane to catch. We have to split. Thank you for…"

"That boy, he be bringin' anger into our church. I could feel it leavin' with him. But now the children are gone, are you sure you do not want to be partakin' of the sacrament?"

"Brother, you don't give up. I told you, ganja's not my thing."

"No problem. All ways are the ways of Jah. But I'm sorry you must leave. Usually we give visitors a tour of the gardens. We feed them healthy food in the kitchen. And we be showin' them of the school."

"We don't have time. Again, thank you…"

"Wait, let me walk you to your van. I didn't get your name."

"Lisa."

"Lisa before you leave, would you consider a contribution to our I-tal School Fund? The money will go to repair the roof and for books for the kids."

"Brother, Peace on. One Love and all that, but, I'm a student…we have Ethiopian family…"

"Not five dollars? A hundred birr for the school? This is how we live. Please, Sister, most visitors leave something."

"All right Brother, OK, STOP! Here's a hundred birr."

"Thank you Sister. Go with Jah. We will meet in Zion."

"Dejen, please open the door."

"Jesus God, can you believe it? Brother Issac would not give the fuck up. Rastah be beggin' You, You. You. Money. Money. Money."

"Mom, don't swear."

"Mrs. Lisa, not all Ethiopians are beggars"

"Whoa. Fikir I wasn't saying that."

"I told you, they are criminals. But why do so many farange love them? Are they all addicted?"

"Fikir, it's because of Bob Marley. He was a total dope fiend. To this day he keeps the Rastahs in business. 'Herb is the healing. Alcohol is the destruction.' That 's what he said."

"Oh my God, Mom, look at those people. And the guys on the camels. Take a picture. Wow. Look at those knives. Are those AK 47s?"

"Mrs. Lisa, please do not take their picture. Those are Afar, they have come in from the Denakil. They do not care for cameras and you see they have Kalashnikovs. They will shoot in the air if they see your camera."

"They are beautiful."

"Ha ha. Ask Selam, would you marry a beautiful Afar?"

"I could never marry Afar. They are primitive. They stink."

"Mrs. Lisa, all their women are cut. They go where they want and obey no laws. The government leaves them alone because they are apolitical. They only cause trouble when their animals have no water. Then they take what they want and will fight anyone. They are proud. They never beg. They steal. And they are the oldest people. All people come from them. They are the people of Dinknesh. You call her Lucy."

"Lucy? You mean the oldest human? Oh. I want to see her. Fikir, where do they keep her?"

"In the National Museum. In Adis."

"Fikir, do we have time? Before the airport?"

"Yes. I think so."

"Selam, Kay Lee, you wanna see the oldest woman in the world?"

"Mom, I thought that was you."

"Brat. Dejem, drive faster. We're going to see Lucy in the Sky with Diamonds. Come on Fikir, come on Selam, Kaylee, sing...

Lucy in the Sky with Diamonds
Lucy in the Sky with Diamonds
Lucy in the Sky with Diamonds
Ahh, Ahh...."

Grandma's Bones

Fikir, Lisa, Kay Lee and Selam: **National Museum, Adis Ababa**

"That's Lucy? That's all? Fikir, I didn't mean to drag you here for just this. I thought there would be a whole skeleton, not just a couple of bones."

"But these bones tell the story…"

"And is that how they think she looked? Like a chimp?"

"…of our ancestors. The first ones to walk upright."

"So do chickens. Does that make them wonderful?"

"Mom, shut up."

"Mrs. Lisa, her knee and hips were different. The arms were shorter. Dinknesh and her people could walk and run and used their hands while they stood. And so they were the first people."

"But they were monkeys. They were hairy and they had little brains."

"No, Mrs. Lisa. They were something in between. I studied Dinknesh in biology. It is proven. We come from her genetics."

"Selam, are you OK?"

"Yes, I am praying to my Grandmother."

Grandmother Dinknesh, you have lost many bones but the ones I see are pretty.

Grandmother Dinknesh, when you were a girl, were there trees?

Grandmother Dinknesh, did you swim in rivers and play with your brothers and sisters?

Grandmother Dinknesh, were you embarrassed if you did not wear clothes and everyone could see you?

Grandmother Dinknesh, did you kiss your sons and daughters and throw them in the air to make them smile?

Grandmother Dinknesh when there was water in the desert, did you eat pineapple with mango?

Grandmother Dinknesh did your husband protect you from the other males when they wanted to mate you?

Grandmother Dinknesh, how you did stay safe from lions?

Grandmother Dinknesh, if you were the first person, then who was your mother?

"Fikir, look there is Helen. Oh my God. That must be her German. Now she sees us. And so she stands behind him. Why does she hide?"

"Selam, Don't look at her. She probably makes some trick with him, making up shit that she is an orphan. She does not want him to meet those who know her family. Now he looks at us. Now he looks away."

"At least he is not fat."

"These farange just want concubines. Let's go. We do not want to hurt Helen's chance."

"Mrs. Lisa, Kalki, come on, before we take Selam to her school, come see the Room of Haile Selassie. His clothes and his jewels. Then you will understand Ethiopia. Come on."

"

Helen Introduces Helmut To His Grandmother
But Then She Has To Hide
Helen and Helmut: National Museum, Adis Ababa

So, Helmut, now you must make a promise to your grandmother.

Good God, Helen, why do you insist on doing this?

I always wanted to see her but I had no one to go with. And because I want you to promise her.

But why does she have an English name? I thought she was Ethiopian."

She is, but the Europeans found her and called her Lucy. But she is really Dinknesh. Helmut, on the paper it says that when the Denakil became desert the children of Dinknesh went in all directions to the whole world and became all different colors. I think what happened was the ones who went to Europe saw snow and turned white, the ones who went to China became yellow, and the ones for Somalia became more black than a leopard. But on the inside in the genes all of them stayed blood red.

But she is so ugly and hairy. How can she be your grandmother?

Helmut, no Ethiopian man has hair on his back such as you, so why do you insult her? She is your grandmother too. In the picture, see her husband, he is the same hairy as her, so of course he would think she was beautiful. See, she carries the child and he holds her hand just like a husband.

Helen, you too funny to imagine that these baboons were married. This picture is an artist's fantasy. Who married them? Did they have a dinosaur for a priest? These monkeys had no concept of being married. They had sex with whomever they wanted and then somehow there was a baby and no one knew why or who was the father or any of that. So how can they be married?

Some monkeys mate for life. I learned this in biology. And so it comes from nature. So now I want you to promise our Grandmother. You will come back from Germany. You will be a true husband. Do you promise to Dinknesh?

Helen, if that will make you happy I will swear by these bones. Why not? It is the same as kneeling to a wooden cross. Or praying to a flag. Should I kneel? What are you doing, Why do you stand behind me?

Wait. Shut up. Stop. Don't move. Don't ask. Just please, Helmut, keep in front of me.

Oh, Helen, I see, ha ha, you hiding from those people.

Helmut please. Quiet. Don't move.

Do you know the woman with the American hair? Or the older girl? She is so beautiful.

I will tell you later. Shhh.

Or is that boy your old boyfriend?

Later. Don't move. Tell me when they have left.

The older girl is nodding at me. Should I say something?

No, but shake your head to her. And then just look at Dinknesh.

OK. Now they look away. Now the girl is collecting the others. Now they leave.

Thank God. The girl is my friend but I did not want that boy to see me. He is from my town. He would have told my parents I was with farange.

And so what is bad with being with farange?

It means you are a bad woman. A prostitute. Unless you are married to one. And then you are gold. One day we will go back to my town and they will be proud. I have been sending my mother money and she will not send it back. But I do not want her to know about me until I am married. So, come on, they went into the room on the left, let us get out of the museum now and go back to the hotel. You are leaving tomorrow and I think we must make this day for love. Unless you are tired from this morning. What do you think?

Fikir Remembers His Dad Remembering His Dad Remembering The Downfall Of The Lion Of Judah.
Fikir, Selam, Lisa and Kay Lee: National Museum, Adis Ababa

The House of Solomon claimed lineal descent from Solomon of Israel and the Queen of Sheba, the latter of whom tradition asserts gave birth to Menelik I. These claims of Solomonic descent make the Ethiopian royal house among the two oldest in the world (the other being the Imperial Dynasty of Japan).

You see that picture? If you meet my grandfather Hagos he will tell you the story of when my father was little and the Emperor came to Dodola. He stood in the back of his Rolls Royce in his uniform and feathered helmet and threw coins at the people from the back of his car, just like in the picture. My father fought the other boys for a coin and then he refused to give it to Hagos until Hagos beat him. Hagos was proud of my father for his lion heart. It was a 50 cent piece. Hagos said in those days it bought food for three days.

Haile Selassie expected the people to treat him as God. The atom bomb had been invented, America had sent a man to the moon, but still in Ethiopia people had to pay a tax to the landowner, and also to the church. The whole country had one train and no paved highway. The literacy rate was only 10%. At the same time other African countries were becoming independent and all people laughed at Ethiopia for being the most backward of countries. The Emperor was ashamed, and so he made his first mistake; he started schools and universities. Of course, the students, learning of Marx and the French Revolution made protest against feudalism, but the Emperor could not accept any challenge to his privilege; his army killed the protesters and the prisons filled with students. His last mistake was to starve the soldiers who were protecting his dynasty. There were riots for more pay, and mutinies. Two coup attempts were beaten down. My grandfather said, it was obvious to everybody what was coming. Ras Tafari was arrogant; he would not tolerate rebellion. The army revolted and joined the students and that was the end of Haile Selassie.

Now all the young people worship Haile Selassie. I fight with them about feudalism but few of them know what that means. How can you argue with those who are ignorant of their own history? All they know is Bob Marley and Facebook and that the Derg killed so many people. They think it was better before the revolution.

You know that the Derg killed my father. He made the revolution strong and then the revolution crushed him. The Derg prison was where he got sick and died. My mother had to fight for his body. He had been beaten. I had just been born. I do not remember him

This is the story my grandfather tells about the last days. Hagos took care of the horses and gardens of Ras Mekonnen, a cousin of the Emperor. His palace was in Dodola.

When the revolution started in Negele, my Uncle, who was in the army, sent a warning to Hagos that the soldiers were on the way to arrest Mekonnen and his family, so Grandfather hid, at his sister's tukol, two horses and a wagon full of tef that he took from Mekonnen's granary. When the soldiers came to Mekonnen's compound they ordered all the guards and tax collectors to run away and then they chased them on the main road shooting them from their trucks. They took the landowner Mekonnen and his brothers and beat them, then put them against the wall of their own jail and shot them too. They made all the workers watch this – to give them fear and to let them know that the days of the landowners were over; the army would be the ruler now. My grandfather always says that that was unforgettable, and that we should pray that we never will see people shot up close. The soldiers took all the furniture from the palace and loaded it in their trucks, then led away the horses and the cows, telling the people that they should take the goats and chickens to feed themselves. That was to make them part of the overthrow. That night my Grandfather traveled, with the wagon of tef and the horses he'd stolen, by the rural road to his father's compound at Asamana. He hid the horses and the tef there until the violence was over and then he found a tukol by Lake Gumare where the city of Dice Dota is now. That is how our family came to live there. My grandfather used the horses to plow land, then he bought cattle and started increasing his herd. He finally invested in a minibus, which is how he became a driver.

Look at this. This is Haile Selassie with his pet lions. See, that is the brother of Kennedy when he visited Ethiopia before the revolution. He too was assassinated. Every Ethiopian knows this picture.

Would you like to learn now of all the peoples of Ethiopia? Here on the top floor they show the 93 tribes and their history.

Wait, my Uncle is on my mobile.

Oh my God, we must go now, or we will be late for the airplane. Come on, Selam, Mrs. Lisa, Ms. Kay Lee. We must take Selam to Adenech and then to Bole. If you miss the plane, then you will have to stay here for your life. How would you like that?

Genet's Big Day Outside The Museum
Genet: **Adis Ababa**

Megdes. Come here. Promise not to tell? Look here's ten birr. We can eat tibs and have Fanta. Maybe candy.

This was a good day. First I encountered that country girl I met and guided, Selam, the one that is a friend of that whore, Heaven, from Seven Nights. Remember, I told you, she let me stay in the room with her at the Jerusalem Hotel and she had all this money Heaven had given her to give to Heaven's mother and I only took 100 birr and she never noticed, she did not count it, can you believe it?

She was there, this afternoon, where I was selling Ras Tafari shirts outside the National Museum for that fucker Miruts, coming down the steps with Ethiopians and another woman and a girl, who, I could tell from their hair and their shoes, were American. Selam saw me and shook her head to tell me not to greet her. I tried to sell the American a shirt, but she wouldn't buy. They are the hardest, these Black women from other places. But then I saw her daughter was Selam's sister, you could tell, it was so obvious, and so I told Selam's sister in English that I knew she was Ethiopian, and she was surprised and said to me, "How did I know?"

"My eyes," I said, so she got her American mother to buy two t-shirts and now there will be 10 birr after I pay Miruts. And right after they got in their minibus, out comes the whore Heaven with the German, the same one who gave me 10 birr the night I met Selam. And she tried to kick me off so I begged him and he gave me one birr, but I said in English, "No, one hundred, please, for my mother. She is sick. I must buy medicine." And the whore, Heaven, says that I am liar, but he laughs and laughs and gives me 10 birr and says, "Don't forget your mother."

So in the whole day I made 20 birr.

Are you hungry? Come on Megdes.

219

Freezing In Dubai
Kay Lee: **Dubai Airport**

Miranda, why am I emailing you? I'll be back home tomorrow and at school on Monday. I know, I'll read it to you. That'll be so cool. But you gotta turn your phone off, that's the deal.

It's 3 in the morning and Mom and me are at Dubai Airport. Sleep is not an option. All the seats in the Dubai airport have these fucking armrests. You can't lie down. Our flight to JFK is at 6 so I have hours to kill. And I'm freezing.

For me the main attraction here at overly air-conditioned Gate G7 is a pile of little women in black burkahs camped out in a pile on the floor in front of the desk where you check in. I counted 35 of them, most under 5 ft, they're like between normal and pygmy, like 7th graders, but they're grown women and they have little babies that you can sometimes hear crying from somewhere deep within the pile. Every once in a while a little brown foot gets pulled out and its irate owner gets fed or changed or rearranged, but most of the action is all under the burkahs so who can tell what's going on? Some bigger kids sleep by their mothers. I wonder where they are from and where they are going and why they are so tiny? I asked Mom if malnutrition hurts the birth rate? She said it makes you stupid before it makes you infertile and that's just part of the whole grand bad design.

What I like about these little women is the way they curl up together like kitties. I'd like to snuggle up with them right now; the air-conditioning here is killer. Outside its 120 degrees and you can see the sand blowing, but inside this ice cube guys in turbans ride huge noisy vacuum cleaners past acres of shuttered duty free stores and empty halls and freezing people trying to sleep while the fluorescents flicker.

Leaving was breaking hearts. My big sister Selam asked if we would take her to America and my Mom said no. My little sister Lushi asked too and my Mom said no. My real mother asked for more money and my Mom said no. Should I feel bad? My Mom says life's not fair, you can't unwin the lottery you won, just give what you can and be kind.

We left Dice Dota this morning and took the van to Adis. Outside of town in this kind of desert area I saw a wart-hog, this little hairy pig with curly tusks coming up from its bottom jaw. They are so cute? Wouldn't it be cool to tame one and keep it for a pet and dress it up? Can you imagine us walking a wart hog in a little red vest on a leash in Lincoln Park? With us was our family friend and kinda sorta protector, Fikir (my Mom says he also is a bit of a parasite), who is an amazing gymnast and who has (he says) graduated from University. Also Selam, who we took to this special school in Adis that Mom helped get her into because she had to run away from home where my creepy real father, Gyorgis (Mom calls him "Gyorgisaurus," you should see him, he's got one leg and is like the BAD DAD in that movie we saw who kills his daughter because he caught her kissing a boy) wanted money to buy a taxi, so he tried to marry Selam off to an old fat friend of his whose wife had died. Gyorgis is usually high and everyone hates him. My Mom says he beats my Mother and that's why Fikir is so important, he protects her and the kids. Selam wants to finish high school and go to college, so Mom and I are going to use some of the money we brought to pay for her to go to a special school in Adis, the House of Adenech. We took her up there on our way to the airport. But first we went to see Lucy in the National Museum.

Lucy is the oldest person in the world. Three million years old. Her skeleton is laid out in the "Lucy Room" in a case in a big museum in Adis. She was tiny, the size of a chimp, and Fikir and Selam say that she is our "Grandmother" because she had a human pelvis and knees, which means she walked upright, which somehow proves that Ethiopians were the first people and we are all descended from them. They are really proud of her.

The museum was full of tourists, church groups from the US and Sweden, Ethiopian school kids in their uniforms, and, what was intensely creepy, these old White men with these young teen-aged Ethiopian girls, they were like barely sixteen with dresses up to their ass cracks, and the men, Germans, I think, were all over them, in a FUCKING MUSEUM, of all places, no kidding, it was gross. What I liked best about my Ethiopian Culture Tour was when we were leaving, outside the gate by our van there was this crazy street girl selling these Ras Tafari t-shirts. My mother tried to brush her off, but she wouldn't take no for an answer, she kept saying, "You will like, three dollars, three dollars", and my Mom kept shaking her head and Fikir was about to slap her, but she looked right at me and my sister Selam and said to me, "You are her sister, give her a present." That kind of stopped every one in their tracks, like she had ESP or something, and so how could we not buy two? I got you a black and white one with a picture of Haile Selassie on it and writing in Amharic. He looks like a little freak, you will love it, it's tight.

On the way to the airport we dropped Selam off at her school, the House of Adenech, which is this big modern building stuck in the middle of a sketchy Adis neighborhood full of crumbly houses and goats and cows wandering around and people living and begging on the street. It's a safe house. These girls and women who live there have men trying to kidnap them – fathers, husbands, boyfriends, pimps even, Fikir says. The girls and women are escorted to the local schools. Women with children can leave their babies and small kids at Adenech while they're at school – and they live and study there, and work, weaving tablecloths and napkins on these awesome looms the Danes bought. You'll see, we bought some tablecloths for your Mom and napkins too. The Principal lady, Misrak, spoke good English, and she was nice, but you could tell she was strict. You knew you didn't want to break any rules or she'd throw you out on your butt. I don't know if I could stand it. You have to go to bed at a certain time and no boys, no dope, no fun, me, I might rather want to be a bargirl, JUST JOKING.

Selam cried when we left and so did I, but you know, I don't know if she was crying about saying goodbye to Mom and me, I think it was more about Fikir. Their goodbye hug was like so obvious, they just wanted to lean in, but they couldn't with everyone around. They both are really hot. She's slim with nice boobs and gorgeous skin (like me!!!) and he does all this gymnastics. Minus his shirt he's got like a 12 pack, and thick ribbony muscles around his shoulders. Mom says he's mostly trustworthy – he'll keep Gyorgis in his cage is how she puts it – but she knows he's getting kickback money from the van guy who is his relative, and she says he also hit on her to guarantee him for immigration so he can come to the states and park cars and try to score an American wife like all the other Ethiopian guys who hang out at Gondar Restaurant. She just loves his Mom though. Eden, who will be dealing with the money we send, so that part is OK.

Oh my God it's 5:30 Dubai time and someone is now opening up the gate for our flight. I've been writing for two hours. Now the little burkah women are sitting up and gathering their babies who have all started to cry. I can't wait to get home. This trip made me so tired of being the girl who got adopted. Fuck Ethiopia. I can't wait to be from there but not there. I will read this to you next week, if you promise to turn your phone fucking off. Ooops, sorry. I promised not to swear like my Mom and there I went. Love you, KL.

2010

God Chooses Fikir To Go To China
Fikir: **Adis Ababa**

From: fikiracroboy@yahoo.com
To: Kayleechicigal@gmail.com
Date: Wed, Feb 19, 2010 at 3:01 PM
Subject: China
Mailed by: yahoo.com

Greetings Miss Kalkidane and Mrs. Lisa.

I hope that you and your family are in the best of health and that your work is successful. Please convey all my regards to Mr. Marc, a man I will appreciate to meet in future times. I write to tell you that big wonderful things have happened. As a surprise gift from God, I was given a scholarship from the Ethiopian gymnastics federation to go to China to Acrobat School.

All through my boyhood days and in high school I trained with my friends and won many gold medals in the gymnastic competitions in Adis. Then when I went to University this stopped and I had no more dream to continue with Cirkus. But two weeks ago they called me and said I am one of five Ethiopians who will go. This was because my friend Alemayhu, who is now the chief of the Federation, chose me to replace a boy who was hurt.

Can you imagine the many things I will learn? The juggling of tables and chairs with the feet, the spinning of the plates on sticks, the German Wheel? I have seen these things in videos but now I will be taught them by China masters and then I can play in Europe with an African Cirkus, or Turkey or even America. I will have money to build a house here for my family. That is what my friend did. She was chosen three years ago. She called it the China gymnastic prison but after she got out she first worked in Germany, then Turkey and now in the Sea World Cirkus in San Diego, USA. She comes here twice a year. All year they have been building the house and it is just now finished.

I have been at the Gymnastics Federation in Adis for the last week waiting for my papers and now finally we have our passports and visas and can go. There are six of us, one each from Tigray, Amhara, Sidama, Adis, Harrar and I am represent Andamu. The training is two years and the China government pays for all.

Last week I said goodbye to my mother and to my friends. Do not worry about the money for the Nigest family. My mother will manage your money to make sure that tuition will be paid and that Gyorgis will not steal it. You will be glad that we have seen Selam at the Adenech house and she is placing in the top three in her high school and she has very good grades in social progress as well as all the academics.

I have given away all my things to my friends who have not been so lucky. Everything: my clothes, my bicycle, my camera. Tomorrow I will take my first plane ride. To China. They will have Internet there and I will write you.

How can I be picked? I thank God for this chance.

All of my wishes and best love,

Your friend, Fikir.

Helmut Carries On Two Conversations At Once
Helmut: **Hamm, DE**

Helmut?

Helen. Just wait one second please.

Crystal, one minute.

Helen, what is the matter?

Who is "Crystal one minute?"

A colleague. Helen, it is good to hear your voice.

It was a woman.

Yes, In Germany women work with the men. Some of them are above me.
So I must listen to them. Which means I can't talk long because I am meeting
with my boss, Frau Crystal Hildeburger.

Helmut, why haven't you called me?

Helen, I'm sorry. I am reaching for the telephone to call you and then I get
another call. And then I call you and the phones are down. This has been going
on all this week. I hate it. Tell me, how are you? Do you enjoy the apartment?

Helmut, when are you coming back to Ethiopia?

I told you, in six weeks. Only six weeks and then you will be in my arms again.

Have you heard from the Embassy? Will they have the visa? Every time
you say six weeks. This has been going on for months and months.

I called again but still they did not return my call. I will make another call
tomorrow.

Helmut, the landlord…he is not a good man.

Moment, please, Helen.

Helmut what are you doing in there? I have to use the bathroom.

Moment, please, Crystal.

Helmut, Are you on the phone?

Baby, I'm talking to my boss.

Of course, that is why you hide in the bathroom. Look, I don't really care who you are talking to. When are you coming to bed? I thought we were going to have a meeting before we picked up Marlene.

Hey, go put something on? That black thing I got you.

Why should I?

So I can take it off you.

Only if you are good.

Give me two minutes Crystal and I will be better than good.

Meet me in the bedroom.

OK.

Helen, look I'm sorry we got cut off. I have to go.

Helmut, the landlord is bothering me. He wants favors. He knows me from Seven Nights.

Look, I will call you tomorrow. I will deal with him. I have to get back to the meeting now, we are discussing serious business and my boss Frau Hildburger is calling for me. I have to humor her and do a good job. I love you. I will see you in six weeks. Goodbye.

Helmut,...I am missing...

Helmut, where did you go?

To the kitchen to finish this call.

Go into the bedroom.

My darling, is this the way you talk to your husband?

Sorry. My Love, give me your hand.

Please.

Of course.

Now.

Selam Sneaks Out Of The House Of Adenech
To See Helen At Seven Nights
Selam and Helen: **Seven Nights, Adis Ababa**

Helen?

Selam! Please call me Heaven.

Hey Henok, this is my sister. She came from Andamu. My mother is sick and she doesn't know what to do. We have to talk. Tell Tati I will be back in an hour.

Come on Selam, walk with me.

Selam, remember this place? We had coffee here when you ran away. Waiter, two cappuccino.

So what's going on? The last time I saw you was last year at Dinknesh in the museum and I almost peed. I didn't want anyone from home to see me. Was that your sister and her American mother?

Yes. And was that your German?

Helmut. He was on his way to the airport.

Did he come back?

Oh yes. And he will be again in six weeks. And then I go to Germany. So how are you? Are you in back in Adis? We haven't spoken since I gave you money for my mother.

Yes. I am at the House of Adenech. Weyzero Eden and Mrs. Lisa sent me there to get away from Fat Tadesse and my father. I will finish high school here and then I will go to University.

Oh Selam, that is your best chance. I am so happy for you. But you look so thin and tired. Is there food there in this house of Adenech?

Helen, there is more than food. The first rule is you have to go to school. On weekdays some women go to morning school and others stay at the house and take care of children and cook and clean and then they switch and go to afternoon school. Helen, there are girls like you at the House of Adenech who have worked in Kasanchis. Now they are finishing high school. You could come there and then you would not have to work at Seven Nights. You could learn for your future to be a nurse. This was your dream. Why are you laughing?

Oh Selam, you are a sweet sister but a nurse here earns nothing, you work for long hours, and still you can only make enough to rent a little house where you shit in a hole and your electricity goes off all days and you can barely afford to send your kids to school. You cannot buy nice clothes and your Ethiopian husband will beat you and take your money and will not use a condom so you are always pregnant. Or he will give you HIV. Don't worry for me. I have my own apartment with Helmut here in Adis. And I have my future in Germany. That is where I will go to school.

You have an apartment with Helmut?

Yes.

Could I stay there? When Helmut is gone?

When will you go to Germany? Last year you said…

Selam it is almost final. It has taken more than a year to get the visa. But now it is almost done. And then, when I have the visa, we will be married in Germany so I can become a German. He says they will not honor an Ethiopian wedding there.

Oh Helen, I'm sad I cannot be at the wedding.

Yes, I know. I wish my mother and my sisters could come…but no, there is no way they can get visas.

What will you wear?

Once I am in Germany I will ask my mother to make me a dress and I will send her money to make it.

Helen, let us make your wedding dress at Adenech. There is an old weaver Saphirra who teaches us the traditional way to weave and sew things that farange will buy; table cloths, napkins and dresses. And I am learning to sell these because I have English and Facebook and computer. The Denmarks have given computers and I go on the Internet and communicate to Europeans and Americans who want to buy the cloths. We would make you a dress. I would send it to you.

Selam, I will send for it.

Waiter, thank you. May we also have two cakes? Selam would you like a cake?

Helen, this Helmut, he must love you too much to give you an apartment and let you work at Seven Nights and then to marry you. How is that?

He doesn't know I am still there. When he is in Adis I keep him away from Kasanchis.

But then, if he pays for your living…why do you continue there?

Selam, you are on a better path, a much better path, to go to University, to become a lawyer or a doctor and to stay a virgin until you are married. That is all good, but know that I think this: if you are a woman you must have your own money. Whatever these men say about friendship or love, they first want what is between your legs. They cannot help themselves. It is too powerful. And Selam, if you are not cut, there is a world of pleasure from men. God has made it this way, and this pleasure gives you children, so who can deny this? I am young so it is good now that Helmut wants me. He will marry me, I will become a German and I will have his children as soon as I can. If he leaves me I will still be secure. For his children he will support me. And then, if he doesn't leave me, he will die 20 or 30 years before me, God willing, and then I will go to California. Have you seen on Facebook these pictures of San Diego from Maritu?

Oh yes, it looks like Paradise.

How is Fikir?

Oh, there is fantastic news. He is in China at the gymnastic school. He was chosen. It's the place where Maritu went. He left four months ago.

How long is he gone?

Two years.

So, you have no …friend? No boy you are in love with?

No, and if I did I would not be allowed to see him and if I got caught they would ask me to leave. There are many rules at Adenech. I am breaking one now to see you. But I am thankful that Mrs. Lisa has sent me there. I have my own room with my own table for my studies and needlework. When I close the door – there is no one with me. It is like being far way from anyone. It is good. But I am very lonely.

Helen, that is a nice watch. What time is it?

It is 10 in the Day.

I must go back. If I am late I will get a warning. Please give me your phone number. I have a paper and pen. I will call you.

Selam, here it is. Call me in the next week. Here, take a cake. I will pay.

Thank you Helen. I would like to see your apartment. You are really often there alone?

Yes. Goodbye, Selam.

Goodbye.

Skype Between Kalkidane In Chicago And Fikir In Chinese Gymnastics Prison About Pig And Dog And God
Fikir and Selam: **Wuqiao, China/Chicago**

So can you see my hand and my arm?

No. I can see your legs down to the waist but your feet are on top. Are you upside down? What did you say? Is that Chinese?

No, I speak Amharic to Tilahun. He is one of my roommates, from Desse. I asked him to move the laptop to the back. Now can you see?

Holy shit. You are upside down and standing on one hand.

This is nothing. Here in Wuchow little children can do this. Others do one hand while on the rope and others jump with one hand from stick to stick. I am learning the foot juggling on one hand. OK I come down. Ha. There is your face. You are very pretty. Here is mine.

Wow. Amazing. How did you learn that?

Kalkidane, you know, here is like the army, the Chinas make us train and train. Before breakfast and then until lunch and then we rest and in the afternoon we train again until dinner and then after that too until sleeping. But it is good because there is no other way to learn these techniques. These Chinas are experts at very hard training but they are great. They gave us a camera to make videos that go into the computer. This is how we call you. And you know they eat pig and dog?

They eat dog?

Yes. In the village at the market, they sell dogs in little prisons made of wood. The Chinas buy them and cook them.

Gross.

And every China keeps a pig in their house for eating. They eat dog and pig. How can they do that? To eat pig and dog is forbidden by God.

Fikir, in America we eat pig. I eat pig.

This animal is dirty.

Fikir, in America the pigs are clean. And they are delicious. Bacon? Listen you better watch out if you come to the US. You might smell some ribs and make God very angry. She would have to punish you.

God is not a woman.

How do you know?

Don't you know? It is written.

Yes, Fikir, but I have a different religion. My own. And my God is a woman. And an eagle. And an ocean.

Listen, I will not argue with you, you are a child so you can insult God without fear. But when you are a woman you will have more respect. Listen, others wait to use the Skype. Kalkidane, I've been sending Facebook to Selam but for one month she has no answer.

I haven't heard anything from her.

OK, I will email Ebe to set up a Skype with my mother. She will know about Selam. Listen, this is important, Kalkidane, my friends and I have a plan for our own circus. I can't say more because the Chinas listen to Skype but...you might see me soon.

You mean...in Chicago?

Shhh. Say nothing, but I wanted to tell you this. I have to go now. The others are waiting. I send my love to Mrs. Lisa and Mr. Marc. And to you my special sister.

Fikir...

Kalkidane...

2012

Eden Phones Selam About Lushi Going To Work
In The Emirates.
Eden: **Dice Dota,** *Selam:* **Adis Ababa**

Hello Selam. How is your life?

Weyzero Eden? Hello. I am fine. And you?

Yes, my health is good. And you?

Have you heard from Fikir? How does he like China?

He calls it "gymnastics prison" but he says with the training he can work anywhere, so it is a great chance. He emails me every two weeks. Tomorrow I will go to the Internet and I expect to find his message.

Please Weyzero Eden, give him the address of Adenech and ask him to write me. He does not write me. And my family? Is this why you call? Is everything OK?

Yes, all are in good health. And there is good news. Geta has placed first in his class and has taken the examination for the Jesuit High School. The results are out and he has been accepted. And because of this your father has forgiven Geta and accepted him back into the household and promised no more beatings. But there is a problem.

Of course. The tuition for the Jesuit school.

Yes. Your family does not have the money for this school. So now Gyorgis has persuaded Lushan to work in the Emirates so that there will be tuition for Geta. Nigest has told me this.

But this is terrible. Certainly Lushan will want to finish school. The Arabs treat Ethiopian girls like slaves. Everyone knows this. Why would she do this?

Gyorgis has told her that if she works for two years it will be her turn. And she has accepted this.

But she is too young.

Gyorgis bought her a false passport for working that says she is seventeen. Many girls do this and the government does not care; they get money from the agency to let the girls pass. And Lushan will do anything to escape living in Dice Dota. She knows that Mrs. Lisa will not take her and that the American money is spent on Adenech for you. For her she says this is her only chance.

Listen, bring Lushan to your house. Let me speak with her. I will forbid her to do this.

So did her mother and so did I but she did not listen. Now it is too late. She told her mother today she would go to Eskadar's to do hair. But Mechtid saw her this morning leaving with other girls from the Southern Sun Agency in a van. They go to Bole. She will fly to Dubai this evening. This is why I call you.

But what can I do?

I don't know. But maybe you can find her in the airport and stop her from doing this.

But, they do not let us leave here. And I have no money for a taxi.

I will ask Mother Misrak.

No, please Weyzero Eden, do not. I left the school already once and she has given me a warning so I do not want to bring attention to myself. This is very bad news but I do not think I can find a solution to this problem. It is in God's hands. All I can do is pray for Lushan.

Well then…I will do the same. Goodbye Selam.

Goodbye Eden. Please… my love to my mother, and Geta.

Selam Goes To Helen To Get Help But Helen Is Working
Selamawit: Seven Nights, Adis Ababa

You are American, that is my guess. Am I correct? Ha, I won. So now you must buy another Champagne. Henok, please another Champagne for Jimmy and me.

How do I know? By shoes. Americans have Nike, not Adidas.

My God, there is Selam. In her school uniform. I told her not to ever come here. Can't she see I'm working?

…And the English are not so, how do you say…undressed? No, I mean, there is more attention to clothing. And the French ooh la la, they are chic. But I do not mean to offend all Americans, Jimmy, *you* are well dressed, this hat, what does it say, *Save the Children?* And always, for fun, you Americans are the best…

Now Henok is going to her. Now she is pointing to me. Oh, he is taking her hand. He will offer her a job and this will be a life of trouble for Selam.

Henok, please the Champagne!

…because you are not so cold, you want more than just doing business and then going away, you want to have fun. Do you like to dance? No? One American friend, Martin, he is from Boston, do you know him? He loved to dance. He has taken me to see Lucy. Do you know her? Lucy, the oldest woman?

OK, you do not like parties with old women but this is different. Lucy is not for having parties…she is… historical. I think you do not understand.

I'm sorry. He is not paying attention. Please excuse me. I will get the champagne.

Henok, get the Champagne or I will lose this American! And, do not start your tricks with this girl. She is my sister and she is going to school.

Selam, so you have run away from Adenech? How is this possible? No don't say anything. I can't deal with this now. NO, I really CANNOT! Here take this key and go to my apartment. I write the address down for you, here, 235 Churchill Apt 411. It is a new building. Everyone knows it, across from the Dashen Bank. Now go. GO. Wait for me there and do not leave. I will be there in the night.

I'm sorry, Jimmy, This little girl is my relative from my hometown. She is telling me news from my Mother.

Yes, she is beautiful, but no, no, please no, I cannot invite her, she is too young, she does not go with men, she studies now and must return to her school.

Selam. GO!

Excuse me, Jimmy this girl just will not listen. Ah, here is the champagne. Come here and sit close. Give me your hand. Do you say "Cheers" in America like the English? "Bottoms Up? " Oh ha ha yes, my bottom. Drink now. More Champagne? And then will we go to the Sheraton? Henok, bring!

Selam Finds Genet Selling Water At The Depot And Persuades Her To Help Stop Lushan From Flying
Genet: **Adis Ababa**

So this girl, so lucky to be forced to take the best path, will fight her way through ten fences to make the wrong choice. Here, she throws away a bed at Adenech and food and school at no cost. What more could she want? I am selling water outside the Depot waiting for the vans to arrive from Harrar, Bahir Dar and the South. It is an hour before night and so far it's been a good day; I've made 20 birr, sitting outside the National Museum selling t-shirts, and now these mini-vans will have many farange coming in from the countryside looking for taxis to the airport or to hotels. They will have been traveling all day and will be thirsty. I hope to make 20 more birr and then have a feast with the children behind the Church.

Then there she is standing next to me. I have not seen her for six months. Two weeks after I sold her American sister t-shirts, I was picking up water from the Arab Mamoud and there she was across the street, wearing the uniform of Empress Tati School. I followed her and some women and girls and a guard back to the House of Adenech and watched them enter the gate. I knew this place and understood that there would be no chance to know her there; it was so strict. But now she is at the Depot in the red and black of Empress Tati. What is her business I wonder? Does she travel back to Dice Dota?

We look at each other. Still she will not speak. The vans arrive and the farange come out of the minis with their big backpacks, and I move from van to van, calling water, water, 5 birr, and she follows me from a distance. OK, I am thinking, she will wait, I will wait and we will see what happens, but whatever it is, I will not be giving her money. She has a sister in America.

So now the farange find their taxis and I have sold all but five of my waters and I have 40 birr – 20 for Mamoud and 20 for me. With the t-shirt money from the morning, this is a very good day. I sit on the stones by the electronic store. I do not look but I can feel her watching.

"So, are you fine?"

"You are at Adenech?"

"Not any more. Today I left Adenech. I do not know if they will let me back."

"So why do you come here? There are no vans for Dice Dota until tomorrow."

"I'm not going to Dice Dota. I need to go to Bole. You must help me."

"Why? You are rich. I saw your American sister."

"I am not rich. I have no money. My other sister goes to work in the Emirates. I want to stop her. Come with me to Bole right now. I will pay you back."

"How will you pay me back if you have no money?"

"Look at this key. Remember my friend who works at Seven Nights? It is the key to her German's apartment on Churchill in the tall building by Dashen Bank. Her German pays for this. She has given me this key. I am going there tonight to meet her. If you help me go to Bole, she will let you stay there too."

"How will she let me stay? She is a fancy prostitute. What does she want with a water girl?"

"She is my friend. She will let you stay. Come on, let's get a van to Bole. I need to find my sister."

So OK, I think I will take a chance with this girl. Even if she does not find money to pay me back I would like to sleep in her whore friend's apartment and there will be more opportunities if I help her. She has an American sister and she is beautiful. She is an OK investment.

"OK, give me your hand and promise that you will pay me back. Remember, if anyone lies to me I never forget it. They always have trouble."

I find the van to Bole. It is full of farange and Abesha going to the airport and there are many rucksacks and suitcases on the top. The boy says no, no, no more room but I push in the girl and myself and give him 10 birr for both of us. Of the Abesha sometimes you can tell who are leaving for the first time. They are dressed in new clothes and you see in their eyes the fear and excitement: *What awaits me? Will there be money? Will I ever come back?* We go past the new hotels and buildings and then we see the new airport building, all glass. We leave the van and stand by Passport Control.

I know Bole. Sometimes, if I can find a ride in the weeks before Meskel and Timkat when everyone returns to Ethiopia, I go there to sell water, and from the passport control gate I look through the glass into the terminal at the people in line and I think of how it will be on the day I leave Ethiopia, I will go through the gate with my suitcase and fly to Minneapolis. In Minneapolis I will meet everyone from everywhere in the world. And when I come back to Ethiopia, I'll bet you a hundred birr, I will have a whole cart of suitcases and I will be a radiology technician.

"How will we find her?"
"Everyone passes here. If she goes by you will see her."

We wait thirty minutes, forty minutes. We see so many different peoples. When I was little I only saw Ethiopians but in the eleven years of my life many more people have come to Ethiopia and so many more Ethiopians go out. There, waiting, we saw the traveling farange with their backpacks, Ethiopians married with farange with their children and suitcases, Abesha who live outside going back with bags full of berbere and wat, students from the Protestants and Latter Days who have been working with NGOs, Ethiopian Islam going to Mecca, Arab mens who make business, groups of Indias and Chinas returning to their countries, many World Health, UN and embassy peoples, and then yes, you see them, the most scared, the Ethiopian girls with their directors, in groups of twenty, leaving to be house workers, bringing just one shopping bag of possessions, with their eyes on the ground, not one looking up, as if, should they look out upon Ethiopia just once, it would pull them back by their eyes and they could never leave.

In the third group Selam saw her sister.

Selam Tries To Save Lushi And
When The Guards Go To Arrest Her
Genet Makes A Distraction
Selam: **Bole Airport, Adis Ababa**

I saw her. I was with Genet watching the people in line for Passport Control before the entrance to Bole. She was in one of the groups of girls with clothes in bags and old shoes, all wearing scarves and led by men and women dressed in business suits. I recognized Ato Mikal from Dice Dota, because he is much taller than a normal man and with a beard. Behind him was Lushi in a yellow dress that had been mine.

"Come on, Genet," I said. We came into the line and I walked beside Lushi, saying, "Lushi, you are making a big mistake, we will find money for your school, we will write Mrs. Lisa, come, walk away with me now," but she said in a low voice, not looking at me as if she was not talking to me, "Go away Selam, please, you cannot change my mind, go away," so then I took her hand and tried to pull her away from the line, saying, "Please Lushi I cannot let you do this, you know the stories they tell about the Emirates, you must finish school," but she pulled back into the line, still walking, saying, "It is impossible, I have signed a contract, my employer has bought the ticket, how will I pay him back? Let me go!"

I had always had my way with Lushan because I was bigger and stronger, but this time, when I grabbed her arm and pulled, she dug her nails into my hand like a cat and I had to let go.

The people and the police were noticing, us, so I made my plea. "Listen this is my sister, she is fourteen, she cannot go to work in the Emirates, this is illegal, her papers are false, you must stop this." That is when Ato Mikal grabbed me by the hair and took me to the Guard saying that I must be arrested for making a false accusation and when Genet struck him on the back of his head with a plastic water bottle so that the water ran down his suit, and he and the guard chased Genet through the people in the passport line.

I snuck away to where the taxis were and peeked between two vans to see Ato Mikal holding Lushi tightly by the hand, talking to another passport lady, explaining and explaining. I wondered how much money he gave her before she waved him through with Lushi. The other girls followed and passed through the glass doors of Bole into the place between worlds. In my heart I prayed for Lushan, God protect her. And I wondered: if Genet is caught, will she go to jail?

Lieutenant Giron Opens The Gates Of The River
So The Girls Flow Out
Lieut. Giron: **Bole Airport**

You are making a video? Then you cannot use my real name or show my face or have my real voice speaking. You must promise: *No name, no face, and you will change my voice.* If you betray me you will have the hunger of my children on your soul.

OK, this is how it is; every Monday, Wednesday, Thursday and Saturday they take the girls to Dubai and Abu Dhabi. Always there is a man and a woman who are the brokers, they hold the passports, twenty or thirty of them. The routine is so regular. On Wednesday and Saturday the guy Mikel brings the girls from Andamu and the South. The Wollo and Amhara girls come from the North on Monday. The Somali and Afar girls come with the woman from Harrar on Thursday. Often, you can smell the new glue on the passport and see where the old date of birth has been covered by the new one by photo computer. Always there is an hundred birr note for you folded with the papers, so you do not ask.

Unless it comes down from Immigration that there is a "misunderstanding." Then you take the people aside and tell them that the work permits are not verified, and they must talk to Ato So and So to straighten out the problem, but he is at a meeting and they must come back on Tuesday with proper documentation for all the girls. So then they must take the girls back to their dormitory and they have to pay their guards and drivers for more days. On Tuesday the brokers must stay in line all day to make the bribe. It is expensive if you don't get the girls through.

Oh, and how nervous these girls are; desperate to get out and at the same time terrified that they will be allowed to leave. Some of them look to be as young as 14. They do not meet your eyes when you question them, they cannot find their voice and can barely remember the date of birth stated on their passport. They have never flown in an airplane before and are scared they will fall from the sky. And they all know what they will face working for the Arabs. Everyone hears these stories, but still so many sign up.

I have seen the girls who return from being servants to the Arabs kiss the ground of Ethiopia, they are so happy to have survived and come back home. Some of them have run away from their employers because of beatings and rapings and then spent time in Arab prisons until their families find money to bring them home. I have seen scars on their faces.

This is an insult to Ethiopia. These are our daughters and we sell them as slaves. If I were ruler of the Department of Labor I would not issue these permits. But if I protest I would lose my job. Who would pay for my children's school? Would my girls then be on this plane to Dubai?

Here comes my boss. I will pretend to look at your documents. Remember you must keep your promise. Use only my words. *No name, no face. And change my voice.*

You may pass. We hope you enjoyed your stay in Ethiopia.

Lushi In The Sky Without Diamonds
Lushan: Bole Airport, Adis Ababa

Mother Nigest, I pray that you can hear me.

I am on an airplane ready to fly.

I am scared that I will never see you again.

I am scared that I will never be myself again.

I am scared that God will forget me.

I am scared that I will disappear into the sky and that my life will be like a cloud that is there for a minute and then it is not.

I do this to become nobody because nobody has the force to shape my circumstance other than myself.

I do this so I can be a Saint for my family.

I am sorry I did not tell you of the plan I made with Gyorgis about the Emirates.

I am sorry I did not tell you of the day that Gyorgis took me to the Southern Sun Employment Bureau in Dice Dota to meet with Ato Mikel to sign the paper for two years of work in the Emirates and receive the passport Gyorgis bought me that says I am 17.

And I am sorry I lied about spending the night at Eskedar's. Instead I went with Mikal with other girls in the van to Adis to the Southern Sun Office and then to Bole.

So I am sorry. I cannot help you with making injera tomorrow. This night I will be in Dubai.

But I can tell you about this plane. It is moving on the ground and I am high up sitting by a window next to a woman who speaks Gurage on her phone and a farange who sits by the aisle. I watch out the window as this plane backs up and turns and joins other planes moving slowly like oxen in line to drink at the water well. When they reach the front of the line they stop and turn and then one at a time they come back towards you on a road next to yours, with the loudest noise you have ever heard, gaining speed until they pass you, and you cannot see them behind you, but you hear the sound change from low to high until it goes away. After many planes your plane is at the front of the line and it changes direction and stops. A voice in the plane says: *in case of emergency you must do this and that and this and that* and a pretty woman in a uniform checks to be sure that your belt will hold you. You wonder if the plane falls from the sky how the safety belt will save you and you imagine death by crashing, and what will you think on the way down, will you be scared, will you pray, will the others scream, will you be at peace enough to think to say goodbye and to thank God for your life just before you hit? Will it be fast, all of a sudden black and crushing, will it hurt; will you survive the crash and then burn? You think how sad it will be to die before you are old. Now this plane starts to move slowly and then faster and faster on the ground, faster than any car you have ever been in and so very loud with a high and low pitch and the wheels bumping on the road. The buildings of the airport rush by you until they all join together and now the front of the plane points into the air and the sound changes, there is no more bumping, the wheels have left the ground, you are pushed back in your chair, the plane is climbing steeply and your ears have pressure. My God you are in the air. Some of the girls cry out. Your stomach comes into your throat. You look out the window, you are above the city of Adis Ababa; the people walk on the side of the road like ants, the cars are small and move in lines, the roofs of the buildings flash the sun back to you, and now there are endless hills with tukols on them and ribbons of roads and paths by the little fields, and you are above tops of mountains. It is very beautiful.

And now there is no land below, just cloud all around you like smoke, like heaven.

This is the truth: I go into a cloud. I disappear.

2013

News Of Nigest's Family
Eden: **Dice Dota**

Dear Mr. Marc and Mrs. Lisa. We have sent the money to the House of Adenech for Selam but in the last week Mrs. Misrak telephoned to say that for three days now she has left the house and if she will not come back that she will certainly lose her place at Adenech through disobedience. I promised Misrak that Selam would return but I do not know if this will be the truth. There is no contact and I have told her friends to tell me if they hear from her and to tell her to return. In some days, I must go to Adis for my job training and while I am there, if she is still missing, I will search through her friend Helen.

Gyorgis has made peace with Geta and so he now lives at home. This is because Gyorgis has hope for Geta's success and then for support. Now the money we received from you we give direct to Geta for food and uniforms But this is not enough. He is first in his class and has passed the examination for the Jesuit High School, which is the best high school in Andamu. This is his big chance for life, but there is no sponsor for his tuition. Gyorgis told Lushan that she should go to Dubai to work and send money for Geta's school, that if she did this, he would sponsor her high school learning when she returns. Nigest and I were against this but Lushan did not listen. She saw no chance for herself in Dice Dota except to marry and she would not do that. Gyorgis paid money for a passport that stated that she was 17 and now she has signed a contract for two years. For three days now she is gone to the Emirates. We pray she will contact us soon. You must know that Fikir is in China, learning the China acrobatics. The Chinas pay for everything. In two years he will be finished and then will come home. We miss him very much.

Here there is much inflation of the price of food but the wages do not increase. The power is often out but in the meanwhile, the development of the town increases rapidly, many streets are paved and they have forbidden horse taxis from the town center. All is bajaj now, and when before there were few autos, now many and even more motorcycles. This is good for transportation but bad for pollution. Now is winter and no rain and some days when there is no wind, you cannot see across the lake. For many people and children this makes asthma. Meanwhile the people are busy. Everyone who finds a little money invents an Internet café or a cell phone business, and here are more and more farange, working for NGOs or making business with coffee and electronics and especially the Chinas, who make big farms and textiles around Dice Dota and build new roads and many of the hotels. So while the wage is poor there is more work from all this activity. I am a nurse and there is always work for little pay – is this not the way of this profession? That is, if you have the connection. My Tigray cousin is a health official high up in the Regional Bureau. She protects me, so I thank God for this security.

I will inform you about Selam and your family as is my promise. I send my love and with deep respect to you and Mr. Marc and Kalkidane, I pray to see you in this year in Dice Dota.

Your friend, Eden.

Lisa Gets All Upside Her Own Head
Lisa: Chicago

Eden, please ask Selam, since she's blowing off the $500 we didn't have but scraped together anyways so she could get away from her dad and go to school, to please start selling her pussy like her friend, so that when she's saved up enough dough to pay us back, she can send it to us by Western Union so we can pay down Kay Lee's orthodontist bill, as soon as possible, no problem?

Shut up Lisa, Jesus Christ, don't jump to conclusions. You don't know what's happened. Maybe she's kidnapped. Maybe she's dead. And even if she's decided to be a bar girl, what's better, selling your body or not having one to sell? Look at Maya Angelou. Collette? People have a lot of lives.

Right, that's a great life, fucking strangers, risking AIDS, getting pregnant, having abortions, getting tied up and pissed on by some pervert. I'd rather milk goats and live in a shack.

So go trade places with Nigest. Gyorgis would be more than glad to have you milk his goat. And Marc would get along fine with Nigest, betcha she'd do all the cooking and the dishes and the laundry, none of this shared house-work crap –just a good African wife, no clitoris, but he'd have to learn to work around that.

Oh fuck you; you just want your own goat and your own shack and not some goddamned husband. Even Marc.

So why don't you write Eden and tell her that even though we are broke, we are sending her $50 to give to a bajaj guy to run Gyorgis over with his bajaj. And to please ask that he run him over – forward and backward – to be sure that he is really dead and to send us the photo of his corpse so that we will know that he will not try to sell any more of his daughters, even though it seems he has none left. We believe that this will help Nigest's family much more than sending medicine or school uniforms.

Aren't you funny? Selam is missing and now Gyorgis has indentured Lushan to be a slave in Dubai so her brother can go to Jesuit school. What a fuckin' nightmare. Ever since you got involved with these people NOTHING has gone like it was supposed to.

Ha, listen to you: *these people*. You mean *those* people, the corrupt immoral lyin' stealin' Ethiopians, the ones who sell their children for a song and practice barbaric acts of mutilation upon the genitals of their daughters while taking every farange for a ride? Good thing you don't mean *these* people, *your people*, like your gang-bangin' crack head cousins or your pops in jail or even Marc's brother singin' Hare Krishna in San Diego? *Those* people are different from *these people*, right? Good thing you ain't one of *them*.

OK, OK, take it easy on yourself, you're freakin.' But what are you going to do about Selam? And Lushi? And how did their lives become your fault? Will this ever end?

Lushi Works In Planet Dubai
Lushan: **Manar, UAE**

Are you looking for an Ethiopian maid or nanny? MaidHelpET.com offers the largest selection of housemaids. Select a candidate based on experience, nationality, skills and age. Unlike other maid agencies we find candidates who are already in the UAE, most often Dubai or Abu Dhabi.

Dear Selam, I'm living in the house of Amudah, which is in Manar, a suburb of Dubai. It is far from the center, but at night you can see the lights of the city; the buildings are twice as high as any in Adis. It is hard to believe that a place like Dubai is not just in the movies, but I saw it from the sky and then when I came from the airport to the city from the van through the valleys between the buildings to meet my employer. It is real.

I don't know yet where there is a post office or if my employers will allow me to find one, but I don't care. These are my first hours not working ever since I got here two weeks ago and there is no one here to be a friend or a sister to talk to, so even if this letter never finds you, still, to keep from being lonely, I write it.

First I must tell you, I am sorry for the trouble you caused at the airport and at the same time I thank you for it. You almost destroyed my life but I understand it was coming from love, so don't worry about me being angry with you; you are forgiven. Ato Mikal was furious, he nearly threw me out of the airport, but the ticket was bought so he didn't want to throw away money. We will laugh about it the next time I see you.

In my first two weeks here I have learned my place, my job and all the rules. My employer is Ato Amudah. His wife is named Sharnah but I must call her "Mistress." Really, Ato Amudah's mother is the boss of everyone. And that's what she does, boss and boss and boss. In the kitchen, in the house, with the children, she is always there watching when I do wrong. I speak no Arabic and she only one word of English, which she uses very well: no, no, no, no, no, no. This may be a problem so I am careful with the Old Mother. She will bite me when my back is turned. I know it.

I live in a small room behind the kitchen. It has a bed, a table, a stool and a light. It is the first bed and room I have ever had for myself and it is where I must go when the children are asleep and all the cleaning and cooking are done. When I shut the door and turn off the light the room is completely dark. In the bed there is no brother or sister to pull the blanket off and whisper with; it is so quiet I can hardly sleep.

Each day I am woken by an electric radio clock which comes on at 11 in the Night, an hour before the sun. Then I begin my duties which go on until 3 in the next night; cleaning the house, the clothes and the bedding, preparing the Arab bread and cutting all the vegetables and fruit for the day, setting the table for the meals and always washing the dishes and the kitchen after eating, and in the day, for many hours, watching the three children of Amudah. The littlest one feeds from his Mother's breast or, when she is out of the house, from a bottle, and the girl is so little, if she is by your side she is happy, but the boy Mahmud is a devil. He fights me whenever I ask him to do anything he doesn't want to do or when I try to stop him from doing something that is forbidden. He calls me "Abid" which means "slave," and runs to the Old Mother who then yells at me like I am a dog. She is one of these old Arabs who think Africans should be their slaves. I stay as far away from her as I can for fear that she will hit me.

Oh my God, Selam, how rich these Arabs are. It is as if they can piss oil and it turns to gold, their houses are like the American's in the movie Home Alone except they are Islam style and of course no crucifix. This is a new town by the sea where the houses are so large you could put our whole compound inside one of them. They have 7 or 8 rooms and they are all air conditioned. What they spend on electricity in one month must be what I will earn in two years. And the machines they have: electric knives to cut the meat and blades that spin in circles to slice vegetables and mix the dough, electric stoves to fry or roast, electric brooms to sweep, cleaners with sucking hoses for the rugs, washing machines and machines that dry the clothes too, even though the sun is as hot as the breath of Satan. I am surprised they do not have machines to clean the baby's shitty bottoms, but I guess I am that machine. At night they have large feasts and always there is meat, lamb or goat or camel, fish, rice, couscous, and vegetables and fruit. The Old Mother does not let me cook, except for the Arab bread. I am only supposed to help cut the food and prepare the table. The wife does not do either. When she returns in the late of the day from shopping or visiting, if her husband is coming home, she dresses for her husband and plays with her children until the meal is served. I bring in the dishes but do not eat with the family; I eat in the kitchen and listen for their call in case they need me to bring a dish, or if the children need help eating or have to be removed in case of crying or non-cooperation. After dinner I prepare the children for bed and to play with their mother and father if they do not go out. Then my job is to put them to bed, to dress them in their sleeping clothes and to wash them. In their children's room I sing them Amharic songs or read them English children's books, which they do not understand, but they enjoy the pictures and they teach me the Arabic words for the animals. I wait for them to sleep to wash the dishes and then I ask the Mother or the Mistress if I am dismissed, and if I get the sign I go to my room. If the boy refuses to go to sleep he runs to the Mother and then, after she scolds me for him not being asleep, they watch television.

I have little contact with the man, Ato Amudah. He is an Arab man with a headscarf and a mustache but handsome and taller than most, a busy man with the oil business who leaves in a suit by car in the morning and returns just before dark. He is polite when he requests you to do something. The Mistress is the kind of mother who may have been beautiful when she was younger but now after two children she is getting fat and she has another child beginning in her belly. She is not so polite, often you can tell when she is not happy with your work, she sighs and rolls her eyes, and says in English, "No, this is wrong, you must learn the right way, here I will show you and I don't want to show you again," but then her child might cry or her sister might call on the telephone and she loses interest and does not finish demonstrating anything, really she is much more concerned with her clothes and her appearance than anything else. I think she fights to keep her beauty for her husband. Still her life has no work. She meets with her sisters and other mothers every day, sometimes at her house. When they come over they go into her room and laugh and eat candy and play with clothes and makeup while I watch the children and the Old Mother watches me. I am her television.

Selam, this is the day off they give me every other Sunday and my employers say I can find a mini-van to take me to the City Center and go to Church. Everything here is Islam so I must travel far into Dubai for this, but I am hoping that there at the Church I will see other Abesha girls and make friends. There is no one to talk to here and I am so lonely. Really, except for the Old Mother that is the only bad thing about working here. My problem is that my employer has given me no money yet for the work I have done since I arrived, so I have been waiting in the kitchen ever since before sunrise for Ato Amudah to awaken so that I can ask him for my wages. I will use some to pay for the van to take me into the city to Church. For two weeks I have not left this house. Now I hear him coming so I will finish this letter. Please give my love to my mother and Geta. I will attach the address of Amudah and the phone number when I send this. Your sister, Lushan.

Fikir And Kay Lee FB While Kay Lee Does A Lot More Than Homework With Her Friend Elijah
Fikir and Kay Lee: Chicago/Wuqiao, China

Hello Kalkidane. Are you there?

Come on, woman, what are you doing? Put that phone down.

Stop Eli. Hey, check this out, see, this is my Ethiopian cousin Fikir in China.

What, is he Rastah? Does he do ganja?

No, actually, he's like a fanatical anti-ganja guy.

Well then I don't care about him. What do you think of this?

That tickles. Wait, this could be important. I haven't heard from him in months.

Hallo Fikir, How are you. Are you still in China? Eli, I mean it … Here take another toke. Don't worry. My parents won't be home until really late; we've got all the time in the world. Look, look, he's answering. Where is the lighter?

Yes I am still in China but I have left the WuChow Academy with some other Africans. We wait in a hotel in Beijing for a plane. There is Internet here. We have a circus contract to go to Germany.

Holy shit Eli, you gotta meet this guy. He's like fantastic at gymnastics and juggling and stuff. The Chinese brought him from Ethiopia to go to Chinese Acrobat School, which is amazing, because the Ethiopian government won't let anyone out; it's like a prison. No wait. I've got to answer him. Here look, I'll take it off. OK? Just let me answer.

Awesome, fantastic Fikir. Does that mean you will come to Chicago?

Kay Lee. You're beautiful.

You should see Miranda's. They are like 34 Ds. Wait, now it's your turn, take yours off. Go on. Hey look, what he says.

This is my hope to come to America, but first we go to Europe.

Wow Eli, you must work out. Your stomach is like all bumps. No, wait, give me another toke.

This is a secret. The Chinas and the Embassy think we are going to Ethiopia and then returning to China and so have given us our passports but we have a ticket to Moscow and then to Munich.

One minute, Eli, one minute.

Kay Lee, don't tease me.

Just let me finish this message. Here, wait. Let me do it. It's a weird button. OK. Here I am. Now wait.

Please if you email anyone in Ethiopia do not tell them this. My mother does not know. I will wait until I am in Germany, then I will phone her.

Don't worry, Fikir I will keep your secret. Have you heard from Selam?

No, she is not on Facebook for some months now. OK, I must say Goodbye.

Goodbye Fikir. Write me from Germany.

Kay Lee, So now put the phone down.

OK, like this is embarrassing because, like, there's going to be blood, like, right, like, is that OK?

Kay Lee, I know what to do. I will be so gentle. And look. I've got this.

Wow. OK, but first now give me another toke. Where's the lighter? Oh here. Thank you. I'm so nervous. Wait, I'm getting a call, I won't answer it. Now you lay down first and don't move your hands so much. Keep them there. Good. OK. You just lie there. I will put it on you. OK? OK? Now, give me your hand.

Heaven And Diamond Drink At The Sheraton
And Discuss Wolf's Hair
Helmut, Wolf, Helen and Selam:
Gaslight Nightclub, Sheraton – Adis Ababa

"Yah so Heaven, this is Wolf. He is my friend from Hamm. He plays football in our region and has come to work with Ethiopian boys training football. And you are Heaven's friend?"

"My name is Diamond."

"And you are from Heaven's town?"

"Yes, she was my classmate."

"And now you are working in Adis?"

"Helen, why does he have so much hair coming from his nose and ears?"

"Shuttup Selam, don't make me laugh. I mean Diamond. Farange men have hair everywhere, even on their back. Where did you get that name?"

"I found it on the Internet. There are many girls with names like that: Gold, Silver, even Platinum."

"Ahah, you two are laughing. You make a joke?"

"Helmut, she says that this friend of yours has such red hair, she wonders if he is from the devil?"

"Aha, she must know him well. Back in Hamm they call him Der Rote Striker. And what would you beautiful young women like to drink? Heaven, would you like to drink wine? And Diamond?"

"Please Helmut, wine."

"Always say "wine" to be high class. Champagne is for bar girls."

"So Wolf, what do you think of Madame Diamond? Isn't she beautiful?"

"My God, yes. I have never seen a girl with such eyes. Are they violet? This with her brown skin, and her lips and breasts. There are no women who look like this in Germany. But how old is she?"

"Do you really want to know?"

"Well I don't want to rob the cradle."

"Yes, you do."

"So Helmut, what do you say?"

"Wolf says that he has never seen women as beautiful as they are in Ethiopia?"

"Oh come on, you...I don't know the English word. You lie to fool women. We see German women, their hair is soft and yellow, and they are very tall and strong with their men, they would never be beaten. We want to be like them."

"Aha, yes, but they are too much like men. Don't you think Wolf?"

"German women are too fat. Their love is the love of a farmer for his sheep. She feeds you and fucks you so you follow her. Then she kills you and eats you."

"Ha, ha, ha!"

"Now, what does he say?"

"He says that he thinks that if all Ethiopian women are as beautiful as you and Diamond, then, except for his mother, Ethiopia wins. Here is the wine. Shall we drink to the beauty of Ethiopia?"

Say 'Prost.' And would you like to eat? Wolf, you must have the Ethiopian cultural food, injera with the meat combo. You eat it with your hands. Helen, what would you like? "

"Pizza California."

"And Diamond?"

"Hamburger."

"Hamburger and pizza? What, you do not want your cultural food?"

"Mr. Wolf, injera is our flesh. Everything here is injera. So you do not want to eat your own every day. It is hard to get out of Ethiopia, so this our way to escape, by eating hamburger and pizza."

"So, Helen, you eat German food?"

"There is none here. But when I come to Germany then I will learn this food and I will cook it."

"So you are coming to Germany. When do you do this?"

"Very soon. Helmut and I will be married."

"Ah, Helen, this was supposed to be a surprise for Wolf, and now you spoil it. I was waiting for the visa to make the announcement."

"Oh, Helmut, I am sorry. I did not know."

"Please let me congratulate you Helen. And Helmut, such a surprise! We must celebrate. I am speechless with happiness. We must have champagne. Waiter! Helmut, you must let me stand up for you at the wedding. And so, Helen, you will be the daughter to Madama Stromfurst, Helmut's mother. She is famous in Hamm. Ha ha!"

"Shuttup Wolf, you are drinking."

"And Helmut, I know Crystal is adventurous, but will Helen enjoy sharing the bed with her? Or will you pretend she is your sister? And what will you tell her about Marlene?"

"Dear Wolf, please shut the fuck up. I will tell you later."

"Helmut, what do you say?"

"We speak of my mother and sister and my family. When I will tell them and when the wedding will be. Please ladies, finish your wine, here is the champagne."

"Oh Helen, I can't believe you will leave Ethiopia. I will miss you so much. How do you think it will be?"

"I will live in a castle and drive a Mercedes Benz. Everyone will be very fat. The men will be big and hairy and the women will have huge tits like the black and white milk factory cow the Germans brought to the Children's Center. The one that ate 20 birr of hay every day and then died of the heat."

"Ha ha ha. I remember that cow. I think I drank milk from it at the Tekle's."

"And so now why do you laugh?"

"Oh, Helen is so funny. She says that when she goes to Germany she will buy a big German cow so that Helmut's children will have milk every day."

"Ah, so Helen, you want to be a farmer?"

"No, I want to be respiratory therapist."

"Oh why are we so serious? Come drink to the marriage. Helmut, Heaven, much happiness. But Diamond, you do not drink. You do not bless this marriage?"

"Oh yes, I am happy for Helen though I will cry when she leaves. But I am not used to so much drinking. I will fall down."

"Don't worry Ms. Sparkling Diamond. If you fall, I will carry you. Helmut, after we eat, are we not going to hear the Ethiopian music and see the cultural dancing? Diamond will you love to dance?"

"Yes, Wolf, I will take you to Kasanchis. To the Azmari Hotspot. So now please drink."

"To the marriage of Helen and Helmut and Pizza and Burger and Injera. How do they say in English?"

"The English say, 'Bottoms up' ".

"Ah, dear Helen, yes, I see your English has improved. I will drink to that. So, to all our bottoms: Up and up and up."

Lushi Runs Away
Lushan: Dubai

Dubai Times, 15 April 2013: Referring to the recent case of three children who were stabbed by an Ethiopian maid in Al Warqa recently, the officer said that the maid claimed she was ill treated by her employers. The maid, he said, claimed that she was not paid for three months and that her sponsor was "aggressive" with her, because of which she committed the crime. The terrified Emirati children, who sustained serious injuries after the maid allegedly attacked them with a cleaver, locked themselves in the bathroom, from where one of them managed to call the police.

Mommy:

I don't know where I will be if you get this letter, but please, if it reaches you, try to show this to someone in the Ethiopian Embassy, and ask Eden or Geta to email Mrs. Lisa. I am in a lot of trouble here and hope that I can find a way to escape from Dubai and come back home. Here is what happened: Ato Amudah tried to rape me, and the Old Mother and the Mistress beat me with an electrical cord and said that I was a prostitute who should die. So I ran away from their house. The problem is about the contract with Amudah and the debt to Ato Mikal; I am afraid I will go to prison because I cannot pay them back. In the meantime I have nothing here. I have no money for a plane ticket and Southern Sun Agency holds my passport, so I am trapped. Maybe the embassy will help me.

And if they say that I was a whore, do not believe them. In no way did I indicate to Amudah that I would give him sex. Even after he offered me a lot of money, I said no. I cried. I reminded him of his wife and kids, and asked him please to let me do my work, but he would not leave me alone. So when he entered my room while I was sleeping and touched me below the waist, and put his mouth on mine, I screamed at him and fought him, I bit his lip and scratched his face, so then he hit me and yelled that I was a prostitute. Then his wife and mother came in the room and the Old Mother whipped my legs with an electrical cord while Amudah sat on me and the mistress said she would kill me. Even the little boy was beating me and calling me, "Nigger." Then they locked me in my room. Oh, Mommy how I cried for you to help me.

In the next day, I called and called that I had to use the toilet and that I was hungry. Finally Amudah unlocked the room and said that his family was away and that I could use the toilet. I tied my things in my scarf and went into the toilet and locked the door, then I opened the window, climbed out the window, jumped to the pavement and ran to the little building behind the house where the air conditioner motor is, and closed the door. I could hear Amudah calling my name but I did not answer. I waited all afternoon in the shed with the door closed, so scared that he would open the door. It was so hot I thought I would die. And there were spiders. Just before it was dark I opened the door and saw no one, so I used a waste bin on the side of the shed as a step to climb onto its roof. Behind it was a road bordered with sand and many cars. I waited until there were no cars and then jumped into the sand. Then I walked along the road with my scarf tied around my head like an Islam. When cars did come I turned away and covered myself because here if the police see an African walking they will stop you and ask for identification. Soon I came to a bus stop. Then came a van that Bangla Desh workers take back to their quarters in the city. The cost was 3 Dirham and I was lucky to have it in my pocket. It took me to a place in the Center near where the beggars sleep.

Oh mother, you think Dubai is richer than even America but there are many desperate people on the streets from other countries. Many beg and are arrested. Others die in the road and then their body is picked up. In the beggars square I did not sleep but sat in there all night on the stone steps always apart from the other women and their babies, and without water. In the morning they said a Kenya woman was dead from sickness and dehydration, so I quickly prayed for her and then left that place. By asking, I found the Church where the Ethiopians go and waited for the Ethiopian time there – it is shared with other Christians, Catholics and Protestants. More Abesha came and waited with me. Finally in the hot middle of the day the Catholic time was done and an Orthodox Priest summoned us into the air conditioning and gave us food and water. "Oh Father," I asked him, "please you must call the Embassy, my employer tried to rape me," but he would not call because he said that the Embassy told him that if he brought them any more complaints from maids the Emirati would ask the Ethiopian government to replace him, and this was a good job that he could not afford to forfeit. The priest said that many Ethiopian girls and women who have run away live in an apartment together and that I should go there.

So now I am here with five other girls. We have no money and only food brought by a woman from Ethiopian Airlines who helps us privately. I gave her this letter and she promised to bring it to Ethiopia and mail it. Oh Mommy, if you get this, please contact the Ethiopian Embassy and also ask the police to arrest Ato Mikel. Also contact Mrs. Lisa and Mr. Marc. I don't know how I will live. The Dubai police sometimes put girls who have run away in a prison, where there is much disease. The sick and the well are all crammed together and the prison guards rape the young girls and give them HIV. Gelila here has been in the prison, and she says that there are many suicides. Her family sold three cattle to buy back her contract but still the Agency will not give her her passport.

Mommy, I am praying that this letter will reach you and that I will soon be going to school back in Dice Dota. I promise you I will never leave again and that I will stay with you and help your life until you are the oldest woman in the world.

Your daughter, Lushan.

Marc Discusses The Nature Of Statutory Rape
With Elijah, A Prime Offender
Marc, Kay Lee and Elijah Johnson: **Chicago**

"Kay Lee."

"Kay Lee. Open the door. I know you are in there. Open the door."

"Kay Lee I heard you. Who's there with you?"

"Nobody."

"Kay Lee, I heard you. Open the door."

"Nobody's in here, Dad."

"Look, who ever you are, I am Kay Lee's father and you better come out of that room right now, or I'll call the cops. She's fifteen."

"Dad it's not his fault. I told him I was seventeen."

"Kay Lee, you stay in your room. Listen whoever you are, get out here right now. I've got the phone in my hand. I'm dialing. 9...1..."

"Dad, don't have a cow."

"Kay Lee...you stay in your room."

"Please shut the door. My name's Marc. I'm Kay Lee's Dad."

"You're not my real Dad."

"Kay Lee you stay in there, or I'll become your unreal Dad real fast."

"Excuse me Mister, what's your name?"

"Elijah. Sir."

"Last name?"

"Johnson. Sir."

"How old are you, Mr. Elijah Johnson?"

"Nineteen. Sir."

"Nineteen, and Kay Lee's fifteen. So Mr. Johnson, can I call you Eli? How do you want spend your time in jail, Mr. Eli, lifting weights, working in the laundry, taking a course or just staring at the wall?"

"I told him I was seventeen, Dad."

"She told me she was seventeen, Sir."

"We used a condom, Dad."

"Where do live, Mr. Johnson?"

"I live with my Mom and Dad, Sir, in Rogers Park."

"How did you meet Kay Lee?"

"I met him online, Dad."

"Oh Jesus, Kay Lee."

"It's not what you think Dad, it's for kids who are adopted."

"So you are adopted?"

"...from Ethiopia, Dad."

"From a place called Wallo."

"That's up north?"

"That's what they tell me. I left when I was little. I came from an orphanage in the town of Desse."

"And your parents?"

"They say that my parents died in the drought of '94. You know, the one that was on TV. My Mom and Dad found me through an agency in 1995. They thought I was two. We celebrate my birthday on the day I left Ethiopia. It was Michael Jackson's 38th birthday."

"What do you do now, Mr. Eli Johnson?"

"I go to Truman. I study music. And I go out on jobs with my Dad. He's a plumber."

"Well, Eli, I'm sure you've got some scales to practice or some sinks to install so why don't you leave now, but before you do, give me your phone number. And don't let me see you around here. I will call you in a couple of days and tell you whether I will press charges."

"Dad, you won't press charges. I seduced him."

"Cook County. It's a hell of a place. I get kids out of there all the time. You ever been there?"

"DAD, stop, I seduced him."

"Is that true Eli?"

"Sir, my phone is 773-889-9376."

"Is that yours or your parents?"

"Mine."

"I'm writing it down. OK, please leave now. Close the front door behind you."

"OK Kay Lee."

"Don't come in Dad."

"Why not?"

"Because I'm fucking naked that's why."

"Kay Lee, please don't curse in the house."

"Mom does it all the fucking time."

"Kay Lee, give me your phone."

"No way, Dad."

"I said give me your phone."

"Dad, it doesn't fucking matter if I give you my fucking phone. I can still get in touch with fucking Eli on my fucking computer, which by the way I need to do my fucking homework, so you can't take that away, and it's a fucking phone too in case you didn't know, and if I have to I can use Miranda's fucking phone or any of my friend's fucking phones, or use a computer with a fucking phone at the fucking library. You can't fucking stop me from fucking talking to Eli."

"It looks like I can't stop you from fucking Eli, either."

"Dad, it was consensual."

"But you are underage."

"Dad, how old were you when you got laid? I chose him. I chose him. He's beautiful and he knew what to do."

"You better tell your Mom right away. I can't keep this from her."

"How old was Mom when she did it?"

"Didn't she ever tell you?"

"Yeah, but she told me not to tell you."

"OK Kay Lee, I want you to know something. Of the six billion members of the Human Being Club, three billion of them have balls, loaded with 280 million sperms *per ejaculation*, all pointed at you, Sweetie."

"Dad, that's really romantic."

"And every month for the next 35 years or so, you will, unless you modify the process through a process known as birth control, present a target called an egg that sends out messages to any of the 3 billion times 280 million sperms saying Hey, Hey, Hey Spermyzoa, don't dry out and die, get into me, come visit, I'm the girl next door, come on in, let's replicate."

"Dad, in Ethiopia I'd already have a kid and another on the way. Or in the projects for that matter. So what's the big deal? I'm not stupid. At least we used a condom."

"That's your Mom coming in the door. Go tell her."

"Yeah, but Dad, first I have to use the bathroom."

"I mean it. I don't want to be the one to tell her."

"Dad, you're standing in the door and I really have to go to the bathroom. MOM! I'LL BE DOWN IN A MINUTE. I'M TAKING A SHOWER. HOW'S GRANDMA? Dad, so can you move?"

2014

Abeynesh Risks Her Job At Ethiopian Airlines
To Help A Runaway Maid
Abeynesh: **Dubai**

IOL news April 15th, 2011: A housemaid chopped off a man's penis after he pestered her for a massage, police told the Daily Mail. The Ethiopian woman, who is in her 20s, told the officer that she had reached the end of her tether following abuse at the hands of her 70-year-old Emirati boss and lashed out with a knife – slicing off his private parts. The maid has been charged with assault, the paper said, while the Emirati man is recovering in hospital. It was not clear if his severed member had been re-attached..

Oh, I have committed a crime so now I risk losing my job and going to hell in an Arab jail. All this for someone I hardly know. Why do I do this?

Yah, this girl is one of the runaway maids I brought food to. Stupid me, running from work to do this charity. I didn't have time to change, so when we met the women in the apartment, this one saw from my uniform that I was at Ethiopian Airlines and immediately asked me could she get work with the airline too. She was smart and alert like a hungry cat, waiting for her chance. Of course she lied when I asked her age, she said she was nineteen but obviously she was no more than fifteen; she was just getting her woman's body and you could tell from how she moved it was new for her. And she lied when I asked her how much school she had; she said 11 years but I knew only 8 or 9, she had not even taken her exams for high school, this lost girl. Of course I said that it would be impossible for her to find work at the airline, she would have to finish university to be considered, but now I see she asked me that question just to find out where I worked. And she gave me a letter to mail to her mother in Dice Dota, which I did.

Some days later I am going into my building after work when suddenly there is a burkah at my elbow, asking in a girl's voice in Amharic, please Weyzero, remember me, I am the maid in the apartment who gave you a letter, please I must talk to you. How had she found me? She had hidden herself in a burkah and walked miles to wait by the Ethiopian Airline Building door until I came out from work Then she had followed me home.

My heart is soft, I want to let her in, but there is the guard at the door of my building. For an Arab woman to go in with an Ethiopian woman, that is not normal, the guard might notice and ask us for identification and they told us at work that the helper of a runaway maid goes to prison. These Dubai devils would punish me. So I tell her to act like she is the Arab mother and to clap her hands for me to follow. An Arab woman ordering an African woman to follow will not seem irregular and the guard will not ask her for ID. This works and so we take the elevator to my apartment. It is obvious that this girl is not used to an elevator. When it starts to go up she presses her hands flat behind her on the elevator wall, her fingers and nails scrabbling the metal siding for something to hang on to in case the elevator were to fall. She is really from the country.

This girl comes into my flat and emerges from the burkha; she is very young and ragged and dirty, and she needs a mother and a sister and a friend; she is a beautiful Abesha girl and now I am really in trouble.

Yes, yes, I know, dear lost girl, the labor immigration officer has your passport and visa, you have no money, you have no clothes and you are indentured to a job broker. You have run away from your employer and now your worst fear is that if the Arabs catch you they will send you to the woman's prison where the guards will rape you and then you will get sick and pregnant, you and your baby will die there, and no one in your family will ever hear what happened to you. "She disappeared in Dubai," they will say, "we hope she's still alive," and no one, NO ONE will ever know your name or who you were or what you did in your life, and your family will gradually forget you and your memory will die with your mother and your brothers and sisters. Even if your family sold everything they had they could not buy your freedom from the employment agency. You are lost, lost in the coldest hot place in the world.

Diamond And The Wolf
Selam and Wolf: **Sheraton Room 314, Adis Ababa**

So, Diamond, how do you find the Sheraton? Please don't call me Mister you must call me just Wolf. You know it is the most beautiful hotel in Adis; the rooms are as big as an apartment. Wouldn't you like to stay here? Of course, you are welcome. And please have a drink. Would you like Scotch? No? Wine? No? Yes, I understand, there was much drinking already and much dancing too, you must be tired. Me, I can go all night. Yes, well then please do not stand, here come sit here with me. Let me help you get comfortable, let me take your shoes. No, I *want* to, this is what men do for women in my country, yes, we make ourselves crazy so that they feel good. It is not the same as the men here.

Here, put your feet up, I will massage them. Don't be ashamed of your shoes. Listen, you will have much better shoes tomorrow. I will buy you some. Would you like that? No, you must not thank me. For me the cost of the shoes is no more than the cost of chewing gum. And you are worth much more than that. Am I rich? Well, they do not think me rich in Germany, but here, yes, I think so. What do you call rich?

How does that feel? Oh come on, relax. Isn't it a pleasure to have your feet rubbed after dancing? Don't your boyfriends do that for you? You have no boyfriend? How can that be? A girl as beautiful as you? Your legs are very beautiful. And the skin is very soft. There. And there. Here, how does that feel?

You should relax. What is the matter, didn't you think this would happen? Come on, why else would you come to this hotel if you did not expect this? Look at you, it is like you are made of sticks, come on, let go, don't stop me, let me take it off so I can see you, don't be ashamed, please, you are lucky you are so beautiful. Your beauty will bring you power and money if you want it.

Men will give you everything if you let them make love to you. It's a natural thing. You do not have to be ashamed.

How do you like that? Boys have done this before with you. No? Oh. Here, here let me see you. You are perfect. You should be a model. Yes, I am not lying, I have never seen anyone as beautiful as you. Why do you repeat this? I know you are fifteen. You have told me this. There is nothing I can do to make you older. Except this.

Oh yes, of course, you are scared. Really, Diamond, this is your first? With this little dress that shows everything and all this make-up and drinking champagne like a little whore, it is just acting? So, this is good, I am the right man, I will not hurt you, I will use a condom, I know what I am doing, you will feel good, you will feel better than you have ever felt. I will teach you. You will become an artist at this, an artist at love.

So now, let see all of you. Lie there and I will take them off. Oh yes, here, come on, yes, let me hold you. There, that's better. And you do the same. You hold me. It is not just the man who does everything. It is a dance. It is like a dance. It is where dancing comes from.

So here, now I will kiss you, see, is that good? No, no, no, you must relax, or it will not work, nothing will work if you don't let go. Can you? Give up all this tension? Can you kiss me? No, not like that, you must relax your jaw and open your mouth. Not like the dentist, my dear, this is not a tooth pulling. This is soft. Love is soft.

Can you speak? Diamond, can you speak?

OK here, give me your hand. Here feel this. Here open your eyes. See this. So you will not look? If you would open your eyes, you would see, I am putting on the condom. So there is no need to be scared. You will not get pregnant.

No, no, no, don't cry, Diamond, it's OK, it's what every woman must learn. Your mother learned this. So here, I am putting this here. Now open, open your legs. Diamond, I cannot do this unless you let me.

Diamond, please, stop crying, please, shhhhh, shhhhh. Jesus, STOP. Where are you going? Look you broke the glass. What, will you cut me? No, no, NOT so loud, the whole hotel will hear you. Stop. Stop. Please stop.

No, stay here. Do not go out from the room. I will not hurt you. Please put down the glass. You will hurt yourself. OK, then go into the bathroom. It's OK, it's OK, I will not force you if you cannot accept me. It's OK. It's OK. You are too young for this Diamond, put the glass in this wastebasket and here take your clothes, go in the bathroom. Go. Take your clothes. Be calm. It's OK. It's OK. Go in there. Forgive me for thinking you might want this. You are not ready.

Diamond, you do not need to lock the door. I will not follow you.

You are welcome to stay here this night.

Do not worry, I will not rape you.

It will be like with my daughter, Regina. She is nine years old.

If you want, I will read to you in German.

How Abeynesh Brought Lushi To Meet
The Gujarati, Hedeyat Pakir,
Who Hires Lushi To Cook On The Dhow "Sea Tiger"
As It Takes A Boatload Of House Paint To Somalia.
Lushan and Selam: **Adis Ababa**

Selam, hey look, there's an Internet Café, we must go there. Come on. I want to see if I can find that woman from Ethiopian Airlines on the internet, Abeynesh, the one that saved me. Will you help me find her? If we look for the staff of Ethiopia Airlines in Dubai maybe we can find her. I want to tell her I am safe and that I will send her 20 pairs of panties when I have money. I want to tell her that I will name my daughter after her. When I have a daughter she will be Abeynesh, I swear it.

All the computers are taken. Can we wait? Can we order coffee? Do you have money? Thank you, sister you are too generous, someday I will buy you things too, someday when I have my own business.

OK, I *will* finish the story. So I told you, I followed her from Ethiopian Airlines and she took me up to her flat. Once we were there we could speak Amharic. She was very nervous that she would get arrested. She told me that at her work they all were warned; the government was cracking down. If she got caught helping a runaway maid she would lose her job *and* go to Dubai Woman's Prison for three months. So she had to get me out of her place. But still, she would help me, she would take me to the Somali Souk and introduce me to a man who might be able to get me to Somalia on a boat.

Jesus, Somalia. When she said that I remembered what Poppa said: when the Angel Lucifer left Heaven before he went to Hell he stopped there. And to cross the Arabian Sea on a boat? I was thinking; I do not swim, sharks could take my leg or my arm. But how else will I get out of Dubai with no money and no papers? I will be arrested the minute any of the Guardians ask me for identification and these Guardians are everywhere and then I will go to the woman's prison. Hell would be better than that. And the women say that Somali men, even though they love to kill and will steal the nails from your fingers, they respect women. So I decided the boat was the only way.

That woman was so kind, like a mother, she fed me injera and wat, and let me wash in her shower. She gave me a blouse and slacks and her own panties. I promise, some day I will buy her twenty pairs. I wished so hard I could have stayed there and that when I was a woman I would have an apartment like hers. In that hot room with the other maids, we were crowded like animals and could not wash ourselves or our clothes except in the kitchen sink. Always one of us was menstruating. We could not go out. To be clean, to have clothes and food and not be in the rain or dust, sometimes there is nothing better than just that.

So then she said we must go. I covered myself again in the burkah and we both went down in the elevator and out the door past the guard, me snapping fingers at Abeynesh as if she was too slow. And then she led me from behind to a metro stop where she bought tickets from a machine and then, oh my God, we boarded a train with no driver. The train went into the ground and then rose back up to the light of day, past the tall buildings along the harbor and then along the waterfront where they have built cities on the water. Those Arabs have so much money; if they wanted, they could construct a mountain range higher than Ras Dashen out of rocks they got from the moon. And they would hire Bengalis and Filipinos to build it.

We got off the train at the Gold Souk. There, for the first time in Dubai, I felt safe. I was not just an African with Arabs. I was with everyone in the world, all in the street, and no one could tell me from anyone; there were Chinas, Africans, Whites, Arabs, Indians and Indonesians, men and women. The reason is the gold. Oh Selam, in this neighborhood of Deira there is shop after shop full of gold jewelry; rings and pendants, earrings and necklaces, such beautiful treasures to wear, I have never seen anything like it, and all races and tribes of people are there because all people love gold. They are buying, trading, trying things on and bargaining. Oh my God, I could look at these beautiful things for the whole day. One ring would buy me a year, one necklace – my life. But I could not stay to look. Abeynesh needed to get me away from there, so we walked through the Gold Souk to the Somali Souk to find her friend with the boat.

On one side of the Gold Souk is the Somali Souk where they sell everything you can imagine. This is why everyone comes to Dubai. It is the market for the world. In one store that sold paints and building things she found Ato Hedeyat, the Gujerati who owned the dhow that would be leaving for Somalia. I waited in the store while Abeynesh spoke with him in the back. I don't know if she gave him money or what, but when they came out she took my hand and said, "Goodbye, good luck my daughter, you will go to the boat, you will cook, you will clean fish and you will do what you are asked. This man is Gujerati Hindu, he and his family do business with my brother in Harrar. I have told them you are a relative. They will protect you and help you get to Ethiopia once you land in Berbera." Then she left.

Oh Selam, so when we are finished with the coffee,can I go on a computer and find her? I am so grateful.

This Ato Hedeyat was a small man, only some centimeters taller than me, wide-shouldered and hard, maybe 35, leather colored, I thought from sun on the sea, an Indian man with a square head of straight black hair and a mustache, who wore the long white shirt of Indians and tire sandals. The first thing he did was take the cloth of my burkah in his hand and shake his head. He pointed to the back of the shop and said, "Toilet."

OK, I understood, for him, a Hindu man, to walk with an Arab woman could mean trouble with the Social Police. When I returned dressed in the clothes that Abeynesh had given me, he handed me a shopping bag for the folded cloth. Then after speaking to a Somali behind the cash register and embracing him he gestured for me to follow. We walked through the Souk to the river where the dhows are all tied up.

Hundreds of them and hundreds, tied to platforms in the river that goes from Dubai to the sea, some so big you could put all the little boats in Lake Gumare on one of them and still have room to put on a car or many motorcycles. There was a fence and a checkpoint with a guard between the road and the floating pathways that led to the boats, but this did not disturb Ato Hedeyat. Before the checkpoint he turned back to me and spoke to me in English without even knowing I could understand: "You are my wife." At the checkpoint he spoke to the Guard in Arabic and pointed to me. Oh my God my heart was beating like when I got on the airplane. If the Guard asked for ID, how would I escape from the woman's prison? It would be impossible. I would die.

But I did not need to be scared; there was no problem. Ato Hedeyat put his arm around the Guard's shoulders and smiling held him close. At the same time he gave him something in the hand. The guard laughed and gave me a sex look, up and down my whole body, then opened the gate and so I passed through the first door to escape Dubai. But how many other barriers would there be? If there were a storm would I drown in the Arabian Sea? Even if I escaped the sharks, how would I find Somalia?

We walked to the outermost platform past all sizes and designs of dhows full of cargo; motorcycles, wooden crates, oil, lumber and metal drums. Men moved the freight on wagons and carts shouting and giving directions and a tower with a cable lifted a car over my head and put it down next to another car on a dhow. Behind us were the tallest buildings of Dubai, the highest in the world some said. Only two months before I had known only Dice Dota and now I felt I was in the middle of all of life. Selam, do you know the edge where fear turns to excitement? That's what I walked when I entered the dhow of Ato Hedeyat. Suddenly I knew I would never die.

The boat was large and sat low in the water. On the back was written *Samudra Vāgha*. Ato Hedeyat pointed to the words and said, "Sea Tiger." The open part was filled with barrels of paint and men were tying them down with ropes and chains. Between the walkway and the boat was a plank onto the boat and Ato Hedeyat gestured for me to cross over on it. I did not show my fear of falling as I stepped across it. All the men stopped working and looked from me to Ato Hedeyat who followed me. Once on the boat he took my hand and spoke to them in his Indian language. I think what he said was like a father; "You must respect this girl." Then to me in English, "What is your name, Abesha?"

"I am Lushan," I said and pointed to myself for all the men to know. "Lushan."

"Here," said Hedeyat in English, "Sagar will show you where you sleep and work and be your teacher."

One of the workingmen put down his rope and came up the stairs to the raised part of the back of the boat where we stood. He was really a boy, not so much older than me. The eyes that snapped a quick glance to take me in and then looked down and away were just like his father's. He was Heydeyat's son, Sagar.

The men's looks burnt my back as I followed the boy to a small enclosure at the rear of the boat, a kitchen with shelves, a knife rack and cutting place, two gas burners on a table with a gas tank underneath, and a water barrel and a washbasin. Bowls, spoons and sacks of food and drying things; dates, lentils, onions and garlic were kept in nets on the walls. This is where I would work, cooking. But where would I sleep? And wash? Was I the only female on the boat?

Oh my God, Lushi, you must have been afraid with all those men.

Selam, let me tell you, after being with the Arabs, if the Somalis had been lepers I still would have thought it better to go with them.

But how are these Indians?

They are different. And the boy Sagar, he was…oh, here is the coffee.

How was he?

Selam I will tell you, but first, would you mind if I ordered some cake?

Life In China Acrobat School And The Many Tricks Fikir Learned There, Especially How To Escape
Fikir: New Orleans

"African students have fairly good physical condition and relatively better balance and flexibility compared to their Chinese counterparts. The students will stay at the school for two years. During that time they will learn acrobatic skills and complete internships with two major troupes in Hebei. The school has assigned professional trainers and Chinese language teachers to assist them in their daily lives." – Ma Shumin, a teacher at the Wuqiao Acrobatic Art School: http://www.ecns.cn/2013/11-04/86970.shtml

Selam, I have asked my mother to find you and give you this letter. I write you from New Orleans in the USA. Yes maybe you heard and didn't believe it but it is true. I am in America. And, I am sorry that I stopped writing you. Someone wrote me that you had joined Helen at Seven Nights and were sleeping with Germans, so I was angry. But I don't care now. Whatever you have done, I still want to be your man and I promise you that when I have money I will send for you and we can marry in the USA. I promise you this.

You know that I was in China. After China I went to a circus in Germany and then to Atlanta in America for another circus, but, the Director in Atlanta, I fought with him and so I ran away to my cousin Binyam's in New Orleans. But now I have to get out of New Orleans, I have trouble here, so I will go to Chicago where your sister Kalkidane lives. And I will find a job there and send for you.

My God, the places I have been since I left Dice Dota. I think I barely remember how life was back home. Here in the USA nothing is like they say. It is a tough and dangerous place with many criminals. There is no structure.

Not like China. Everything in China was structure. You would not believe how it has changed me, China and all the training. I am more disciplined than a soldier now. Anything I want to do, I know I can achieve. Even here in the capital of gangsters.

I have nothing to do for hours until my bus to Chicago so let me tell you about China. After I was chosen by the Gymnastics Association we had a party and then I went to Adis and met the others, and then we took the plane, my first one. I know, my stomach jumped, but looking down, how fantastic. We flew for hours until we landed in China and then in the dark we drove a long way until we got to the Gymnastics Academy of Wuqiao. The first week was easy – orientation. The Chinas showed us around and told us what we would be doing. They were very nice. We were amazed to see the hard training and how the hundreds of little Chinas knew so much more than we did of acrobatics and juggling. How we all wanted to start work to learn the tricks they knew! We all remembered Mullanae who had gone to China two years before and then had won an invitation to join the African Circus in Munich. He had built a house for his family and was going back and forth to Germany all the time. With this training we knew that we could take same path he did, to get out of Ethiopia and work all over the world. Who could believe this chance?

They gave all the Africans rooms on one floor, 23 of us, Kenyas, Tanzanias and Ethiopians, four to a room, with two bathrooms and a common room with a television, refrigerator and a computer! You know my house in Dice Dota was not poor. We had electric and a gas stove from bottles, but still, to live in a big hall with an inside bathroom and showers that came out of a wall, and no animals outside. In the first week I thanked God a thousand times for selecting me for China.

Our social director, Ying Wjen lived on our floor too but in her own room. She didn't speak Amharic so our language was English and in this she was not so advanced. She showed us how to eat with sticks and how to say "no pork" in China language. She showed us the town and introduced us to the shopkeepers. I think that we were the only Black people in the region. In two years I didn't see any others that were not in the school. You know the Chinese people in the town were really nice. I loved them.

And they are the smartest race when it comes to control. If you are late you are not punished by hitting or told to go away like in Ethiopia. No, they act kind, and tell you that this is a problem they will help you solve by extra training, which is only available in the early hours before the regular training or on your day off, which is one day every two weeks and is your only chance to leave the school. So they help you instead of punish and it works better; I always had a problem getting to school on time in Ethiopia, it was hard to leave my bed. In China in the first month I was late twice and so I had to get up one hour earlier than the others for extra training and could not leave the school for a month. And the extra training was not real training. It was cleaning the gymnastic mats and disinfecting the equipment. That helped me never to be late.

In the second week the training began and what we thought was God's luck became gymnastics hell. Up before breakfast for stretching, then gymnastics drill until lunch, then a rest, then aerial and trapeze until dinner. After dinner – acrobatics, then juggling, then stretch, shower and sleep. This was before our muscles and hands and feet got hard; we hurt so much. After evening training and shower we would be in our rooms and the girls would start talking about how much they missed their families, and how much their legs hurt, and that their hands and feet were bleeding. They would all cry together, and when we heard them, us boys in our rooms, because we were in the same shape they were, we would cry too, except we would never weep together as women do, no, we would just sniffle alone in our beds. Oh how we all wanted to get out of there.

And we would talk big in our beds about who would lead the revolution against the Chinas and be the spokesperson the next day to demand they let us out of gymnastics prison. But then we would argue; if the Chinas send us back to Ethiopia, would we get in trouble with Woyane and the gymnastics federations for disgracing Ethiopia and lose the one chance we had to get out of there and be big people in the world? Would we have to live with our parents and suck the ass of the government for years to get any kind of job? If these little Chinas could submit to this training then why could not we? Were we just lazy and weak? And then because we were so tired in our rooms with our sore muscles and bleeding we would fall asleep and in the morning we would bandage each other and go to training without any word of rebellion.

And this was all part of the China's plan, they really are smarter about people than any other race. They knew that if you present an athlete with an impossible task and then slowly build his strength and endurance to accomplish it, then he will learn to do tricks he never believed he could do, and he will change, he will become excited for himself, he will believe he can learn anything, he will know that pain is part of achievement and he will search for more pain. The China students know this from when they are little but we had never learned to work like that. The teaching in Ethiopia is all based on fear of being dismissed, not on talent. If you are an obedient donkey you advance even if you know nothing. At the end of three months we had learned how to work. There were new materials, ribbons, and trapeze, foot juggling of heavy things, pyramids and balancing and many new gymnastic tricks. I grew new muscles, and more important, I learned: the more pain – the more power.

None of the other Africans bothered to learn China language. So, after some months, even though I was not the best acrobat, I became a leader because I got the language fast. I would study during the rest time. The Chinas don't speak English. Ying Wjen was the only translator in the whole school and she was at grade school level which was a problem with medical, you could be dying and she would think you were just in pain from the training. My China language saved Tikun. He was a boy from Desse, really strong, one of those who can be the base of the pyramid and hold up seven or eight, but he got a sickness in his kidney and was in too much pain to train. I told Ying and told her, "Sick, sick, die, he will die, he is pissing blood," and she came back with aspirin pills and China medicine saying, "Two weeks, two weeks." So I practiced my speech before I went to the Director's office.

"I want to speak China to you," I said. "Your translator does not understand, Tikun has a kidney problem and he needs to go to hospital immediately." And so they called the Embassy and they took Tikun away to a hospital. We heard that the Embassy flew him back to Ethiopia. I don't know where he is now – maybe he died. If not, with this sickness, it was probably the end of his chance.

After that, for communication, the directors went through me and so did the African students. And then a good thing happened. I told the director that I knew video and asked if I could have access to a camera and so they let me have a camera and I began to video our training. That is when the whole idea started…of sending video to Europe to get an invitation to a circus.

On the Internet we contacted Mullanae at Circus Mama Africa. He told us that in the next year the promoter would need a new group. We should start practicing different tricks, working with silk, perfecting "standing towers," making a love act in the air and always with comedy; acts they did not have. And only when we were excellent should we make a tape to send to Germany and not one with edits, but our whole routine in one long shot. The group was me, Mekeda and Kifle, and the girls, Nyala and Sintayehu; we had to make the tape in secret, for if the Chinas had known that we were making video for Europe they would have taken our equipment away. We told our teachers that we wanted to watch ourselves on video in order to improve and so the teachers let us stay late after they left at seven. Every night we worked on the act and the video; practicing, arguing, laughing and shooting. We made three scenes: JUNGLE LOVE in the ribbons; a falling in love between two birds up high and two lions down below in which the lions want to eat the birds for their wedding feast and the birds want to steal the lion's hair to make their wedding nest; LIFE ON THE OMO; acrobatics with painted masks and costumes like the Mursi tribe, standing on each other to find fruit in the trees, juggling sticks and baskets and changing shape with different ones somersaulting in the air to the top place; and then SPAGHETTI; making fun of farange. We are African waiters dropping and catching trays of food, juggling and spinning them until the hungry fat farange gets angry and chases the Ethiopian thief on the wire with fallings, catches and saves, while the waiters juggle chairs and cabbages.

It was cold in the rooms and the training hall and we worked very hard. Everybody was hurting. But we finally had a good tape using costumes and props that we made and hid from our teachers, with close-ups and good music that we got from the Internet. Now the next problem was how to send the tape? To buy a stamp we needed a passport and the Ethiopian Embassy had given our documents to the school. A good thing about China is that in terms of corruption it is like Ethiopia; many people do not take the law so seriously so it was not hard through the butcher Ying Li to find someone in the town to buy us stamps and then to find someone in the postal service to put the DVD into the mail. And it worked; Mullanae emailed us back saying that the producer liked this and would send an invitation and money for plane fare to his contact in the Ethiopian Embassy in Beijing to hold for us. If we made the connection, then we could get visas from Germany. But how would we get to Beijing and find this contact? The Chinas only let us walk to the town from the school once every two weeks. And there was no way to sneak to Beijing without being noticed. No Chinas are Black.

But actually this was why I was able to go to Beijing and get the invitation. You see, the Chinas are happy when they see Blacks doing the same tricks that only they do and the rulers of the school knew that to amaze their people and become more famous they should put some Blacks on their tour, so they took us with one of their student groups –THE AMAZING CHAMPIONS OF WUQIAO, six China boys and China girls, all under fifteen, and the five of us – the ETHIOPIA STARS. So in the winter we traveled in vans to more than six or seven cities. It was the first time I had been to any of China outside of the school and the town close by, and by traveling I saw their agriculture and factories and realized that Ethiopia was only as big as one province of China and that Adis was a village compared to Shanghai or Beijing. And, surprisingly, the tour all worked without problems and I think that was because all the Chinas are of the same tribe with the same language and with the identical religion of communism, so there is no tension between peoples like at home. And here was the luck; the top performance was in Beijing at the All African Union Brotherhood Festival. Can you believe this? The China Prime Minister was there and the Ethiopian minister *Yonas Kidame* too, *Yonas* from Tigre, who hates all Adamu people and keeps us down below the Tigre and the Oromo, *Yonas* whose police shot Andamu farmers by the GDZ when I was making gymnastics at the Children's Center up the hill. I heard the shots. I saw the trucks pick up the bodies.

Here's my secret: God help me if I ever tell my mother, she will forbid me to be her own son because I did not turn away; *Yonas greeted us and embraced me.* And I smiled and made my eyes big while I looked through him, thinking of the next day, our sight-seeing day, when we would miss our appointment with our guide and meet Mullanae's contact from the German Embassy, Mr. Otto, at a Japanese Restaurant close to the dormitory. That is where we signed a contract for ETHIOPIA STARS to be in Germany on April 15 for rehearsal, and filled out the visa applications for Germany. This was all kept secret from the Chinas and the Ethiopian Embassy. Mr. Otto would contact me by email when he had the visas and then he would buy the plane tickets to Germany and meet us in Beijing. He gave us Euro to buy our own laptop. Now we could edit our video and photos and talk by skype to anyone in the world.

So we were back in the school, making promotions, continuing training and now doing the politics to leave China. This is when we contacted Mekeda's friend at the Ethiopian Embassy whose name I cannot mention, but who I will call Ato X to protect him, because of course we gave him money to ask him if he could help fix a problem; we have contracts for jobs and visas for working in Germany so can the Embassy please ask the school to release our passports? First, as expected, the school disagrees; it says the agreement with the Ethiopian Gymnastics Federation is that the five Ethiopian students will spend two years in the training program and then return to Ethiopia. But then Mekeda's Ato X, asks again, insisting, please, the Gymnastics Federation is not the government, do not argue, can you release their passports so these children can return to Ethiopia? So then the school says yes and gives us our passports. The school has a special ceremony, they give us a diploma and pictures. We pack everything, all our costumes and props and we get ready to go to Beijing. The school sends a teacher in a van with us to Beijing. His mission is to drop us at the Ethiopian Embassy At the Embassy, Ato X is there to greet us, the teacher leaves and then we immediately move with all our stuff to a hotel where Mr. Otto is waiting with our visas, our tickets for Germany and our Euros.

The school has notified the Chinese Embassy in Adis that we would arrive in Adis. But instead we take a train to the airport and catch a plane to go to Germany. All our papers are correct and they let us onto the plane. But we get stopped at Moscow airport when we are changing planes for Frankfurt.

Someone had called because we had missed the plane for Adis. The Russians take all our passports and give us a guard and put us in a room. Oh my, I am thinking, the trick has not worked. Either they will send us back to China or back to Ethiopia but either way we will be in jail.

But then I call Mr. Otto who calls German immigration at the airport who takes us from the Russians. They check all the papers, fingerprints, visas, passports and everything and call Helga the artistic communicator for Mama Africa Circus in Munich. "Put them on the plane," she says "They have working papers," so OK, soon we are in the air out of Russia. It is only two hours and we land in Munich and Miss Helga shows up. Everybody hugs her, we have water and juice, get into a van and she takes us to a small town outside of Munich to a guesthouse.

This is a beautiful time in our lives. It's summer and we are free. We love so much Germany. Next day we drive two hours from Munich and we meet the director of the circus, Eric, a Black artist from Kenya. And then the next day the bus comes with the African circus crew, Mullinae, the girl Mofu that I know from Dice Dota and everyone else. Then we start working and practicing every day in a tent. Eric likes the acts that we had prepared. He puts the Love of Birds and Lions after the opening dance, and the Omo People and the Clown Waiters in the second part of the show. There will be 1,500 people in Augsburg. We practice with a live band.

Everybody is very excited. It goes very well. The tent is shaking, no mistake, everybody loves us. The producer is so happy because he paid a lot of money for us. He tells the designer to improve our costumes and pays for them. This show is never taken out of the circus.

And we got better. With our larger troupe we made a great beautiful African acrobatic pageant with three and four in the air at one time and juggling many swords and fire torches, while doing the jump somersaults. The audience cannot stop their applause. Now we are touring all over Europe, Germany, Belgium, Italy, Holland, Austria and Switzerland. Zurich is clean and nice and Austria – Salzburg is so beautiful. I found a girlfriend in Austria, and had a beautiful time; no stress, no problems. We five Ethiopians stay in Germany and start a street show, performing in Munich and Köln. That time is difficult – our visas are finished – but we have permission to stay. Then Mother Africa delays another month. Either we get work or else they would send us home. We find a small circus – Big Africa Circus – to tour in Germany. Big Africa pays only 300 and no per diem while Mother Africa had paid 500 Euro a week plus hotel and food. This is when I start thinking about getting to the States and contact my friend Kofi at BlacKafro Circus in Atlanta.

Oh wait a second. Oh no, I have to go, really, oh no, no, it is about my cousin Binyam…the Rastahs are looking for him and now they are in the bus station. I press the send button and now I run.

Dolphins

Lushan and Sagar: **In the Arabian Sea**

Look how they jump.

Yes, when they jump they turn. They call them the Spinner Dolphin.

They are fish?

No they are animals like us. They breathe air.

I have never seen this. There is no ocean in Ethiopia. How long do they follow?

There is no telling. Sometimes they follow all the way across to Somalia. Sometimes they just come to say goodbye when we leave the harbor. They know us.

They know you?

Oh yes, they are more smart than dogs. See that one with the wounds on her nose, and the black on the bone on her back. I have seen her many times. She is the leader. We call her Leela. That means in Gujerati "to play." We call her that because she will jump and dance for hours. Look at this. I do not even need a fish.

Oh my God, she touches your hand.

Yes, and if I tell her to go away, and make the sign with my hand, she will go. Look. I say, "Dura Jaya". And she goes.

No, no, don't send her away. I want her to follow all the way to Berbera. Call her back.

Mara prema pacha Avo.

Look, she is coming back. What did you say?

I said, "Come back my Love". Lushan, please get me a fish from the pail.

Oh my God. She jumps for it like a dog and takes it from your hand.

Now hold out your hand. She will lift her head so you can pet her nose.

She will not bite me?

No, she knows you are my friend. And dolphins love this touching. They are like dogs. They are like us.

How do you know she is female?

The man dolphins, they do not swim so close. Maybe now that you are on the Tiger a man dolphin will visit.

Maybe she has fallen in love with you and she wants you to be her husband.

Don't be stupid. She is a mother. Here she gives you her nose. She wants to be your friend.

She will bite me. She is jealous. She will pull me in and give me to a shark.

Here, I will hold so you will not fall. I promise I will not let you go. Go on. Go on. I've got you. Hold out your hand.

Oh look, she turns to look at me.

Yes, and she will remember you now.

How many days before we come to Berbera?

Usually it is five days and nights.

You have crossed many times.

Oh yes, with my father ever since I was a boy. When there is no school I work. And I have crossed with him across the border to Harrar. Now we make that journey without him. Oh hold on to me, here comes a wave.

Wooh, this gives my stomach fear. Oh you are strong.

Yes, and I can pull the anchor alone. Some of the older men cannot do this. Oh now my father calls. I must let you go.

Sagar, what are you doing?

I am showing her Leela and how to play with her.

And this is why you hold her from behind?

Yes, she asked me; she does not swim. She is scared.

Sagar, pull your shirt out so it covers you. I'm sorry to laugh, forgive me, but no man has brains when their pants do that. Sagar, it happens to me still and when it does I thank Kama, but I do not act on it. Listen, I know what is going on with you, but you must know *you cannot have her.* Even if she would give herself to you, and for love she might, *you cannot have her.* I trust you with her here on the Dragon and then across Somalia to Harrar and then to Adis where you will put her in a van for her home and *she will be virgin,* and I mean in spirit as well as in body. You will not kiss her except in greeting and leaving and you will not touch her except as a brother. And I will speak to her too to be like a sister. She has goodness in her I am sure she will be strong and not betray a promise. Listen, I know, she is beautiful, she is more desirable than a Queen – and if you deliver her safely you will have shown me real strength.

Dad, does that mean forever?

That is part of the learning. But you must promise for this journey.

I promise.

Now go set the fishing lines and see if there is something there for her to cook. Go.

Hey Girl, Madame Lushan, our cook, come here, I would like to talk to you.

Diamond And The Wolf: Part Two
Selam and Lushan: **Adis Ababa**

So no, he did not take advantage of me. I came out of the bathroom covered with a towel and still with the broken glass in my hand. I asked him to please turn while I put my clothes on. Then I laid down next to him on the bed, not touching and still with the glass in my hand and he told me a story of a girl and a jibi. And the strangest thing is that the jibi had the same name as the farange. Wolf. Who would name themselves after a jibi? You might as well call yourself Satan.

Oh my God, you are in the bed in the Sheraton with big hairy naked rich German and he does not rape you? And with all his money you do not let him?

No, listen Lushi, if I could have done that believe me I would have. But God would not let me make sex with the German. He chose Helen for that, to use her beauty to find a German and leave her people. But God told me to stay virgin even if I died; I had the glass in my hand and I would have cut him and myself and the German knew that.

I will never forget the story. The jibi ate the Grandmother and then pretended to be her and then he swallowed the girl but then a hunter came and cut open the jibi. The girl came out and the Grandmother too. They put stones in the jibi so he could not run so at the end the girl was the winner and the jibi was dead.

So was he angry that he could not have you?

No, when he saw that I would cut him, he became like a father and so I played daughter as he spoke and closed my eyes and pretended to fall asleep. And then when he was done he drank more whiskey and turned off the lights and turned on the television. I waited a long time until he fell asleep and, for a while I watched him, with my eyes almost shut, his white and pink body covered with red hair and blue veins, his chest rising and falling, while he snored. He was not such a bad man. Another man would have raped me and no one would think it wrong, after all it was I who played the game of being a little whore. I thought about Fikir and how would he ever find me, and you cannot tell anyone this, I thought of letting him touch me between my legs. Then I prayed to Mother Maryam and very quietly got off the bed and left that room and walked out of the Sheraton Hotel into the night in Adis holding broken glass.

Where did you go?

Lushi I tell and tell and you say nothing. But you, Lushi, you must tell me, how in the name of Jesus did you get from Somalia to Adis? And what of this boy Sagar? I'm sorry I have no more money for coffee. Will you walk with me?

Where are we going?

Where I stay, in the apartment of Helen. Let's go, OK? The sun is going down. And tomorrow you will go back to Dice Dota. I will find the money for the van.

Where?

From my friend Genet. You will meet her. She knows how to find money. And she is not a whore. Come on.

2015

Sagar And Lushi On The Sea Tiger: A Father's Perspective
Hedeyat: Dubai

Oh, Abeynesh, this girl Lushan you brought me, she hypnotized poor Sagar. He took one look at her and immediately became her protector and her slave, and that was a good thing; she made him brave. I told him, "I will leave you and the girl in Berbera. I will buy you an Indian passport. You will take her and thirty barrels of paint through Somalia across the border to Harrar. Everything is fixed: Ahmet will drive the truck and I will give you money for the bribes to get you through. In Harrar you will get the agreed price for the paint, $2,000, then you will take her on the bus to Adis, leave her there, fly from Adis to Mumbai and then take the train to Amedabad with the money. If you do this and get back by December you can be captain of this dhow on the next voyage and then I will send you to university in March."

He accepted and from that moment, whether he was steering or fishing or singing, one eye was on her. And his was not the only one, she was a hard girl not to look at, as are all you Ethiopian women, and though she was proud and her back did not bow, it was good she kept her eyes down and always slept next to Sagar's blanket. I knew enough Arabic to tell what the Somalis said about her; sometimes they would talk with disrespect about having sex with her and mocking Sagar for being virgin because they knew his desire was the strongest. Not that I didn't trust them, these are dreams all men have about being King and having every woman. Women yearn too for the young men, I know, but I have seen desire turn red when men kill for beauty. It doesn't matter if you are Hindi or Islam or Christian, the Gods of Lingam and Yoni, Kama and Rati, can win over any law. Ha, Abey, you blush. Are the names of sex parts not spoken of in your language? In Hindi we treasure them and speak of them without shame.

And this girl, though she was Devi virgin, she was Rati in her eyes and face and body, and she vanquished my son. It was the same the first time I saw you, Abey, when I sat next to you on the plane to Dubai; Hindu Lingam begins a conversation with Christian Yoni. Wasn't it about the gold you were wearing, no, Miss Ethiopia Airlines? I tell you, you Ethiopian women are witches. Now, for ten years your enchantment still holds me.

No, there was no problem at the harbor; this girl was not by far the most illegal cargo we have taken to Somalia. The inspectors are our friends; we cross every month and have all the papers for the paint from India and the license from the Emirates. When they pretended to search we covered her with ropes and tarps. Even if they had found her they would not have sent her to prison. These are not the kind of Arabs who would keep a house slave from escaping; they would have seen her pride in her face and let her pass. They worry about the smugglers of guns and SAMs, not girls.

Once we were out to sea I watched how the nets of desire tightened around them, up to the point where I questioned whether they could keep control. So I cut through and shook them out like fish on the deck, challenging them to be careful, not of me, but for themselves. So they could keep their desire burning as pure as flame, so they would not tarnish their golden feeling with trouble and disgrace. He got her to Adis and swore to me he did not take advantage.

This Lushan is a good girl, do you agree? She is Orthodox not Hindu, but I don't care for my mother's thinking; to me Krishna and Jesus are brothers. Now they write on the Internet about going to school in Germany. And if this comes to pass I will not let him go there unmarried. I want a good brave girl for Sagar and she is that.

But it is late and tomorrow you fly to Rome and I return to Kandla Port, so let us not speak any more of young lovers. So give me your hand to kiss, and then your lips. We must do as they would do, don't you think? We must show them the way.

Fikir Mess Up Bigtime
Amuzu (Fikir's Nigerian Roommate): **New Orleans**

Yeah dat boy Fikir he one stupid mofah, comin' in from Africa, don't know shit, says he with ze circus and for sure he a clown, he lose his gig in Atlanta cuz ze boss is a horndog, shows up in New Orleans to see his Ethiopian homie, Binyam, think he going to college or something, gets some wack under table job with ze Beaners at El Taco zat pay garbage but only last two days because ze Immigration raid ze place and he run coz he all illegal, but Binyam been doing ganja deals with Rastahs, burns ze mofahs and splits for Denver and Rastahs come round looking for Bin and find Fikir and figure one Ethiopian mofah just like another and mess Fikir up pretty bad, so what's he do? He run to Chicago, end of story. Now I'm stuck wiz rent for ze crib and got Rastah's on my ass cuz they donno the difference between Ethiopian and Nigerian mofahs, and no way I'm staying NOLA, I'm going Houston, that's the wave, I gotta cousin there, he Igbo like me, his wife American Black, gotta good teacher job, he drive cab, got green card, they got it together bigtime, I'll stay wiz them, meet some Black American soul girl, get married, get legal, go college, none of zis restaurant bullshit, Ima gonna help ze people, be physical therapist, learn ze acupuncture, alla dat shit.

Fikir Surprises Mrs. Lisa
Fikir and Lisa: **East Rogers Park, Chicago**

"Who is there? Oh my God, Fikir, I thought you were in China."

"Kay Lee! Marc? Fikir is here on our doorstep. Fikir from Dice Dota is in the house.

"I'll be damned, I'll be a monkey's uncle twice removed, Fiker, let me hug you, My Lord, is this is a surprise? Come in, come in, why don't you take off your coat and stay a while. How did you get here?"

"By bus from New Orleans. And then I walked from the Center. Chicago is very beautiful. What ocean is that?"

"Fikir, don't you know about the Great Lakes? That's not an ocean, that's Lake Michigan. It's a hundred times bigger than your Hippo Lake. What were you doing in New Orleans? How did you get here? Do you want coffee? Are you hungry? Where are you staying? What happened to your face?"

"I am just here since this afternoon. And for coffee and food I say please, yes and thank you. I have not eaten since yesterday."

"Kay Lee, look, here's Fikir. Where's Marc?"

"He said he was going running."

"Kay Lee, you make Fikir comfortable. I'll get him food. Fikir, Do you have a place to stay?"

"No, Mrs. Lisa."

"How long have you been in the States?"

"Since the summer."

"Why didn't you call us? Hey, I know you're going to tell me all about it. But first let me get you food. Where did you say you were staying?"

Lisa

That boy's a mess, somebody beat him up, he hasn't bathed in days, hasn't eaten, got mud-colored bags under his eyes, seems to have no belongings other than what is in that backpack, has no place to stay, we will have to put him up, and for how long? That's the question. I can't refuse, he's family.

No he's not. He's not even related. How'd he get here from China is what I want to know. I shouldn't worry, the fucking boy is as smart as they come, in two years, he will be married to an Irish Catholic Girl from Bridgeport who needs to piss off her cop dad by marrying an African and in ten years he will be Senator from Illinois.

And Kay Lee, that little whore, she will be on him like a fly, who am I to speak, good thing no one round here knew me when I was sixteen at Lane Tech and he is so pretty, looks just like his Momma, that's it, we'll call Eden, we'll call his Mom, then we'll find out what's going on with this boy, then we'll get it straight.

Fikir

She is not happy to see me. She doesn't want me to stay in her house. She is afraid I will ask her for money. She is afraid that I will go after Kalkidane who is so beautiful any man would want her.

I will be true to Selam if she is true to me, but if she has left The House of Adenech and graduated from the School of Helen and is now a bar girl sleeping with Arabs, Chinas, Germans, and Japans, and giving them her pussy and putting their sex in her mouth I will make money here from ganja, then I will go back to Ethiopia and watch her from the street until I know the best time and then kill the men with an AK and escape to Kenya. Then she will marry an Italian.

Stop, do not think that, she is no whore, she is fine, she is in school, she is waiting for me, she is still virgin, I must call her but there is no phone at Adenech, I know, I will ask Mrs. Lisa to call my mother, I will ask my mother to look for Selam and give her my message, that's what we will do, we will call my mother. And Selam will not marry an Italian.

"Fikir, I did what you asked. I didn't tell them you were coming."

"Kalkidane, are you fine?"

"What happened in Atlanta?"

"Can I call my mother?"

"What happened to your face?"

"OK, there was a problem with BlaKafro Circus: the director wanted sex from Nyala, the girl who had gone with me from Dice Dota to China and then to Germany and the States, she was like my sister, but she sexed with him to keep the job and get the green card and I was angry and fought him and so I was expelled. I went to New Orleans on Greyhound to stay with my cousin Binyam who got me a job with Mexicans but he was dealing ganja and owed money to the Rastahs, so he ran to his sister in Texas and the Rastahs found me and beat me for his money. Then the immigrations raided the restaurant but I ran from them and left New Orleans on Greyhound and came here. How is Chicago? Can I call my mother?"

Helen Gets A Phone Call She Didn't Want To Get
Helen and Crystal: **Adis Ababa/Hamm DE**

Hallo.

Hallo.

Du bist Heaven?

No German.

Du bist Heaven?

Nicht German. Kein German. English.

You speak English?

Yes. Who are you?

Are you Heaven?

No, who are you?

You are Heaven. I know it. I am Crystal, the wife of Helmut. I am his wife now 12 years. Our daughter is Marlene. Did he promise you to bring you to Germany and to marry?

He has no wife.

Oh Heaven, I apologize. He makes this promise to all women when he is working in another land. You are not the first.

No, you lie, this is impossible. Who are you?

I am Crystal. I learned of you from the wife of his friend Wolf. She found your number. Please, Heaven, tell Helmut that Crystal says for him not to be so cruel to you. And that she will see him next week. How old are you? Listen, you should find another man who has no wife. There are many people who want this and children and everything. But Helmut is taken. Goodbye.

No.

NO.

NO!!!

Selam And Lushi Go To Work Selling T-shirts
Genet: **Steps Of The National Museum, Adis Ababa**

Wasser? Agua? Ambo? Water? Thank you. You are English? Austrailenya? Will you buy Haile Selassie T-Shirt? Lucy? Bob Marley? 100 birr? 90? 85? Chicle? 5 birr? Oh you walk away. Fuck you.

OK, Ha, Oh no, Selam, there she is again, always she comes looking for me when life squeezes her, and now, look, that is her sister with her, the one at the airport, the one who I got arrested for who went to Dubai. I don't believe it, how did she get back?

Look at her now, no more school uniform, new clothes, look at those jeans. Maybe she has money now that she gets from being a whore like her friend Heaven. I will hide here under the umbrella and watch her some more before I call out.

The sister though, she has no good clothes, just a gabi and only flip-flops. Oh, she looks at the Chinese shoes from the blanket of the Gurage. But her sister shakes her head, she cannot buy. Now she asks the little sniffer boy where to find me and so he points and now the hiding is over.

Hey Selam!

So you are here. And with her. She is back from the Emirates already? I thought the Arabs kept girls for two years. What is your name?

Lushan.

I am Genet. I was the one at Bole with your sister when she tried to save you. I hit the tall man with a bottle so she would not be arrested.

They beat me and then they took me to children's jail. But it was OK. I was there two times before so I know how to make money there. I work it with my friend Demekesh, helping her to get messages to families. She gives me a percentage of what they give her. I was there three nights and I got 40 birr.

Selam, You are not in school, I see. Are you working in Seven Nights? Like Heaven?

Oh she doesn't want to talk about this, she shakes her head and ha ha! her sister sees this. She does not want her sister to know that she is a whore.

You were looking for me? So did you come to pay me back the money I wasted for the van to the airport? Hey I know. You promised to take me to the apartment of Heaven. Is the German there or can we go?

Yes? We can go? Fantastic. Selam, I love you. Can I bathe? Oh good. OK, but first I must sell these t-shirts because I owe Mamoud. Hey, you can help me. You both are so pretty; the men and girls will buy. The women will hate you, but you can send them to me. They will have pity on a street girl.

Here, Selam, you take the *Bob Marley One Love* shirt, and you, Lushan; you take *Haile Selassie, Lion of Judah*. I will sell *Lucy, Mother of Humanity*. People say I look just like her. Ha ha. Selam, go to the steps where they come out of the museum, and Lushan, go to where they come from the taxis to enter, and show them the shirts. Speak English. Everyone knows "T-shirt." Look for the farange with shopping bags and coffee. They are leaving Ethiopia and shopping for presents. Show them the shirt, say "present, present," and then point to me, and if they are farange and they let you, take them by the hand and bring them and I will do the deal. If they are Abesha, do your best. For farange I start at 100 birr and go down to 60. The ones for kids I start at 90. For Abesha or Chinas I start at 70 and 60 and go to 40. The cost is 30 birr.

Here are the shirts. Watch out for the glue sniffer boys. They will run up and grab a shirt, so always hold on to the shirts. Do you see that ugly boy there with the t-shirt that says *OHIO?* He is very aggressive. If he comes close to you kick him away. If we sell all the shirts we can buy a lunch before we go to the apartment of Heaven's German. Won't that be nice?

Phone Call To Weyzero Eden
Lisa, Fikir and Eden: Chicago – Dice Dota

Hello Eden? This is Lisa from Chicago.

Oh Mrs. Lisa. Oh it is good to hear from you. Are you fine?

Yes, are you fine?

Yes, and Mr. Marc, is he fine?

Eden we are all fine. And listen, I have news: Fikir is with us.

Fikir is with you? Thank God. Is his circus in Chicago?

In a manner of speaking his circus is definitely here. But he will tell you more. Listen, I will give him to you but first I want to know: where is Selam?

She is in Adis. She telephoned in the last week. She has left the House of Adenech and is staying with her friend Helen.

The one who is a…who works a bar?

Mrs. Lisa, this I cannot say. But the news is very good about Lushan. Her employer in Dubai abused her but she escaped from Dubai and is now in Adis with her sister.

And Nigest?

I spoke with her yesterday. She was in fear about Selam and Lushan but now she is happy. Gyorgis has bought a bajaj and though he does not beat her because Geta is there, everyone knows he drinks alcohol and goes with prostitutes so she is scared for acquiring HIV from him. And Geta…he is making politics in the high school about the election. She tried to stop him but he will not listen. He goes and makes protest with the university students. So now there is tension and Woyane soldiers are everywhere. Geta wants to fight them and there is no telling him to take care. He will not listen. He does not know what an army can do when it moves to suppress opposition.

Oh baby, that sounds bad. We don't hear about that on the news here.

314

Mrs. Lisa, if you do hear of this it will be too late. But let us talk of happy things. When do you return to Dice Dota?

Eden, I know you are just dying to talk to Fikir.

I'll put him on. Mrs. Lisa, why do you say this? I am not dying.

No, Eden, it's an expression in English. I meant you must want to talk to your son.

We miss you very much.

Eden, I will try to come back. But listen, give our love to Nigest. And be safe. Here's Fikir.

Mom.

Fikir, I can't believe you are in America. You said you might get a contract with a circus but then I didn't hear from you and now you are calling me from Chicago. So tell me, is everyone rich? Are the buildings so high? Do you have an auto? Is there snow?

Mom, ha ha. Look, all that is propaganda, except for the snow and I have not seen that yet. They say it will come in December. But as for the rest, if you have no money it is the same as Ethiopia, everyone steps on you and you are last. And there are many prisons for the poor. But don't worry. I am here now with Mrs. Lisa and Mr. Marc and Kalkidane. They will show me what to do.

And how is the circus? Is there much money? Are you famous now?

Mom, ha ha, not yet, but when I am, soon, I will send for you. You can run my house, supervise all my servants and make injera. And even though the servants will all be farange, I know you will treat them very kindly, just as if they were Ethiopians. You would give them one day off a week and you would not beat them, right?

Not unless they cursed me and disobeyed. Fikir, you are too funny. So where does the circus go in America?

Mom, how is Selam?

Fikir, I spoke with her last week. She has left her school, and, you cannot tell Mrs. Lisa, but I think she working at a nightclub with Helen.

She would not.

Well, when Alemnu was driving farange to hear the cultural Azmari music in Kasanchis he saw her and Helen with Germans.

Look Mom, I think they were just friends with Helen, not...

Alemnu said Selam was dressed for business in miniskirt and high heels.

Mom, no, that is not Selam. She has high morals.

Fikir, no one can stop her from doing what is her choice.

Mom, I must know. Will you find out?

I will Fikir. But if I find the truth, will you accept it?

Fikir this is costing money, can I speak to Eden please?

Goodbye Mother. Look for email. I will write you here from Mrs. Lisa's.
Goodbye Fikir.

So Eden, Please, write me for Selam and Lushan and tell them...

Wait, Mrs. Lisa, there is a noise. Oh, I know this sound, it is shooting, It is coming from the Town Center where they are demonstrating. Geta is there, so, I must go now. I will write you. Please tell Fikir...

Eden? What? Are you there? Eden? Fuck!

How Can A Girl Get Ahead In 2015?
What's Her Business Plan?
Selamawit, Lushan and Genet
2205 Churchill Road, Adis Ababa

So Selam, what is your idea?

For what?

For making money to pay the rent for this apartment.

What? Genet, this is Helen's apartment, not ours.

I thought you said her name is now Heaven.

Yes, I know but the apartment is hers, the German pays for it, so why should we pay rent?

When she goes to Germany and is married then he will not keep it.

How do you know? Maybe he will keep it for another Ethiopian wife.

Yes, but even if he did, Helen would be gone, so how could we stay here? No, we must rent this ourselves.

How could we afford that? The rent here must be 20,000 birr a month.

Well, you could do what Helen does. And so could Lushi. Even if you are not virgin you could still make 500 birr a day.

I could never do that.

Why not? It would be fun. You could have a lot of sex. They say it is enjoyable if you are not cut. And you are not cut. You could do that and make a lot of money.

You just wait until you grow up and men want to have sex with you. Then you will not talk like this.

They already do.

Ha, you? You have no titties. You don't have hair.

I do too. Look.

Wow you do, you have a lot. But who tries to get you?

Look you are schoolgirls, you don't know this, but when you are on the street men think you will do anything for money. Ever since I was six years old they have chased me. They try to fuck the boys too. In their bootie.

So what do you do?

I show them this knife and I tell them that after I cut their avocados off then my father and my brother will make them eat them before they kill them.

You are fast with that.

You should have seen what I did to this old guy once. He was so surprised he started to cry when I cut his leg. Right behind the knee so he could not chase me.

This man in the Emirates, my employer, he tried and tried but I fought him.

Ha. You should have seen this German, Wolf, who took me to his room at the Sheraton. He would have given me so much money if I had let him. He took off his clothes and his penis got very big and he wanted to kiss me in my thing. I broke a bottle and ran into the bathroom.

Yes they like to do that. And they want to put their penis in your mouth until the seed comes out. I've have seen it. The woman drinks it.

You have not seen that. How did you see that? You are little.

Selam, the Arab Mahmoud, he shows me this in an English magazine when I come into his place for the t-shirts. The man's penis is big and the women have the seed on their faces. He wants me to do this. I show him the knife and tell him to go fuck a camel. I asked my friend Tenech, who works at Las Vegas Bar. She says all men want this and they will pay. She likes it better than the other. She says it is safer. No HIV and no baby.

I will never do this.

What if your husband wanted it?

No it is disgusting. The big penis in your mouth. What if he pee-peed?

You could bite it, ha ha. Then you better run.

What if he would lick you?

Shut up. My husband will only want the right kind of sex.

What is that?

You know what that is. The penis in the pussy. Like God designed it to be.

Yes but God is a man, so it is designed to his advantage. If he was a woman she would have made the places for pleasure and for babies different.

Yes and if he was a woman she would have planted trees that condoms grew on. So you would always have one and would not have to pay.

Yes, and if he was a woman she would have made the man's penis with a condom made of skin already on it and only if the woman opened it up would the seed come out.

Yeah, And if he was a woman she would given men periods not women. The blood would then go easily into a bottle and there would be no mess. Every month he would bleed and then his seed would be renewed.

Ha ha, and if he was a woman, she would have made the man a lot smaller, so he could not rape the woman. The woman would just pick him up and throw him off her and then kick his ass.

Ha ha, and if he was a woman...mmm...she would have given one breast to the man and one to the woman so the man would also have to feed the child and carry it around.

Ha ha ha. But God is not a woman, this is obvious.

Look, this is stupid talk. We better make a plan. First. May we stay here?

Genet, I have to ask Helen. I mean Heaven. The German has gone for business to Kenya for a week. I have been here since he left, and now Lushan is returned from the Emirates and now you are here. Helen will probably say OK - but the German returns in two days and then we will all have to leave and find another place. Where can we find that?

That depends on if we find money. Like I was saying...you are beautiful... and so is your sister, and it would be easy for you to...

I told you, I will not do that.

What about you, Lushan?

Shut up, we are virgin and I would rather marry a hyena. I would rather beg.

But what about you, you little t-shirt girl with no titties and all that hair in your panties? You say so many men are asking. You could do it with the mouth like you say so you wouldn't get HIV. And you would stay virgin.

Selam, I will not do that. I am not pretty and I do not like men and their penises. They are always hitting you. But, here is my idea: if you help me sell the Arab's t-shirts we could find enough money to rent a room. And then we would save so we could rent a portapotty and charge 2 birr. I have street friends who do this with the musician Mola Abera. He delivers and takes away the toilets and you watch it all day and collect the birr. People pay not to shit in the street and women when they have their period to not stain their dress. Then, when we have enough money from the portapotty, we will buy gold from these glue boys I know who grab purses and crawl into houses. They have rings and necklaces and earrings and when they want glue they sell them for nothing. We will buy these and sell them to my friend who sells gold in the Merkato, and then we buy more gold and sell that until we can rent a table from my friend in the Merkato. And then, when we have enough money, we can rent our own store in the Merkato. We can run the store and go to night-school. After some years, I will go to America to study in the state of Minneapolis and I will leave you the store.

Selam can run the store here. I will open a store in the Gold Souk in Dubai. I was there. You would not believe how much gold they have; there is enough to build a whole house out of gold. All the rich people in the world are there. Hey, look at this television here. Let's turn it on. Maybe we can find this American program I saw when I was with the Arabs in Dubai. It was great. The woman was a magistrate and the people came with their problems and she would decide who was right. Her name was Judy.

Hey, Selam look, on the table there is wine. Would Helen, I mean Heaven, mind?

Hey, you girl Lushan, tell me, how did you escape from Dubai?

I came on a boat and then in a truck and by bus with a boy. A nice boy.

On a boat? You came from Dubai on a boat with a boy? My God, how did you do that?

Lushan's Tale: The Voyage Across The Arabian Sea, The Whale She Saw And How The Gujeratis Saved The Pirates With Water

Lushan, Selamawit and Genet: **2205 Churchill Rd., Adis Ababa**

Like I told Selam it was a woman from Ethiopian Airlines in Dubai, Abeynesh, who saved me when I ran away from my employer. She got me on the Sea Tiger, the boat of her boyfriend, Hedeyat, the Gujerati. We crossed from Dubai, taking paint to Berbera for transport to Abeynesh's cousin in Harar. We were on the sea for five days. Three days we saw no land. When you are so far from shore, let me tell you, the world is different, it is always moving beneath you, you see only water, dolphins, birds and sometimes other boats. In the day the light comes off the water so hot it burns you in a minute and you wait for the cool of the dark. I cooked food for the sailors and I found a boyfriend Sagar, Hedeyet's son. Dolphins followed us. One time we encountered pirates. And I saw a whale. It came right up below to take a look at my butt when I was going pee-pee. Really, it was the most scary thing that ever happened to me, but also like a miracle.

On the boat, every night after I had cleaned the supper dishes, I would put a cloth over a rope on the back corner of the boat so the men would not see me, and then I would wash with a bucket and pee and shit. I had been holding it all day and the men knew that this was my time. On the night of the whale the moon had just come up and it was big and bright, reflecting off the sea, shining, almost like the day. I was squatting with my butt over the side of the boat, holding on to the ropes, feeling the cool wind on my popo, which was like a breeze from Paradise because the day had been so hot. And I was looking down between my legs at the beautiful green sparkling splashes that my pee-pee made when it hit the water. Selam – did I tell you that in some places the sea at night is full of little lights? When there are waves from the boat, or when you throw something into the water, or if, you go pee-pee, each drop makes an explosion of green light and the sparkling is so beautiful you just want to pee forever. But then something rolled up from the water with a big swirling green cloud of light, first a long nose and then a huge eye as big as a cup came out of the water right under my ass. The eye was above a long mouth. I screamed and got my butt away from the side of the boat and pulled down my dress and the big eye rolled back under and up came a big black and white body that went on and on rolling up and under. It had a paddle arm on the side and a black fin on the back and then a long black and white tail with two fans coming out to the side. Before it went back under the whale lifted its tail and slapped the water and the whole world sparkled and splashed like green rain. When they heard my scream the men came through the blanket because they thought I had fallen in, and we all saw, there in the water, in a green glowing cloud, the whale, twice as long as the boat and swimming on its side.

Did the men see your butt?

No, no, and no one was thinking of that, it was like there was a big angel in the water, something that came from a heaven in the deep. The men said that I had been blessed by the Prophet Jonas and now would be lucky.

And then you saw pirates?

Yes, the next night, all of sudden the sound of a motor and then a bright light. They came up on us so fast that the men barely had time to hide me under the sails. We thought they would steal our paint, but that did not inter-est them. They were out of water. They told us how they were pretending to fish but really following a Swede boat hoping to take hostages, until they ran into the American Navy who took their weapons and most of their food and water and told them to go home. So we gave them water.

Were you scared they would take you?

Not at all. They only take the rich and who would pay for us? Their leader was Somali Issaq clan like most of the sailors, so they were relatives. The leader bragged that he was cousin to the one who went to prison in America for kidnapping the American captain. Actually they were nice guys. They had khat and they gave some to our sailors. Hedeyat told me to come out from under sails and to make food for them. I made shark rice. And we gave them water so they could return to their home. Then we sailed two more days to Berbera. My God, that is the hottest place in the world. It is famous.

Oh someone is at the door? Do you hear?

Oh it's Helen.

Helen, here is my sister Lushan and my friend Genet. Can we stay here?

Helen, what is the matter?

Welcome To The North Side; The Rules Of East Rogers Park
Eli and Fikir: **Chicago**

Hey Fikir, whachu doin? Where you goin?

Mrs. Lisa says I should go to the Ethiopian Community Center and see Ato Sisay.

Wait. You can't go out wearing that jacket. You'll get shot.

Who would do this?

The Peoples.

The Peoples?

Right, so Fikir, pay attention, here are the rules of East Rogers Park. You may think this is your American dream, streets paved with gold, freedom to park cars and work at Mickey D's and alla that bullshit, but here is the reality; you, being what your profile would call a "young Black male," present an equal opportunity for a gangbanger or a cop to shoot your ass.

In this neighborhood you don't wear blue. Folks wear blue. Right, see Fikir, you must know this; around here there are two families, the Peoples and the Folks, East Rogers Park is Peoples – Black P Stones and Latin Kings. Kings are the worst, man, nasty little scorpions who will sting you if you move too fast or not fast enough. So remember this, because it's important, blue means Folks.

And Folks are the enemy of the Peoples. And if you wear your hat to the right or show the five-point star, you signify Peoples and you will be stopped and checked by the Kings or the BP's and more than likely they will mess you up bad. Now, if you go east, past Ridge, it switches to Gangster Disciples. The GD's. They are Peoples.

So you don't wear red or yellow over there and you don't wear your hat to the left or show anything that looks like a pitch fork, because they will assume

324

you are Folks and the same thing will happen, you will get hurt. Devon and Barrow is Black P's, Peoples; Ashland and Farlow are GD's; Folks. Anywhere on Western in between Peterson and Touhy is all Peoples.

So, if they come up to you and say, "What's up, what you doing here, are you Folks? Are you gangbangin?" Then you gotta get real Ethiopian on them, ask them, like you are fresh off the boat, "Please sir, how to find the Red Train?" Then they won't hassle you. School uniform works good too. I knew one kid, he was a freak, he'd wear like a jacket and tie and carry around a bible like he was an Adventist or Jehovah's Witness or something. He got insulted but he never got hurt.

What is the advantage of this control? Do they make a tax to pass through the area. Is it about who can sell the ganja?

No, everybody sells, ganja, shit man, my aunt sells weed, no it's not about the drugs so much any more, it's about revenge, like for who shot who in 1978 and they've just been whacking back ever since.

And it's not just the gangbangers. It's about the cops. They are twice as dangerous. Up here on the street in Chicago, if you are profiled as "young Black male" brother, go to Afghanistan to be safe, go hang out in Syria, don't stay around here. In East Rogers Park, shit, the cops patrol everywhere, and if you fit the profile they will stop you, and then, señor, you are in danger. So remember: Rule Number One for cops is *don't run, don't ever run,* because, if you run, they will say they thought you had a weapon and *they will shoot you.* And if they stop you, move *really slow,* cuz if you do anything fast, like reaching in your pocket for your ID, they will say they thought you were going for a piece. A "piece" is a gun, Fikir, like a Glock or an M...and *they will shoot you.* And shoot you and shoot you. And if they start hitting you and you fight back, they will say you were grabbing for their gun, and *they will shoot you. And shoot you and shoot you.* They don't give a fuck. That dude in Ferguson, they shot him six times. And he didn't have a weapon, didn't have nothing.

Rule Number Two – which comes before Rule Number One: don't draw the cop's attention; don't stand in one place too long, keep moving, but don't walk around too energetically, try to be invisible, be a ghost, and don't gather in groups either, brotherman. If the cops see a *pack* – and get this, a *pack* is a gathering of more than two, that's right, two of the rapidly extinctifying species of Homo Erectus Black Malus – you will be stopped, and then for you, being of the subgenus – Illegal Africanus – it's all over, they will trap you, cage you, shackle you and take you before the judge and the next thing you know your ass will be flying on the big bird straight back in Adis where you will be free at last to go nowhere forever. It used to be you could stay in IMS jail for at least a year, and you'd have time to appeal, and ask for asylum and all that shit. But since Obama, man, they they ship you right back. It's like he doesn't want the native Black genus to have the competition. So Fikir, do you understand?

You said that some things that are like Ethiopia. In Ethiopia too, the tribes have different language and wear different colors. But some things are different. Here the government permits everyone to have weapons, even children. In Ethiopia, the government knows what happens when the people are armed, they were revolutionaries once. Unless you are a farmer or a nomad who needs a weapon to protect his animals, or a soldier or a guard for a business or NGO, if they find you with a gun they will put you in prison, and then you are lost. No matter how hard your family fights they do not let you go. They beat you. They deny medical care and food. Eventually you get sick and die like my father.

So thank you Eli for this lesson. But now I must go see Ato Sisay. And this is my only coat. It is blue. And there is wind.

Just turn it inside out man. Like this. And tuck the collar in. Good.

So now, do I look like a person who is not a Peoples and not a Folks?

Oh yes, Fikir you look just like a real "Merican, no color, just grey. You will be fine.

I will be invisible.

Right, like a ghost.

And I will be safe.

Ghosts can never die. But just in case, I'll walk with you to the El. Come on. But keep your eyes open 360. And...shit, see that car? That's police.

326

How can you tell?

The antenna. Just act natural. They're watching. Fuck. They're pulling up. They gonna wanna ID us. Just do what I do. Let me do the talking. Don't say nothin'. You don't want them to hear your accent. Here they come. Put your hands like this so they can see them. And *remember*, do everything slow.

Helen Vows To Defeat Crystal
And Teaches Her Friends A New Dance
Helen, Selamawit, Lushan and Genet:
2205 Churchill Rd., Adis Ababa

"So Helen, all your dream is smoke? You will not have fat German babies and a Mercedes and the stone castle in that picture you showed me before? I am so sorry."

"Selam, she said she is Crystal, she is married to Helmut twelve years with a ten-year old daughter and that he has done this before. Wherever they send him to build a road, he finds a girl and promises to marry."

"So what will you do? Can you go with his friend Wolf? Maybe he has no wife. He is hairy but he is kind. He did not rape me."

"Selam, Jesus, do you think I am just a whore to go with anyone? Helmut is my life. I love him. He gives me pleasure and presents and I will marry him. This is what I will do. I will tell him: 'Divorce her. When the divorce is final you will marry me and I will go to Germany to take care of you and give you more children.'"

"You will ask him to choose?"

"Yes, that's exactly what I will do. But I will not ask him. I will tell him."

"And what if he says, 'Yes, I'm sorry, I love you, I'll return to Germany and divorce her.' And then you never see him again. Why would you believe him? He lies and lies. Do you think you can change a liar?"

"My plan is to marry Helmut, have children and learn German, to send money home and to study so that in five years I will be a nurse. Jesus, why do you think I will give that up so fast, just because he has a wife. If he lies or doesn't lie, it doesn't matter, because *I will take him from her.* She is old. I am young. He tells me he will do anything I ask, if he can have me. He thinks he is lying when he says it but I know better. I can get him. Look, he is coming from the South tomorrow, and you cannot be here past the morning."

"What will you do? Will you do it with your mouth?"

"No, Lushan, you are so stupid, it is much much more than any sex trick. It is more about casting your spell. So when you find the right man, you make the time he spends with you like a dream world which he cannot escape, so that the thought of you is always there where ever he is and he has to have more, he has to smell you and touch you and make you happy, he cannot live without you, you are an addiction stronger than glue. If you put this spell on him then you will keep him. He is a good lover and he is rich, so I choose him to give me children and get me out of Ethiopia. No other girls at Seven Nights have half a clue about this. They just give sex and get money and are lucky if the man uses a condom and they are not abused. Look, you must leave here in the morning, so I can prepare the place for his return. I will spend the next days with him breaking the spell of Crystal and tying him to me. And, before you leave, you, street girl, Genet, I want you to find me something. I will give you money and then I will let you stay with me after Helmut goes."

"Find what?"

"The Abduction Potent. You know where to get it?"

"Of course I do. There is a pharmacist in Piazza who has the best. All the men who want to be married save up their money to buy it, and it is expensive, let me tell you. It will cost 250 birr for a good dose and if you give me 300 birr I can bring you this."

"Sleeping here it will cost you 50 birr, so that is your pay. And I will pay 200 birr for the drug, not 250."

"I don't think I can get it for that low a cost."

"Would he take 210?"

"No I don't think so, but probably 215, and that is only because he is a friend. He usually sells it for 250 or 275."

"All right. I accept 215. When will you bring it?"

"When you give me the money I will go look for it."

Here. And if I get pregnant, you'll get a hundred more. I promise. And you can visit me in Germany.

"OK, I will be back here in two hours. And I can sleep here tonight? And take a shower? And wash my clothes?"

"I will buy food. We will have a feast. Right Selam? Lushi?"

"And we will watch Judge Judy?"

"No, Lushi, tonight is Ethiopian Idol. And guess what? Hosanna will dance tonight on the program. She's a contestant."

"Hosanna? No, you don't mean Hosanna from Dice Dota?"

"Yes everyone is talking on Facebook. She will do this new dance. She came for the audition and she was chosen. If she wins she gets 20,000 birr."

"But she is not the best dancer of all the girls. What about Sebbie or Adis? Did they audition?"

"Yes but they just did Crunk. All girls do this now. This is a different dance. It is not like hip-hop. The steps are not important. It goes like this."

"Oh my God."

"Wow! Helen, where did you learn this?"

"I saw the Hosannah video. Then I looked it up on YouTube and practiced."

"It's not a real dance."

"Lushan, it is very popular in America and everywhere. It is called the Twerking."

"It is all your butt? Every way and fast and slow?"

"Look, I can do it. Is this right?"

"Can you make one side jiggle and the other be still? Yes, Selam, that is twerking. Can you go up and down? With legs apart. High and low. Yes. Lushan, look at you. You have enough back there to get moving. Go around too while you jiggle. Yes. Go Go Go. Genet, you have the moves but you just need a bigger butt. And you will get one. You will. A beautiful big butt."

"And I will take it to the state of Minneapolis. I will be a radiology technician and I will do the Twerking."

"Yes you will Genet. Come on."

"And I will sell gold in Dubai."

"Yes you will Lushi. Do it."

"And I will be a woman pilot for Ethiopian Airlines."

"Yes Selam, yes you will. Faster."

"And Helmut will divorce and marry me and I will be a nurse in Germany."
"Yes you will Helen. Yes you will."

"If we twerk it we can work it.
Yes we will. Yes we will.
We will make it if we shake it.
Yes we will. Yes we will.
Shake it. Shake it. Shake it. Shake it."

Five Days In March, 2015
Various Newspapers: **USA**

*3/13/15 – Manhunt Is Underway After Police Officers Are Shot in Ferguson –
NY Times*

*3/12/15 – Police Shooting Forces Discussion Of Madison's Racial Divide –
Houston Chronicle*

*3/10/15 – Aurora, Colorado Police Shoot And Kill Yet Another Unarmed Black
Man – News One for Black America*

*3/10/15 – White GA Officer Shoots, Kills Black Unarmed, Naked Man - USA
Today*

*3/4/15 – Family Of Roshad Mcintosh, A Young Black Male Fatally Shot By
Chicago Police Officers, Files Lawsuit Against City Of Chicago – Chicago Tribune*

Eli Got Shot
Kay Lee and Marc: **East Rogers Park**

Oh no, oh no, OH NO NO NO NO NO NO! The motherfuckers shot him. They shot him.

What? What? Who got shot?

The pigs, the pigs, they shot Eli, he was on his way to the community center with Fikir and they got stopped. And they shot him. They killed him. THEY KILLED HIM. Miranda just called me. She heard it from her brother. I HATE THIS FUCKING COUNTRY I HATE IT.

Oh my god, Kay Lee, I'm so sorry I'm sorry.

No you're not, you *hated* him. You were gonna send him to jail. So now you're happy.

Honey, you don't know what you're saying. I didn't hate him. He was in your room. I was being a Dad. He was a great kid. Look, I understand, you loved him, and now he's gone for no reason and you're totally furious. It's OK, it's OK, be mad, say what you want, let me hold you. Come on. Come on. You gotta get through this.

And the thing is, he *knew* how to act with the police – he taught other boys how not to get shot. He was a mentor. And that's why they killed him. This is horrible, SO HORRIBLE.

Do you know what happened?

I don't know anything. He went out with Fikir to show him how to get to the Community Center. He was going to meet with Ato Sisay.

Where's Fikir?

I don't know. They might have shot him too for all I know.

Oh honey, I'm so sorry, I'm so sorry. It's so sad. It's so unnecessary. Just cry, just cry.

I gotta call his folks. He's got a little brother. Oh My God! I was over there yesterday. I was cooking with them and we ate together. I stayed over. That was our last night.

Maybe you should wait. Maybe they are overwhelmed.

No I gotta talk to them. I gotta find out what happened. THEY JUST KILLED HIM BECAUSE HE WAS BLACK. THEY KILLED BECAUSE THEY COULD.

Calm down honey, calm down. Or go freak. It's OK, just don't do anything for a minute. Don't go outside until you know what you are going to do.

I gotta call Benito at Rainbow Free House. They're going to be organizing something; they'll be marching to the Police Station. They'll be at the Police Station. This cannot happen. THIS CANNOT HAPPEN. Can you give me a ride to West Rogers Park?

A Poem While Waiting To Talk To Fikir
In Immigration Detention.
Marc: **Illinois Immigration Retention Center**

gun tunnel

bullet through softness

blood

fire shatter

flesh

gut piercing

cave in

automatic

splatter

ravage perfect

fat charring

breath taking

gas

splinters

in the body cage

gouged out

steel

in the heart

Guards will be Kings

our Wives

their pleasure

your body

your breath

your will

your flame

your torch

your story

your story

your story

wire shards

of the sigh

Sons will be Slaves

our Daughters

our pain

your battle

your shield

your sword

your love

to pass

your story

your story

your story

Fikir Gets A Visitor
Fikir and Marc: Illinois Immigration Detention Center

Hello Lisa. No I'm still waiting. Did you talk to a lawyer? Oh. Well then he's gonna go home, that is, if they don't connect him to...what happened. Here, they 're bringing him in now. Bye.

Hello Fikir. *You don't know me.* I am Marc Levi. Ato Sisay...

Mr. Marc...

Although *you know we have never met*, it's a pleasure to meet you now, even though I wish circumstances were different. Do you speak English?

Good. Ato Sisay sent me from the Ethiopian Community Center. I volunteer there and sometimes I visit Ethiopians who get picked up by immigration. *I am a volunteer from the ECC. Do you understand?*

You are volunteer.

Yes, and my name is Marc.

Thank you Ato Marc.

Good. I think you understand. Ato Sisay asked me to tell you that he has found you an immigration lawyer. Her name is Pamela Oliphant and she will represent you at your hearing. She will be asking you some questions. Ato Sisay wants to make sure that you understand the questions and he sent me down here to go over them with you. The first question is – since *you do not have any family in Chicago, why did you come here after you left the circus in Atlanta? Was it to visit a friend of yours that you thought lived here – but who you couldn't find?*

Yes.

And that friend's name?

Zeri. But we call him Zizi.

But *you could not find your friend, Zeri?*

Yes.

So you *slept by the lake?*

Yes, I slept by the lake.

And when the police picked you up you were looking for your friend who lived at *1204 Farwell.* Do you remember the address?

Yes, the last I knew my friend Zizi lived at 1204 Farwell.

Can you repeat the address?

1204 Farwell.

But you couldn't find him at 1204 Farwell.

I couldn't find him at 1204 Farwell.

Good, because you know there was a shooting very close to where the police picked you up. A boy got killed by the police. They said they thought he had a gun. His friend ran, but they couldn't find the friend. It's a good thing *you didn't know that boy.* If you did, you could be in prison for a long time before they decided your immigration status. It's a good thing *you know no one in Chicago.*

I only know Zizi. But I couldn't find him.

Oh, that is a pity. Perhaps he went to another city. And there is something else that Ato Sisay would like to know. In Ethiopia, *there was no reason for you to leave there* other than to work for the circus in Atlanta that you ran away from, right? *You are not asking for asylum* here, is that correct?

Mr. Marc…

Because that could get complicated because of the boy who got shot and the boy who ran, you understand, you *probably would not want to ask for asylum and spend a year or two in immigration prison* while they investigated your history in Ethiopia, Correct?

Yes, Mr. Marc. I will not ask for asylum. There is no reason to do that.

Good. Well, I must go. Your lawyer Ms. Oliphant will come to interview you in two weeks. Good luck. Fikir. I will give your regards to Ato Sisay.

Please give my regards to…all peoples, Mr. Marc.

I will, Fikir. If you do not seek asylum, in a month or two you will be deported. Obama has really sped up the process. Keep in touch from Ethiopia. Here is my card.

Thank you Mr. Marc.
Goodbye Fikir.

Kay Lee's Coming Home (She Says)
Kay Lee: **Chicago**

Dear Weyzero Eden and sister Selam. Please tell my mother and all my family I am coming to Ethiopia for a long visit, maybe even to live there. Many years ago I was taken against my will from my country and now it is time to come home and be with my people. Fikir is here, but he got into trouble and I don't know what is going to happen to him. Don't worry, though, he is OK. I hope to live in Dice Dota and learn Amharic. Once I get to Adis I will contact you. I am earning money for the airplane and think I will be there by the beginning of February next year, but I will let you know more when I have made my final travel arrangements. Weyzero Eden and Selam, please send me your phone numbers and of all my family so I can reach you by phone. Don't forget to tell my mother that I am coming. I send all my love and cannot wait to be home. Marc and Lisa send all their love. Love, Kalkidane.

Lushi Has A Fantasy About Helen And Helmut And Dreams Of Sagar
Lushan: Adis Ababa

Why does Helen Heaven want the sex potent? Will she give it to her German and then while he is sleeping cast a love spell on him so he awakes with a big penis and must have her, but she says, no, no, you cannot have me, only if you leave your German wife and marry me will I ever make sex with you again, otherwise I will go back to Seven Nights and meet a richer man than you and have his children?

And so drunk he is with her beauty and smell that he promises to leave his wife and marry her, and he tries to kiss her, but she hisses and shows her nails and says, you've said that before, what is the proof, because without the proof the thing you want so badly you will never have again, and he says, no, this time is the truth, you are the most beautiful woman in the world and I want you to have my children, and so she says, if you lie, my curse will follow you everywhere in the world and you will never have happiness again, so think about what you saying, because, look at me, look at my body, I can find another man, but can you find another Heaven?

And he says, I never want to be apart from you, and so she thinks *he is all penis, and he thinks he is lying but he is not,* he will not be able to keep the promise of this lie, because she, Helen Heaven, has cast all her woman's power behind her spell, the power of Maryam the Mother and Dinknesh Lucy the Wonderful, and so she exhausts him for the whole day and night, with her hunger for his seed, pulling it out of him again and again in all the different ways, from the front and back and standing and kneeling, stopping only to sleep and eat, and he, because she has truly bewitched him with the sex potent, he cannot believe that he has the strength to do it many times, more than he has ever done since he was a young man.

And so the next day he flies back to his wife in Germany, but there is nothing like those two days ever with his wife, and every hour he thinks of Helen Heaven, because she has truly bewitched him in the hotel, he has never been caught this way and in the meantime Dinknesh's spell is working. Once his seed takes root in her womb the magnet of her is irresistible even from Africa to Germany and when the wife Crystal knows this, she divorces Helmut who moves to a separate house in that town with the very tall pointed church that we saw in the picture. And then he comes back to Ethiopia for the birth of his daughter, and then, in Ethiopia, they marry and go back to Germany, and then sponsor me to work as their housemaid and babysitter, and I go to university in Germany to study business and there I meet Sagar as planned, and we marry there and move to Dubai, and with the help of his father and Abeynesh from Ethiopian Airlines we open the Store of Gold.

2016

Geta Videos The Death Of Betlihem At The Protest
Captain Abinet: Dice Dota

On 15 May, the Ethiopian Peoples Unity Front issued a press release that condemned the "tragic and deplorable killing of innocent Ethiopian university students. While news of the shooting of unarmed protesters has caused great concern among many Ethiopians, there has been little coverage overseas. The government strictly censors domestic media; it ranks as one of the world's chief jailers of journalists. Independent reporting of events in the country has become increasingly difficult. – The International Sentinel, Thurs. May 21, 2014

Ethiopians should stand up for your rights NOW or NEVER!

It is so predictable. I have seen it the last two elections and now again. They gather at Piazza with their loudspeakers and give *the speech*, always the same, about corruption and democracy and the domination of Woyane, and then they march to the Regional Office in Dice Dota to present their manifesto. And as they turn off the main street to approach the government compound we come from the Telecom office behind them to cut them off and chase them towards the office. Then our other squad comes out of the gate, so they are squeezed between us; we beat them and they run; we chase them, catch some of them, beat some more and take the ones we catch to the truck and then to jail. Others run down the side streets and this is as planned; those who run cry out, "they are beating us, they are beating us," and this serves to warn any one else who might protest. It happens before every election. And it is organized from within; one of the leaders of the students, I forget her name, is a spy for the Regional Government.

Except this time was different. I don't know if there was an order from the top or if it was an improvisation of Captain Melech, but no doubt it was he who fired the AK. I saw the flame from his barrel. And everyone saw the bullet take away the front of the girl's head. I've seen this before but this was a new thing for the students; when they saw and felt the blood splatter on them and the fragments of bone sting their cheeks they became frenzied and ran towards the soldiers instead of away. How could these students think to run at armed soldiers when they had no weapons? They should have just fallen down. The problem was that they could not think. They just were mad like a hurt ox that will charge a wall. Of course, we fired to keep them from tearing us apart with their hands. For a minute I thought I was back in Eritrea when the Eritrean females ran out of bullets and fought us with their hands. Like then, I fired up. But others did not.

And now there were some students dead and others wounded. We did not chase the ones who ran. We were too astounded at what had just happened. Really, many of us had brothers and sisters in university and high school in Mekele and these students could have been them. One thing Woyane does right, though, all soldiers in the South come from the North and East, and soldiers who suppress the North are from the South or West, so there is little chance of oppressing your own family. For certain if we had been facing our own clan, our guns would have been pointed at whoever would shoot them.

No matter, whether ordered or not, the shooting was a big mistake. Because one of the students used his phone to video the shooting of the girl. I saw him do this, he was young, not from the university but wearing the colors of the Black Lion High School, and I should have shot him, but I was so disgusted with what had happened I held fire. Other soldiers sent bullets his way but he ran into a side street and was gone. It seems that he instantly sent the pictures with the sounds of the screaming hurt ones to other students who sent it to others and soon there was a big angry crowd in front of Saint Abraham, many, many and growing all the time. Not just students now but members of the UDJP and other known oppositionists, some of whom had been jailed and then released after the last election, ones who usually are careful not to stick their necks out, but on this day they were fearless. Our soldiers at the Church called Major Mengistu for instructions and support; we all gathered by the radio telephone to listen. They said that now this boy had the loudspeaker and was waving his phone, saying: "Send the video of the Dice Dota massacre to everyone everywhere, in Ethiopia, to the USA and Europe, by email, Twitter and Facebook, so that the whole world would know that the face of EPRDF was stained with the blood and brains of those who hated corruption." It was the same kid I declined to shoot, now causing big trouble. Then the soldiers said that the number one UDJP guy, Ato Tewedros, the one who had just been released last year, now had the loudspeaker and was calling everyone to march back to the gates of the Regional Government to save the wounded and bring the dead to their families.

What should we do? Shoot, make arrests, do nothing?

Mengistu told them, "Stay in the church, ask the priests for the priest vestments, put your AKs under, go out the back door and follow at the back of the march. Keep your eyes on them and if you are discovered and attacked, threaten but don't be aggressive. If there are stones, shoot in the air as you retreat. There are too many of them. If they all run at you, you could be trampled.

Meanwhile the bodies are lying on the street and the wounded are crying for help. It was so sad. I said, "Hey Major, shouldn't we do something about these wounded, call for the medical truck and arrange the bodies before the people get here?" I thought if the people saw the bodies lying there and the wounded crying for help with no response, they would go berserk and attack the soldiers and then we would have to shoot them.

Melech gave me a look that spoke: he was the Roman who slept well after he'd hammered the spikes through the palms of Jesus. He cared nothing for the waste of these young people's lives, their family's pain or the agony of the wounded. To him, enemies of the government were cockroaches. His look said "OK you feel for these Southern insects. Go help them die," and with a toss of his head he indicated I should tend to the wounded and arrange the dead. I looked to the other soldiers and thanked God when Lisbe, Semret and Jibril came forward with no thought of punishment.

All of Ethiopia saw this video. I am in it. I am the soldier firing his AK in the front. If you rewind it and look carefully, you can see that I am shooting high, but to the millions who have seen this, it looks like I am trying to kill the camera. If the government does not fall, I can use this to my advantage for promotions. It is documented – I am the famous soldier in the video who stood by his commander and his government and fired on command. But also, if the government falls, when they look closely, then I am the famous soldier in the video from the North who refused to kill the students in Southeast Peoples Region. So either way I am a hero. But the government will not fall, not yet. Melech will make me a colonel. And then when there is an investigation of the student massacre, he will go to jail and I will become commander. And this will put me in the position to go higher in the army. If I play my cards right I could get in High Command in Adis and then be part of the strategy meetings with the Minister of Defense. Oh, how I long for the day when I am at a meeting with him, in the palace of Haile Selassie and then I can take out my M9 and avenge the death of my father.

The Student Demonstrators Hide In The Cave Of All Religions
Iman Muhammad: **Shashamene**

Their names were Kiflu, Antoneh, Sebbie and Geta. They came at night by the east path, up the cliffs from the fields of Ali Dulani. When the dogs woke us, my sons and I got the dogs and took our lights and rifles to go greet our unknown visitors. So many bandits think we hold money and are rich from the Cave. With Allah's help we are careful and always ready. The dogs held them against a tree until we turned the lights on their faces.

They said they were students from Dice Dota. One of them, the boy Kiflu, knew the Cave; he had once come with his friend Fikir the guide, bringing tourists. They asked if they could find sanctuary; there had been violence in Dice Dota and the government was looking to arrest them. Could they hide from Woyane in the Mosque of the Church in the Ground? I told them that it was for Allah to decide. I sent my daughter for Fanta and biscuits. Then after they had drunk and eaten I asked them to follow us into the most secret chamber, the mosque of the chapel of Theodosia so that we could pray without fear of discovery. By flashlight they followed us down the ladders and through the tunnels to the house of Theodosia. As is our custom before we speak with God we waited in the dark to listen for his voice. When Allah told me he was ready, we made the lights. I told the children to pray first, and then to ask. Always visitors to the Cave are confused about how to pray. Is it Islam or Orthodox, is the Cave Mosque or Church? They do not understand that it is both and that Allah is God, the father of Jesus. The students were all Orthodox so I told them to do what is their custom. They made the cross and prayed to Jesus and John. Then they showed Allah the video on the phone of the youngest boy named Geta, of the soldiers killing the girl and then they told us of the shooting and killing of the others outside the Government Office. I let them tell him their story directly in prayer. They spoke of how after the shooting the people became furious and gathered in the square, then marched again to the Government; how the soldiers used the gas to disperse them and did not shoot, but then came to their houses looking for them, calling them "ring-leaders"; of their escape in the night through the fields to bypass the border checkpoint at Red Pasture and enter into Oromia, and of how they walked at night through the mountains to Ali Durani's land and then, by the back way, up the cliffs to our chapel in the ground.

And Allah listened and told me to ask them: Why did they make a demonstration that upset the order of the town? Why did they come here and put me and my family and the Mosque of the Church in the Ground, in danger? And, if they were innocent of all crimes, why had they run?

Their answer was that they were only asking the government to act justly as God would want, that no student had been violent or had meant to make social disorder, rather, they had sought to make society more peaceful by asking for an end to corruption and favoritism, so that students from all tribes would have the same opportunity for advancement; that opposition candidates would not be put in prison; and that officials in city and regional government who abused women would be punished. They ran, not because they were guilty, but because the army had already murdered and beaten others and was now looking for them. And that, if they were caught by the government, who knew what would happen. They were sorry to put the Cave of All Religions in danger, but they thought that no one would think to look for them here, and that as soon as possible they would leave at night for Shashamene.

After a while God told me that their request was reasonable. I told them that I would return after the next day and let them come up to wash and eat, to see the stars and breathe the air of Allah. In the day we would be conducting tours in parts of the cave close by, so they must be quiet and careful with the light so no gleaming would come from under the door. My son would bring them flashlights and food and water and we would check in on them from time to time. It would be a long day for them; they should pray and meditate that God forgive the soldiers and keep all peoples safe. Then I left the Cave.

Genet Discovers The Revolution And Money To Be Made From End Products
Genet, Helen, Lushan and Selamawit:
2205 Churchill Road, Adis Ababa

Helen, here is the Abduction Medicine.

No, there is no change. It was just like I said. He wanted 250 and I talked him down to 215.

What, do you think I am a thief to keep your money? If I was, this apartment would be empty by now, just believe it. My way is always true, that is why I will be more rich than any thief because all thieves will trust me and I will have all their business. Now please, Helen is your cell phone charged? Let me use it. We must contact Mola Abera immediately. Selam, Lushi, I know how we all can make some money. I have a perfect idea. Do you know about the Unity March? Everyone in the Merkato is talking about it, the students are marching to Shashamene to call for no shooting in the election time and freedom to speak, thousands of them will gather there on Bob Marley's birthday. And the Army of Love song, everyone is singing it. Have you heard it?

So when they come to Shashamene with so many freedom words coming out of their mouths, then a whole lot of waste will come out of their other ends and where will they piss and shit? Not in the fields where they are sleeping and cooking, no, that would make disease. And where will the girls do their sanitation? If we can get Mola Abera to bring a truck of 10 portapotties down there, we could make so much money, 700 birr a day *each*, by managing them. Look at this paper. I figured it out: a lot of University students are rich and many of them are used to sanitation in their sleeping halls; they will find the money to use the toilets. If we charge 2 birr for five minutes, if we knock on the doors when the time is up, they could be used 12 times an hour,

15 hours each day. There are 10 seats so we can collect 3,600 each day. 40% would go to Abera for transport and the pumping, and we would all split the rest of the 60% three ways. *What do you think of 720 birr a day?*

Don't be afraid of what might happen. If the soldiers start shooting, we can hide until the shooting is finished.

No, I did not learn this mathematics in school, because I could not go to school. I learned this from making business, the same way I learned to read, playing student to the children who went to school so they could play teacher and pretend to punish me, and later trading cleaning for learning with a woman from Shell Ethiopia. If you are smart you can always find a teacher. There are many who need to teach the same way a child needs to learn. And there are few who learn as quickly as me.

So please, give me this phone. If this demonstration goes on for only a week we will be rich enough from all this shit to buy gold from my friends and rent a stand in the Merkato. I need to call Johannes who used to be a glue boy. He is now the captain of the shintabet team behind the Holy Trinity Church. He knows how to contact Mola Abera. I have his number. Helen, give me your phone.

I apologize. I am lacking a mother and so I am impolite. Thank you for the correction. *Please*...the phone. *Dear* Helen. Thank you.

Hello? Hello? Is that Johannes? Johannes it is Genet. Genet with the t-shirts, Genet with the chiclets, you met me in the Children's Jail. Are you stoned? Of course not, I know that, I was just checking. I congratulate you. It is hard to stay straight and truly, I am happy that you will have a brain to work with in the future. Look, I need to find the number of Mola Abera. You have it? Fantastic. I will give you 10 birr for his phone number. Text this number with it. Listen, you know I will pay you. I always do what I say. Who else does that? Why else do they call me *True Word Girl?*

The Unity Wave Rolls On Shashamene
Getachew: **The Field Behind The Rastah Museum, Shashamene**

Abesha the time has come
To throw off the rule of the gun
to fight like Ghandi and King and Mandela
that we may all rule Ethiopia With The Army of Love
The Army of Love

The Singer predicted One Love
Feelin' All Right and what about One Heart?
An end to the fightin' and killin' and shootin'
Army, policemen, their jails and their trucks and their guns
The Army of Love

Abesha our song is our prayer
To speak our minds and not be scared
To vote and travel and live where we please
To throw off the rule of the gun with the Army of Love
The Army of Love

The name of the river is Blue
The water is me and is you
We grow in Abesha the flower of love
in the hearts of all people to fight against torture and guns
The Army of Love

To Shashamene we come
To throw off the rule of the gun
To fight like Ghandi and King and Mandela
That we may all rule Ethiopia With The Army of Love
The Army of Love

OK, you call me the father of the Unity March but really I had no intention to start anything, I was just lucky enough that Ahmet lent me his phone and that it was charged, so I could shoot the killing of poor Betlihem and the other students. With the way the front of her skull blew off and how her face disappeared in blood, and the students falling and screaming and the wounded boy wailing, "Oh Jesus, Jesus," the gun bursts and the man shouting, "You kill your children," my video did more for the Unity Movement than any speech ever. After they showed it on CNN and Al Jazeera, suddenly millions of people all over the world remembered Ethiopia. The last they'd heard of Ethiopia was of the famine in the 90's. Who gave a damn when Ethiopian students were killed in 2001 and 2014? But with that cruel picture of Betlihem's head exploding, the world took notice.

But we only found this out when we got to the Rastah Museum. We'd had no news in the cave. We passed easily through a checkpoint in the night, wearing black cloth on our heads, and herding the donkeys of Muhammad's son who accompanied us, so the soldiers took us for Arsi tribe and didn't ask for ID. When we finally got into the Rastah Museum and onto Silverstone's computer what we found amazed us; the video had 400,000 hits from Ethiopia and three million from the Diaspora in the USA and Europe. And then was a big miracle as if a hyena gave milk to a lamb: Abesha calling themselves *Bahadir/Chicago* appeared on Facebook and Twitter and all the Amharic dating sites, calling, in the name of Ghandi and King and Mandela, for everyone in Ethiopia who wants freedom of speech and assembly and fair election, to meet on Bob Marley's birthday, February 6th in Shashamene, to show love against guns. And the song *"Army of Love"* they made was great, you cannot forget it, you hear it once and you sing it too: "To Shashamene we come, to throw off the rule of the gun." In one day it started and all last week it grew and grew. Really, after my video, the Unity March was a secret that everyone knew.

Silverstone was shitting scared – would the government blame the Rastahs for making revolution? No one had asked their permission to invite the world to Shashamene. At first he blamed us, but I explained to him that it was just because the power of Bob Marley was so strong and that so many worship the Redemption Song and One Love that the Chicago/BaHadir group had called for the march to Shashamene – and now that the Unity March would wash over the town – this was his chance to make the Rastah Way the Ethiopian Way. Students from everywhere, high school and university, technical college and vocational school, from Arba Minch to Mekelle, Bahir Dar, Jimma, Gondar, Jijiga, Dire Dawa to Assosa, from all tribes – Oromo, Amhara, Somali, Wolayta, Gurage, Sidama – from all regions, were not returning to classes after Timkat. By foot, marching and singing along the highways, by bus, van, donkey and motorbike, the students were coming. The government could not stop them; it was like trying to stop a river with a hand. Wherever the government set up a check point, it was posted on Facebook with maps and alternative routes, so the Unity surge flowed around, came through the fields and on footpaths through mountains, walking, by donkey, by bicycle or hidden in trucks.

Now there are 30,000 students in Shashamene camping in the fields all around the north and east side of town behind the Rastah Museum. Silverstone is happy because he is selling ganja; the Shashamene shiftas have a corner on the khat business, the Rastah women sell injera and the local Oromo, goat, firewood and umbrellas; witch doctors push remedies against tear gas and bullets and the Protestants predict the end of days. In fact, the whole Unity March is as much a festival as a political event. And an amazing thing happened: when I waited in line to use the portable shitters, *the girl who was the attendant was my sister Lushi.* How could that be? I thought she was in Dubai. And then when she saw me, she called out and *there was Selam,* also working the shitters. They said they were working for Mola Abera who had fixed things with the army to provide sanitation so no cholera would come to the Shashamene region. Tonight they will come to the Army of Love HQ so we can catch up.

The feeling is good; there has never been a gathering for peace like this in all the history of Ethiopia. When there was a fight over the best table place between the "Blue River" t-shirt vendors from Ziway against the "Let's Get Together and Feel All Right" vendors from Hawassa, the bystanders jumped in and stopped it, telling the sellers that peace was the point, not money. Some of our friends from the One World Circus took the back roads around the Chinese plantation and brought their generator and lights; now they entertain us at night with their band and with juggling and there are many guitars and singers and dancers who join them. Always the song is "Let's Get Together and Feel All Right" and "The Army of Love." Meanwhile the military is gradually tightening the ring of soldiers and checkpoints around the encampment and cutting off cell phone reception. What will happen? In three days is Bob Marley's birthday and tomorrow there will be a meeting of all the Army of Love leaders. Two people will represent each region. Because of my video I was chosen with the girl, Eden, to be part of the Dice Dota team. We will meet to decide the next Unity action. Can we bring the soldiers to our side? And if we do, what then? Can we turn all the blood of the past into clear blue water?

Fikir Gets A Free Ride Back Home
Fikir: **Midway Airport, Chicago**

I could make it here. I could marry for my green card, work at the airport, park cars or drive taxi like the other Ethiopians and send money back to my mother and her family, but then I would never have my big chance. You think I am upset because they are throwing me out of America? Not at all. I accept their gift of a ride in a van to the airport and a free flight to Adis; it is worth at least 20,000 birr. The handcuffs are a small price to pay to get out of this cold place.

My God, my life is a better movie than has ever been made. It surpasses Spielberg or Bruce Lee. You laugh, but I think I will have the last one. Why? Because it is my time. You could not have imagined me three years ago. I am only 23 years old, a poor boy from Ethiopia but I have already been to China and Europe and America. Now with antibiotics, my life expectancy is 64 years in Ethiopia so, if God is willing, I have a big life ahead of me: houses, women, children and grand-children and, with the investment of Marc and Mrs. Lisa, my business will become bigger than Ali Durani's. So what is my idea you ask? You would like to see my business plan? Ha ha. Good try! The idea is secret. I cannot tell you or you will steal it, but I will give you a clue that is a question: What does Fikir know that a billion others want to know? What? You cannot guess. Well then, I will give you a hint. The plant we call "banana," some call "shung jow." Do you get it? What do I know that everyone will want to learn? And is this not worth a lot of money? And once I have some profit from this first business, it will not be a problem to find a loan to buy property and then to build and sell and rent houses and shopping centers. With the way Ethiopia is growing now, who can stop me with such an idea?

Join Our Family Of Extraordinary Egg Donors
Amethyst Kolkawalski: **Compassionate Fertility, Chicago**

We pioneered egg donation and blessedly became the most prestigious program in the country. Due to our ranking, reputation and high volume of matches, we offer a superb opportunity at being matched very quickly. The gift of donation has immeasurable emotional reward but we also offer the highest compensation.

Hey, I'm not supposed to talk about donors, but just as long as you promise not to write it down I will speak about the girl in question, OK, but it has to be completely *off the record*, right? If you don't mind me asking, what did she do? Oh, right, that's confidential. Where are you from again? Right, the UN. A great organization. I always give to UNICEF.

She was something else, Ms. Anonymous, cool as a cucumber. She really didn't seem to have a lot of doubt like the some of the others. She was good-looking, had 145 IQ, 3.8 average, partial scholarship to college and she was Black; the demand from Black couples is enormous. She knew her eggs were golden. The big question was genetics; she was adopted from a couple in Africa. We couldn't fact check what she told us about her natural parents, and we couldn't call her adoptive parents because she was over 18 and an adult, so all could do was the standard stuff; the ovarian exam, bloodwork for CF, Tay-Sachs, sickle cell, thalassemia, and, in her case, malaria. And, of course, the mandatory talk with our shrink, Dr. Linda. She did fine. Then she knocked it out of the park at the staff interview, spoke about helping other Black couples and going to school without debt, and really, the way she used her body and her eyes when she talked, (she must have practiced) had us all mesmerized. We *all* wanted her to have our baby.

Of course, it's mostly about looks, we all talk about the "right fit," but the reality is, everyone wants eye-candy for a kid – and she was. We had this Black couple on deck – he worked for Comcast and she was a lawyer with the City and they lived like on the 95th floor of Lakepoint Towers – who'd been looking for some pure African genetic stock for over a year and once they saw her picture they were slain; they were calling every day to see if they could get her eggs in their basket.

She wasn't fazed by the self-injections, didn't complain of torsion, never called for counseling. Once she'd synched up her cycle with Mrs. X's and bloomed, it went like clockwork. She took the drug to release the eggs, came in 36 hours later, did the sonogram – which was fine – and *Bam!* We harvested 20 ovules in thirty minutes. That girl was *fecund*. We fertilized them in the lab with Mr. X's sperm, let 'em incubate, selected the most vital and got the little gonna-be up in Mrs. X's uterus five days after the extraction. A classic non-complicated procedure. Follow-up went fine, no OHSS, we cut the check for how much I am forbidden to say and that's the last we saw of Ms. Anonymous. She said she might be back to do it again for next year's tuition and we said fine, please, you were great. We haven't heard from her. She was going to some college up in Iowa. I hope she's having a great year.

Oh really, she's in Africa now? What's she doing, a program with you guys? My niece went there as part of a project at her college, working with kids, teaching English, you know, trying to make a difference. It wasn't Ghana, but close to Ghana. Kenya. She was there for three weeks. She loved it. She said they need so much and it's amazing how a little goes a long way.

Oh, right, I understand, you can't say, it's "confidential." I hope she's not in trouble. And if you see her, tell her we're glad it all worked out for her. She can come back any time.

Kay Lee Flies To Ethiopia To Shashamene
Kay Lee: Queen Alia International Airport, Zizya, Jordan

Hi, Miranda.

Kay Lee! Where are you? I've been texting but...

Amman, Jordan. It's a 6-hour layover between Chicago and Adis.

What? You bought the ticket and just flew away? You're amazing. How much did you get?

Seven.

Seven? Helaine only got five.

She's White. And there was a Black couple who *loved* my picture and wanted, like real African eggs, and my rhythm synched right up with the Missus so I got more. I guess they thought I was an heirloom tomato or something.

That's sick. How much was the ticket?

Two grand. Look Miranda I want you to...

What about your folks? Do they know?

Marc drove me to the airport.

No, about how you got the money.

Duh. I don't hide shit from them. If I'd just bought the ticket they would have thought I was dealing or selling bootie, or something, so like, right, I told them. They didn't have a problem with that. It's my body.

And your Ma? What does she think about you leaving?

Her uncle went to Ghana for 8 years after the cops murdered Fred Hampton, so she gets it. She says she'd do the same if it weren't for Grandma and Marc and Marc's folks, but she's just saying that, she'll never leave Chicago.

And you know she did the sweetest thing. Before I left she gave me this tiny gold bracelet. She told me that it was from Nigest my real mother, that it was around my ankle when they adopted me and that I should take it with me as my birthright. That I should carry the Gold of Ethiopia with me for luck. And that if I ever had a daughter I should give it to her.

Hey, so Miranda…just in case I lose the connection, tell them that I told you I am going to Shashamene. Write it down. S-H-A-S-H-A-M-E-N-E. It's a town. Everyone in Ethiopia is going there for like this huge party for Bob Marley's birthday, called the Unity March. Did you hear the song The Army of Love? It's gone viral. It's from these Ethiopian kids. Some from Chicago, I know them. And these Ethiopian guys on the plane, they are Rastahs, they are flying home to go to it, they invited me to go with them. They say it's going to be bigger than Woodstock, except it's for peace, not just music. Hang on a second.

OK. Look, Miranda, we are going to go see if we can find a place to lie down. Me and the Rastah guys. Yes they are hot but no way am I going to get involved with an African guy. To them you're just a green card. It's like 3AM here and we fly at 6 to Adis. I need to sleep. Tell everyone I'm OK and remember, tell them, *Shashamene*, Kay Lee's going to *Shashamene*. To Shashamene she comes.

An Ethiopian Farmer Speaks His Mind To The Students
Ato Abdella: Kuyera Debeda

These students think they are so far above. They walk through our fields on shoes we cannot afford to buy for our kids, and they don't even take them off when they are in the dirt, they are so rich. Their parents are connected with Woyane. How else would they be accepted in the college and afford to stay there? Look, one of them takes a banana, the little bastard.

Hey, you, do you want me to kick your ass? Do not take my banana.

No, I will not give you. It's 2 birr for banana. Water? 2 birr. We carry this from the well; do you think we carry it for you? If you do not want it, there is water after 10 km. in Shashamene. And please get out of my field. Use the path. You do not know what I have planted there. If you are hungry my wife would make you some wat and give you injera. 15 birr for each one of you, no, not 12, 15. And for the injera, 2 birr each.

So then go, suit yourself, walk to town and buy it, if you can find it – but I can tell you, so many students are coming through there may be no food left in Shashamene. And tell me, you who tried to steal my banana, how can you leave the university and come here to make trouble when you are supposed to be learning? It is clear that you should be studying, because, if you think the soldiers will not hesitate for one minute to shoot you, it is obvious that you know nothing. It won't matter to them if your father is Woyane or working at Dashen Bank, if the captain says shoot, you will eat bullets. My sister is stationed in the Ogaden, and she has been ordered to Shashamene. All soldiers will be coming to meet you.

Oh yes we have heard of the song of the Army of Love. We love to sing it. Are you sure you would not like to buy some wat? Injera? Water?

Dear Sagar
Lushan: **Marley School House, Shashamene**

Greetings Sagar this is Lushan on FB. Please friend me. You will find me @ LuZena99 on FB. I am sorry that I did not message you sooner but I lost the FB address you gave me until now. I found it in the end of a shoe where I had hidden it and I was so glad. There is Internet here in the library of the Rastahs in Shashamene so now I can say hi. My sister Selam helps me with the English. In this she is perfect.

How is your father? Does he have health? Are you fine? Please let me thank him and you for saving me from my employer and helping me return to my country. You brought me safely to my home and I am forever grateful for this service. I hope that some day I may repay you and your family.

And please excuse my English. I missed too much school when my father sold me to Dubai. Now I am in the town of Shashamene with my sister and her friend Genet. There is a great gathering of students and my sister and I hope to make much money with portapotties and then open a gold business in the Adis Merkato, which they say is the biggest in the world. There is the possibility of returning to Dubai for this gold business.

Another plan, Sagar, is to study in Germany. There is the possibility of my sister's friend marrying a German and going to that country. If she does this she will sponsor me working there and then I will learn German and go to university to learn business. All day I think of my future, when I will have a job and a house and a family. And perhaps a husband, though the men here in Ethiopia often abuse.

Are you in university in your country? Do you study biology in the way that you hoped? I am wondering if you go to university in Germany we could meet. You were very kind to me and I often pray that I will see you again.

One thing I remember is our journey on the Tiger when the whale came up and then with you and Ahmet in the truck through Somalia for two days and never leaving it except at night and dressed in a boy's clothes. When you were strong with the soldier at the border who wanted me to get out of the truck, telling him I was sick with the lung disease and giving him money, telling him to be careful from infection and how I coughed and coughed and how we laughed once we got through.

Sagar, please write me back. You see here is my Facebook and now we are friends. There is Internet here in the library of the Rastahs in Shashamene so now I can say hi. I am also trying to find your father's friend, Abeynesh. I had Internet in Adis and tried to find her but I was not successful. Will you send me her email? I want to thank her so much.

With great thankfulness and respect, Lushan.

A Not-So-Bad Interrogation
In Which Fikir Gets Slapped Only Once
Officer Abselo: **Immigration Bureau, Bole Airport, Adis Ababa**

You say you left the employment that you had in the city of Atlanta and then were robbed and beaten by a gang of Jamaicas. Then you went to the city of Chicago to look for a friend but the police found you without your visa and identification, and put you in the immigration prison and then deported you. Surely you know, Mr. Fikir, since you have been deported from one country, that now it will be almost impossible for you to get permission to leave Ethiopia again. So, why did you not fight the extradition? This is unusual. Most who are caught will do everything to avoid returning to Ethiopia.

Ahmed, come over here. Listen to this kid's bullshit. What a joker. He says he came back to Ethiopia to make money. Ha ha. That's the first time we've heard that one. Should we show him how we find out the truth?

So, you do not cry out. Are you used to it then, Mr. Fikir? Would you like more? How about telling us the real story? What did the CIA ask you to look for? Are you working for Israel? We know you ran from China and broke your contract with the Gymnastics Federation. And then you went to Europe and then to America. Why did the Chinas let you go? How much are they giving you? And we know why you went to Chicago. It was not to see a friend; we have read your emails to your relatives there. We know your family history and we honor your father and the sacrifice of your mother, but don't think that we will be easy on you just because they were enemies of the Derg. And we see that, when you were a student in Dice Dota, you were making political trouble with your Club Against Harmful Tribal Practices. We need the truth from you and, believe me, if Ahmed smells a lie then you will have an unforgettable experience; he is an artist at getting people to remember. He is not a crude slapper like me; he uses special devices and he leaves no bruises. So tell us really, why did you come back to Ethiopia?

Ahaha. Well then, that is interesting. You say to *teach China language*, and that so many will want to learn in order to get jobs with the Chinas that you will make enough money to buy property and build houses and hotels and become the next Ali Dulani. Well Mr. Fikir, this is interesting, this is original, this is almost plausible. Let's say, just for the moment, that this is your dream for real. What do you say Henok, do you smell a lie? Will you have to plug in your truth machine?

No? Well, this is a surprise. Mr. Fikir, I must say, it is a rare day when Henok does not take the opportunity to demonstrate his talents. Hennie, is it that you want to learn Chinese and get a job with the Chinas? Hahaha.

Mr. Fikir, I apologize for my little slap. Often we do this just so people know that we are serious about the truth. Would you like some coffee? A beer? St. George? Bedele Special? Henok would you call and order. And for me, a Johnny Walker. Red please, not black.

Hennie will not touch alcohol. He is Muslim. So guess what? If he cannot find khat he is so unhappy he becomes like a monster.

Listen Mr. Fikir, I like this idea of yours, I like it very much, but you know that in order to open a language school you will need a license and, if there is suspicion about your deportation, well, that could be a problem. What would you do then? Go to the side of the road and sell watermelons and bananas? You know, with your gymnastic training you could probably do well, you could juggle watermelons and tomatoes; you would attract all the business and all the other poor beggars will starve. You would be the Ali Dulani of the Tomato on the road to Moyale. Hahaha.

You don't laugh. So, you are a very serious man, I can see, you do not like anyone to joke about your dream. Well, look, do not be discouraged. I told you, I like the idea of a China school and if you cooperate with us, we will not stand in the way of you getting a license, and actually, we could make that happen very fast. You know how these things are; usually it takes a year but we could make it happen in two weeks if we put the right word about you in the right ear. What do you think?

Oh, you do not need to thank us, but, come to think of it, there is something you could do that would be very helpful to us. You know your famous relative, Getachew Zena? The one who shot the video of the soldiers killing the girl Betlihem?

You don't know about this? Everyone in the world knows about this. It has become a virus on the Internet. Ah, you were in the immigration prison, so you did not see. Yes, Betlihem from Dice Dota. She was a student who worked in the café called Metro. Maybe you knew her. You did? She was a friend? Oh, you will be very sad to see that video. It is very disturbing.

Well listen, your brother, all right, he is not your brother, but this little bastard who is like your brother, Getachew Zena, is now a leader of the Unity March. You haven't heard of that? Well, now many students are going to Shashamene to fight violence. And he is their leader. Surely you want nothing bad to happen to him. And, neither does the government. If he is shot or exposed there will be hell to pay.

What did I mean by "exposed?" Aha, you are very quick. No, of course not. Who would think that Getachew was working with the government? No one, I'm sure.

Here is the beer for you. Do you chew? Ahmed, come on, be a good guy, share your leaves. Is there khat in China? No? Yes, opium, of course. But they execute for that. They are so serious. So, first we will chew and have beer. And then we will go to Seven Nights. They have the most beautiful girls, better than Stars of Heaven. My girlfriend Tati, she runs the place. Ahmed, bring the khat. Will you cut it?

So, Mr. Fikir, what do you think about making a stop in Shashamene for a couple of days before you go home to Dice Dota so you can give your friend Geta a message. These kids, they are so reckless, they will march right into the guns of the army and then some idiot captain will start the shooting and there will be a big mess, someone will make another video of the "Shashamene student massacre," the farange will complain, there will be a counter movement and all the old liberation bandits will dig up their old rifles, just to pretend they are still fighting for Amhara, Oromo, or Somali independence or, even more stupid: "Bring back the monarchy," the same old shit. What do they want, another Syria? And it will all be so unnecessary. Now Ethiopia is developing so quickly, who needs all this violence and revolution from the feudal time?

Come on now, let us drink our beer. Bottoms up! You know that one? I learned it from the English. And "Jolly good." Please, Mr. Fikir, tell us something about the USA? Did you meet my brother? He is in the state of Denver Colorado. His name is Sessay. Well then, say more about your China school. It is a brilliant idea. Will you do this here or in Dice Dota? There is a China girl at Seven Nights. Maybe she will be available and she can practice the r sound with her tongue. Hahaha. Will you chew?

Fikir Gives Kay Lee The Secret Way To Join The Army Of Love
Kay Lee and Fikir:
Shashamene/Bole Airport, Adis

Kay Lee. Are you there?

Fikir? Oh My Fucking God. Where are you?

You should not curse God.

Sorry. Where are you?

Ethiopia. Shashamene.

No way. How'd you get out of jail?

Deported. Free ticket.

Guess what? I just landed in Bole. I'm going to Shashamene. I will see you there.

Listen, don't come here. We are surrounded by soldiers. You can't get through. And there will be possibly shooting and killing.

Then I will feel at home. I will fight the guns. Did you hear about Charleston? Insane.

Racist mens. Here is tribal. Or government. Or criminal. Ha ha, they are the same. But they would not shoot in a church. Selam and Lushi and Geta are here.

Oh My Fucking God. Oh, sorry. Well then I am definitely coming.

You will not get through.

What can I do?

Wait. Maybe there is a way. Your sisters are here. They are working for the singer Mola Abera. He brings in the sanitation for the army and the demonstrators. The soldiers let the trucks through. But it is very dangerous.

I am writing this down. Mola Abera. Fikir, how can I...?

Fikir? Fikir, are you there?

Officer Abeselo Puts The Bite And The Make On Kay Lee
Kay Lee and Captain Abselo: **Bole Airport Immigration Office**

So, you are American?

Yes Sir. I was adopted. I intend to renounce my American citizenship and become Ethiopian.

You will give up American citizenship? Hey Hennie, come here, listen to this girl. She says she will give up American citizenship for Ethiopian.

Why will you give up American citizenship?

Because I am Ethiopian. I want to live with my people.

But your passport is American. And you have a tourist visa.

Yes sir, but once I am with my family in Dice Dota I will apply for citizenship and then an Ethiopian passport. The law says I can do that because I was taken to America against my will when I was a child. I have done the research.

And you are staying with your Ethiopian family in Dice Dota?

Yes sir.

Do you speak Amharic?

Tinesh. But I will study and study.

How are you transporting there?

My uncle has sent a van.

You know the road is closed through Shashamene. He'll have to go around.

He is a professional driver. He will know how to do it.

Are you here to join the Unity March?

What's that?

It is a song on the radio. Don't you know it?

The Unity Match? No sir. They do not have it in the USA. Is it soccer?

It is the Unity *March*, and it is *from* the USA. Listen, take my advice, stay away from Shashamene.

Excuse me? I don't know anyone in that town.

It is full of bandits.

Thank you for your advice.

OK, Ms. Kay Lee Levi. What is your Ethiopian name?

Kalkidane.

Do you know what it means?

Yes. Promise.

Yes, so what is your promise?

What?

What is your promise?

My promise is that I will honor my mother. Ethiopia.

Very good answer. Here is your passport back. And, thank you for your gift. Oh, and when it comes time to give up your American passport, here is my card. Do not just give it to any official There is so much corruption. We want to make sure that it doesn't fall into the wrong hands.

Thank you Sir.

Where are you staying in Adis?

Sir, my uncle is waiting outside the airport. He will take me to Dice Dota.

Well if somehow you miss him, you have my number if you need assistance. Do you understand?

I think I do. May I go now?

Hennie, can she go?

Right, the entry fee, Oh yes, I forgot. It is $20.

But I paid that for the visa.

This is different. This is for entry. Very good. Much luck becoming Ethiopian. Next.

Captain Melech Watches Geta On The Eyes Of Solomon And Reports That The Students Will Have A Mass Meeting. What Are His Orders?
Captain Melech: Behind The Rastah Museum

Hello Captain Abinet? It is Melech. Yes, I am watching the students on the Eyes of Solomon drone. My God, the resolution is so perfect that I can read the captions on t-shirts. *What About One Heart?* Ha. How can they get such good pictures from two thousand feet? These machines, they must be from Germany.

Are you tuned in? So now, can you see? The leaders have come out of their meeting in the Marley schoolhouse. The one with the braids and the shirt that says *Blue River* is the Geta who took the video in Dice Dota and who started this whole mess, the little bastard. Now he and two others are moving to the big field where there is a stage. The rest from the meeting are going into the campsites with their megaphones. What are they saying? Hang on, I will call our boy Fikir, he is right down there, he will be hearing this. It is ringing now.

Hello Fikir. We are seeing what is happening on our phone screens but we can't hear. What are the people with the megaphones saying?

Oh Good. In two hours. At nine?

Good. I am looking at your relative right now. He is on the stage behind the Marley School. You should go there and stay with him. Find out what they are planning. Then call me. OK. Goodbye.

So, Abinet, Fikir says they will call the committee to a meeting in two hours. He doesn't know their plan but I told him to try to find out. You must call Major Daoud and ask him what will be the strategy? Do they want the meeting stopped? And, if so, how? Do we take the hard line? There are so many. It could be a disaster. Try to get orders and then get back to me. And that girl, what's her name, Deborah, the one who is on the committee, you are her handler, so if she checks in tell me what she says. OK, we will keep watching. I sign off now.

Eden Calls A Bajaj To Take Her To Shashamene
And Finds To Her Surprise That The Driver Is Nigest
Who Fills Her In On The Death Of Gyorgis,
The Imminent Arrival Of Kalkidane
And How It Is Impossible To Get To Shashamene
Unless You Are A Soldier
Nigest and Eden: **Dice Dota**

Hey Bajaj! Bajaj!

Weyzero Kalmata where are you going?

Nigest. Now you drive a bajaj? I can't believe it. God helps me because I was looking for you. I have news. How are you?

I'm in health. And you, are you fine?

Listen Nigest, Fikir is back from America and he has joined the Unity March. He called me. I am going to Shashamene to bring him home. Can you take me? And listen, Nigest, he says that Kalkidane…

You can't get there. I had someone this morning who wanted Shashamene. I drove 90 km, half the day and then we had to turn around. The roads are full of trucks of soldiers and they won't let anyone through. They have surrounded the north part of town where the students camp behind the Rastah Museum. You must go around in a big circle by Langano to get to Shashamene. All my kids are there. Geta, Lushi and Selam.

Listen Nigest, Kalki…

Fikir is back from the USA?

Yes, he called me from Shashamene yesterday.

Eden, you are the expert in politics. Do you think the soldiers will keep their heads? Or will there be more shooting?

I lost my husband to these government people. If they take my son

I will not speak of what I would do. How is it that you drive a bajaj?

Since Gyorgis died.

He died?

Four months ago.

Why didn't you tell me? You did not invite...

We kept it quiet. He owed so much money. We didn't want all the vultures to come around to collect or we could not have paid the priest and bought the coffin and the resting place. Of course his khat and tej friends showed up. They were very disappointed that they could not chew and drink after they finished off all the food we put out for them. Fat Tadesse was there; he must have eaten half of all we made. And, of course, the next week he and his sons came to take back the bajaj but by that time the army had sent the death payment, so when I waved money at him he could not resist selling it, and because my cousin is working in the license department, it was not expensive to put my name on Gyorgis' permit. At first it was very frightening because I did not know how to drive, but my passengers helped me. Now I am perfect.

Listen, about Gyorgis, I am so sorry.

Are you joking? Please be happy that he can no longer try to make everyone around him miserable. For fifteen years, ever since he lost his leg, he was like a scorpion lashing his tail out to sting anything that moved. I was the closest so it was me he stung and stung. Really, if it had not been for the children I would be in prison for murder. I had many chances. Now I have peace in my life for the first time and my children, whom he drove away, can come home. That is, if they do not die in Shashamene.

Isn't it unbelievable? My 8-year old niece told her mother that she will not go to school, no, she will go to Shashamene for the Unity March to join the Army of Love. She knows every word to that song. My sister had to walk her to school to make sure she didn't turn around and go to the road. And you know about Geta?

Oh yes, he is famous. I heard him on the radio and then I saw on the television the phone film he made when they killed Betty. He told me he does not expect to live.

Well, that is the way with this country. My poor husband is the proof. But listen, I've been trying to tell you, Kalkidane is coming.

Kalki...?

She contacted Fikir. She hates America. She will live with you and learn Amharic and become Ethiopian. Can you imagine? How can she hate America?

Oh my God. That is fantastic news. She will come to Dice Dota?

Nigest, Do you know if there is any way to come around the soldiers to get to the student camp?

She will live with me and help with the bajaj?

Fikir says she will meet him in Shashamene.

But it will be impossible for her to get there. There are checkpoints on all roads. The army is letting water in and pump-outs for the toilets, but they turn everyone else away. Now the whole town is full of students who cannot get into the encampment. These the soldiers threaten and beat with their sticks so they will run back to their schools. I saw this at the roadblock.

And the students do not fight?

No, they are schooled in the ways of Ghandi and Mandela. Listen, Nigest, in my dream Fikir was chained to a wall like his father had been. He said, "Mommy, bring me home." I pulled his hand to get him free. He said, "Stop, stop, you are hurting my hand," but I kept pulling so hard that the wall fell on him. Listen, Nigest, my heart tells me to go to Shashamene. Lets take this bajaj and bring back our children.

I don't know. Unless you are a soldier you can't get in.

Well then, we must be soldiers. I will call my friend Jolenee who drives truck for the army. She knows every trick. Wait, I am calling Jolenee?

Hello Jolenee? Oh great, God gives me luck today. I want to talk to you. Look, I am coming to your house in half an hour. I need help. Beautiful. Thank you. God's blessings. I am on my way.

Nigest, we go to the Harrari Road. Nigest, be careful, Nigest, BE CAREFUL! Oh Christos, is this how you drive?

Kay Lee Rides The Portapotty Truck With Genet
Which Hits A Donkey And Causes a Riot
Kay Lee:
The Unity Camp Behind The Rastah Museum, Shashamene

Miranda, there are no phones or internet where I am now in Shashamene so I'm back to writing letters in my notebook, which I like better than on a computer, because somehow when my wrist travels across a page the flow doesn't break as much as when I'm tapping down on a key stroke one letter at a time. Also, who knows if I'll ever send this, I mean, I could lose the notebook, or forget I wrote this and in ten years rediscover it in some old box of my shit or, if things go bad here, these words will be bulldozed by the army with the rest of the encampment and buried with my body. In that case this account of me will live for just this hour and I will be its only witness.

I'm looking for Fikir, but good luck finding him. There are thousands of young people here and we are surrounded by soldiers. Everybody's camping. I got here a couple of hours ago and I don't know a soul. That I got here in the first place is a miracle. It's been three days since I landed at Bole and since then, holy shit, it has been intense.

At the airport, the immigration officer's uniform was so pressed and ironed he could have cut you with the crease of his pants. The minute he figured I was alone, no family or boyfriend with me, his vibes were clear: alpha male control. Unless I sucked ass he would hang me up entirely, keep me in the airport and make me report back on Tuesday the whatever at 8 AM and then again on Friday before I got a visa. He looked at my tits and then in my eyes and then back to my tits just so I'd know. He wanted to know where I was staying. If I needed help I should call his phone number. He put his hand on my arm. He offered to sell my passport. Then he and his punk buddy, another officer, soaked me for a phony entrance fee after I had already paid $20 for a tourist visa. I slipped a $20 in my passport just to speed up the process. That's the last fucking bribe I do. Once they know you are soft, they just keep chewing on you.

Anyways I got me past immigration and my backpack through customs without getting detained or having to give blowjobs to any officials, *barely*, and changed money, so then I was waiting by the airport door for the Rastahs I met on the plane to Amman who said I could ride with them to Shashamene. They were beautiful guys with the dreads and the hats and the Kingston jive, *yah man*, and *dah ting, and neddy dis* and *dreddy dat*, which spoken with an Amharic accent is really sexy, but I could hardly understand a word. What I *thought* they said was that they were students at Illinois Tech on winter break coming back from Babylon to Ethiopia for this big gathering on Bob Marley's birthday, but I figged that was bullshit, they were really dealers flying home on the golden wings of ganja because I never met a Rastah who wasn't a dealer and what Ethiopian student could afford to go back for winter break unless their dad was President of the Universe or Colonel of the World? Anyways, it was all set up, they said, their *breddah* was picking them up at Bole with a ride to Shashamene, but wouldn't you know it, out they come from this room with the same dickhead officials that put the screws on me, soldiers on either side lock-stepping them towards the luggage carousels, and the Rastah with the red dreds, Jamal, looks at me and shakes his head so I fig they're busted, I'm on my own in the no-so-hospitable and ungentle carnival they call Adis Ababa, which means "New Flower." On the other side of the airport door is a swarm of would-be guides and porters and taxi-drivers just waiting to buzz all over me. I remember from when I came to Ethiopia when I was a kid, how my Mom dealt with it. You have to be very clear about yes and no, and no and no and no, and what's Amharic for *Fuck Off!?* Then through the door and out into the teeming womb of Mother Ethiopia goes Kay Lee Kalkidane Levi Zena the Third. The taxi men don't even bother speaking Amharic to me, even though I'm Black they smell *farange*, and so I swim into a breaking wave of *You You, Miss girl, taxi, taxi...*and me – *back off, no hands, bekkah, bekkah!!!* They're fucking pulling me by my backpack to get me in their taxis and I am l fending them off until goddam am I happy to see a tall fat guy holding up a sign that says "Kalkidane Levi" and I'm thinking how can this be? But, I wave to him – *here I am, I'm Kalkidane* – and he sees me, wades in and yells something at them in Amharic so they back off. He's older and bigger than most of them, bald and has a gut which parts the waves.

"Miss Kalkidane, if you please, I am Ato Tedros. Fikir asked me to meet you. Might I carry your backpack?"

He gives the other taxi guys a look and they fade. It's clear…he *is* king. Actually his British accent is so unexpected that I'm thinking maybe he went to Oxford and is an expert in Shakespeare but he couldn't make a living teaching Hamlet in Adis so instead he drives a cab. I let him take the backpack off me and I follow him to his car, one of those beat up boxy old blue taxi sedans that were lined up in the parking lot, but his is less dinged-up than most. He puts the rucksack on the roof rack and bungies it down. He opens the door for me and I get in the back and smell the old leather. I'm thinking, maybe it's his wife who has hung those frowzy red-checkered curtains on the backseat windows. Wouldn't it be nice if he took me to his house and I would meet her and she would smell divine and serve supper on a red-checkered tablecloth, and there'd be my room with a shrine to Ethiopian Jesus and my bed under a blue and white Ethiopian bedspread. The next morning I'd go to school in a purple school uniform and I'd speak Amharic and love Beyoncé and Jesus just like I was an instant Ethiopian girl.

So, we're driving into Adis on the Bole road from the airport, breathing monoxide, smelling cinnamon, coffee and shit, passing hotels, shops and shacks, the same streetscape I remember. We whiz by this huge, very lived-in ravine below a church enclosed by one of those fences with broken glass embedded on the top, and it starts to rain; a sun shower spits from tall, billowing black clouds over Adis and big drops splatter on the dusty windshield. Ato Tedros hits the wipers and the fence-tops sparkle through the dissolving grime on the glass. I see people on the side of the road opening umbrellas, boys pulling their t-shirts over their heads and girls arranging their scarves to protect their hair.

"Will you go to Shashamene?"

"Yes."

"Well, I cannot take you there, they will stop me," says Ato Tedros, and then he looks around to see if anyone is listening, *(Is everyone paranoid here? We are alone in his taxi and still he looks around)*, and he says, "*I am already known,*" nodding his head like I know what that means. "But there is another solution from Fikir and your sisters. I will tell you."

He says that Fikir and my sisters have arranged a ride for me to Shashamene on a truck that is bringing in WCs for the army. My sisters have the connection and I can get through from the army side to the student side because the company does sanitation for both. It's all fixed with the people I ride with and the whole thing is being run by Mola Abera, a musician who provides children a way to make a living by improving the sanitation of their neighborhoods. As he tells me all this I'm wondering, what the fuck is a WC?

In a minute the sun is steaming the rain off the pavement and roofs. This part of Adis is full of little shack shops selling food and shoes and clothes. yards full of tires and lumber and cars, and little three-wheeled taxis in various states of disrepair. We come into a compound full of blue portapotties. The WCs. There's a flatbed truck with maybe twenty of them tied to the bed. Tedros gets out of the van and unties my backpack from the roof. He opens the passenger side door and beckons.

"There's your transport to Shashamene." He points to the truck. "Here are the people from your clan."

He carries the pack for me and we walk over to the truck. In the driver's seat sits a tall grey-bearded man with a bulge of dreds trailing from a Rastah hat, all yellow and red with black swirls. A scrawny little girl with a sharp face in a pink headscarf gives me the once over from the passenger side. She motions me to climb in and sit next to her.

"You are Kalkidane. I am Genet. I am sister to your sisters. Here, for your head."

She gives me a green headscarf.

"When we come to soldiers you go there. "

She gestures to the back of the truck. And I'm thinking, OMG, holy shit, *no way.* Does she mean I will have to hide in the pottapotties? What if I get locked in there and no one finds me. I'll die in there.

She sees the look on my face.

"It is required."

She gestures to the back of the truck again to be clear... *you'll go in there.* Then she speaks to the driver in Amharic, he revs the motor and we're out the gate, on a road jammed with cars and trucks and vans. I want to start a conversation with the girl and find out, how much English she speaks. How about an alternative to toilet entombment? But she falls dead asleep the minute the motor starts and is leaning on my shoulder, sniffling quietly through her nose and drooling on me through a half smile. I look down into her scarf. Her right ear is small and saddle colored, tight to her skull and she's one of those people, like Marc's sister Laurie, who doesn't have earlobes; the cartilage just curves right into her head. She smells like sweat and toilet disinfectant and her face is sharp and pretty. We're coming down a long slope and heading towards a hat-shaped mountain miles away in the distance. Along the side of the road folks are waving frantically trying to flag down anyone to buy their bananas, potatoes, tomatoes, watermelons and charcoal. Others drive donkey carts in the dirt alongside of the pavement. There's a big concrete plant on the uphill side of the road, then a replica of a fighter jet plane up on steel posts by a huge stone gate manned by men in uniform. It's an airbase. I remember it and the mountain. This is the same road we took to Dice Dota when I came here with my mother when I was twelve. A sign says "Debra Zeit."

We pass through a town into the countryside and cross a river surrounded by eroded gullies. From the bridge I see women washing clothes and naked kids swimming. The girl is dead asleep on my shoulder, still drooling and snoring like a little goat. The guy driving doesn't say a word and I'm about to ask him if he is the Mola Abera, when suddenly he slams on the brakes, too late for the herd of donkeys crossing the road. The portapotties crash together in the back of the truck and if I hadn't straight-armed the dashboard and held the girl's head we would have hit it hard, but the truck doesn't stop in time, there's a horrible crunch as it hits a donkey who, with a god-awful squeal that I will remember for the rest of my life, flies into another donkey, and now both donkeys are on the pavement, squealing. The rest of the donkeys are bucking and screaming, herdsman on horseback are surrounding the truck yelling at us and waving their rifles and swords, yes Miranda, these people had fucking swords, and their women, all with black bobbed hairdos, are beating on the hood of the truck and pulling at the driver side door. I'm paralyzed, thinking: after all this, after leaving home to return to my people, I am going to be lynched for donkeycide and I truly think I deserve death. I could see the bone coming through the poor animal's leg and *anything to stop the donkey screaming!* The little girl doesn't waste a second, she grabs my hand and, quick as a rabbit, pulls me out the passenger side door. I somehow land on my feet, she grabs my hand and starts beating on the door of the truck and yelling as if we are part of the mob, signaling me with head nods and bulging eyes to save my ass and do the same. I do, and nobody knows the difference, they are intent on murdering the driver, and I'm sorry to say, I'm not thinking about him, I'm thinking: what about my rucksack, my camera, my notebook, my underwear, my shoes? I run to the side of the truck and climb up the back rail. The truck bed is slick with blue goop that's spilled out of the portapotties but there is my pack stuffed in the corner between the cab and the rail, standing on its frame so it's out of the mess. Reaching down from the rail I pull it up and lower it down to the girl like I'm a looter, she catches it, I jump down, and we scoot through the crowd and the donkeys, down the road, each with one hand on the rucksack. There's a wall of cactus on the side of the road and we cut through a gap and crouch down behind it. We can hear the crowd yelling and men shouting. Then gun shots. Holy shit. I start to stand up to look, but the girl pulls me down, hissing....

Miranda, I have to stop writing. I think I see Fikir. I've been calling him but the phone doesn't work. And if I never finish this then you'll never know about the Arsi guy on a horse who saved me. He played a mean guitar and toted a Kalashnikoff. Maybe I should have stayed with him. He was all muscles and rich in donkeys. No, we didn't fuck. He would have had to formally abduct me, and he did not have the time. He had to get back to his donkeys.

Sergeant Jolenee Is Shameless
In Service Of Her Cousin's Wife Eden
Sergeant Jolenee and Captain Tessema:
Army HQ, Dice Dota

Good afternoon, Captain.

Good afternoon. Sergeant.

Captain, this is my cousin, Rodeat and her friend, Tesfanesh. They are with the 3rd Division.

What are they doing here? The 3rd Division is based in Jijiga.

Yes Captain, but they were home on leave. Now instead of going back to Jijiga they want to be reassigned to Shashamene. They are concerned about the situation there.

Sergeant, why are you asking me? You know that they have to work that out with their commander. I cannot reassign somebody else's soldier.

Oh I know that Captain, but...if you requested them for your division, there is a special circumstance, which is very personal. Can we discuss this in private?

Soldiers, please wait outside. And close the door.

Jolanee, so you know that already this makes me uncomfortable.

Jembere, sorry, but...

And what is with your relatives? Don't they know how to wear their uniforms? Look at their belts. And their boots? And how old are they? Surely they are close to retirement.

Look, Jembere I need a very special favor this time. Really, my relatives are very grateful people. They have brought you a gift. See? And I would be so happy if you would help them. I would really want to thank you.

Stop that. There is no privacy. What is your schedule?

My husband is in Adis. I am flexible.

How can I help?

Give them orders for Shashamene.

But then I must call their commander in Jijiga.

That would be a problem. They say they will be back on Jijiga in time, and that their commander will never know.

Yes but the situation is very serious in Shashamene. If there is fighting with the students and something happens and they are involved, my signature is on their orders.

But once they are through Control, they can tear up the orders. And if they are discovered, then that is *their* problem. No one will ever connect you to them.

One interrogation and they would tell everything.

Tesfanesh's cousin is high up in the Judicial Police. If they are caught, I think there will be leniency. And, their gift is very generous. See? That will certainly help you with the house you are building. And I will make you very happy that you helped them. We can have so much fun like we did at Langano. Did you look at the video?

I told you, not here. But can you meet me at Hotel Heron tomorrow at noon to discuss this further?

Yes, should I bring the camera?

Certainly we should document the meeting. All right, I will process the orders. Give me their IDs.

Well, there is a problem, their house was broken into and they lost their wallets.

Well, how can I issue orders?

Here, see the paper that is with the present? It has their names and ID numbers. Just fill them in.

My God, do you know the penalties for impersonating a soldier? Is nothing easy with you, Julanee?

Some things are easy. Especially when I am with you. I can't wait until tomorrow.

I told you, not here. Please. Wait outside with your relatives and I will make out the order. And tomorrow, don't forget the camera. And that uniform you wore in Langano. The red one. All right, Sergeant. You are dismissed.

Yes Sir. Thank you Sir. Very good. Sir.

Shut up! Go!

Ouch!!! Captain, Such discipline. Will you do that again?

Kaylee Finds Fikir And Her Sisters And Tells Them
Of Her Rescue By An Arsi On A Horse
Kaylee, Fikir, Selam, Lushi and Genet:
The Unity Camp Behind The Rastah Museum, Shashamene

Fikir? FIKIR it's me, Kalkidane.

My God, KALKIDANE. Genet said you are lost on the road with an accident of ahya. I called my friends in Zwai to find you.

She got here? That girl....

"Yes, Genet. With the truck and the driver and the portapotties. How did you come to Shashamene?"

"How did they ever get here? I thought the donkey people were going to rip that driver to pieces. After the truck hit the donkeys they attacked the driver, so we ran down the road and hid. Then we heard shots. I was thinking, Chicago, Ethiopia – same ol', same ol.' Then an army truck came up the road and went towards the accident. Genet told me to wait and she went back to see what was going on.

I waited and waited for her, but nothing. I figured she'd gotten arrested or something. So I stuck my head out of the cactus to take a look just as this guy came down the road with a horse, one of the donkey people. His hair was all plastered down and he had a gun, and a sword and a guitar stuck in a saddle bag. I guess he vibed that I was lost. He said something which of course I didn't understand, so I told him, 'Tinish Tinish Amharic, Englishenya?' 'No English,' he said, so I said, 'Shashamene?' He nodded OK and motioned for me to get on his horse. So I did."

"You went with an Arsi?"

"He had a guitar."

"Was he Islam?"

"Yes. He'd get off his horse to pray. And he smelled like his horse and put butter on his hair. I saw him put it on."

"You stayed with him?"

"For two days. He had perfect respect. More than the dickheads at home. We rode around this big lake with a lot of hotels on the other side and camped one night. He shared his food and water and when I washed in the lake he did not look. He didn't speak English but we got along OK. He was nice. His name was Goro. I taught him Amazing Grace and All You Need Is Love.

Is that Selam? SELAM! Selam…It's me. It's Kalkidane."

"SISTER!!! I prayed you would come. I prayed. Lushi, Here is our American sister. Come greet her. Genet, look!"

"Selam, Fikir said you'd be here but I thought I'd never find you. Is my brother here? Geta?"

"Yes, he is leader of the Unity Movement. You will see him."

"Selam, what's she saying?"

"Genet asks why you did not wait?"

"*I did wait*, tell her that, but, Fikir what are you saying? Why are they laughing?"

"I told her you got a ride with an Arsi on a horse to Shashamene. And Lushan asks if he did stink from the donkeys? It is a joke. Because they are primitive."

"She shouldn't talk shit about him. He was my protector."

"But sister, how did you get through the soldiers? They let no one in."

"We came from the lake over the fields. Then as we got close to the town we heard the music and then saw the line of soldiers. I pointed to Goro that I wanted to cross over to where the students were. We rode up to the soldiers. I didn't know what was going to happen, they all had guns, but Goro spoke to them in some language that wasn't Amharic and one of them answered and then Goro got down from the horse and they did some kind of soul shake."

"Oh, the soldier was Oromo. The Arsi are the same. They spoke Oromo."

I guess so. Anyway, it felt safe so I got off the horse and asked the guy if anyone spoke Englishenya. So the soldier went back and another guy came out. I told him, "Please, I must talk to you, my sisters are in the Unity Demonstration, I have to get in," but he said, "No, go away, we cannot let you in, you are farange." So I fake cried and told him that I had to see my sisters, so many years apart, we are from the same mother, sob, sob, and I gave him five dollars. And he pointed to the other three guys so I gave him $20 for all of them and they opened up the line. I said amaseganalehu to Goro, and my time with the donkey man was over.

So here I am. With my passport. But, Selam, how did that girl get here with the portables? And what about the driver? I thought he was dead meat."

"Genet told us that the army mens came and protected the driver once they knew he was from Mola Abera project. The driver called Mola Abera and he said, no problem, he will pay 2,000 birr for the donkey. So the Arsi got money from the driver and released him and the army let the truck and the portables pass to Shashamene. The government does not want a health crisis so they let them come in."

"And Fikir, how did you get here? Man, you were in immigration jail and then you got *deported*. What happened? How did *you* get through?"

"Kalkidane, my God, the prison, it was in Missouri. Your father and mother helped, they sent me things, but it was so bad, there was fighting and sex abuse and you could not pay the guards for safety. I was so glad they threw me back here. Look, wait one minute. Here is my phone. I must go meet Geta now. I am helping him organize the demonstration."

"Tell him I'm here. That I left America and came here to join Unity. And that I'd like to meet him."

"I will. Now I must go. Stay with your sisters."

"Don't You Worry About A Thing.
Every Little Thing's Gonna Be All Right." – Bob Marley
Kay Lee, Marc and Lisa: **Shashamene/Chicago**

"Hey Dad."

"Kay Lee!!! LISA, IT'S KAY LEE. Kay Lee we were so worried."

"I'm in Shashamene. With Selam and Lushi and Fikir."

"SHE'S IN SHASHAMENE. FIKIR'S THERE TOO. I'M PUTTING HER ON SPEAKER PHONE."

"Miranda told us you were going there. In the news it says the students are surrounded."

"It's in the news?"

"Because of that song. They're playing it everywhere."

"ARE THEY GOING TO SHOOT YOU?"

"MOM. Stop. There is no "they." We *all* are the Army of Love. They are the same army, they just don't know it yet. We will come together on Bob Marley's birthday."

"MARC, SHE IS OUT OF HER MIND."

"Kay Lee. If I were you, I'd get out of there. Soldiers love to kill students. It's a tradition. Kill the students. Cairo, Kent State, Mexico City, Bangkok, Tienanmen Square, Dice Dota. The list goes on and on."

"Dad, how many people got shot in Chicago this week? Five? Ten? You are in as much danger as me. Or at least Mom is."

"That 's not the same."

"Yes it *is*. Look, I worked really hard to get here, so if I leave now, then what the fuck? Guns win. Peace runs. My brother Geta is one of the leaders. They are meeting to decide a nonviolent strategy. And my sisters have a plan to control the situation if it gets heavy."

"MARC, WHAT THE FUCK IS SHE TALKING ABOUT?"

"Look, I want your blessing for this. It's important to stand up to guns. Give me your blessing. Come on. Can you send me some courage? I need all your courage. This is going to be so great. You'll see. Look, Fikir wants his phone back. He's got the only phone that's working. Here's Selam."

"HELLO MR. MARC. HELLO MRS. LISA! ARE YOU FINE?"

"Here's Lushi."

"HELLO MRS. LISA?"

"And Fikir." "HELLO ATO MARC AND MRS. LISA…"

"Hello… Hello…Hello…FUCK! Lisa, the phone's dead."

Fikir Minds The Store While Genet Plans
To Protect The Toilets, The Girls And The Cashbox
If The Soldiers Shoot And The Students Run.
Genet, Selamawit, Lushan and Fikir:
The Field Behind The Rastah Museum

"Hey Mr. Fikir, now you are back, could you watch the WCs? Selam, Lushi, come on, we need to talk business.

Oh, come on Fikir. Look, you can take the money for yourself. See those lines? In half an hour you can earn 2 birr x 6 x 10, 120 birr, if you are strict about the five minute time limit. But don't be a dictator to people. Sometimes they are having problems with their stomachs. Or women have their periods. Remind them by beating on the door and after ten minutes ask them if they need a doctor. Or more paper or a sani-pad. Don't be embarrassed. This is the new day when we are not afraid to speak of what everybody knows. You can sell them for two birr. Here's the timer.

You, American…go with Fikir, help him, OK? Thank you so much.

Hey girls, we must have a meeting. Come on out here by the tree. Jesus it is hot. We should buy an umbrella. Lushi, here is 10 Birr. Will you go over there to the Gurage with the umbrellas? Look, everyone is buying from her. She is probably making more money than we are.

Selam, quick while Lushi is gone, I am thinking, this Fikir, your relative, I know you are his girlfriend but…

Oh, ha ha ha, you are such a bad liar, you lick your lips and rub your hands and look at him like he is a watermelon. But what I'm saying is, he is definitely working for Woyane.

Yes he is, can't you see? The way he looks you in the eye when he says something and will not turn away? That is a sign of the liar trying to seem true. He says he was deported from America, but yet he comes here two days after landing at Bole, he gets through the roadblocks and he has a phone and money? From where? Woyane got him the minute he was off the plane. But the good part of this is – he might know what the soldiers will do and if we know their plan we can protect our money and ourselves. Can you get him alone and ask him? Say you are scared that the soldiers will shoot and that Geta and all of us will die. Remember what he tells you and tell me. But don't tell him you know he is a spy.

You know this game of chess, when you think so far ahead, if they do *this*, I will do *that*, and if they do *that*, and then I will do *this*. So we must think through the possibilities, to protect our toilets, our cash and ourselves. If we lose our money, these two weeks will be a total waste of time and we will never be able to buy gold. Really! We must make a plan. Here is my pen. Selam go get toilet paper to write.

What? Look, I know you are oldest girl, but I am the manager of this project so you should be the one to get the paper. OK, I am sorry I am not polite. So I say, 'please.' Here is Lushi with the umbrella. Is there change?

Look at this umbrella, such cheap shit from China. Be careful when you open it, it will break in a week. OK, that's better. Oh shade, you give us life.

OK. So, what if the soldiers shoot and shoot and there is gas and running like what just happened in Dice Dota? You see, we cannot predict where the soldiers and the students will be, so we must plan for all possibilities because once a riot starts, you cannot tell who will go where."

"What if when we hear shooting we hide in the toilets?"

"Lushi, the bullets will go right through the toilets."

"What if, if there is shooting, one of us grabs the cashbox and lies down on the ground as if she were shot, and the others also fall to cover her and hide the box?"

"Selam, if we are lying down and everyone runs in fear they will trample us like at a football riot. If there is shooting, the risk is even greater."

"Genet, here is the solution, we lie down behind the toilets. That way they cannot trample us because the toilets will be a wall that we will hide behind. They must run around on either side. Then when the shooting is done we can get up."

"Yes, Lushi that is the best idea. If there are many AKs shooting and gas and people running, we will lie down behind the WCs with the cashbox. OK? That is the plan. But, we should now do investigations. Geta is meeting with the student leaders. Lushi can you find him after the meeting? To find out what the students plan to do? And Selam, maybe you can take a walk with Fikir. He is so smart. Maybe he will have some idea of what the soldiers will do. I will watch the WCs. Can you believe it? I counted the money an hour ago and already we had made 240 birr. It is only 11 in the Day and it is always so busy after supper.

All right. Selam, so go get Fikir to walk with you. Lushi find Geta. I will watch the toilets.

Fikir, we're done. Thank you. Did you collect a lot of money? Oh yes? Maybe you will buy us a Fanta?"

Notes On The Meeting Of The Army Of Love
Coordinating Council
One @ Night, Thursday Feb 4
Deborah: **Rastah Library, Shashamene**

"Getting rid of the panic eliminates a lot of the effectiveness of the anti-riot gas. Educate yourself about the tear gas and pepper spray challenge. Print this page, and share it with all your friends. Stock up on cloths, goggles, vinegar, lemon juice, and water – The Crooked Bough: Tear gas self protection and decontamination - http://www.crookedbough.com/?p=2370

1) 2 Reps from all the regions 19 people in the circle, including me. 3 missing.
   a) Vote for leader. Candidates:
- Geta – Dice Dota – I nominate him, as ordered.
- Lemma – Bahir Dar
- Mehret – Harrar
- Worknesh – Adis.

   b) Geta wins big; though he is High School not college he is famous for video.
- Lemma is VP (connection with Chicago Bar Hadir & the song).
- Worknesh is Sec. (she has laptop – Apple, WOW! Is she rich?)

   c) Geta thanks committee for confidence. Welcomes all spies on the committee!!! *Looks at me and Mehret from Harrar!!!* Mehret protests but then sits down.

   d) Geta asks to act as communications connectors between Army of Love and the Army. He will thank them for service to country. He will tell them all our plans. Total Transparency. No secrets.

   e) Government cannot block Internet. Students get around blocks.
- It's simple, use email, FB, Twitter, You Tube. Spies must tell Government

394

that Ethiopian Army will be famous for One Love and One Heart
and No Violence.

   • Total Transparency. No secrets. Looks at me and Mehret again.

f) I argue: We should not give away our strategies. I am told that that is
the Old Way. Mistake? I am suspected? Does it matter? Not a spy. I work
for my country and to protect students.

2) Analysis: 30,000 students. 2,000 soldiers. Estimate.

a) Latest Development: Army says students must leave by Marley's
birthday tomorrow. No more food, water, sanitation coming in and out.

   • Do we leave? Discussion. Harrar Mehret - loud in saying NO. Is
   this because he knows everyone thinks he is a spy, so we will vote YES
   because he says NO? And then, when we leave, they will pick us
   off in small groups as we travel back to our schools and homes.

   • He will file his report and you can read his version.

   • Vote: Unanimous. We stay.

b) Publicize BIG meeting on BM birthday. Committee spreads word
throughout the camp. Sound system and stage. Use One World Circus
generator. Band will play. Petrol for generator will come from Sanitation
Truck. Committee will organize.

c) What do we ask for?

   • Freedom of Expression, Free the Journalists, Free Political Parties,
   Freedom to Travel, Gender Equality

   • End of shooting students and opposition

   • End imprisonment for speaking, writing,

   • End tribal favoritism, political favoritism, bribes, sexual extortion

   • Renounce violence in politics. Keep strong army for national defense

   • Punish violence, but permit all forms of expression except hate

3) Synthesis:

a) Army pressure on students: no food, no water, tear gas, guns, tanks, planes.

b) World pressure on army, government: If there is violence - stop aid, stop
military support, impose sanctions.

   • Stupid. We have no power. Woyane doesn't care. Government
   is Tigre, Christian; between Sudan & Somalia are Islam, ISIS and

Al Qaeda. West will never cut aid to Christian Ethiopia.

d) What will Army do?

  • Gas, Shoot, Beat, Arrest.

  • Geta speech: Status quo. They will kill or certainly arrest all members of the committee, unless you are a spy (looks at me and Mehret again), Result: huge loss of morale, more protests, violence.

    We are here because we do not accept this, we are non-violent BUT we are soldiers and so must be ready to die, like Ghandi, King, Mandela.

e) Girl from Jimma: But if you don't want to die, is it OK to run? Laughter.

  • Discussion - Running is more dangerous because when one person runs everyone runs, and people can be crushed. Better to walk slowly, surrender with hands up. Or lie down. Gas? Wear scarf over face. Try not to run.

  • What if Army does nothing and there is no food, water, sanitation? Stalemate?

  • Many students will leave but core group will stay...hunger strike... continuing publicity. Will they care? Will world lose interest?

  • Lemma: Not if we keep making #1 songs.

d) What will we do?

  • Ask for Freedoms

  • Sing

  • Go home

  • What if army attacks as we try to leave?

  • Lie down when attacked. Cover your head!

4) Action Plan

  a) Publicize BIG meeting on BM birthday. Committee spreads word throughout the camp. Sound system and stage. One World Circus Band will play. Petrol from Sanitation Truck for generator. Committee will organize.

    • Who leads Publicity? Alemhu (Jima) and Escandar (Desse).

    • Call for general meeting at 10AM. Everyone.

    • Make handouts with Rastah copying machine.

    • Announce what we will do ahead of time. Hand out Non-violent

Guidelines and Survival Manual
- Everyone, distribute the flyers and go throughout compound telling all.
- Set up by tonight…One World Circus…publicize from stage. Who does set up, stage and sound? Lemma (Bahir Dir) and Minihya, Mekel, Tesfaye (Ambo). Generator??? Stage???
- Cables/Amps/Mics. Figure it out.
- Who organizes security? Caleb (Dire Dawa), Dag (Gondar).
- Core of 20. Wear yellow armbands.
- Who does Press and Communications? Hewan (Bahir Dar), Social Media – Geta & Lemma.
- Government Liaison – He looks at us again. Me and Mehret, says do you have connections? We say NO. He says he will give us his connections. Asks if anyone has access to telephone? Looks at us again. I keep my eyes down. I had put my phone on silencer before the meeting.

5) Time Running Out. Other Business:

a) First Aid. Girl from Yir Gallum volunteers (she is a nurse and knows other nurses) – they will have Red Cross and tear gas, pepper spray instructions to read at the meeting. Collect scarves. No lemons.

b) Drugs and Tej: PR committee put on poster – Don't be stoned. Don't be drunk. Don't be high.

c) Relations with Rastahs deteriorating because of ganja war with khat vendors. Fighting & knives.

- How to enforce non-violence? Without being violent.
- Use of hula hoops discussed. Semret (Arba Minch) says what if security was equipped with hula hoops they could place them around fighters to pull them apart. She saw this on a video. Also the technique of falling into the fighters until they have no room to fight. Risky with knives. What would Ghandi do?

6) Meeting interrupted by helicopter flying over with search light and loud-speaker saying that all students must leave by noon tomorrow on orders from the President of Ethiopia, the Prime Minister and Chief of the Army. All who stay will be arrested.

a) Decision is to disregard. Meeting adjourned 4 in the Night. Next meeting noon, tomorrow.

I send this to you via soldier at gate, folded inside Army of Love songsheet. I will report again after tomorrow's meeting.

Face Off

Captain Melech and Captain Abinet:
Rastah Museum, Shashamene

"PLANNING: Organization. The development of an effective force capable of controlling civil disturbances depends largely upon proper organization. The following five principles of organization should be considered in planning for all civil disturbance operations: a. Essentiality. b. Balance c. Coordination. d. Flexibility. e. Efficiency – CIVIL DISTURBANCE OPERATIONS, Subcourse Number MP 1005, EDITION C, United States Army Military Police School Fort McClellan, Alabama 36205-5030: 6 Credit Hours Edition Date: April 2006

Melech. Are you ready?

Yes, Captain Abinet.

Review the sequence.

We move from behind the stage, facing the assembly while Nataye's Division presses them from behind. We leave only one opening for exit - approximately 5 m. wide, West by Northwest at 290 degrees, between my right flank and Nataye's left. My division takes over the stage and the sound system. I state the violation: Illegal Assembly and Refusal to Obey President's Order. Inform the illegal assembly that they are forgiven, that we want peacefulness, the government will consider their demands and has provided buses for them to return to their towns and schools. Order them to leave through the opening of soldiers. Both divisions press the demonstrators toward the exit passage, batons held horizontally to push, not to strike. Myself, on the stage will ask Zena to speak with me off stage. Then I arrest him and send him under guard to you in the command truck.

Be careful not to have this be seen by the crowd. It must happen offstage.

Yes Sir. No one will see the arrest or know where he is being taken. Then, as the students pass from the field to the road, ten soldiers from each division on either side of the exit passage will slap the students as they pass, with sticks, not batons, to sting them into hurrying, but not to damage them. I have picked these soldiers carefully and issued them the correct equipment.

Not batons.

No Sir, we have whipping sticks like they use in the high school, and my soldiers understand that this is psychological, to treat the students as if they are naughty children, not criminals, so that they will not mingle but will hurry onto the busses which will be waiting to take them to Adis, Arba Minch, Jimma, Hawassa, Dice Dota, Harrar and Dira Dawa. One bus is for those identified as leaders. Silverstone, the chief Rastah will be by the busses and he will help in the identification. He has already pointed out many. They will take them to jail at Maikelawi.

That is good, Melech. I will be watching via the Eyes of Solomon from the command truck. If it does not go as planned then we will go to plan B.

Yes Sir, if the students will not move, then we will set off the tear gas canisters on the east side of the field so that the students will run west. And both divisions will then present batons vertically and will use them to create pressure as the students run.

But not on the head.

No sir, we have briefed our soldiers to only hit on the body and not so hard that anyone falls down and runs the risk of a trampling. And if a student is shooting with a cell phone, they should try to break the phone.

Right. This time there will be no provocative images to feed the vultures that hate Ethiopia. All right. You must be in starting position by 3:30. Call me then. The action is planned for twenty minutes after the start of the demonstration, which the organizers call for 4:00. But these students are lazy. I don't count on it starting until 5:00, or even noon. OK, this is Abinet signing off, Lieutenant Melech.

This is Melech, signing off, Captain Abinet..

Whipping Sticks
Eden: **Behind The Rastah Museum**

That Jolanee, my God, the way she got the Captain to sign the papers! She said: "He is a slave to my vagina." Eden told her to be careful, what if her husband finds out about her adventures? She says he is an expert in whores and beer and selling bricks but she is a soldier and an expert with guns and knives and judo and if he gets physical she will kick his ass. How she speaks! I was ashamed for Eden.

So there we were in uniforms that didn't fit. Jolanee said the Captain noticed this, obviously we needed to do better, so after we dropped off Jolanee we went to my house, and improved the uniforms, shortening the trousers of Eden's, and taking in the seams on my shirt, ironing and starching the pants with strong creases and polishing the boots and buckles. Then we packed up some injera and fruit in the army sacks Jolanee gave us, and, in uniform, after filling the bajaj with petrol, off we went to Shashamene.

We were lucky to get through. After miles and miles going west, there was a roadblock. Who was the lead guard? A friend of my friend, Mulu. OK, Satan is working against me today, I thought: she knows I'm not a soldier, now I will be arrested, but she just shook her head and gave me gave me a funny look that said: *Nigest, what the hell are you doing?* I asked Eden to put 20 birr in the papers that we had to show her, and Mulu took it, gave us back the documents and said, "Good luck." Before Shashamene, after the famous Cave of All Religions, there was the roadblock where I had been refused entry the day before, but this time as a "soldier" it was easy to get through with the crush of others in uniform coming to join their divisions; the Inspectors took no time to examine our orders. In Shashamene we drove to my brother Tsega's to park the bajaj at his compound. This was a surprise for him, but he did not refuse me; he is a religious man and always loyal. I told him that all the kids were trapped in the demonstration, and that we were going in to get them. He said that two of his children were there too and that he would pray for all of our luck and safety.

Shashamene is always a crazy town, full of people, buses, trucks and mini-vans going all directions at the crossroads, to Hawassa, Moyale and Kenya, Adis, Bale and Arba Minch. The tourists from Lake Langano stop there and every khat truck in the Southern Regions passes through at top speed on the way to Bole, always having accidents with livestock and gharis, they are in such a rush to keep the leaves fresh for the planes to Yemen and the Emirates. Then there are the Rastahs from Germany staggering around, high on ganja that they buy at the Marley Church, and more thieves on the street than in any jail in Ethiopia. And this time it was more chaotic than ever with hundreds of soldiers on the street called up to take their positions against the Unity March and angry students who could not get into the Love Demonstration wandering around by the Bus Depot, looking for food, water, bathrooms and a way out of town. The town felt like a dry roof, just waiting for a spark, and you knew that when it caught fire a thousand bugs and rats would emerge in a frenzy. We walked through the Center and then, with many other soldiers, up Rte. 7 north past a line of tanks and pickup trucks mounted with machine guns to the gate of the Rastah Museum where there was another checkpoint. Our orders said we were to go to Captain Melech's Division. The soldiers at the checkpoint said to go to the Marley School, find our division, and get our orders and equipment.

"Where are the students?" I asked.

"Oh you'll see them soon enough, Mother," the soldier at the gate said to me. "Right down the sights of your rifle. You will feel their bones break at the end of your stick. And then you will load their bodies onto trucks and clean up their blood. That's what we did in Dice Dota. It's ugly work. But then I guess when these little rich bastards are shot there will be more room in University for students who respect their country."

Oh my God! Was there any way to stop this old class murder talk from the days of Haile Selassie and the Derg? I was scared to give him the answer he deserved but Eden was so smart: "Oh, come on my brother," she said, "you are the lucky one, you have a job. When they these kids get out of University you will see them in the cafe, borrowing money for a cappuccino and playing the immigration lottery, while you can buy a motorcycle and drink Johnny Walker. And, you, you are a good loyal soldier, a protector of Ethiopia, you would not be bribed like so many others and maybe you will be a General one day. But, my brother, these kids don't know anything yet. A protector would spank them and kiss them and send them home to try to grow up. So, if you are ordered to shoot, well then you must obey, but who knows where you will point the gun. Think about that!"

She did not wait for an answer, but signaled me to follow her to a new concrete building with a sign that said 'Bob Marley Community Development School.' We entered into a big room and went to the table to check in. It was chaos, with soldiers looking for their divisions and all the Captains shouting out for their soldiers. We asked for Melech and were directed to a big-bellied man with a mustache. He looked at our orders and then at us and then at our orders and then at us as if he smelled a rat, and I thought we would be arrested. But no, he just smiled and told us that he had special duty for us, we would be on the front line as the students left the demonstration, and he would issue us special equipment to help them leave. And he gave us the whipping sticks.

Fikir And Selam Try To Live Before They Die
Fikir and Selam: The Field Behind The Rastah Museum

Genet says you are a spy.

What do you think?

I wonder why your phone works. Please get your spy hand off of me. All I ask Fikir is that you tell me everything.

I'll tell you if you'll tell me what happened with you and Helen.

What do you mean?

What did you do when you left the House of Adenech?

Are you asking me if I was a whore at Seven Nights with Helen? Well, what if I was?

Were you?

Why do you ask?

My mother says that you were seen with Germans.

Oh, you *are* a spy. What difference does it make to you?

No difference.

So why do you spy on your brothers and sisters? When we are shot, will you get money? Will you be behind the window for the interrogation? Will you watch them rape me?

Jesus, not so loud…

Don't touch me.

SELAM! They told me they would release me and help my business if I went to Shashamene and reported on Geta. So, of course, I said yes, but not to betray anyone, only so I could get out of custody and get to Shashamene and *see you, and protect you and your sisters and Geta.* The first thing I did when I got here was to *tell Geta* that I was supposed to report on him. *I told him,* so now I tell them whatever Geta wants me to tell them. I am a spy for peace. I will not put anyone in danger. Do you believe me? Look in my eyes Selam, I would do nothing to hurt you. I would do everything to protect you.

If you are lying Fikir my heart will forever be closed to you.

Do you mean it is open to me?

What did they tell you? What is going to happen?

They told me to tell Geta that they would shoot some students if they made illegal assembly, and then they would let the rest run. They were laughing. But they could easily have said that just for intimidation, so that Geta would call off the demonstration. They play with the truth like a dog with its bone. They kill it and bury it and then dig it up new again. The committee is going ahead anyway. There will be a confrontation. Who knows what can happen?

I know. We could all die tomorrow. My sisters have a plan if they start shooting. To hide behind the portapotties. You can join us.

Thank you, Selam. But I will be next to Geta. I am his bodyguard.

Fikir, I don't want to die if I have not lived.

What do you mean?

Fikir put your arms around me. Hold me and look me in the eyes.

Selam, everyone is looking at us. Is that what you want?

I want them to see us, so then they will know that we are together. Why did you ask me about Seven Nights and if I went with Germans?

Because I would hate you if you were with other men.

Should I hate you if you have been with other women?

Yes.

Well then, maybe you will hate me too.

Do I have reason?

Your hate is up to you. Where can we go? Where I am sleeping is Lushi, Genet and Kalki. Where are you sleeping?

On the other side. There is a closet in the back of Rastah Museum, where they keep the ganja. The smell is horrible. I have a pass and they let me go back and forth. For money, they will let you pass too. We can be alone there.

How can we get back to the student side in the morning? I want to be here for the demonstration?

There is a door in the back of the building that opens onto this side. It is locked from the outside but you can open it from the Rastah Museum.

Wait here, I must tell my sisters.

Why?

So if I never come back they will know to look for you.

Don't you trust me?

I don't trust men except for my brother. This will be a test. Wait.

Genet Tells A Reporter About The Confrontation
Between The Army Of Love And The Army Of Guns
Genet: **Shashamene:**

Where did you get this newspaper? From Adis? Yes, that is me. I am the girl on the tank with the Captain. Now I am a famous girl.

Yes I have time. I wait for a truck to take me and my friends to Adis. We have to return the portapotties from the demonstration to Mola Abera.

You are from the England radio? Yes, your Amharic is England Amharic. I can tell.

They would not let you in? Well I can tell you everything that happened. Yes I saw everything. Everything. I will tell you. But how much money will you give me?

10 birr? No, look, now I am a famous girl. So, I want 40 birr. Do you think I can be paid for the picture by the newspaper as well? Isn't there a law that I must be paid?

Thank you. Good. OK, I will speak while you record.

I am Genet. I am the chief of the Mola Abera portapotties.

I am 13.

No I am not in school. I have never gone to school. I am a street girl. I learned numbers and reading and writing without school. I learn very quickly. My mother is dead. She never went to school. Her family forced her to work in the tukol and raise her brothers and sisters, and that killed her courage for learning. I must have got the fast learning talent from my father, but who was he? My mother's story is that she was raped in the dark by many soldiers, so there is always that question. My uncle disagrees; he says it was Mengistu and my mother made up this rape story so Mengistu wouldn't kill her. Wasn't that Mengistu so smart, he had so much aradanat, really, the most of all the ones who killed Haile Selassie. What is the proof? Meles is dead six years but Mengistu is still living rich in Zimbabwe. And how old is he? Over 80? And how many did he kill? One million?

~~But really this is nonsense.~~ My uncle's brain was scrambled by khat; he would make five from two and two. There is no way Mengistu could have been my father. Woyane threw him out 10 years before I was born. The truth is I was lucky that when my mother died I had no father to make me his slave and then to sell me in marriage; I had to teach myself every day how not to be hungry and to always look for my chance. This is why at the Unity Demonstration I have established the portapotty business, turning shit into money, and now my friends Selam and Lushi and I will open the Habesha Sisters Temple Of Gold Shop in the Merkato and we will turn the shit money into gold.

Yes, we will open a store for gold in Adis. Will you please say that on the radio? Everyone come to Habesha Sisters in the Merkato. Opening in two weeks.

OK, I will tell you what happened. My friends, two sisters from Dice Dota, and I, were managing portapotties for Mola Abera to make sanitation for the students. I came down with a truck of them and they let us through because they did not want cholera to come to Shashamene region. We had all planned to alternate our duties through the whole demonstration and we were making good money, but on the Marley birthday morning the sisters deserted me. Some students had told them that charging people money for sanitation was "too much capitalism" and the Rastahs had called it "The Way of Babylon." One sister, Lushi, went to the demonstration in the morning to be in solidarity with the students. The other sister, Selam, had gone with her boyfriend Fikir the night before and not come back.

OK, you cannot put that in the radio. You will erase that. You promise? OK? About Fikir and Selam? Thank you.

Part of the problem was that a third sister, Kalki, who had been sold for adoption to America when she was little, had just come back to Ethiopia to join the Unity March. She spoke about as much Amharic as a child of one year, and the other sisters, Selam and Lushi, were both hungry to improve their English, so English was what they spoke all the time. They thought I knew little English so they spoke in front of me thinking I didn't understand. Did they assume I was more stupid than a dog to not know my own name when they said *Genet, Genet,* and looked at me out of the sides of their eyes? I heard the word *bullshit* and *piss me off* many times.

I knew they were angry words. I had saved these sisters and given them jobs, and still they bitched. I could have bitched too, but what a waste of time! And Kalki didn't understand anything about life in Ethiopia, she had been here not one week, still, she would argue in English about things she knew nothing about and the rest would pretend to agree with her because she was their farange sister and no one had any idea of how much money she had or what she could do for them. I didn't care. I wasn't going to kiss her ass so she would take me to America.

OK look, my vision is to be boss of Habesha Sisters Gold Business and the younger sister, Lushi, will be Vice President. She is the only one of them who understands business. For all her talk of "Babylon", when she told me her dream of meeting an Indian boy she loves in Germany and then going to Dubai to trade gold, I saw the love of treasure glinting in her eyes, and thought perhaps someday we will make gold business in India and Ethiopia by way of Dubai and Germany.

Selam, the older sister, as expected, didn't come through. The night before she had told us she had much to discuss with her boyfriend and that she would go with him that night to "work things out," and we were not to worry, she would be back in the morning, but, if she didn't come back, we should blame *him.* Lushi, and I tried to talk her out of that, but the American Kalki said: "No, go do it, if you want him," and then Selam got mad and said "Could you mind your own (she cursed) business?" She said she could take care of herself and who were we, her mother? Kalki offered her some condoms from her purse and Selam got furious and walked out into the darkness. Of course she didn't come back in the morning.

Oh I am sorry, I am saying too much. My words are like a flood now. I was very frightened with the shooting, and now I am like a big bottle of beer that has been shaken and all the beer comes out when the bottle is opened. I am sorry, do not put the part about the condoms on the radio. Please, these are secrets of the sisters. Please, erase these last words. Thank you.

Yes, yes, I will tell you about the shooting. You heard it from outside? Well I saw everything, so now I will tell you of the demonstration and nothing more.

So it was morning and Selam had not come back. Lushi and the American had got up with the sun and gone to the field where the stage was. They said they would spread their blanket right in the front, so they could get a good place at the demonstration. *A good place to be shot or trampled,* I thought. I was left alone to collect money for the portapotties and, because morning is a busy time for everyone to piss and shit after having coffee, and there were ten porta-potties, I had to run up and down to collect the fee. Most of the students had spent all their money by then, so they would come out and run away without paying and if I caught them they would say, "Sorry, I am broke," or they would yell a curse to me and keep going. I could not chase them far and leave my station. So I was losing a lot of money.

Over the loudspeakers came the call for everyone to meet for the Marley birthday, and then music, a band and a singer singing the Army of Love song. It sounded like Devorah B from Dessie. I couldn't believe it, she is the most famous singer, so I came to the back of the portapotties and looked towards the stage, and yes, it was her. No one wanted to miss seeing Devorah B and for the next half hour all the students came from the sleeping field to the front of the stage, so many standing together that all I could think was how many would be trampled when the shooting began. Soon it was only me by the portapotties and the vendors with no customers at their stands in the sleeping field. Now I was frustrated; if I guarded the portapotties I could not see the stage and that worried me. How could I tell what would happen?

Then there was a big surprise; from the hill behind the sleeping field came a grinding motor sound. I knew it from the days in Adis after the election when I had seen a tank come into the Piazza and crush everything, so I grabbed the

410

money from the money box and twisted it into my scarf underneath my shirt. The tank came up the back of the hill and then appeared at the top with a line of soldiers on either side and then swept down into the sleeping field, grinding the tents of the students and the vendor tables into the dirt. The vendors yelled and cried but the tank and soldiers did not stop and now they were heading straight for my portapotties, so I ran to the front of the tank waving my hands and yelled loud above the motor: "Stop! Stop! Stop!" The Captain, riding high on the tank, motioned me to get out of the way, but I did not; I challenged him to roll over me with the tank. One thing you must know about me: if I have a job to protect the property of anyone, I will never run away. I will die. In this way I am better than most soldiers. So OK, he stopped the tank and beckoned me to climb up. Oh no, I thought, this is a trick, when I am on the tank he will go forward and knock down the portapotties and attack the students. If stay where I am, he will crush me. Always the best thing in these situations is to give a present. So, I took a chance that he was like all soldiers, and folded three 20 birr notes in my palm. He swung me up to the top of the tank and the money was in his hand when I yelled to him above the motor sound, "These are the property of Mola Abera. He sent me here with the WCs so no one gets cholera. Please, my Father, go around. Mola will thank you. He will reward you even more if you keep his property safe." He felt the notes and looked down hiding his palm by his side. "All right little daughter," he said, "because it is Mola Abera we will leave these for him." He put the money in his pocket and spoke into his radiophone, so the tank and the army went to the side of the portapotties and then around, and reassembled behind the students. I was up on the tank with the Captain now, whose name I now know was Captain Netaye. See, in the newspaper, the picture of me and him? Netaye and "the unidentified girl." That's me. I am "unidentified."

The soldiers came around the portapotties to the field. They held their sticks with both hands in front of them as if to push and not to beat. In the front, up on the stage speaking into the microphone, was Geta, the brother of Kalkidane, Lushi and Selam. I had never met him but he was famous as a leader of the Unity March and his face was perfectly like Kalkidane's so I knew it was him. Beside him on the stage was Selam's boyfriend, Fikir, the

411

spy. Oh, I should not have said he was a spy. But everyone knows he was. He told everyone.

Just as the soldiers took their position behind the students, hundreds of others appeared from behind the Rastah School and then jogged out to either side of the stage. The ones I was with did the same, jogging to encircle the students from behind. Now the students were surrounded by soldiers carrying clubs, and some with pistols and rifles. I thought: what was going to happen? Oh my God, so many will die…

A big man with a captain hat came from the back of the stage and held out his hand for the microphone, but Geta was too fast for him. He skipped to the front of the stage, then turned to the big Captain Man and said into the microphone: "Brothers and Sisters in uniform, Police and Soldiers, I welcome you to the Army of Love." And then he bowed to the big Captain Man and turned out to the crowd and said, "They are joining us. Everyone, can you say: "Enkuan dehina metachihu?"

And so all the crowd shouted out their welcome. *This is when the soldiers will start shooting,* I thought, and got ready to jump off the tank and run like hell with the money away from everything. But this Geta was so smart as an agitator, he called again through the mic: "All of you, if you have your cell phones, take them out and let us record this day when the students and the military and the police all came together to end the violence."

Hundreds of people held up their phones. Now the army knew that whatever happened, the world would see. Then Geta held out his hand with the microphone to the big Captain Man and called out: "Our Captain wants to speak, now listen," and handed him the microphone. The big Captain Man took the mic and said: "Greetings from the President and the Prime Minister of Ethiopia. Know that the government supports the Unity March for No Violence and wishes Bob Marley Happy Birthday." Then he put his arm around Geta's shoulder like a father.

This was a surprise and the crowd cheered, but that was the end of his kindness. His hand tightened on Geta's shoulder and he told everyone to leave the demonstration. If we refused we would be arrested and charged with the crime of *Illegal Assembly* and *Incitement Against the State* and *Refusal to Obey*. If we left peacefully there would be no problem, we would be forgiven, and could return in buses provided by the government to our towns and schools.

At this moment he gave a signal and the soldiers made an opening in their circle and took positions on either side, so now there was a way for the demonstrators to exit, along the side of the Rastah School and then by the Museum out to the road. Then he looked at Geta and said into the microphone, "Tell your people to disperse," and, still holding Geta tightly, he held the microphone up for Geta to speak.

This was his mistake. As quick as a snake's strike, Geta's hand came for the mic and he ducked away from the captain, danced to the front of the stage with it and started the call. Everyone knew this call because they had repeated it over and over on the loudspeaker to teach everyone in the days before.

No killing people
No stopping speech
Give us freedom
To say what we think
Come on Ethiopia
Lets have fun
Many parties
Not just one

That was the chant that everyone had practiced and, as they sang it, many held up their cell phones to film the big Captain Man taking his revolver from his belt. Geta pointed to the gun in the Captain's hand for all to see. Then he swept his hand to the back of the stage to the soldiers who were shouldering their rifles, and then back to the students, shaking his head, saying with a big mouth for the cameras, *No, No, No*. Many phones shot the big Captain Man coming forward to strike Geta with the handle of the gun, but Geta was too fast, and made a dodge away to the side of the stage and called, "EVERYONE LIE DOWN, EVERYONE, LIE DOWN NOW."

Then the biggest surprise of all; Captain Netaye suddenly pushed me down onto the tank and gave the order: "Elevate 20. Rotate left 35. Correct right 5. OK, FIRE", and the tank's cannon moved to point above the stage, and BLAM, there was the explosion that hurt my ears for life; when flame flew from the barrel of the cannon and the shell rushed with its tail of smoke above the stage over the Rastah school and into the air; when everyone screamed and fell down to kiss the ground like Jesus had just walked on it; and when Geta jumped with the microphone off the stage into the crowd and disappeared. I think the explosion of the cannon was a signal to the soldiers with Captain Netaye because, right after the missile flew, they pointed their rifles to the stage at the big Captain Man and his soldiers, and Captain Netaye, standing on the tank with an electric speaker held to his mouth, called out across the field: "Soldiers let us all point our rifles to the sky. I speak with the authority of the President who has called for non-violence. We will shoot a round for Bob Marley. And then we will all go home. Students keep down." And he looked across from the tank to the big Captain Man and his men on the stage, to see if they would follow this order, and he called down instructions to the gunner in the cockpit so everyone saw the cannon shift down to point exactly at the big Captain Man and his soldiers. And then he yelled into the megaphone, "Soldiers, for our children, point your rifles to the sky."

Right then Captain Netaye pulled me up from the hot greasy metal he had just pushed me down on, and held my hand. That was when the student turned around and took that picture of me. Such a good picture of me with the Captain. Don't you think I look like a hero of the girls?

Thank God the soldiers lifted their rifles as if they were going to shoot down the clouds, so that when Captain Netaye yelled, "Fire" their rifles roared and the field filled with smoke but no students were hurt. The mistake was that the gunner in the tank thought that the order to fire was for him too, so again came the noise that tore my ears and rocked the tank, and when the shell flew with fire from the muzzle of the tank's cannon it blew up the stage and the Captain and some of the soldiers with him, and then tore a hole in the Rastah School. I saw it all before the smoke from the guns made seeing impossible. The Captain blowing up. Fikir the spy diving off the stage. That is what I saw.

Oh yes I was scared. Of course. When I saw the Big Captain Man blow up, I thought, "Oh my God, now the bullets will start flying," so I jumped from the tank and ran behind the portapotties and threw myself down on top of the money in my scarf. I did not move and waited for the longest time with my hands over my head in the dirt and my eyes closed, but what a surprise! There was no gunfire, only the voice of Captain Netaye through megaphone: "Soldiers, return to your divisions. You will receive new orders from the new leadership in Adis. And I promise you, you will get a raise." And to the students: "Children, get up and go home. Now follow me," and then I heard the sound of the tank grinding forward and the cheering of the students as they rose from the ground to get out of the way of the tank. By the time I opened my eyes and came back around the portapotties, they were following the tank out to the road and to the waiting buses. And soldiers were picking up the dead and wounded on the stage.

So now I wait for the driver to come. He has taken the portapotties to be emptied and then we will return them to Mola Abera and I must pay him his share. The sisters are with their mother here in Shashamene and they will take the bus tomorrow to Adis and then we will start our business.

OK, here is the truck. Thank you for the money for my story. Oh, can I say this on the radio again for the English tourists: "Habesha Sisters Gold Business. At the Merkato in Adis. Please visit."

Selam And Kalkidane Discuss The Future
Selam and Kalkidane: **Shashamene Bus Depot**

Selam, What are you going to do?

Fikir wants me to go with him to Arba Minch. He says the money from the world now pours into there. The American military have come with their drones to kill ISIS and the Chinese build farms and roads in all directions. He says he will teach Amharic to both and he will get rich.

Are you going to Arba Minch?

He wants to marry us and have children. He is the only man I have been with. He is a strong sexy man and modern. He would not hit me, he would not keep me down. He says he loves me.

I'm happy for you.

But Kalki, I told him no. Yes, I could love him, but this Fikir love would keep me down. I want more than that, more of what I do not know. I will go to Adis and work with Lushi and Genet in the gold market and get some money. That is one thing that my friend Helen told me. A woman must have her own money. I told him this and now he hates me. What will you do?

I'm going home.

When do you fly?

No, not back to Murder Land, no way. I'm going to Dice Dota. I'm going to be Ethiopian.

Kalki, do you know that when I was young I wondered many times why God chose you and not me to be American? And now you throw America away and say you want to be Abesha? Do you remember when I kissed the foot of Mrs. Lisa and asked her to take me to Chicago to be your sister? And then she kissed the foot of Nigest and said I should not act as a slave and told me "No." I was so angry. What do you think, can we ever become the other?

I'm *adopted*. Selam. I've always been the *other*.

Where will you live?

In Dice Dota with Nigest. This morning, after the demonstration, we saw her and Weyzero Eden. Lushi and I helped them get rid of their stupid uniforms. Then she told me she had something to say to me and asked Weyzero Eden to translate. She asked me to come live with her and to let her be my mother. She cried and said that with all you gone she comes home from her work with the bajaj and there is no one there to cook for or talk to, and she feels she's a dead woman alone in her grave. I cried too and told her I would come to live with her and be her daughter and I hugged her and kissed her and called her "Mom." I showed her the bracelet that Lisa gave me before she left, the gold that was around my foot when I was adopted, and Nigest cried more and would not let me go.

I have the same bracelet. And Lushan. Kalki, are you sure you are going to do this? It would be a sorrow to tell Nigest this if you change your mind. There is so little trust with farange. They always promise and then...

I'm not farange.

You speak no Amharic.

I will learn it.

How will you live?

For bread? I will drive the bajaj while Nigest cooks.

No, you will not.

OK, then I will be a bar girl. The Ethiopian men will pay double for a farange. I will get rich like Fikir.

Kalkidane! You will not.

Right. I will not. If I am careful I've got money for one year. That will give me time to learn Amharic and become a citizen and figure out what to do. I want to start a project in Dice Dota.

What project?

I don't know. What do you think? What is needed?

My God you ask me a question with ten thousand answers. You know there was a German man in Adis I met who worked with World Health Family Planning. Martin. He loved to dance and he did not want to buy sex.

417

He said the problem with Ethiopia was too much antibiotica. If there were no antibioticas then many more children would die as they used to and there would be not too much population, so not poverty.

He was joking.

Yes. But there is truth in this joke. What is needed for Dice Dota is the same as for all Ethiopia and all the world. God's mercy for all people. The same for the poor as for the rich. The same for women as for men. And for everyone, a house for everyone like in Home Alone. Are you so rich to give all this?

Look, Kalki, there is the mini-van to Adis. I must go. There's Lushi, she is already in the van. Genet has returned to Adis with the WC's in the truck. I am meeting them tonight in the apartment of Helen. Over there is the place for you to wait for mini-van to Dice Dota. Look the boy is calling. Go. Do not pay more than 30 birr.

Selam…

I will see you and Nigest in Dice Dota in some weeks. Buy the SIM card and I will Facebook you how to call me. Goodby Kalki. Kiss our mother.

Selam…

Goodbye Kalkidane.

2019

Genet Sells Some Gold And Tells An American About Her Famous Connection
Genet: Habesha Sisters Table: Merkato, Adis

Oh yes, the ring is special, yellow gold, 14 karat. Three hundred dollar. Two hundred twenty-five? Ha ha. I pay five thousand two hundred birr for this ring. It would cost three hundred fifty dollar in Dubai.

You are American. I know from the shoes, OK, I like American, so two hundred seventy-five, you can buy.

Not two hundred fifty, two hundred sixty-five.

Two hundred sixty. OK American, here is my hand. Such a beautiful ring. Do you want a box? Here. And take this present, this ring from the Omo, it is copper, from the Mursi people.

I am Genet. And you?

Jane. Yes, thank you. I have taught myself English but now I study. I study Americans. Here is the question I ask them. Who is the leader of Ethiopia?

Aha, you don't know. Not even one per cent of one per cent know. My friend Kalkidane from America tells me that people in America think that all countries in Africa are next to each other and that Ethiopia is by Nigeria.

See this picture on the table here? Who is that girl? Correct. That is when I was 12, the girl on the tank, and the soldier, do you know who that is? It is Netaye Worede who is now the President. And you see this writing on the picture. It says, "God Bless Genet." That's me. I was with him on the Day of Unity. Now he is my friend and benefactor.

Jane, do you know any Ethiopia history? Haile Selassie, OK. The famine, OK, but do you know about the Day of Unity, three years ago when President Netaye killed his enemies in one shot from the tank. That is how he saved the students. From this day he now is President.

This was the turning point in Ethiopian history, when the government made peace with the people. Now you see, everything is different. Afewerki in Eritrea makes peace. The Denakil solar fields make Ethiopia so rich as the Emirates. But my secret that I will tell you is - *this shot from the tank was a complete mistake.* Netaye did not mean for the tank to fire. I know this because as the fire came from the cannon he let go of my hand and cursed the gunner, beating his head in the cockpit, calling him *fool* and the *son of a hyena* for shooting. This mistake is why the non-violence won, because the soldiers who remained believed the tank would destroy them too, so they put their rifles in the air and the demonstrators won. I tell you this because you are not Ethiopian. President Netaye would not like everyone to know. He wants all people to think he was strong to kill his enemies, but really that was not his desire. God chose to do it.

You are correct, I am young for business, but now that the Canadians have built the great solar field, and the Afar have Mercedes and many cameras, they love gold so much we make great business in the Merkato.

And you, Jane, what is your profession? A nurse? I study in medical profession too. I work at Habesha Sisters in the morning but learn in the afternoon at the St. George school. This is where the children of President Netaye go. I study science so I can later learn the MRI. Of course you know this. It is such a miracle to look at the inside of a person to find the disease. I cannot wait to see this. When I finish high school I will leave the gold business to my friends and go to the City of Minnesota in the USA and study radiation technology. Why Minnesota? Because this what my friend's sister Sintayehu did. She went there and is now a radiology technician in the hospital. And she is rich. She has her own auto.

You must go? I am sorry. Come back tomorrow I will have more gold. Oh but wait, listen, I love all Americans so I say too much, I am not careful. About the mistake of President Netaye, it was not really a mistake. He was pretending that it was, so he would seem kind. Please do not tell anyone I said this. Now that there is freedom to speak in Ethiopia we must be sure that everything we say is true or things could be difficult.

Happy Birthday Momma
Kay Lee, Lisa and Marc: **Dice Dota/Chicago**

"Hey. Mom, Dad, sorry, the phones and the Internet have been down."

"Kay Lee, We got your message. What's going on?"

"Well first I wrote you a song:

Happy Birthday Momma
You are the bombah
You fed me and clothed me
And kept me from harma
You gave me tough love
You taught me Double Dutch
Happy Birthday Momma.

So, what's the matter? You don't like my song?"

"Kay Lee, very funny, look, you can't just pick up and leave the whole project."

"Mom, your hair looks great. Did you get it done for the Skype?"

"Kay Lee, for Christ's sake, get real girl. If you just suddenly split everything will fall apart."

"So why don't you come on over here. Save the poor Africans. Me, I'm done."

"Marc, did you hear that? Kay Lee's bailing from the Nigest's Temple, so now she wants us move to Dice Dota to finish what she started. Listen, Kay Lee. That's the last thing I want to do. You're the one who made all those promises. So what happened? You moved to Ethiopia to find yourself and the self you found was a liar."

"Mom, see this? Fuck you. When they shot Eli, I had to get out of Chicago. *I sold part of my body to get out!* I came to Ethiopia to find out who I could have been if you hadn't *bought me*, to get away from the shoot-the-nigger shit I grew up with. And a history that wasn't really mine."

"You mean my slave past? Look, I am proud to come from slaves."

"And their fucking owners?"

"Look, Kay Lee, you don't get to choose who you come from. Or where they take you if you are sold. And yes, *you were sold*, to the barren farange, the cruel Mom and Dad overseers who gave you time-outs, forced you against your will go to school, take piano lessons and brush your teeth. But remember if you'd stayed in Ethiopia you'd have two babies by now and no clit. Nigest knew that. That's why she sent you away."

"Momma, I get it. But get me. When I lived in Chicago I just wanted to be a barefoot goat-chasing Ethiopian girl, but when I got here I found that Little BoPeep was going ghetto as fast as she could, taking selfies, twerking her butt and playing the immigration lottery so she could get the fuck out of Donkeyville, go to Hollywood and become the next Beyoncé. Everybody here is becoming what I ran from, what I despise. And at the same time I know that's just bullshit; Abesha peeps just want what we got; food, love, kids, a job, a nice house. And fun. How 'bout a car? A convertible? Yeah everybody here has their hand out but so do they at home, hands out to show you the way, pick your pocket, pet you, dance with you, beat you up, do your hair. Who the fuck am I to pass judgment?

Ethiopia doesn't need me. It needs to be itself. Since Unity Day it's getting better. Now you can travel, they don't jail the opposition, the journalists are out of jail. Meanwhile, what the fuck is happening at home? The clowns are in control. Closing the clinics. Building the wall. Defunding birth control. Ending Obamacare. Holy shit. I need to go home.

Revelation: the cops killing Eli is the real Taste of Chicago, the *Bad Taste*, like drive-bys, Crips and Bloods, kids packing guns, Cook County Jail. And now the whole country is one big battlefield; the lines are drawn. I want to take a stand on ground I know. GeoNiger, you remember him, Dave McCray, he was Eli's bestie, he's been telling me what's going on, how they brought down the Police Chief and the Mayor and now they are going to bring down the School Board and take the City Council. The plan is to block Michigan

Avenue again. Surround the Federal Building. Join the General Strike. I'm gonna be there."

"I understand, Kay Lee."

"Thanks Poppa. You're not pissed?"

"How could I be? Look what you've done. I mean you started Nigest's Temple, raised money, rented a building, put all these good people to work, took in girls and women and built a safe place for them. How many babies did you say are there now? Fifteen? You did that."

"Yes, I'm proud I did that, Dad."

"You got real jobs for your own birth Mother Nigest and your aunties, sainted people who were meant for this, and you gave them a vocation. And so now you teaching them a lesson that it is *so important,* it's one they've known for centuries: *don't depend on farange for fucking anything.*"

"Don't guilt trip me Dad."

"It's courageous Kay Lee, the tough love you're showing these women and their kids, a great lifetime learning lesson about *sustainability.* You set up a whole project that is dependent on you and then you leave it high and dry. In case of *Project Abandonment* break glass and sell your ass to feed your kids. Or be a slave nanny. Or go back to your husband and get beaten up when you don't want to fuck him. Good lesson Kaylee."

"Dad, I'm gonna hang up. This is such colonial bullshit. You know what you're saying? That Ethiopians can't run their own projects without the presence of PC Bwana Massa Marc & Missa Lisa and Kay Lee - *who don't have a clue about how things really work in Ethiopia.* Listen, Ethiopians have been running their own show a whole lot longer than the United Fucking States of Racism. They are the only…"

"…country in Africa that has never been colonized, I know. But, look, if you leave…"

"Dad, I got my ticket. I'm leaving in four weeks. So take a breath and please don't interrupt me. Nigest's Temple will do fine. My Mom, my sisters, my brother, they're kicking butt, beyond anyone's wildest dreams. Gold is way up and Abesha Sisters is making more money than they ever imagined. Genet is running things, but she is going to school too and wants to go to America.

Selam is stepping up to take over. They are sending Lushi to Germany to learn business. They can help support the Temple. Fikir got married and his school in Arba Minch is expanding; he says he'll contribute. Geta is in Adis working with the new Unity government's Department of Youth. When I leave, Eden is ready to run the Temple until they find a new director. There's an intern from Brandeis coming from the States, an Ethiopian-American kid who knows Amharic and who will write grants. So don't worry things about falling apart.

Listen I gotta go. There's a lot to sort out before I leave. The money you sent, guess who I have to fight with to get it released? The Tekles. Tsehay and Rodeat. God knows who they bribed, but now they are high up in the Unity Party, in charge of Dice Dota's Department of Woman's Affairs. They're the ones who OK all foreign money for women's NGO's. And believe me, they haven't changed; some still sticks to their hands. Same vultures, different feathers. But I'm not worried. They'll be clean with me. They know Geta is high up with Unity. They'll fork it over.

Meanwhile, farange keep coming. Ethiopians keep leaving. Mom, Happy Birthday. Dad I love you. Here, I kiss the camera, *mwuuuuuh*, and say skype bye. And remember, if you come to Ethiopia *don't do it to help anybody*. Do it for yourself. Do it to be selfish. As for me – full circle. I go home from my home."

FINIS

Glossary:

Abesha – A person who is Ethiopian (from Abbysinia)

ahya – donkey

Amedabad – capital of Gujurat, home of Hedeyat Pakir and his son Sagar

Ambo – a popular brand of bottled water

Andamu – a fictional province in southeastern Ethiopia

aradanat – courage

Ato – Mr., adult male

bajaj – a three-wheeled motorized taxi

Barentu – site of a fierce battle during the Ethiopian-Eritrean war in May, 2000

Bek ah! – enough!

Berbera – port in Somaliland on the Arabian sea, traditional gateway to Ethiopia

Bilharzia – also known as Schistosomiasis and snail fever, is a disease caused by parasitic flatworms called schistosome*s*

Bole – airport in Adis Ababa, major airport of Ethiopia

buna – coffee

Denadur – Good night (to a man)

Denakil – desert in North Eastern Ethiopia; one of the hottest places in the world

Devi – Hindu female divinity

Dodola – town in Arsi district, Ethiopia

doro wat – Ethiopian chicken stew

farange – person of European descent (white)

firfir – Ethiopian dish made from left-over injera

gabi – traditional white dress of Ethiopia, often worn at church by women and men

GDZ – German Development Corporation

ghari – a horse-drawn, two-wheeled taxi

gomen – spinach

Gujerati – a person from Gujerat, a state on the east coast of India

Gurage – tribal group in Southern Ethiopia

Harar – town in Eastern Ethiopia. Gateway to Somalia

injera – tradional Ethiopian staple, fermented tef pancake – basis of Ethiopian cuisine

jibi – wolf

Jijiga – town in eastern Ethiopia in the Ogaden desert, near the Somali border

Jinka – a town in far South Western Ethiopia, gateway to the tribal regions of the Omo Valley

kabele – neighborhood, smallest political district

Kambatta – tribal group in Southern Ethiopia

Kasanchis – the nightclub and red light district of Adis Ababa

khat – herbal stimulant grown and used in East Africa and throughout the Middle East. Fresh green leaves are chewed. Perhaps Ethiopia's second largest source of income after coffee.

kik alicha – split pea stew

konjo – pretty/handsome, nice, cool

Lake Langano – Rift Vally lake 200 km. south of Adis Ababa, popular with tourists as it is the only fresh water lake free of Bilharzia (schistosomiasis) and safe for swimming

Lalibela – a town in Northern Ethiopia, home to the famous sunken churches. Perhaps the premier tourist attraction of Ethiopia.

Meles – Meles Zenawi, leader of Ethiopia 1993-2012, Tigrayan leader instrumental in the overthrow of the Communist Regime of Mengistu Hailemariam

Mengistu (Hailemariam) – ruler of Ethiopia and leader of the Derg Party from 1973-1995. Allied Ethiopia with the Communist block. Known for bloody suppression of political opponents and rivals.

Meskel – an annual religious holiday in the Ethiopian Orthodox churches commemorating the discovery of the True Cross by The Roman Empress Helena *misir* – Ethiopian dish made of ground red lentils.

Ogaden – region in Eastern Ethiopia and Western Somalia: site of border conflicts 1960-2010.

Oromo – largest tribe in Ethiopia. Both Christian and Muslim. Traditionally out of power, dominated by Amhara and Trigray tribes.

pina – pineapple

Ras Dashen – Ethiopia's highest mountain

Ras Tafari – Haile Selasse's real name: Ras (Chief) Tafari Mekonnen

Rati – Hindu goddess of female carnality

Shashamene – crossroad town in the rift valley, gateway to Southern Ethiopia, site of Jamaican Rastafarian resettlement in the late sixties

shifta – bandit

souk – Arabic word for "market"

tef – traditional grain grown in Ethiopia, used to make injera

tej – homebrewed beer

Timkat – (baptism) is the Ethiopian Orthodox celebration of Epiphany. It is celebrated on January 19 (or 20 on Leap Year), corresponding to the 10th day of Terr following the Ethiopian calendar.

tinish – little

tukol – traditional round house of Ethiopia

UDJP – Unity for Democracy and Justice Party – opposition party to EPRDF (Ethiopian Peoples Revolutionary Democratic Front,) which presently (2019) rules Ethiopia

waba – mosquito

Weyzero – Mrs./Ms. (adult woman)

Wolayta – a tribe of several million living in South Western Ethiopia in the Wolayta Region

Woyane: Tigrayan Nationalist Movement that later became the Tigrayan Peoples Liberation Front which, in 1993, defeated the Communist Derg regime and took over the Ethiopian Government and army in 1993. Woyane is commonly used to describe the present (2019) regime which is dominated by the Tigrayan ethnic group.

yegodana lejoch – street kids

Yir Gallum – a town in southern Ethiopia famous for growing coffee and khat

Ykerta – excuse me

zinjero – monkey

About Fomite

A fomite is a medium capable of transmitting infectious organisms from one individual to another.

"The activity of art is based on the capacity of people to be infected by the feelings of others." Tolstoy, *What Is Art?*

Writing a review on Amazon, Good Reads, Shelfari, Library Thing or other social media sites for readers will help the progress of independent publishing. To submit a review, go to the book page on any of the sites and follow the links for reviews. Books from independent presses rely on reader to reader communications.

For more information or to order any of our books, visit
http://www.fomitepress.com/FOMITE/Our_Books.html

More Titles from Fomite...

Novels
Joshua Amses — *Ghatsr*
Joshua Amses — *During This, Our Nadir*
Joshua Amses — *Raven or Crow*
Joshua Amses — *The Moment Before an Injury*
Jaysinh Birjepatel — *The Good Muslim of Jackson Heights*
Jaysinh Birjepatel — *Nothing Beside Remains*
David Brizer — *Victor Rand*
Paula Closson Buck — *Summer on the Cold War Planet*
Dan Chodorkoff — *Loisaida*
David Adams Cleveland — *Time's Betrayal*
Jaimee Wriston Colbert — *Vanishing Acts*
Roger Coleman — *Skywreck Afternoons*
Marc Estrin — *Hyde*
Marc Estrin — *Kafka's Roach*
Marc Estrin — *Speckled Vanities*
Zdravka Evtimova — *In the Town of Joy and Peace*

Fomite

Zdravka Evtimova — *Sinfonia Bulgarica*

Daniel Forbes — *Derail This Train Wreck*

Greg Guma — *Dons of Time*

Richard Hawley — *The Three Lives of Jonathan Force*

Lamar Herrin — *Father Figure*

Michael Horner — *Damage Control*

Ron Jacobs — *All the Sinners Saints*

Ron Jacobs — *Short Order Frame Up*

Ron Jacobs — *The Co-conspirator's Tale*

Scott Archer Jones — *And Throw the Skins Away*

Scott Archer Jones — *A Rising Tide of People Swept Away*

Julie Justicz — *A Boy Called Home*

Maggie Kast — *A Free Unsullied Land*

Darrell Kastin — *Shadowboxing with Bukowski*

Coleen Kearon — *Feminist on Fire*

Coleen Kearon — *#triggerwarning*

Jan English Leary — *Thicker Than Blood*

Diane Lefer — *Confessions of a Carnivore*

Rob Lenihan — *Born Speaking Lies*

Colin Mitchell — *Roadman*

Ilan Mochari — *Zinsky the Obscure*

Peter Nash — *Parsimony*

Peter Nash — *The Perfection of Things*

Gregory Papadoyiannis — *The Baby Jazz*

Pelham — *The Walking Poor*

Andy Potok — *My Father's Keeper*

Kathryn Roberts — *Companion Plants*

Robert Rosenberg — *Isles of the Blind*

Fred Russell — *Rafi's World*

Ron Savage — *Voyeur in Tangier*

David Schein — *The Adoption*

Lynn Sloan — *Principles of Navigation*

L.E. Smith — *The Consequence of Gesture*

L.E. Smith — *Travers' Inferno*

L.E. Smith — *Untimely RIPped*

Bob Sommer — *A Great Fullness*

Fomite

Poetry

Stories

Fomite

Odd Birds

Fomite

Plays

Essays

Made in the USA
Middletown, DE
08 July 2022

68407600R00267